Something About

ABBY

SEVEN VIRTUES RANCH ROMANCE BOOK 7

BECKY DOUGHTY

Something About Abby: Seven Virtues Ranch Romance Book 7
Copyright © 2020 by Becky Doughty

Published by BraveHearts Press

The story, all names, characters, and incidents portrayed in this production are fictitious. No identification with actual persons (living or deceased), places, buildings, and products is intended or should be inferred.

Book Cover by BraveHearts Press Designs

Author Information: BeckyDoughty.com

ISBN: 978-1953347459

ABBY

"But if I close my eyes and sing
With the cicada serenade
In the maples on my street...
For a moment, that's home to me."

Ranae

ONE

... And home is still out of reach to me,
But if I close my eyes and sing
With the cicada serenade in the maples on my street
For a moment, that's home to me.

The words poured out of Abby like a lament, the homesick child inside her aching with every note, every syllable. It wasn't how the tender song was meant to be performed, but she couldn't help it. The longing for that old familiar sky, the rich and ruddy earth beneath her feet, the tangy scent of fresh hay bales stacked rafter-high in the barn. The background music of the feminine voices of her sisters—tears and laughter, too—filling every corner of the ranch house.

But I don't think that I'm sad now,
I'm not anything more than I was when I left.
But maybe that's my problem.
I'd sooner crack in two than let myself forget.
All I can do right now is take a breath...

The rumble of a tractor, the lowing of cattle, the pounding of horses' hooves marking the pulse of life at Seven Virtues Ranch.

And Jedediah Goodacre. *Oh, Daddy. I miss you.*

How does one hold onto this?

How do you keep from losing what you never had?
Standing in the whirlwind,
Trying not to let all of the change make me sad.

It was all she could do to keep the quaver from her voice as she sang. She swallowed the lump of emotions that kept trying to close her throat, and pushed the poignant words out—words meant to make people smile and remember, not weep.

The moon has fallen from that old familiar sky
In both of my hometowns....

She bowed her head over her guitar as she gently plucked the last notes of the song and let them hang there.

A smattering of applause jarred her out of her reverie, and Abby lifted her head, her wide stage smile in place, and nodded in acknowledgment.

It was time for a break, wasn't it? A bead of sweat trickled down her spine between her shoulder blades before getting absorbed into the fabric of her shirt. Her hair clung like spiderwebs to the back of her neck, the fans in front of the stage doing little to counteract the sticky summer heat that pushed in through the open windows at their backs.

Glamorous was not a word she'd use to describe gigging on Honky Tonk Row in Nashville. In fact, if the Seattle music scene hadn't already laid claim to it, Abby was certain someone would have coined it Nashville Grunge. Not for the music style, but because of how a person felt performing on the tiny front window stages in the packed bars and restaurants all along the busy downtown street. The owners and managers knew how to draw folks in and sell them lots of drinks—as long as the weather cooperated, the plate-glass windows were opened wide to the elements, and the better the band sounded, the more attention they got from passersby. The more attention the band got, the more likely it was that those passersby would duck inside to listen. And then eat and drink. Spend their money.

Abby didn't judge people for eating and drinking. She didn't judge people for spending their money. In fact, lately, she was doing a little too much of both herself.

She leaned closer to her microphone. "Folks, y'all are fabulous," Her speaking voice was naturally husky, so she was pretty sure no one would notice the catch in it. She poured on the twang, just in case. "You remind me of my people back home, and that's sayin' a lot."

Someone at the back of the room called out, "We love you, Abstinence!" A dark-haired woman waved from where she sat leaning casually against the shoulder of a barrel-chested man. Regulars for the last couple of weeks—Starla and Robert? Bob? No, Bill, maybe. She couldn't quite recall. She was usually great with names, but his wasn't coming to her. Tonight, she was finding it difficult to focus on anything except getting through this gig.

"Hey, you two lovebirds." Abby pointed in their direction. It was still weird to hear strangers calling her by her full name. She'd gone by Abby her whole life, but Remington Sounder had suggested she use the unique and memorable Abstinence to give her a leg up in the industry. "Do I need to call for a hand check?"

That got a reaction out of the crowded room, lightening the mood that had settled after her song. She raised her voice to be heard over the catcalls and wolf whistles. "Listen, we're going to take a quick break. Ten minutes, then we'll be back for more. Y'all behave while we're gone now, ya hear?" She waggled a finger at Starla and her man again. "I'm talking about you two, especially."

Amidst another round of hooting and applause, Abby unplugged her guitar and set it on the stand behind her, skirted the conglomeration of microphone stands, cables, and monitors, and headed off the side of the raised platform.

She intentionally did *not* look at Bucky. His eyes bore into her as she made her way to the tiny room at the back of the bar used by the different bands. She hoped the guys would mingle and let her have the space to herself for a few minutes. She needed to get her act together, and ten minutes was hardly enough time to use the bathroom and touch up her heat-warped makeup.

"What the hell, Abby?" Bucky's voice caught up to her before he did, but his hand on her upper arm made it clear that he had no intention of leaving her in peace.

She didn't even flinch at his abrasive language, even though he knew she didn't like it. It could get a lot worse when he was really ticked off. She stopped mid-stride and waited for him to continue, partly because she wasn't sure how to answer his question, and partly because she knew it wouldn't matter, anyway. He wasn't really looking for answers. At least not ones she could give him.

"Let her be, Buck." Tad wasn't far behind, shoving his drumsticks into his back pocket as he approached. "Everyone has a rough night now and then."

"Yeah, maybe," Bucky shot back, still gripping Abby's arm too tightly. "But the princess here doesn't seem to get the whole 'now and then' part of that equation."

Had it been so obvious that she was in a funk? Could her audience tell, too? Abby grimaced and let her hair fall forward to hide her face from Bucky's glare. A bubble of anxiety behind her ribs threatened to burst into a full-blown panic. She tried to pull away from his bruising fingers, to no avail. "Give me a minute, okay?" she ground out, doing her best to keep the tremor from her voice as she met her guitar player's eyes. Hard, unyielding, and definitely condescending.

She hated when he called her princess. He was the only one in the band who did, and it had been a long time since he'd said it nicely.

"You've got ten. No, make that eight minutes." Bucky pointed at the digital clock mounted crookedly on the wall just outside the small band room. "You better find your happy place and make it snappy. We have an audience to get fired up, and you're acting like a wet rag."

From behind him, Tad gave Abby a bolstering smile, but said nothing.

"I'll make it snappy," she retorted, snapping her fingers emphatically. But her voice cracked on the last word, and Bucky didn't miss a beat.

He bent forward, his face too close to hers. "Don't—"

"Hey." Tad moved around Bucky to step between them. "Let's not do this here, okay?" He eyed the clock pointedly.

Abby jerked her arm from Bucky's grasp and pushed open the door of the little storage room. It should have been locked, but she didn't bother acknowledging it. She knew well who'd been the last one out of there, but she wasn't about to point fingers at her guitar player right now. Fortunately, her most important possession, her Hummingbird guitar, Blossom, was up on stage under the watchful eye of the band manager. She snatched up the backpack she used instead of a purse and shoved past both guys. "I'll be in the little girl's room. Don't come looking for me."

"Don't make me!" Bucky called after her, the warning coming out on a snarl.

Abby was relieved to find the bathroom empty. It didn't happen often, and she lifted a quick "Thank you for small mercies," heavenward. Ripping several paper towels from the dispenser, she let the water run as cold as it would get and held them under it. Then she peeled her shirt off over her head and pressed the cool towels to her neck and chest, then tucked one under each arm. She smelled just fine, thank goodness—the Pixie Cut deodorant Prudence made for her worked like nothing store-bought ever could. But she knew a thing or two about how to keep from overheating; she'd spent far too many long hours rounding up cattle in the dog days of summer not to. Closing her eyes, she leaned against the vanity and counted backwards from twenty-five.

She could get through this. She had to get through this. They still had an hour-long set to go.

Two minutes later—which left her fewer than five remaining before Bucky came looking for her—Abby tossed the paper towels and slipped her arms back into her shirt. She eyed her makeup and hair. Actually, her hair seemed to be holding up all right despite the humidity, but her eyeliner was smudged and her lipstick sung clean off. "I look like one of those crying clowns," she muttered to her reflection, just as the bathroom door swung open. It was the woman from the audience.

"Hey, girl," Starla said when her eyes met Abby's in the mirror. The woman didn't exactly smile at her, which made Abby wary. "You okay in here? That hot guitar player of yours is out in the corridor waiting for you." She came to stand at the counter, too, but kept studying Abby. "And when I say hot, I don't mean his appearance. Although I do have eyes in my head and he is easy to look at." She waved a hand dismissively, as if to flick away her own comment, then continued. "He just seemed a little riled up to me, that's all. Hot under the collar, you know?" She leaned forward and made a kissy face at her own reflection. "I'm trying to be a girlfriend, but if I'm just being nosy, you can tell me to hush and mind my own. Do you like this lipstick on me?"

For a moment, Abby didn't respond. She swallowed hard, resisting the urge to ask the woman for a hug. Something about her reminded her of someone from Plumwood Hollow, someone good, someone genuine. "You remind me of..." Who? Abby shook her head in frustration. Not any of her sisters. None of them were quite so—so *vivid*.

Starla let out a good-natured, albeit slightly self-deprecating, chuckle. "Well, I hope it's someone good and kind. And pretty," she added with a wink.

Cass Whitehouse. Starla reminded Abby of Cass and her baked goods. The cinnamon rolls at Serendipity's. Her mouth began to water. "Good and kind and pretty. That's exactly right. You remind me of someone from home." She thought her voice was steady, but Starla was more than just good and kind and pretty. She was also astute.

"Need me to run interference with Mr. Hot and Bothered out there?" Starla pulled a tube of lipstick from the depths of her suede leather shoulder bag. "And you never said if you like this color on me." She uncapped it and held it out for Abby to see. "It's called Girl Talk."

"How à propos," Abby said, giving her a warm smile. "I do like your lipstick. That color is perfect for you. And don't worry about Bucky. He's always in a fit when we're in the middle of a gig. He takes forever to unwind, so breaks aren't really his thing."

"Huh," Starla replied noncommittally, her mouth forming an open 'O' while she applied a thick coat of Girl Talk to her lips. She straightened and dropped the makeup back in her bag. "Well, you just say the word and I'm there, okay?" Then she ducked inside one of the stalls.

"Thank you," Abby said through the closed door. "I'll see you out there, okay?"

"I'm rooting for you, girlie!" Starla said from behind the stall door. "Bert and I are your biggest fans!"

Bert. That was the guy's name. She was inexorably grateful for Bert and Starla being out in the crowded room tonight. She'd buy them another round of whatever they were drinking as a thank you.

Abby smiled at her reflection and decided the smudged eyeliner wasn't so bad after all. "Nashville Grunge," she whispered so the other woman wouldn't hear. "I like it." Then she headed out of the sanctuary of the restroom.

Sure enough, not more than ten feet from the door stood Bucky. Tad was nowhere in sight.

"I still have two minutes," she stated, not even slowing her pace as she tried to veer around him. Bucky stepped forward to block her path, forcing her to pull up short, just inches from plowing into him. "Get out of my way."

Bucky didn't step back. He crossed his arms, one of his elbows grazing her breast. She stood her ground; she didn't even flinch at the inappropriate contact. She would not let him see how close she was to a breakdown. She had to keep it together.

"I said, get out of my way." Abby swung her backpack up onto her shoulder, and Bucky took a quick half step back. She scowled up at him. "I'm not going to hit you."

He narrowed his eyes at her menacingly.

"Move," Abby demanded.

Bucky didn't move.

"Move!" she said, this time much louder. Behind her, the bathroom door swung open.

"Hey there, Guitar Man!"

Starla. *Thank you, God.*

"Sounding great up there," the older woman cooed as she sidled up to Abby. "Our Abstinence has the voice of an angel, doesn't she? You are one lucky guy to be a part of her band." Starla nudged Abby's shoulder with her own. "You know how to pick 'em, woman."

Before her eyes, Bucky's face transformed from dark and foreboding to charming, beguiling, engaging. To Abby, it didn't make him seem any less threatening, though. And definitely just as repellent. How had she not noticed the act back when they'd first started working together? How had she missed it? She was usually such a good judge of character. But somehow, she'd been blind to the real Benton "Bucky" Jarlsburg. Until now.

Well, until a couple of months ago, when his true colors started showing through that pretty outer layer.

"Why thank you, ma'am. And yes, I am indeed a lucky man." Bucky reached for Abby's hand, but Starla intercepted the gesture as if she'd thought he was reaching for hers. His expression registered momentary displeasure, but then he lifted the older woman's hand to his lips and planted a quick kiss on her knuckles.

"I was just telling Abstinence here how much we love her music," Starla gushed. "I bet you're honored to get to work with someone so gifted."

Okay, now she was laying it on a little too thick; surely Bucky would start to get suspicious. Abby had to stop her before she said something that might make him blow. It already sounded like the woman thought he was some half-rate musician for hire.

Technically, Abby supposed he was. Maybe not half-rate; Bucky was a strong, solid guitar player who filled in nicely around her own playing. She'd chosen him for that reason—because he *wasn't* a virtuoso. When Remington Sounder had brought her to Nashville almost two years ago, the man had advised her to hone her own guitar skills so that she wouldn't be dependent on the skill and ability of another musician to keep her afloat. She'd come a long way since then, especially in the last year since being out in the big world all on her own, and it hadn't escaped her that perhaps that was one of the reasons Bucky was always so moody. Over the ten months they'd been working together, he'd slowly come to realize that Abby could play anything he could, maybe even better than he could.

But just because she could play all his parts didn't mean she no longer needed him. The band wouldn't be complete without him, or Tad, or even Gregor. Gregor, who'd be sitting at the bar until the rest of them returned to the stage, she knew. Not for the drinks, although he always seemed to have one in front of him, but for the women who really, really liked her bass player. Who probably bought his drinks for him, too.

"I need to stash this," Abby said abruptly, shaking the backpack that was still slung over her shoulder. "Did you lock the gig room this time?" She wanted to bite the words back the moment they were out.

"You were the last one in there," Bucky retorted. He tried to pull his hand from Starla's, but the woman played dumb and didn't let go.

Abby shot her a grateful glance. "I'll see you on stage then." Abby pushed past him. Oh, she'd hear about all of this later, but she could handle it then. *After* the show was over and she didn't have to put on a brave face for her adoring fans.

TWO

Tuesday night's performance hadn't gone much better than the night before. Bucky had all but refused to acknowledge her, even on stage. By the end of the night, she was wrung out and ready for a day off. She didn't work Wednesdays, thank goodness, at either of her jobs, and she wanted nothing more than to head back to her tiny studio apartment, wash off the clinging vestiges of night life at The Whiskey Vault, and fall into the blissful abyss of sleep.

Tad and Bucky were loading up their gear into the back of Tad's van, but Abby was stuck inside with Stan, waiting for a check. She'd put her foot down early on when they'd first started gigging, refusing to let the guys run a bar tab against the night's payout—Gregor, in particular, since he had a propensity to use their tab to purchase drinks for the pretty faces around him, too. It was shocking how quickly those drinks could whittle away at the total owed them at the end of the night.

Gregor had helped haul Tad's drum kit out the back door, but then he'd disappeared with a girl who'd plastered herself to his side as soon as he left the stage. Abby knew they likely wouldn't see him until Thursday morning when they got together to run through their set for The Stage where they played the rooftop.

Stan, stout and stoic as a tree stump, but wickedly good at keeping the band working, waved at the hustling barman to get his attention. "Can you let Jack know we're still waiting on him?" Stan called out. "My band is done for the night and ready to go."

In other words, pay up. Now.

A minute later, Jack Hindlay came around the end of the bar toward them and gave Stan a sealed envelope—presumably their week's pay—completely disregarding Abby's outstretched hand. "Thanks for waiting," he said, his gaze shifting to Abby, then back to Stan.

Shifting. Shifty. That word stuck in Abby's craw. There was a look in Jack's eyes that didn't bode well. His next words made her heart race. "We need to talk about next month's contract."

"Call me tomorrow," Stan told him, his tone casual, but brooking no argument. "This kid needs her beauty sleep."

"Nah," Jack insisted, just as coolly. "Let's talk now. You and me, Stan. The little princess can go get her beauty sleep without you."

Abby frowned at the exchange. How many ways had these guys just insulted her? Kids? Beauty sleep? And little princess? Really?

"Excuse me." She reached over and snatched the envelope out of Stan's hand, then slipped it into her backpack without even bothering to look at it. "If you're talking about my band playing here next month, then you're talking with me, too."

Jack crossed his hairy, tattooed arms, a gesture that said far more than any words might.

Abby appreciated Stan. He was great at his job, and she was grateful for all that he did for them. When Abby first came to Nashville, she'd thrived under the mentoring of Remington Sounder, an icon in the country music industry. Remington was famous for plucking no-name musicians off tiny no-name stages and giving them a jump start into the big arena. He'd heard her perform at Plumwood Hollow's Smokehouse Grill near the end of her senior year, and he'd offered her a half-hour opener spot on his tour and to produce her first album... in exchange for the rights—and ninety percent of the royalties—to said album. As painful as that concession had been for her, the majority of the up-and-coming musicians he'd taken under his wing had gone on to superstardom, and it had been an offer Abby couldn't refuse. She'd gotten a taste of that super stardom on the road with him and his extensive production caravan, and she'd been hooked. So when the tour was over, she'd opted to stay in Nashville so she could get on the Broadway circuit. Rem had introduced her to Stan, who made her promises that he'd kept for a whole year now. The Abstinence Goodacre Band had indeed been busy.

But there were things about Stan she didn't care for. His curmudgeonly silence. The toothpick he always had sticking out of the side of his mouth, that he somehow kept lodged in place, even when he talked. How he studied her while she performed, like she was a product, not a person. The way he shifted his tone of voice, his language, his behavior, ever so subtly to match those of the people he did business with. Sure, that chameleon ability probably had a lot to do with his exceptional managerial skills, but it always left Abby feeling a little unsettled, unsure of which Stan was the real one.

"Let's talk, then," Stan said after a moment. "The three of us. Shall we step into my office?" He nodded toward the back door that led out into the alley behind the bar. He didn't wait for a response from Jack, but turned and headed that direction after gesturing for Abby to go ahead of him.

Tad was just closing the doors of his van when they stepped out into the night. The heat and humidity of the summer day hadn't let up more than a few degrees in the last several hours, even this close to midnight, but the air was fresher than it was inside the crowded bar, and Abby took a deep breath. She ignored the slight stench that emanated from the dumpster nearby. She turned toward Stan and Jack just as Bucky came around the back of the van to join them.

"What's going on?" he asked, his voice ringing with surliness.

Abby glanced over at Tad, who shrugged noncommittally. Tad was a good ol' boy, a great counterbalance to Bucky's volatile nature. He opened the driver's side door and got in behind the wheel, then rolled his window down so he could still listen in on the conversation.

Without preamble, Jack said, "I've only got one spot a week for your band next month, Stan."

"My band," Abby said, her hackles rising.

"Our band," Bucky interjected, his scowl deepening as he edged in closer to her.

"Nope. We need two nights." Stan ignored them both. "Mondays and Tuesdays."

"You get one or none."

"Why the change? You got someone else better than these kids?" The question came out sounding like the very idea was ludicrous.

"Your band is on the rocks," Jack stated, crossing his arms again. "I can't take a risk on a no-show. Especially the last gig of the night, twice a week."

"Excuse me?" Abby stepped forward, standing shoulder-to-shoulder with Stan. "I don't do no-shows, Jack. Neither does my band."

"Our band," Bucky growled from just over her shoulder. She side-stepped slightly to try to edge him out, but he just moved with her, crowding her obnoxiously.

"That's what I'm talking about." Jack spoke to Stan, but he thrust his chin in Bucky's direction. "You got trouble brewing, Stan, and I don't want any part of it. So Mondays and Tuesdays are going to someone else. I can give you Sundays at 2:45 PM, and that's it. Take it or leave it."

"There's nothing wrong with my band," Stan said, his voice as bland as ever. "You don't want to put an end to a good thing, Jack. You got people in there who come just to hear Abstinence sing." Stan never called her Abby. Nope; to him, she was a commodity, not a small-town girl with a sweet nickname.

Jack lifted his hands at his sides. "I know they do. But I'm not paying for the drama, and my customers aren't, either. There's been talk, and I don't like it."

"You won't get another Abstinence," Stan started to say, but Jack cut him off.

"No, I won't. But I'll get a Sarah, and a Brittney, and a Jessica. Who knows? I might even get myself a Taylor. There's always another pretty young starlet waiting for an opening on my stage, Stan. Don't kid yourself."

The words cut deeply, just as they were intended to. Pretty young starlet. That's all she was to these people. A product. A commodity. And an expendable one at that.

Keep her in her place. Remind her she's nothing special.

"We don't need this kind of crap, Stan," Bucky spoke up, widening his stance and nudging Abby aside. "We walk away."

"Shut up, Benton." Stan's tone didn't change, but the use of Bucky's real name was remarkably effective in putting the musician in his place. To the bar manager, he said, "We'll take it, Jack. But you and I aren't finished discussing this."

"No discussion. Take it or leave it. There's nothing more to my offer, and I'm not budging. I'm already giving you handouts as it is."

Bucky said a foul word and turned on his heel. Behind her, Abby heard the van door open and slam shut again.

Jack cocked his head at Stan with an expression that said, "Didn't I tell you?"

Without another word exchanged, Stan and Jack shook hands, then Jack nodded curtly and headed back inside, leaving Abby and Stan alone at the back door stoop.

After a brief uncomfortable silence, Bucky exited the van again and stomped toward them, his face a mask of rage. He opened his mouth to speak, but Stan lifted a hand to silence him.

"Here's the way I see it," he began, his voice raised a little so they all could hear him. "You two—" he waved a finger back and forth between Abby and Bucky. "You two better figure out who's in charge here. When you do, let me know, and then we'll get back to work."

"I'm in charge," Abby said, her voice shaking with anger and fatigue. "I've always been in charge."

"Well, that's what I thought when I signed you on, but it seems to me that your guitar player is starting to think differently."

"I'm in charge," Abby said again.

"Not if you're letting him walk all over you," Stan argued. "Not if you're letting him dictate the quality of your performance." Bucky made a garbled sound that might have been another bad word, but Stan talked right over him. "Jack's right, Ms. Goodacre. I've seen it a thousand times, and so has he. Your band is on the rocks. You're going down if you don't get this sinking ship repaired. And quickly."

"But—but I—"

"If you're in charge, you don't get to make excuses." Stan pulled the toothpick from between his teeth and pointed it at Abby. She couldn't help it; she took a step backward, repulsed by the disgusting object. The man kept talking like he hadn't noticed. "Like I said. Let me know when you figure out which one of you gets to be on top." And with that crude indictment, Stan headed back inside the bar after Jack.

Abby had no false hope that he was going in to try to get a different response from the guy. Stan often stayed after the band left, listening to the feedback of the unwitting customers, assessing the quality of the band that took the stage next when there was one. It didn't hurt that he got to write off his food and drink that way, either. More often than not, someone recognized him, and his meal would end up costing him nothing but a shared table.

She turned to Tad before getting in the van. "Would you mind dropping me off at my place first?" Usually, they all went back to Tad's place to unload the gear. Most of it was his drum set, but because he also happened to be the only one of them who had a garage, he kept some of the other stuff at his place, too. It was a good time to hash over the night's performance and make any necessary tweaks to the next gig. But tonight had her utterly deflated, and she didn't think she'd be any good to any of them. She tensed, certain Bucky would have something to say about that.

He did. He gestured dramatically in the direction Stan and Jack had gone. "This is on you, Princess Abby."

"Buck. Enough." Tad raised his voice, something he rarely did. "Let's call it a night."

"Fine. We'll call it a night. You can drop me off at her royal highness' place, too."

"Bucky, please," Abby breathed out, tired of his ugliness. To Tad, she said, "Never mind. I'll come help with the gear." That meant getting a ride back to her place from Bucky, which was what she'd been hoping to avoid in the first place, but she certainly preferred that to him getting dropped off with her and then not having a car in which to leave. At this point, she just wanted the night to end without any more drama than was absolutely necessary.

Because with Bucky, drama was always necessary. Which meant it fell on her shoulders to determine how much of it there'd be.

"Nah, I don't think that's going to work," her guitar player said, his tone suddenly smooth. "I just remembered that I've got someplace to be, so I'm leaving straight from Tad's. You'll have to find another way home."

Yep, drama.

Abby wanted to throw something at him. Something hard. She wanted to punch him in that beautiful face. She wanted to wring his neck, the same neck she'd pressed her face into far too many times. She wanted to wind back the clock and undo the things they'd done together. No dancing, no long afternoons in the park co-writing songs, no squeezing together into the one and only armchair in her tiny studio apartment so they could watch movies on her laptop. No holding hands, no holding each other. No kissing. No promises. No roller coaster romance.

"I'll take you home," Tad said, circling the van to open the sliding passenger door for her. She climbed in beside her guitar, glad to be alone in the back with the equipment. Bucky got into the front opposite Tad and pulled his door closed with far more force than was necessary. He shot an ugly glare at Abby over his shoulder while he fastened his seatbelt.

She ignored him the best she could, but was immeasurably relieved when she saw that Tad was, indeed, taking her home first.

She and Bucky didn't exchange another word until she stepped out onto the sidewalk in front of her apartment. Bucky had his head down scrolling through his phone, making an exaggerated point to ignore her, but Tad nudged the controls on the driver's side so the passenger window rolled down.

"Thanks, Tad," she said, looking past Bucky, who still didn't acknowledge her.

Tad gave her an apologetic smile. "Sure thing."

"Goodnight, Bucky," she finally said. How she wished things were different between them. "You sounded good tonight."

"Thanks," he muttered, but he didn't look up.

Abby patted the side of the van, and then turned to go inside her building, knowing Tad would wait until she was safely behind the security door before he pulled away.

The tiny foyer had a bank of mailboxes along one wall, and Abby set her guitar case down so she could check hers. There wasn't a single piece of mail in it, not even an advertisement flier, but that was no surprise. For some reason, the sight of the empty box brought on another wave of homesickness, one that left her weak at the knees. But she had three flights of stairs to climb before she could fall apart, so she took a deep, shaky breath, picked up Blossom, and started up.

A few minutes later, Abby stood at the one window in her apartment and gazed down into the narrow back street—an alley, really—below. She had no view, unless she counted what went on inside the apartments across from her, but most of those residents kept their curtains drawn for that very reason. Bracing herself with a hand on the window frame, she toed off first one boot, then the other, kicking the pair aside before peeling off her socks, too. She needed a shower. She needed something to eat, something that wasn't battered, fried, or eaten with a dip. Why was it that the band always got to eat stuff for free, but only from the unhealthiest items on the menu?

She needed some sleep. She needed to shirk off the shroud of Bucky's anger and the stench of another late night at the bar. She needed some peace. A little bit of oblivion.

"I need a drink."

THREE

Jedediah Goodacre smiled as he watched his five head of cattle cavort around their new pasture. Faith and Cord had helped him haul them across the way from Seven Virtues Ranch just yesterday, but the way the cows were acting, you'd think they hadn't seen fresh grass or the wide open prairie for a coon's age.

His sturdy log home was perfect just the way it was, as far as he was concerned, but his daughters all insisted that he needed things like sofas and occasional tables and stuff on his walls. Jed was more than satisfied with his recliner and the side table where he set his cup in between sips. Right next to the remote, the lamp, and whatever reading material he had on hand.

"But where is anyone else supposed to sit when they come visit?" Faith had asked yesterday afternoon. She'd pointed at the gorgeous hardwood planks under her feet, one hand on the small curve of her belly. "I might brave sitting on the floor right now, but in another couple of months, that's not going to work." She was pregnant again, and the thought of yet another grandchild also lent itself to the smile Jed couldn't hold back.

"I don't *want* anyone else sitting in here with me," he'd said with a shrug. "And I put those rockers on the front porch for visitors. Folks can sit for a spell out there. That way, when I'm tired of flapping my jaw or listening to them flap theirs, I can just leave. Once I let them inside, there's no getting rid of some folk."

"Daddy!" But she knew he was joking. Sort of.

He'd promised her he'd get a sofa soon enough, and she'd shaken her head in surrender. Then the two of them had settled into the rocking chairs on the front porch together, enjoying the lull of the sweet-smelling afternoon breeze that sent ripples across the ripening hayfields like waves on the ocean.

Jed had seen the ocean on more than one occasion. During war—he'd served in two of them—and also on his and Caroline's fifth anniversary. Faith had also been with them; they just hadn't known it at the time. But seeing a summer beach in real life—not just on the television or in the movies—had been one of his wife's fondest wishes, and Jed had squirreled money away in secret to save for a trip down to the coast. At the time, they'd lived in the hill country of Texas, so a trip to the ocean was quite an extravagance. Not just because of the cost, but also because it took them away during one of the busiest seasons for ranchers.

He could still picture her walking along in front of him, reaching out a hand for him, cajoling and teasing him about being afraid of the water. It didn't matter that every time a wave raced up the beach to spill over her bare feet; she was the one who squealed with a mixture of delight and shock at how cold it was. The sun shone down on her long, golden hair, left loose and hanging down her back the way she wore it after her bath at the end of the day. Part of him wanted her to corral all those glorious curls back into the tight braid she contained it in during the day, not because he didn't want to see it, but because he didn't want anyone else to see it.

The beach had been her dream—just one of many—and he'd made it his mission to fulfill her dreams.

His dreams—every one of them, it seemed—had been simply to make his beautiful young wife happy.

Some gave him a hard time for it, calling him names that challenged his position in his household, but it never bothered him. Jed had no need for other men's accolades; he had Caroline, and she had him.

By the end of their week away, his hearty, healthy wife had grown pale and wan, sickly. It wasn't until a month later that they discovered she was a couple of months pregnant.

Caroline, in between bouts of retching, had been ecstatic. They'd been trying for a baby since their honeymoon, and month after month, year after year, had gone by without a child. "It's as if I went down to the shore and got washed clean of whatever was keeping me from being a mama, Jeddy."

The news, although cause for celebration on one hand, did little to appease Jed. He hated watching Caroline go through the intense nausea and vomiting, the inability to keep anything down, sometimes not even water. Hyperemesis gravidarum, the doctor had called it. Even now, Jed couldn't stand the words, his mind taking the sounds and twisting them into the shape of an arch nemesis. Wasn't that what it had turned out to be, after all?

"I'll be fine, Jeddy," Caroline had assured him over and over again from her hospital bed when she was a little over four months along. "We're already halfway there, and then it'll all be worth it. You'll see."

When they'd placed Faith in his arms and her little red face squinched up in newborn angst, Jed's heart had all but burst out of his chest. He'd blinked away tears and murmured to his daughter how beautiful she was. And to him, she'd been the second most beautiful human in the world. When his eyes met Caroline's weary ones, they'd shared a silent joy so intense, the memory of that moment still made him clutch his chest.

Even now, more than three decades later.

In less than two years, Caroline was pregnant again. For the first month, it seemed hopeful that she wouldn't suffer from the same debilitating condition as she had during her pregnancy with Faith. But soon enough, the sickness began. When her doctor insisted she be hospitalized, Caroline had put her foot down, unwilling to hand over her toddler for someone else to care for.

So Jed worked extra hours to pay for the assistance of an older woman in the community. Velma came during the days while Jed worked, and for the duration of the pregnancy, she tended to every need Caroline would admit to having, and she helped with Faith whenever Caroline was too incapacitated to do so herself. Velma also cooked and cleaned, much to Caroline's chagrin. She often had to sit outside while meals were being put together; even the smell of food would cause her to be ill.

But she had insisted that she felt better at home, where she could be with Jed and Faith, where she could sleep uninterrupted by machines and hospital staff and other patients. "The only thing they can do for me is make sure I get enough calories in, but I can do that here, too. I just have to try harder."

Velma had been a gift from the Almighty. She worked her magic with herbal teas and bone broth, and when Caroline threw everything back up, Velma would patiently dole out another serving. Despite his hefty misgivings, between the two women, his wife had not only survived the second pregnancy, but had actually gained six pounds through it. Charity had been born underweight, just as Faith had, but in all other ways, she'd been a healthy, thriving baby.

When Jed told his wife they wouldn't be having any more children, Caroline just laughed.

When Jed moved his blanket and pillow out to the couch just to keep him honest, Caroline just laughed again, and then joined him there, leaving her nightgown behind in the bedroom.

When Caroline smiled softly and told him she was pregnant a third time, Jed nearly wept. When he told her he didn't think he could bear watching her go through that again, Caroline smiled softly, already glowing with that special pregnant woman aura, kissed him on the forehead, then the nose, then the mouth. "Oh, Jedediah," she'd whispered against his lips. "If I can bear it, you can, too, my darling husband."

With Velma's help, they all bore it together. That time, Caroline did much better. Velma had finally found a blend of herbs for a tea that helped assuage the nausea long enough to keep little bits of sustenance down. It took Caroline longer to recover after Charity's birth, but then, she insisted, any woman would be worn thin by having three children under five years old underfoot.

Her doctor, when Jed finally convinced her to go see him six months later, hadn't agreed with Caroline. "These three pregnancies have taken a toll on your body, Mrs. Goodacre. Your heart needs a break. You need a break." Dr. Elender had turned to Jed and reiterated, "Your wife needs a break, Jed."

Caroline had been offended by the doctor's tone. "He spoke to us like we were teenagers without a brain cell in our heads."

"It doesn't matter how he spoke to us, Caro. What matters is what he said. I agree with him there. No more pregnancies."

"He didn't say no more pregnancies," she'd countered. "He said my body needed a break. So we'll give it one."

Jed stopped arguing when she started crying. But he was determined to stick to his guns; by now, he knew her monthly cycle almost as well as she did. He'd made it a point to do so. She wouldn't take oral contraceptives, so he also brought his own birth control to the bedroom. She didn't like it, but she forgave him for it.

Over the following three years, Caroline put on a good face, but Jed didn't miss the tight lines that formed at the corners of her mouth, the way her eyelids drifted shut the moment she'd sit to take a break, even falling asleep in church if he didn't keep nudging her. He saw the shadows under her eyes, shadows that weren't just there at the end of a long day, either. She awoke with them, never quite getting a solid full night's sleep.

Jed had tried to help out in any way he could. He took the older girls to school, he came home on his short lunch break to play with them so his wife could shower or go read in the quiet of their small bedroom. He often cooked dinner for them at the end of the day, too. It wasn't much—he hardly had the energy himself to whip up something more than chili, or hamburgers, or a pot of spaghetti. What he served them didn't matter; it was sustenance, and Caroline was always so grateful for everything he did to care for his family.

Over time, it became their new normal, and Jed grew tired himself. And then he got careless.

Pregnant with twins, the doctor told them, showing them the two fetuses on the ultrasound monitor at the big hospital where they'd admitted Caroline. She'd passed out on the kitchen floor when she stood up too quickly and had been late picking the kids up from school. Faith, only nine at the time, had insisted she could take care of her little sisters at home until Miss Velma got there. The woman had arrived with her small suitcase not more than an hour later.

The next six months had been touch and go. The hyperemesis was the worst it had ever been, and over the course of that pregnancy, Caroline became gaunt, skeletal, her pale skin pulled taut over bones that had never been prominent before. Even her baby bump seemed smaller than it should be, especially considering there were two babies nestled in her womb.

When Dr. Elender joined Jed at Caroline's bedside and told them that he feared for Caroline's life if they didn't take the babies by Cesarean, Jed had readily agreed. Caroline had not. But in time, she'd given in; likely more because of Jed's pleading than because of concern for her own health. The twins were born five weeks early, but despite the ravaged condition of their mother, the babies surprised everyone by being healthy and ready to go home, even before Caroline was.

Then Dr. Elender had made an irrevocable mistake. He'd asked Caroline when—not *if*—she wanted to schedule her hysterectomy.

Two years later, despite their best efforts to prevent it, Caroline was pregnant again, and this time, Jed could not figure out how it had happened. They barely had a moment to themselves at all, no less for conjugal relations, and the few precious times he'd made love to his still-so-lovely wife, he'd made sure there was no way she'd end up pregnant.

And yet, once again, she'd found herself carrying another babe. "It's God's will," she'd murmured into the darkness the night she'd told him about it.

She'd refused to go back to Dr. Elender. Or any other doctor, for that matter.

Velma gave them the name of one of her dear friends, Evelyn Banes, who was a semi-retired midwife. She'd already told Evelyn about Caroline, and the midwife had agreed to come by for a preliminary visit. On one account. "She may not take you on as a patient, but she's willing to see you if you're willing to heed her advice, even if you don't like what she says," Velma had told Caroline. "She won't bother coming out here if you won't bother listening."

Caroline not only listened, but she somehow won Evelyn over enough that the midwife agreed to take her on as a patient. "But if I say it's time to go to the hospital, then there's no arguing from you, got it?"

For whatever reason, whether God's mercy, or simply that every pregnancy is different, Caroline's hyperemesis appeared much less pronounced for the first two trimesters. In hindsight, Jed had figured out that by her fifth pregnancy, she'd just gotten a lot better at hiding her symptoms from him, so he wouldn't worry so much. Because once she'd crossed the six-month mark, things had spiraled out of control.

Evelyn was sympathetic to Caroline's wishes for a home birth, and with Velma's help, she did everything she could to accommodate it. But a month before Caroline's due date, Velma fell and broke her hip, which meant Caroline would be on her own for the next several months, maybe longer. That had been the last straw in Evelyn's book, and she'd sent a distraught Caroline—escorted by an unabashedly relieved Jed—to the hospital for the last month of her term and the delivery.

A week before Prudence's birth, Velma had suffered a massive stroke at the rehab facility where she'd been making a painfully slow recovery from her hip surgery and she'd passed away.

Caroline had come home from the hospital changed, somehow. Diminished, she had seemed to Jed. Caught between the overwhelming pleasure she found in being a mother and the deep grieving she was going through over the loss of such a dear friend, that it was no surprise that she hadn't been her old self. At first, anyway. But over time, she didn't rebound the way she had in the past. Where she used to always be humming a lullaby or an old hymn, now she stayed silent unless a response was required of her. She grew listless, easily distracted by her own thoughts, often drifting off into a place only she could go in the middle of a conversation.

She'd remained an attentive and loving mother, caring for her six daughters with great tenderness, and she'd bent over backwards to acknowledge and encourage Jed. But he sensed a growing distance in her, something that kept pulling her away from them. Something he couldn't nail down.

And if he couldn't nail it down, he couldn't fix it.

Before Prudence was a year old, Jed knew something had to change. His ranch hand job was solid and steady, but he had to be gone for long stretches of time out in the vast open prairies of the enormous Texas ranch, and he knew he needed to be more available to his wife. In the aching void left by Velma, their Faith, barely ten years old, had taken it upon herself to help care for her mother and sisters. Caroline had been grateful, but she'd often expressed her worry to Jed that their eldest daughter was growing up before her time.

Then Jed got word of a job in Kentucky that included the purchase of a parcel of land at pennies on the dollar. To him, it was an answer to prayer. He could take his wife away from the sun-burnt heat and frigid winter winds of the Texas ranch, away from the constant reminder of Velma's absence in their lives, and into the lush green pastures of the rolling hills and valleys of Plumwood Hollow. To a place where she could heal both physically and emotionally, where he could stay closer to home, to her.

Caroline had agreed that it was a fine idea. "We'll make a new start of things," she'd told him. And within a month, they'd packed everything up and made the move to the small two-bedroom row house they'd rented in town while Jed began building a home for his wife and daughters on the land he'd purchased.

Even though he worked long hours for Judge Flanner at Whispering Hills Ranch, he managed to complete the first stage of the house in time to move his family into it before the winter arrived. With six daughters, he'd need to add a few more bedrooms, but the heart of the home was there in the kitchen, the family room, a bathroom, and two large bedrooms.

Seven Virtues Ranch. The seven virtues had become a private joke to Caroline and Jed. They'd had no idea when they started having daughters that they'd need more than the three great virtues listed in the Good Book in the first letter to the Corinthians. "So now these three remain: faith, hope, and charity."

Of course, Charity still always insisted they include the rest of the verse when anyone told the story—"... but the greatest of these is charity."

So when the twins came along, it was Caroline who'd suggested they continue to name their daughters after the seven heavenly virtues, since they were practically halfway there already. "Courage and Justice," she'd said like she was testing the sounds on her tongue. "I think they're perfect names. So strong and brave, just like they are," she cooed over the tiny twin girls nestled between them.

Faith. Hope. Charity. Courage and Justice. Five Heavenly Virtues was good enough for him. He didn't need seven.

When Prudence had been born—and named—his wife had tried to make light of his worries. "Surely the Good Lord won't bless us with an Abstinence since we clearly don't practice *that* virtue," she'd giggled cheekily.

For a while, it seemed that the move had done the trick. Caroline opted to home school the girls so Faith could continue to help with her younger sisters but still maintain her education.

Faith was thrilled about that plan, too. Being home during the day meant that she could work with her father to get his small ranch up and running. "I'm going to be a cattle rancher just like you, Dad," she'd remind him on a regular basis. "I don't want a husband, but I could probably use a few kids to help me when I'm old." She'd been pretty serious about that plan back then.

Less than a year after moving his family to Seven Virtues Ranch, Jed found a whole new reason to worry about Caroline. At first, he thought she might be pregnant again and afraid to tell him. Sometimes he'd wake in the middle of the night to find her standing at the bedroom window, peering out over the dark pastures, and talking quietly to herself. He'd try to make out her words, but they'd made little sense to him at the time. "Wait. So much love. Not ready. I can't."

But her monthly cycle, although not always regular, came and went.

Sometimes when their eyes would meet, it seemed that she saw right through him. She'd smile and say, "It's all right, Jeddy," without provocation. Or she'd cross the room to where he sat in his chair reading, and she'd lay a hand on his cheek and tell him to stop worrying.

Other times, he'd find her sitting in the garden on the bench under the apple tree, apparently talking to the gnarled old dame. Caroline would smile at Jed when he'd approached, acting as though there was nothing unusual about conversing with a tree.

Then came the day he couldn't find her at all. The girls had no idea where she'd disappeared to, and in a panic, he'd headed into the woods that bordered their property, knowing she often collected wildflowers at the edges of it.

It had been a long time since he'd heard her singing, but it had been her voice lifted in the moving melody of "Be Still My Soul" that had drawn him to her. He'd found her standing in the middle of a natural clearing, her arms outstretched at her sides, her face lifted to a beam of sunlight that had found its way between the walnut and poplar branches overhead.

"Caroline," he'd breathed out, and she'd turned to him, a look on her face he'd never seen before.

"There you are, my love," she'd said. "Come dance with me."

Jed had gathered her to him and held her as they swayed slowly in time with the song she sang. When his heart had stopped racing, he hummed along, softly though, not wanting to overpower her soothing, gentle voice. He still recalled how her body had felt lithe and young against his chest, not frail and fragile the way it usually did, and she had moved with a sense of ease that he hadn't seen in too long. She'd always seemed to be anticipating something coming just around the corner, her shoulders hunched, flinching at every sudden noise or movement, but there in the clearing, she had seemed unshackled of all of that.

It had been so beautiful, like a moment out of time, and it had brought to his mind their wedding day. Not their first dance, not the moment they'd said their vows, not even that first kiss as husband and wife. It was the moment she'd left her father's side, stepped in front of Jed, and placed her hands in his. To him, *that* had been the moment they'd been joined as one.

That joining of hands, that dance in the clearing, their hearts pressed together, beating strong and sure in tandem; that was what marriage was all about.

She had asked him for one more baby on the walk back to the house. She hadn't begged. She hadn't demanded. She'd asked.

Jed had refused her, and Caroline hadn't argued.

Two months passed, and she'd asked again. "A son, Jedediah. One named after you. Let's try one more time." Once more, he'd said no, and she hadn't argued.

Several weeks later, she'd come to him again, this time with a look in her eyes he'd been unable to bear. It'd had nothing to do with carnal desire. No, it had been desperation. In that moment, Jed had believed that if he refused her yet again, his beloved wife would simply wither up and die.

The thought of losing her because of his rejection had nearly taken him to his knees.

He'd said yes.

Caroline had, indeed, become pregnant again. And the whole time that baby had grown inside her, she'd been withering up and dying, anyway.

And there'd been nothing Jed could do about it.

FOUR

Morning came with a blade of sunlight slicing through the crack in the curtains and piercing Abby's closed eyelids. She groaned softly and turned away from the light as the thumping of her pulse ricocheted around inside her skull. Slowly, tentatively, moving as little as possible so as not to set off the drums again, she pulled the sheet up over her head, unwilling to face a new day just yet.

Her apartment came with a window unit air conditioner, and the thing ran frigid or not at all. Last night, she'd taken a cool shower and had dressed only in sleep shorts and a tank top, and she'd been glad for the cold air after the sweltering heat that never quite let up in the Nashville summers. But this morning, the recycled air felt like a stuffy winter blast, and her comforter seemed to have disappeared. Abby thought she remembered kicking it off to the floor in the middle of the night, but she was afraid her head might explode if she attempted to look for it over the edge of the bed. The sheet offered little protection for the light or the cold air, but she knew she was in no shape to do anything about either problem at that moment.

She knew exactly how much she'd had to drink last night. She knew, because she'd stared at the half-empty bottle of Vanilla Jack Daniels—a girlie drink, Bucky called it—for a long time before deciding to dive into it head first.

She'd been so tired of the drama, so sick of the ugly feelings that brewed in the unsaid words between the band members, not just her and Bucky, but between all of them. Stan, too, had made things sound far worse than she'd been willing to admit, but the truth of his warning had resonated in her like a harbinger of doom. She wished she could go back in time to that year she spent with Rem and his crew, back before she was really out on her own. He wasn't a father figure to her, not by any means, but she'd looked to him for guidance and support in an industry that was known for being dog-eat-dog. Where little princesses like her got chewed up and spit out all the time. Hadn't Jack's comments earlier that night only validated that? Rem had been there for her, he'd had her back while she worked with him, and even though she'd paid for every second of it with the rights to her first works, in her dark moments—moments that were stretching out into minutes and hours and days and weeks—she admitted to herself that she just wanted someone to take care of her again.

That maybe, just maybe, she wasn't quite ready to grow up this quickly.

Abby was more homesick than she could ever have imagined, but she knew that this was all part of the journey toward being a superstar. She'd heard it a thousand times—if you want to play, you have to pay. In more ways than just financially, too.

And boy, was she paying.

The trouble was, it felt a whole lot like she was in debt. Deep in debt.

She owed Rem for his faith in her, for the boost he'd given her by taking her under his wings. She owed him for helping her find such a talented band, for encouraging her to not settle, to become the best musician she could be, to never stop learning. She'd be paying him in royalties for the rest of her life, sure, but for now, she still owed him big time.

She owed her band mates for how hard they worked to make her rising star shine. She owed them for the work they'd turned down in order to back her up.

She owed Bucky something more, even though she couldn't quite put a finger on it. He seemed to think so, too, but no matter how hard she tried to figure out what it was, nothing she did seemed to be enough of a payoff these days. She knew he wanted them to be dating again, 'to be *his*' was the way he'd put it the last time they'd tried to come to some kind of a resolution, but after the way things had escalated so quickly between them, she couldn't quite convince herself she owed him *that* much.

She owed Stan for his diligent effort to get The Abstinence Goodacre Band on stages in Music City. They played some of the top venues, something not many bands could claim. Thursdays, they performed the last set of the night at The Stage's Rooftop. On Fridays, they ended the night at Alan Jackson's Good Time Bar. That was one of the best gigs to be had, and Stan had managed to land it for them. They also had a regular Saturday and Sunday evening set at Legend's Corner, where some of Abby's most devoted local fans came regularly just to see her. And then there was the Monday and Tuesday gig at The Whiskey Vault. Make that the Sunday afternoon gig now. But that was her fault, not Stan's. Stan did what he'd promised he'd do, and she owed him for his skill set.

She owed the folks back home for their love and support. People she barely knew had gone out of their way to send her off in style, like she was some kind of hometown hero. She'd received financial gifts, cards and flowers and other congratulatory well-wishes, and more. Cass Whitehouse, as capricious as ever, had even sold t-shirts that said *Abstinence will go all the way!* at her send-off party at The Smokehouse Bar and Grill. Abby had been fairly sure the majority of the folks wearing the shirt hadn't gotten the tasteless double entendre, but it had sold like hotcakes, and the wad of cash Cass handed her when all the festivities were over had been astonishing. If she blew it now, she'd be letting down a whole town.

And last, but not least... not least, by far, there were her father and her sisters. She probably owed them more than anyone else. They'd believed in her longer than Rem, longer than Bucky, Tad, or Gregor, longer than Stan, longer than any of her growing crowd of fans. Faith had collected money from all the sisters and presented her with a "Group Project" Christmas gift when Abby turned ten: her first guitar. It hadn't been anything special, but that didn't matter to Abby. It hadn't taken her long to find her way around the instrument and start setting her own lyrics to music.

"If they could only see me now," she muttered mournfully into her pillow. "Wouldn't they be so proud?"

Abby owed her family so much. She had to find a way to make their dreams—no, *her* dreams—come true. She couldn't give up. She had to try harder. Had to sacrifice more. She had to find a way through this dark place she was in to the other side where she could make everyone proud again.

"I have to get up," she said. "Let's start there."

An hour later, Abby sat in her armchair, her comforter draped around her shoulders, a mug of steaming coffee clutched in her hands. She had found a chip clip in her tiny junk drawer and clamped the curtains closed against the sunlight, but she still kept her lids at half mast. Her head felt like it weighed too much for her body, and her eyes ached at the slightest stimulation.

There wasn't much to eat in her little apartment fridge, but she had eggs. They were cheap, and one or two of them, as a meal, could go a long way. Now all she had to do was bring herself to cook them; even the thought of seeing the slimy raw egg made her stomach churn threateningly. Maybe after she got a little caffeine in her system.

Her phone rang from across the room; it was still in her backpack on the floor where she'd left it when she came in last night. Through squinted eyes, she measured the distance and tallied up the number of steps it would take to get there and back, and decided she didn't have it in her. Not yet.

Ten minutes later, it rang again. She was only halfway through her coffee, and she became all the more determined that whoever was on the other end of the line could wait. "No coffee, no worky," she grouched, lifting her mug defiantly.

Five more minutes passed, and the phone rang a third time.

"Fine!" she fumed, pushing to her feet, then pausing to wait for the room to stop spinning.

Bucky. Why was he calling so early? What could he possibly need to talk to her about?

She frowned when she saw the numbers on her phone clock. Surely that wasn't right. It was almost noon? She sighed mournfully. Her day off was already halfway over.

She couldn't talk to Bucky right now, not in this frame of mind. She texted him a message instead. *I'm in the middle of something. I'll call when I'm finished.*

The phone rang almost immediately after notifying her that Bucky had read her text. When she silenced it, a text from him came through, complete with a crass word or two. *Answer your phone. Emergency.*

"Emergency?" she scoffed. "Right. Everything is an emergency to you, Buckster." She lifted her arm to launch her phone at her bed, but something in her made her hesitate. What if there really was an emergency? What if something had happened to Tad or Gregor? Or Bucky? Wouldn't he have said if something was wrong with him, though?

She started to key in *What's wrong?*, then realized she'd only expose her lie about being busy. Instead, she keyed in, *Give me five minutes,* and hit send.

Two, he sent back.

Abby shook her head. She would have rolled her eyes if they didn't feel like they were being squeezed from the inside out. So not quite an emergency, then. If it had been, Bucky wouldn't have given her any time at all.

I'm coming over. You can have your five minutes only because it'll take me that long to get there.

"No, no, no," Abby groaned. "No!" She did *not* want to see Bucky this morning. Or this afternoon. Or whatever time it was. She didn't want to see Bucky any time at all today. It was her day off, for crying out loud, and she had plans.

"I'm going to eat junk food, binge-watch British cooking shows, and go to bed before sundown," she elaborated to no one but herself.

But she knew that Bucky would make an appearance, no matter what she told him. The only way out of seeing him was to ditch her apartment, and she wasn't in any condition to step foot outdoors. It would take her a good half an hour just to be presentable enough to go downstairs to check her mail. "Not that there would be anything in it."

With a sigh of surrender, she set her cup in the tiny sink, crossed to her dresser to pull out a pair of leggings and a clean t-shirt, then headed into the bathroom for a shower. She'd just taken one the night before, but if she was in the shower when Bucky got here, then she'd have an excuse for not letting him in right away. And she could say that was what she'd been busy doing when he'd called. "Two birds with one stone," she quipped.

Except that it wasn't two birds; it was just one. Bucky.

FIVE

The intrusive ringing of a cell phone disrupted Jed's reverie, and he patted the pockets of his jeans before he realized the irritating device wasn't on him. Not a surprise, since it rarely was. The girls had insisted he keep it with him whenever he was out afield alone. He hadn't liked it, but after his near-fatal tractor accident several years back, he knew it was a sound thing to do.

He couldn't recall much about that day, at least not what came *before* the accident. The girls told him he'd gone out to cut back the encroaching woods at the edge of one of the far pastures. Somehow, a sapling had wrapped itself around the axle of his back wheel and the heavy machine had flipped onto its side, dragging Jed down underneath it. He'd come to his senses with the acute awareness that he was in terrible trouble, but he'd found some comfort in the knowledge that he would soon be holding his Caroline in his arms again.

He lay there, his body shaking uncontrollably as the shock wore off, the pain so fierce that every inch of him felt like it was on fire, and as he drifted in and out of consciousness, he prayed. "Almighty God, who sees and hears. Help me, Lord. Take me home. Let me see my Caro."

As time passed, the intensity of his pain waned slowly, and his mind cleared a little. He thought of Faith, just barely an adult herself, and knew she'd take responsibility for her six younger sisters. He thought about Hope and Charity traversing the rough seas of their teens. Of Courage and Justice, of Prudence, and of Abby, little girls who'd already lost one of their parents. His prayers changed. "You see and hear me, Almighty God; this I know. Our girls, they've already borne too much. Help me, Lord. Let me stay. Tell my sweet Caroline that I love her, but let me stay. Let someone find me before its too late."

Faith had been the one to find him. He saw the look on her young face when she saw the condition he was in. He knew, then, that staying would mean a great deal of suffering. But he'd been willing to bear it because of his love for his daughters, because of his love for his wife, who had cherished each and every baby girl she'd gifted him with.

It had been almost a year before Jed had been able to walk the length of his barn without the walker they'd sent him home with. How he'd hated that thing, but he wasn't going to risk re-injuring his leg for the sake of his pride.

Faith had taken over running things at Seven Virtues Ranch. She'd graduated early from high school that year and had poured herself into turning the place into something that now turned a profit. Jed had brought his great big Texas ranch methods with him to the small acreage that he'd called Seven Virtues Ranch after his daughters, but try as he might, he'd never been able to make the land work for him. Faith got a hold of it while he was laid up in the rehabilitation ward and had implemented a whole new way of ranching using a method she'd been researching for her own future place. By the time he was well enough to come home, she'd had the whole operation whipped into shape, and he had no choice but to step aside and let her do things her way. Her way made far better sense than his every had.

Eventually, she offered him back the reins of the ranch, but he presented her with the idea of a partnership. She could use the land to build her own herd—she had a penchant for a sturdy little Irish breed called Dexters—and over time, he'd whittle his herd down to something he could manage easily in his retirement. He didn't admit as much to his daughter at the time, but his doctors had told him that there was little they could do about the pain he still felt deep in his reconstructed thigh bone, or the catch in his low back from the crushed vertebrae, and that over time, he'd have to slow down and limit his hard labor if he were going to remain upright. "Keep exercising, keep moving, but stop tossing hay bales and roping calves," had been the doctor's mandate.

Besides, handing the ranching over to the very capable Faith had allowed him to be available to his daughters in ways he'd never considered possible before. He sold enough of his Angus cattle to put a sizable deposit on Hope's veterinarian school. She'd worked the whole time she was in school and had come out the other end with very few loans, and although she insisted she'd pay him back after graduation, he'd refused. He'd been so proud of her, especially when he saw how proud she was of herself. Now, happily married to Levi Valiente—and with a baby on the way—his daughter made a living as Plumwood Hollow Animal Hospital's own Doc Hope. "A fine investment, indeed," he often thought to himself.

Jed had been there for Charity when her beloved Thad had gone to war. And he'd been her landing place when Thad had returned from that war in a box draped in red, white, and blue. He'd offered the silent comfort she needed when everyone else offered sympathetic, but oh-so-useless words. He'd encouraged her cooking, selling off a few more head of cattle to remodel the ranch house kitchen so that Charity could start her catering business. Now she was had found a helpmate in young Frank next door, and the two of them, having traversed similar traumatic events in their pasts, were making a new future for themselves and for their baby boy, another Frank Flanner in a long line of them.

Courage and Justice. He'd been gifted with time to spend with them. On them. Without the sole responsibility of operating the ranch resting fully on his shoulders, he'd had the time to be there for them, to travel with them, even to participate in some of their shows with them. Their success might not have happened without his investment of time and a little financial aid along the way—first as the trick riding duo, The Twisted Sisters, and now with their new riding school and students already on a waiting list.

Prudence. Sweet, gentle Prudence. Her name suited her so well. She was her mother's daughter in so many ways—her appearance, her eyes, especially, that startlingly dark hair. But where Caroline was fiercely dogged in the pursuit of what she desired, Prudence weighed and measured, taking into consideration all outcomes of every decision. She wasn't a doormat, not their Prudence, but she often sacrificed her own wishes to make way for those of others. Jed's heart was full of gratitude for the reappearance of Collin Stewart and the radiant joy he now saw on his daughter's face. Caroline would have especially loved young Collin; Jed was certain of it.

Abby. Abstinence Eve. Had he cursed her with that name? Last year at the twins' double wedding, the Ransome woman had asked him directly if Abby had endured teasing and maybe even inappropriate harassment over it. He hadn't heard of anything, and he thought he knew his youngest child enough to be confident she would have told him about it. She would have at least told Faith about it—Faith, who had become her second mother—and surely, *surely,* Faith would have shared with him if Abby was struggling.

Then again, Faith had kept her teen pregnancy a secret from him until she was out of other options. When she'd finally come to him, she'd insisted she'd kept the news from him because she didn't want to hurt him. To be a burden to him. To protect him.

How much had his eldest daughter kept from him over the years in order to protect him? When had it become her job to do so? The tractor accident? And wasn't the role of protector his?

Did *all* of his daughters keep secrets from him?

Jed frowned at the thought of all of his daughters withholding their deepest wounds from him; not just Faith. In hindsight, hadn't they all done it over the years? Charity had poured out her grief on his shoulder, but in silent tears, not words. Courage had told no one of her desire to stop performing, not until after her terrifying fall. And Justice... well, he still didn't know what the black cloud had been the year before she married Brandon, and his relief over her obvious happiness after the fact had kept him from asking.

Prudence and that lost look in her eyes. Why had he never asked her about it? "I did, though," he countered out loud. "All the time. Where are you, child? Remember?"

Good grief. What would his daughters think if they heard him talking to himself this way?

But had he done all that he could? He'd asked the same question over and over; why did he think he'd get a different answer? When Prudence insisted she was fine, that she was content, that she liked her life at the ranch, Jed had nodded in acceptance and pushed no further. And yet, it hadn't been the love of a father that had put the light back in her eyes. It had been the love of another man, and that had broken Jed's heart a little.

He'd asked God to let him stay in this hollow for his daughters because they needed him. But had he been the kind of father they needed? Or had he only been one more burden for them to carry?

The phone rang again. Jed shoved up out of his chair and headed to his neat little kitchen. The contraption would be in the silver tray on the counter, along with his truck and tractor keys, the spare change that weighed down his pockets and made wearing a belt necessary, and the wallet that had never been very full, but had always had just enough for what his family needed.

He'd done the providing thing right. He was confident in that.

The protecting thing, though? Looking back, he saw a whole lot of failure in that camp. Was it too late to try and make up for it? Did his girls even need him that way anymore? Did they need him at all?

"I know you have me here for a purpose, Lord. Help me find it. I hate to admit it, but I think I might be a little lost myself."

He picked up the phone. "Hello, child."

"Hey, Daddy. Can you talk?"

SIX

By the time Abby opened her apartment door to Bucky, he was in the exact frame of mind as she'd anticipated. Frustrated, fuming, and ready for a fight. "What took you so long to answer the door?" he demanded.

At least she felt more like herself after the steam of the hot shower had cleared her brain fog a little. "I told you I was busy, didn't I?"

"Are you going to let me in?" Bucky didn't wait for a response, just pushed past her into the room. He had a paper bag in one hand, and the whiff of something fresh-baked and sweet drifted in with him, making Abby's stomach growl.

Not in agony this time, thank goodness. Although, knowing Bucky, what he'd brought might only be for himself. "Come in," she said, gesturing grandly at his back. "What's the emergency?"

He didn't answer her, but crossed to the small counter and plopped the bag down next to her coffee maker before pulling a mug from a shelf and pouring himself a cup. He took a sip, made a face like the dark brew was noxious, then set it down and opened the bag. "I brought you a blueberry muffin."

Oh, the games he liked to play. She made dang good coffee, and he knew it. That's why he'd not bothered to buy any from the pastry shop. He also knew she didn't like blueberry muffins. She loved fresh fruit, but she had an aversion to cooked fruit in any kind of baked goods, with the exception of Charity's apple pie. But that was because the apples were sliced so thin, they practically melted in your mouth; no chewing of slimy fruit chunks required.

"No, thank you," she said. She leaned against her closed front door and watched him pull only one muffin from the bag. Just as she'd thought; he'd known she'd refuse the treat. "I appreciate the generous offer, though," she said in a conciliatory tone. She didn't ask him about the emergency again, but she didn't move away from the front door, either. She hoped he got the message that he wasn't staying any longer than necessary.

Bucky pulled out the one stool at the end of the counter where Abby often ate her meals. Lowering his tall frame onto it, he took several bites of the muffin before finally saying, "I'm assuming you've heard nothing."

Abby kept her mouth shut and just waited. She hated the way he toyed with her. She'd never been around people who behaved this way, not until coming to Nashville. It wasn't the city itself, she knew, but the people who worked the underbelly of it. She wished she'd never seen what really went on behind the scenes. Her naivety had brought her only so far before she'd become disenchanted, and even worse, disingenuous, just like so many others she'd met in the backstage shadows where she now existed.

"Gregor's gone. Cut and run. Snatched up by another artist."

Abby closed her eyes, not wanting to see the look of satisfaction in Bucky's eyes. Why on earth was he happy about this? Shouldn't he be concerned? This was his livelihood, too. Did it mean so much to him to see her put in her place? To know she'd have to scramble to find another bass player before tomorrow night? Someone who could pick up her nuanced music in twenty-four hours?

"Stan's got another guy lined up for tomorrow's gig," he informed her smugly. "But he says it's gonna cost us."

"Well, that's good news," Abby said, breathing out a huff of relief.

"How is any of this good news?" Bucky shot back. "We're losing gigs, Stan is ticked off at us, and now our members are bailing."

She couldn't win with him. "Did Stan say anything about what happens with Gregor breaking contract?"

"Funny you should ask," Bucky said with a derisive snort. "According to our manager, if we can't find a replacement in the next few days, we are all in breach of contract because we signed with him as a band."

Abby lowered her gaze to the floor, but made a point not to show any other reaction to his terrible words. The thing was, Bucky could land another job anytime, anywhere. He'd made a name for himself as a local studio musician and made a lot of money on the side that way. Music was his career, and everything he did in the industry was to get himself a leg up. Breaking a contract was a step in the wrong direction, especially in the small Nashville music scene where everyone knew everyone else.

"Then I guess I'd better start looking." Abby straightened and pulled open her front door. "And you'd better go. I have some calls to make."

He looked at her like she'd lost her mind. "I'm here to help."

She narrowed her eyes at him. "I don't need your help."

"Yes, you do. I'm the one who has to play with the guy you hire. I need to be here."

Abby stared at him, not exactly surprised by his sentiment, just surprised that he'd said it out loud. "We all have to play with him. Or her," she added emphatically. "But it's still my band, Bucky. I'm the one who decides who's in it."

"Not really," he argued. "You thought Gregor was in it, but look how that turned out. I mean, for all you know, Tad might be looking at options, too. Especially now that the contract is on the line."

"What about you?" Abby was getting fed up with this conversation. She needed to find a bass player, *now,* and instead, she was stuck playing head games with a guy she used to think was pretty special. "Are you looking at options, too?" She almost hoped he'd say yes.

Bucky didn't speak for several moments, then finally shrugged. He met her eyes; there was steel in his. "Not if I have a say in who else we sign on."

Why hadn't Stan called her and told her about all of this? She hadn't missed any other calls that morning. "When did you talk to Stan?" she asked. Had their manager gone to Bucky and not to her?

"This morning. We had coffee." He nudged his still half-full mug away from him as if to say hers wasn't worth finishing. "I guess Gregor was at the bar negotiating his new deal when Stan went back inside last night."

"I see." She wasn't going to ask Bucky why they hadn't included her in on their conversation. She wouldn't give him the satisfaction of knowing how upset she was by the situation. In fact, as she stared at him, she realized that she was sick and tired of his petulant pretty face messing up her already lousy apartment decor. She wanted him gone. Maybe not from the band, but at the moment, she thought the sacrifice might almost be worth it. She pulled the door open wider, determined to call his bluff. "Well, you're not staying. So maybe you should go have coffee with him again and let him know you intend to quit, too. I've got my work cut out for me if I'm going to find a bass and a guitar player before my contract goes up in smoke."

Bucky stared at her while he finished his muffin. Then he nonchalantly swept his crumbs off onto the floor, crumpled the empty paper bag, and lobbed it in the general direction of the trash can on the other end of the counter. He didn't even look to see where it landed. "I'll let Stan know where things stand," he said noncommittally as he approached. He stopped directly in front of her, and she could practically feel the angry vibrations coming off him.

She held his gaze, refusing to look away or to say another word. She'd scream herself hoarse into her pillow after he was gone.

"Have it your way, princess." Bucky lifted two fingers to his forehead in a mocking salute, then he patted her cheek none too gently and sauntered out onto the third-floor landing.

With the utmost self-control, Abby didn't slam the door behind him. But she stood with her cheek pressed to the cool wood trim and let herself imagine him tumbling tail over teakettle down all three flights.

Stan answered his phone on the third ring. "Stan." It was how he always answered. Not a greeting; just his name.

"It's Abby. I just got a visit from Bucky. Want to tell me what's going on?"

"He didn't tell you what's going on?"

"He did. I should have heard it from you, though." She shouldn't have to tell him this.

"Gregor is gone. I have a stand-in for tomorrow night—Paul Castor, you know him."

Abby clamped her lips closed to prevent a groan from slipping out. Paul Castor was a terrific bass guitarist... and he knew it. He also charged an arm and a leg, possibly even a lung or two for his time. They'd be lucky to come away from tomorrow's gig with a dime in their pockets after giving him his fare. But Abby didn't know the local musicians the way Stan did, and she wasn't sure she could come up with anyone by the weekend, no less by tomorrow.

As though he'd read her mind, Stan continued, "If you don't have a new bass player by Friday morning, I'm pulling the plug on Alan Jackson's show. That's bad enough, but please don't make me pull you off Legend's Corner over the weekend. That would make all of us look bad, and I don't like looking bad."

"Got it," Abby said, feeling dismal.

"We'll meet Friday morning for coffee at the pastry shop near your place. I'll remind you what your contract says, and you can tell me what you have in mind to keep this ship afloat. Essentially, you have until Monday to get your ducks in a row, Abstinence, or I'm out."

It was pretty much exactly what Bucky had told her, but it got her hackles up hearing it again. "And you couldn't tell me this yourself? Maybe you're in breach of contract." The moment the words were out of her mouth, Abby wanted to scoop them out of the air and stuff them back down her throat.

"I'm going to pretend you didn't say that," Stan replied, his tone not changing at all, making Abby wish all the more that she could indeed retract her words. "I'm going to focus on keeping club owners happy by filling their stages with bands who can put on a good show, whether it's you or some other hungry young thing. You focus on keeping your band whole and happy. I know I can do my part. Can you do yours?"

Abby nodded, then realizing he couldn't see her, mumbled, "I can."

"I'll believe it when I see it." And with those ham-fisted words, Stan hung up on her.

If she didn't figure things out, she was going up in flames. Along with her band, her reputation, and maybe even her future as a professional musician.

Three hours later and what felt like thirty phone calls, Abby had arranged to meet with two different musicians the next day. One of them didn't sound super-thrilled about it; he kept asking if she liked bluegrass. She did, but it wasn't something The Abstinence Goodacre Band performed. But beggars couldn't be choosers, and Ronnie's demos on his website were pretty clean, so she put him on the list of possibilities. The other bassist was a girl named Stena Holder. She'd recently arrived in Nashville and was looking for a regular gig. She had a good online profile and her samples were pretty amazing. Abby was a little surprised no one had snapped her up yet. Stena had that superstar quality about her, an air of confidence that had the potential to take her places.

Abby would meet with Ronnie in the morning and Stena at noon, but she'd asked them both to be at The Stage for Abby's Thursday night gig—the one during which Paul Castor would fill in for Gregor—to make sure they knew what they were signing up for. Stena said she'd been to Abby's shows before, that she already knew several of her songs, and wanted to know if she should come ready to get on stage with them.

Ronnie, on the other hand, asked if there'd be free drinks.

Abby said yes to both, although she was already fairly certain the free drinks would be a complete waste of her money.

Who was she kidding? Her money? What money? She was barely breaking even after paying Stan, her band mates, and all the other expenses that went into climbing the entertainment ladder. She was, in fact, still nothing more than a pay-to-play musician. A hungry young thing. A pretty little starlet. A nameless voice in the madding noise of the music industry.

"I have to do better than this," she whispered as she stood at her window, peering down into the trash-strewn alley below. "I have to fix this mess."

SEVEN

"HAVE YOU HEARD FROM Abby lately?" It was Prudence.

Jed frowned slightly and glanced over at the calendar hanging on the wall next to the refrigerator. He called her every Sunday, and she called him on Wednesday mornings, because it was her day off. Every once in a while, she'd pick up an extra shift at Betty's Grill, a place that served some pretty good made-from-scratch burgers, but she still called home before noon, even if only to let him know she had to work and couldn't talk.

In the busyness of getting his cattle moved and settled this week, Jed hadn't realized he'd missed his youngest daughter's phone call this morning.

"I haven't," he admitted. He didn't like the undercurrent in Prudence's voice, and he couldn't help wondering if she knew something about Abby that he didn't. Especially in light of this recent ponderings over his girls keeping secrets from him.

Prudence hesitated on the other end of the line. He could practically see the thoughts churning around behind her wide blue eyes.

"What is it, child?" he asked, his voice coming out a little more brusque than he'd intended.

"I—I don't know, Daddy," she finally said. "Last night, I woke up with her on my mind, and I can't get rid of this feeling that...." Her words drifted into silence.

"What feeling?" Jed prodded.

"You're going to think I'm crazy."

"Going to?" he teased. "Pru, honey, I already do. But, as you know, I trust your crazy." He smiled behind the words, hoping she'd hear it and be put at ease. This was another way this daughter of theirs was like Caroline. There'd been more than once when his wife rose up out of a deep sleep with something or someone weighing heavy on her heart and mind. She usually got out of bed and onto her knees when it happened; she believed it was the good Lord waking her up to be a prayer advocate for someone in need. More than once, her intervening prayers had been validated when word would get out about a near-death accident or a sick child in desperate need of miraculous healing. This wasn't the first time Prudence had come to him with the same kind of experience, either. Who was he to question the way the Almighty worked? "What is it?"

"I don't even know, but I just can't get her out of my thoughts, and I'm super unsettled about her. I dreamed she was—oh, this is going to sound so silly!" Before he could assure her otherwise, she went on. "I dreamed she was walking in the woods. Not our woods, but some old and creepy woods." Prudence sighed, like she was relieved to be able to talk about this. "Something was hunting her, Daddy, and she didn't know it. That's what keeps freaking me out. She was just skipping along the path like she knew where she was going, all the while, something—I don't know. Something sinister, you know? Something bad was closing in on her."

Jed waited, giving her the time she needed to get her thoughts out before he responded.

Prudence let out a huff of exasperation. "When I say it out loud, it sounds like just a nightmare. A stupid bad dream. But Daddy, I can't get it out of my head. I tried calling her three different times today, but she didn't answer. She's probably at work, but—"

"Pixie Cut." Changing tactics, he stopped her before she worked herself up into a tailspin. She didn't do it often, but every once in a while, Prudence could get overwhelmed by her own deep well of emotions. "I'm glad you called me. I'm sure she'll get back to you when she gets a chance."

"I know. I know." She drew the last word out, sounding fed up with herself. "I don't mean to worry you about it. I really only called to see if you'd heard from her this week yet. I had no intention of dumping all of this on you. Sorry."

His earlier thoughts came back to mind, and Jed frowned. "That's what I'm here for, child. I've grown some pretty broad shoulders over the years, you know."

"I know. But you already have a lot on your plate, what with your move and getting settled in all by yourself over there." She paused before she asked, "Aren't you lonely?"

Jed ran a hand along his jaw, the slight stubble of afternoon rasping against his roughened palms. "On the contrary, my plate seems rather empty, now that most of you girls are doing the kind of work you love to do. And married to men I approve of, to boot. That said, even if it were full, you girls and your wellbeing is and always has been and always will be a priority over everything else this world throws my way. You hear?"

"I know," she started again, but he cut her off.

"Don't placate me, Prudence Goodacre Stewart." He cleared his throat to shake loose the knot that seemed to be forming there. "I hate that you feel you have to apologize for sharing your heart with me."

"I just don't want to bother you with something that's probably nothing."

"If it's unsettling to you, then it's not nothing to me. I want you to bother me with stuff like this." He reached up and rubbed the back of his neck in frustration. "I can handle it."

"Okay," she said meekly. "Well, that's what's on my mind."

"Thank you for sharing it with me. Now I'm going to hang up with you and try calling your little sister. If I don't get a response before this evening, I'll call Betty's Diner. She might have taken an extra shift. Or maybe her phone is dead." How he hated these darn phones that made everyone so accessible, whether or not they wanted to be. He didn't blame folks for letting their phones die now and then; sometimes it seemed that was the only acceptable excuse for not answering a call these days.

That said, it wasn't like Abby to let her phone die. That little pocket computer was the lifeline of her business as a musician. She was too responsible to let a thing like that happen, no less to let it stay off all day long. And surely, if something had happened to her phone—if she'd lost it, or damaged it—she'd have let him know so he wouldn't worry. He supposed that in the busyness of her waitressing job, if she had, indeed, gone in to work today, it was possible she simply hadn't realized the phone was off.

He couldn't allow himself to consider the alternative.

Prudence thanked him and said goodbye, and Jed dialed Abby's number.

When she didn't answer his first call, he didn't let himself panic.

When she didn't answer his second call just after dinner, he realized his jaw was beginning to ache from clenching it.

When she didn't answer his call at nine o'clock that night, he could hear his own racing pulse inside his head.

EIGHT

THE WEEK HAD GONE from bad to worse. After Gregor abandoned ship on Tuesday, Abby had been forced to call off work at Betty's on Thursday so she could meet with Ronnie and Stena. Betty, however, had been more disgruntled than usual about Abby taking the day off, and had told her not to bother coming in the rest of the week. When Abby ventured to ask if she still had a job, Betty's taciturn response had been to call back on Saturday and find out.

"I need someone who can be here when they say they'll be here," Betty told her. "If you can't make it happen, I'll find someone who can. There are a lot of folks looking for work in this town, you know."

Yet another person reminding her of how expendable she was, how easily she could be replaced.

Granted, Abby did take her share of sick days. Not including this one, she'd already called in three sick days in the four months she'd had the job. One of those hadn't exactly been a sick day... unless one called a hangover from hell being sick. She supposed some people would, but it wasn't exactly the kind of illness that garnered sympathy from a boss.

"I really need the job," Abby had insisted.

"Then stop taking days off," Betty had barked, going on to say that none of her other serving staff took near as many as Abby did, and the others always made the effort to find someone else to fill in for them.

"I don't know the others, though," Abby started to explain to the woman. "I mean, we work together, but I don't know them personally. I don't have their numbers." She didn't remember Betty telling her that was the protocol for calling in sick before.

Betty had scoffed into the phone. "I don't care if you are friends with your co-workers or not. I pay you to show up. If you don't show up, you need to find someone else who will. Only call me when you've exhausted all other options."

On Thursday, right before she was to meet with Stena, Stan called and told her Bucky had a family emergency come up and had to leave town for a couple of days. "So you're out for the gig at The Stage tonight—they had another band waiting in the wings for an opportunity like this."

Expendable. Replaceable. Abby hung her head and fought back tears.

"Bucky says he'll try to make it back by tomorrow night and be ready to play, but I'm starting to wonder if you still have a band at all." Stan remained matter of fact, even as he added, "Things are going down fast, Ms. Goodacre. Let's meet tomorrow morning and go over our options."

"Okay," she said with a weary sigh.

"And you still have to pay Paul for tonight," he added before hanging up without saying goodbye.

Of course.

Stena turned out to be the one bright spot in her day. She was shockingly beautiful, with long black hair that hung like a satin sheet down her back. It kept slipping over her shoulder while she played. Stena knew how to work that hair to her advantage, though; she adeptly flipped her head, lifted her chin, and sent the tresses sliding back down her back. The move might have been the result of a whole lot of practice in front of a mirror, but Stena managed to make it look one hundred percent natural.

"You've got the job, if you want it," Abby told a grinning Stena. She was so relieved; Ronnie had been good, but he'd rubbed her the wrong way. His cocky self-assuredness had reminded her too much of Bucky, and Abby was glad she'd be able to call him with a no.

Not only did Stena know several of Abby's most popular songs by memory, she picked things up fast. She played by ear exceptionally well and needed only to hear a new song once or twice before picking up the bass line with a finesse that rivaled Gregor's. The thought of having another woman on stage with her didn't hurt, either. Abby was a little tired of it being just her and the guys. She'd been a bit of a novelty to them at the beginning, but it hadn't lasted. Especially after she made the mistake of getting into a romantic relationship with Bucky.

Stan had warned her not to fall for any of them. "It always turns out bad," he'd said.

Had she listened? Yes, she had. But she'd also thought maybe Bucky was worth taking a chance on.

How could she have misjudged him so badly?

She hated having to tell Stena that hiring her was contingent upon Bucky showing up or not, but Stena waved off her apologies. "Boys. And they call *us* the divas." She leaned forward and put a hand on Abby's knee. "Why don't the two of us go out tonight? We can raise a glass to flaky guys; they make us look good."

Abby wasn't sure her band mates' treachery had made her look good or not, but going out with a girlfriend sounded better than anything had in a long time.

With acute relief, she called Ronnie and told him the job had gone to someone else. "There are no drinks on me, period," she added in response to his insistence that she owed him at least one. She didn't bother telling him that she and her band wouldn't even be performing that night.

By the time Abby staggered up the stairs to her apartment, it was well past midnight. Stena had somehow managed to stay sober—or at least it seemed that way to Abby—and had dropped Abby off at her apartment before driving off into the humid, starlit night.

When Abby awoke to someone pounding on her door, a rush of panic coursed through her. Holding her head with both hands, she managed to sit up at the edge of her bed, albeit very slowly. Her mouth felt lined with cotton, and when she tried to speak, nothing but a raspy whisper came out.

She got to her feet, propelled by the rush of awareness that things were not as they should be, and stumbled across the room to the door. She left the chain in place—she didn't even remember locking up last night—and opened the door just enough to see who was on the other side of it. "Yes?" she managed to say.

"You are an hour late for our meeting."

Stan.

Oh, geez. Stan and their meeting.

The meeting about her band. Her career. Her future.

"I—I'm sorry. I'm not feeling good," she stammered. "Can you give me a few—"

"Here's what I can give you." Stan shoved a manila envelope through the narrow opening. "A copy of our contract. Your guitar player has just informed me that he won't be back until next Tuesday. Your bass player is AWOL—"

"I found a bass player," she cut in, a sense of desperation and dread tap dancing inside her chest.

Stan continued like she hadn't spoken. "I've pulled you off Legend's Corner for both Saturday and Sunday's shows, and the Whiskey Vault isn't interested in an acoustic solo set from you. I already asked."

"But—but I—" she stammered, unable to come up with anything to counter his statements.

Stan let out a scoffing snort and told her, "Your time is up Monday at noon. I'll be at Margaritaville for lunch. If I see you there, I'll know you're ready to work. Otherwise, this is goodbye."

"But—Stan, wait." She closed the door and slid the chain free so she could speak more freely to her manager. "Stan, can't we—"

"It's not goodbye to your future, Abstinence," Stan interrupted her, holding up a hand to stop her sputtering words. He took a deep breath and shifted to a more relaxed stance. For the first time in the months she'd worked with him, his voice came out sounding almost kind, sympathetic. "It's goodbye to right now. This is only a season in your life. You have the talent to go far in this industry, young lady. I've seen thousands of kids come and go on these stages. But its musicians like you who always come back, sometimes again and again. It's all about timing for kids like you."

Abby stepped forward, pulling her sheet tighter around her body, acutely aware that she wasn't dressed for company. "This isn't how it's supposed to happen. Please. Isn't there another way?"

Stan stepped back, the slightest wrinkle of his nose the only indication that he knew exactly why she wasn't feeling so good.

"I'm sorry I messed up today. This week. Everything." She rubbed her eyes with her free hand and shoved her long hair away from her face. It felt stiff and tangled under her palm. She must look atrocious. "I'm sorry I'm such a screwup." Her voice broke, but she refused to cry. "I'll try harder, I promise."

Stan studied her, his stoic expression somehow sympathetic. "I'm going to give you some parting advice, Abstinence Goodacre." One corner of his mouth hitched up just the slightest bit. It wasn't a grin. Not even a half-grin. But it made Abby pay attention. "This time, I think you should heed my words, okay?"

Abby nodded, pressing her lips together. Her head felt like it was about twice its normal size, and the throbbing of her pulse was loud in her ears. Her legs trembled beneath her, but she hoped the sheet prevented Stan from noticing.

"Go home. Take a few months. Maybe a year. Get your head on straight." He held a hand up to his mouth in a drinking gesture. "Get your head out of the bottle. That's the last place you want to be in this industry, and believe me, if you don't get out now, it *will* end up being the last place you'll be."

"I can't go home," Abby replied, her misery seeping out through her words. "Not like this."

Stan closed his eyes briefly, then straightened his shoulders and looked her in the eye. His were definitely sympathetic now. "If you can't go home like this, then where can you go?"

She had no answer for that. She knew she *could* go home. She knew her father would open his arms to her, her sisters would gather her close and offer comfort, that they'd still tell her they believed in her.

But it wouldn't change the fact that she'd failed everyone. She'd be the kid sister crawling home with her tail between her legs, and they'd all pat her on the head and tell her that everything would be all right, all the while exchanging concerned and knowing glances over her head. *Poor little Abby.* She could hear them thinking it, even now. She couldn't bear it.

Stan studied her for a few more moments. Then he glanced down at his watch. Before turning to go, he said, "Call your father. He wants to hear from you."

"My father?" He'd called Stan? Abby had seen the missed calls from both Pru and Daddy over the last two days, and she'd intended to respond to them, but that hadn't happened. Between scrambling to find replacement musicians, the disappointment of canceled shows and cut hours at the diner, she'd decided to wait until last night to call them back. But she'd gone bar-hopping with Stena instead and had gotten home too late—and too drunk—to call anyone.

"If Jedediah Goodacre is your father, then yes," came Stan's long-suffering reply.

"Is everything okay? What did he say?" Why hadn't she called him back before she went out?

"Just call him so he'll stop calling me."

"Okay," she said with a nod.

Stan turned to head back down the stairs. "Had to be the third floor," he muttered to himself. Then he hitched up his pants, gripped the stair rail, and started down.

"Thank you," she said to his descending back. She wasn't exactly sure what she was thanking him for, but it felt like the right thing to say.

Stan lifted a hand briefly, but didn't look back. The moment suddenly felt very momentous.

Inside her apartment, Abby sent a short, apologetic text to her father. *Dad, I'm so sorry I made you worry. It's been a super busy couple of days. I meant to call you several times, but something always came up.* It wasn't exactly a lie, but she couldn't tell him the whole truth. It would have to do. *I'll call you this afternoon, okay? I promise.*

Jed replied immediately. *I'll be waiting for your call.* Abby read all kinds of things into that single statement, but even in her miserable state, she was pretty sure the most prominent sentiment in his text was disappointment in her.

She texted Prudence, too. This time, she did lie. And she was pretty sure her sister would see right through it. *I'm sorry I didn't respond to your calls.*

I worked super long hours the last few days and my show last night went way later than I'd hoped. Got home and crashed. I'm doing great, Pru. Don't worry about me, okay? Remember - this is my dream, and I'm making it happen!

Prudence didn't text back.

She called back.

Through the first three rings, Abby debated whether to answer or not. She finally swiped the phone on. "Hey, Pru!" she spoke in a rushed tone, hoping she sounded terribly busy.

"Abby? What's wrong?" Clearly, the text hadn't done its job.

"Wrong?" Abby asked. "Nothing's wrong. Didn't you read my text?"

"I read your text."

"Yeah, so, like I said, I'm just crazy busy this week. In fact, I'm just getting ready to hop in the shower; I have an appointment in an hour."

"You're not at work today?"

Dang it. "No, I took the afternoon off. I kinda needed a break, you know?" she added.

Prudence paused long enough to make Abby squirm, but then said, "I'm glad you're giving yourself a break."

Abby waited for Pru to continue, but when her sister remained silent on the other end of the line, she said, "Well, I gotta go get ready. I'll talk to you soon, okay?"

"Hey, Abby." Prudence's voice got quiet, serious.

"Yeah?"

"Dad called the Stage last night. Just thought you should know."

Oh, no, no, no. Abby groaned internally. No wonder she'd read disappointment into his clipped text. It had been clipped, hadn't it?

Then again, her father wasn't a verbose kinda guy.

"I didn't play at The Roof Top last night. I was at Layla's Honky Tonk." Not a lie. Layla's was just one of the several watering holes she and Stena had visited.

"You might want to update your schedule with him. He was pretty worried about you."

"I know," Abby said, trying to maintain the carefree note in her voice. She forced out a rueful chuckle. "He called my manager, too. I got the riot act from Stan this morning."

"Sounds like Stan is a keeper."

If only that were so. Out loud, she said, "I know, right? Hey, I really need to go now, okay?"

"I love you, Abs. Call if you need anything. I mean it. There isn't anything too trivial to call home about."

Abby swallowed the lump that rose in her throat. If only that were so, too. "I know. I love you, too. Say hi to your hottie hubster and hug the rest of the fam for me."

Later that afternoon, after she showered and scrubbed whatever the sticky stuff was out of her hair, after straightening her apartment, and after devouring a can of chicken and stars soup, Abby finally worked up the courage to call Stena.

"Hey, girl!" Stena responded after Abby identified herself. "We had a good time last night, didn't we? You okay?"

"I think I had a better time than you did," Abby said self-deprecatingly. "At least until I woke up."

Stena chuckled at the other end of the line. "I have to admit, I was a little worried about you. But at least you're a happy drunk," she quipped.

"I didn't do anything—you know, inappropriate, did I?"

"Nah. I kept you in my sights the whole night. Other than that guy you were practically getting naked with back by the bathrooms—"

"What?" Abby yelped, then clutched her head as the sharp sound assaulted her senses.

"I'm just kidding!" Stena laughed heartily, and suddenly Abby sensed something other than friendship in the girl's teasing. "He was definitely into you, though. Do you still have his phone number? He wrote it on your back. Kyle, I think that was his name?"

"You're still kidding, right? I don't—I don't remember any of this." Abby got up and headed to the bathroom where she pulled wide the neck of her t-shirt so she could see her shoulder in the mirror. There was nothing there, but then, she'd taken that long shower.

"Not kidding. You wrote yours on his chest."

Abby closed her eyes, mortification sweeping over her like a heatwave.

"I had to stop you from leaving a lipstick kiss along with your number," Stena said censoriously. "I can't really blame you, though. You two were really into each other."

Abby couldn't remember any of this. Not the numbers exchange, not the chest, not even Kyle. It was time to change the subject.

"Well, thanks for looking out for me," she said, although, clearly, that wasn't what Stena had done at all. "But the reason I'm calling is to let you know that my other gigs this week have been canceled. As you know, I'm kinda, um, well, my band is going through a—"

"A restructuring?" Stena offered helpfully. Abby didn't sense any malice in her tone, but that didn't make things any easier.

"Yeah. A restructuring of the band. I gave my manager your info yesterday, so he'll be in touch with you when we're ready to gig again. Hopefully, we'll get this all figured out by this weekend." *We. Right.*

"Oh, Stan already called me. This morning," Stena added. "And guess who's coming to see me play tonight? He thinks I've got something he can work with."

Stena's words fell like a lead balloon into the pit of Abby's stomach. "Good for you," she managed to force out. "He's a great manager," she added, doing her best not to choke on the words. She hesitated for just a moment, then said, "I didn't know you were playing somewhere else tonight."

"Oh, it's at a different time than your gig is. Was, I mean. I would have been there for you, don't worry."

It was all a moot point now, but why on earth hadn't Stena at least mentioned her other gig before? "Who do you play with?"

"Oh, it's my own band. Stena and the Steamrollers. Do you know how big a deal people make about a chick bass player around here? And the fact that I can sing real pretty doesn't hurt either. I mean, your voice is ridiculously amazing, but I can carry a tune with the rest of them. Strap on my axe, and according to Stan, I'm gold."

"That's—that's amazing," Abby stuttered, at a loss for words. Betrayal churned inside of her and she thought she was going to be sick. "Look, I gotta go. I'm really glad for you. Stan's a good guy."

But he wasn't, was he? Hadn't he just replaced her with Stena? He was just like everyone else in this stupid city where fairytales, if they didn't come true, turned into nightmares.

Abby hung up and moved to sit on the end of her bed. "What am I going to do?"

NINE

JED KEPT HIS PHONE in his pocket the whole afternoon, waiting for Abby's call. As the minutes and hours ticked by, he kept pulling it out to check the battery, to make sure he hadn't accidentally silenced it or turned it off—something he was apt to do, mainly because he didn't know how to do it on purpose. Every time he did, the phone was on, the ringer was on, and there were no missed calls, no new text messages.

The day was slipping away, and Jed felt a little like his youngest daughter might be slipping away, too.

When his phone rang at 4:45 PM, he almost dropped it while trying to pull it out of his back pocket. "Hello, child," he said, hoping she couldn't hear the edge in his voice.

There was a short pause on the other end of the line, then a voice he immediately recognized said, "Jedediah? This is Charlotte. I take it you were expecting a call from someone else?"

Disappointment and anticipation wreaked havoc inside his chest for a few moments, and he couldn't seem to find any words.

"Jedediah? Is everything all right? Should I call back another time?"

"No, no. It's fine. You just caught me off guard. I am, indeed, waiting for a call from Abby."

"I can call back," she reiterated, but he shook his head, even though she couldn't see him.

"It's fine. These newfangled telephones have no problem interrupting one call with another."

Charlotte let out one of her low, throaty chuckles that made the thinning hairs on Jed's arms stand up. "Ain't that the truth," she quipped.

Jed cleared his throat. "What can I do for you, Ms. Ransome?" Despite her insistence that he call her by her first name, Jed persisted in addressing her with her surname. Somehow, it helped to put a little distance between them, almost like a line drawn in the sand. Not because he had any expectations that it would keep her from crossing over to his side—she'd made a point to do that every chance she got, something that both rankled him and riled him up. No, it was to keep himself from crossing over to her side. He didn't want to think about what might become of him if he let that happen.

Besides, she still called him Jedediah. Usually Jedediah Goodacre.

Caroline had called him Jedediah when she wanted something from him.

"I'm so glad you asked," Charlotte replied. "There's a property I'm eyeing out your way. I was wondering if you wouldn't mind taking a look at it?" He'd been scoping out places for her all summer, and although he pretended it was a nuisance, he really didn't mind. The thought of her living up close and personal, though? That, he was pretty sure he minded.

Charlotte Ransome wasn't beautiful.

She was stunning, but not in the storybook heroine way. No, she could have been chiseled from the side of a craggy mountain, or carved from the towering trunks of a tulip poplar. Tall and straight, lean and muscular, angles and hard lines, that's what Charlotte Ransome was made up of. But that smile could knock a man right off his feet, and those slanted silver eyes... Well, those eyes saw right through his quiet barriers and prodded at things he'd long believed lay dormant deep inside of him.

"Where is it?" he asked, letting his inner turmoil make him sound brusque.

"Do you have a pen and paper? I'll give you the address."

Jed didn't need pen and paper. He knew every square inch of this valley in a hundred-mile radius. "I got one."

"Write this down. 331 Outer Canyon Road. It's twenty-three acres, so a little more than I need, but it's got two pole barns already in use on the property."

"The Gallups' place. I heard they were pulling up and moving closer to their kids."

"You know it, then. Good. What do you think of it?" He could hear the excitement in her voice. "I only really need five acres, but if the price is right, I certainly don't mind the extra. According to the listing, about ten of those acres are woods, anyway. I'm not planning on growing my pasture much beyond five acres—that much keeps me busy enough already—but maybe I could lease some of it, or even let the woods take back more of the land. I wouldn't mind the bigger buffer between me and the corn fields the next property over."

He waited until she stopped to take a breath, then said, "It's a fine property. Larry Gallup takes good care of his place."

"Great," she said. "How well do you know them? Do you think you could go out and take pictures for me? The listing has some good photos online, but they're just a smattering of this and that. And you know how those are—they always use those wide-angle images with fancy filters that make things look twice as big and ten times as pretty as they are in real life. I need to see what the inside of the pole barns look like, how much space there is between them, how far they are from the house. I'd also like to see if the house has a good room for my work. I need a lot of light."

"Hold up, woman," Jed interrupted. "I'm not a Realtor, and I am not your personal shopper. I don't mind giving you feedback on a property, but I am not a photographer, either. I can tell you that Larry Gallup takes good care of his place, like I said. He's an honorable man, and I can also guarantee that whatever he's asking for his property is fair. The Gallups are friends of mine, and I will not go nosing about their property with a camera. If you want pictures of the inside of his personal property, I suggest you contact him directly."

The silence on the other end of the line told him his words had hit home. Finally, she spoke. "Thank you for setting me straight. You're right; I need to just reach out to them myself."

Then why the tarnation hadn't she? She wasn't stupid. Nor was he. What else did she have up her sleeve?

"I guess I was just looking for any excuse to call you," she admitted, plain and simple. "But I'm a big girl now, and I shouldn't have to have an excuse, should I? So Jedediah Goodacre, how are you?"

Jed was so taken aback by her forthrightness that he had to lower himself into one of the rockers on the back porch. She made his head spin. "I'm fine," he managed to grunt the words out.

"That's good to hear," she returned, and he could hear the knowing smile in her voice. "You said you were waiting on a call from Abby. How is she doing? I think about her all the time. I was once a young and stupidly bold young woman out in the big world on my own. It's a wild place out there, but oh, so full of wondrous things."

She wasn't helping ease Jed's mind about Abby, that was for sure. He didn't want to think about his youngest daughter being alone—and stupidly bold—out in the big wild world. It reminded him in an unsettling way of Prudence's dream.

"I'd love to go see her perform the next time I come out that way. I haven't told you yet; I'm planning on being there the first week of next month, and I'm really hoping to put my money down on something then. I need to get my sheep moved before winter sets in, and if I don't find something by the end of September at the latest, I might have to wait until next year, and that just won't do."

The woman could talk, he thought to himself, but instead of feeling irritated by it, he found it entertaining. She didn't gossip or prattle on about useless things. At least, not that he knew of. She just spoke her mind, and her mind happened to be a busy, and from what he could tell, productive place. "Sounds like a good plan."

"You know how I usually stay with Sarah when I come out? Well, she's got company next week—her sister and her family—and from what I can tell, it might take a lot out of her. Especially right now, while Joe and Courage are in the middle of all the work they're doing to expand the place."

Joe was adding on an extension to the back of the modest three-bedroom farmhouse. To prepare for children, Courage had told her father. When he'd asked if that was her way of telling him she was expecting, she'd laughed awkwardly. "Not yet. I want to finish school first. But we hope to start our family in another year or two, and we want space for them before that happens."

Jed couldn't have been more pleased by the thought. He imagined Joe and Courage would make exceptional parents, and Sarah, a fine grandmother, indeed.

But Charlotte's next words had him balking, and he suddenly wished there were a whole lot of extra bedrooms to spare over at the Lynxwilder farm.

"Well, I got to thinking," she said, calm and casual, as if she weren't suggesting something that would turn the world as he knew it upside down. "Since I'm leaning so much on you to be my guide about town."

Guide about town? He wasn't her guide about town, or anywhere else, for that matter. But her next words had Jed struck dumb before he could argue.

"What if I just stay with you? You've got an extra room. In fact, if I recall correctly, you've got two extras, right? I could just crash at your place for a few days while I scout out a few more properties. That would make it so much easier on everyone, don't you think? That way, I could bring home each day's findings and we could talk about them over dinner. Or coffee and pie. That Charity sure makes a mean apple pie. That crumb top is to die—"

Jed let out a garbled, unintelligible noise that stopped Charlotte mid-sentence. He tried again. "Absolutely not. No. You can't stay here. Alone." His heart was pounding so hard he thought it might just lurch right out of his chest.

Charlotte chuckled. "I wouldn't be alone, though, would I? You'd be there."

"Absolutely not," he repeated.

"Why Jedediah Goodacre. Are you afraid of having me as a guest in your home?" Charlotte sounded utterly aghast, but he could hear the grin in her voice. It sent another wave of heat up his neck; she was mocking him. "Are you worried about your virtue?" she asked with an exaggerated drawl. "Or mine?"

"I am not afraid of you, Ms. Ransome. It's my daughters who scare me." Why was he letting her goad him like this? He pulled the phone from his ear and scowled down at the screen as though she might be able to see how disgruntled he was through the camera.

"I can talk to them, if you think that will make a difference," she offered. She sounded like she was trying not to laugh. "They're all big girls. They would probably agree that it makes perfect sense. I mean, we're adults, Jedediah Goodacre. Old adults." She stretched out *old* like one might a piece of chewing gum. "I think you and I can control our hormones after all these years, don't you?"

"No. It simply isn't an option. This is my house," Jed said, irked by the belligerence in his tone, but unable to wrangle it back under control. "I didn't move out of the big ranch house just to fill this place up with company. No ma'am. I moved here so I could have some peace and quiet."

As if conjured by his words, a deafening silence hovered in the air for several moments.

"Fine," Charlotte finally said. "You be peace, I'll be quiet." And then she laughed.

Jed did something he'd never done to any woman in his life. He hung up on her.

Before he could think what to do with the phone—he certainly didn't want to accidentally take another call from that woman—the intolerable device rang again.

Torn between checking the screen and throwing the dang thing away, Jed worked up the courage to see who it was.

"Abby." His greeting leapt through the phone like the wave of relief that washed over him. He just hoped it wasn't a case of out of the frying pan and into the fire. *Please let everything be all right with my baby girl, Lord.* "How are you doing, child?"

TEN

"Hey, Daddy!" Abby forced a brightness into her greeting that she didn't feel. She glanced at her pale reflection in the window and almost laughed out loud at the plastered-on smile she wore. *My stage smile,* she thought, and drew the corners of her mouth up even higher. Supposedly, people could tell by the way you talked if you were smiling or not. Come hell or high water, she was going to convince her father that all was well in her world. "I'm so sorry I didn't call you earlier this week." She went on to tell him that they were restructuring things—thank you, Stena, for the perfect word—and they had some surprise schedule changes, but that things were going along as they should. "I should have filled you in as soon as I knew what was going on. Prudence told me you called The Stage on Thursday night, and that you were worried when we weren't there."

On the other end of the line, Jed made a few understanding noises, but let her ramble about her job at Betty's. "I'm really glad for the good tips, Dad, because Betty can be super cantankerous when things get busy or don't go her way." Wasn't it always best to stick as close to the truth as possible?

"Well," Jed finally said when Abby came up for air. "I'm glad you're all right. I was worried, yes, but Stan—I spoke to him this morning—he told me he'd let you know I called. Figured if there was a real problem, he'd have filled me in."

Abby grimaced, glad her father couldn't see her expression. "Yeah, he told me you called. Again, I'm sorry I dropped the ball. I hate that I made you worry."

"It's my job to worry, Abstinence."

Abby stiffened at the edge in his voice. And so rarely did he call her by her full name that for a moment, she didn't recognize the word. "Okay," she said hesitantly.

"It irks me that you girls are afraid to share your struggles with me," he said, his pitch rising a little as he spoke. "What is the deal with that? Do you all think me so fragile, so weak, that I can't be a shoulder to lean on? I have withstood a storm or two, you know."

In the silence that followed his mini tirade, Abby struggled to find an appropriate response.

"It isn't a rhetorical question, Abby. I'd really like to know."

Finally, she said, "I—I can't speak for the others, but..." She hesitated, chewed on her bottom lip a moment, then took a fortifying breath and continued. "You're the strongest man I know, Daddy. Inside and out. It's not because I don't think you can weather any storm that blows your way. It's just—"

"It's just what?" Jed sounded more frustrated than impatient.

"I don't want to disappoint you." There. She said it.

"How could you possibly disappoint me? You are one of seven of the most amazing women alive on this planet, Abby-girl. You couldn't disappoint me even if you tried."

Abby's head dropped forward, her shoulders slumped. How could she tell him that his words only validated her fears. There was nothing amazing about her right now, unless being amazing at being a loser counted. "I know, Daddy. And I love you for believing in me. In all of us." She spoke softly, careful not to let her misery seep into her words. "I miss you," she added, and those words were truer than anything else she'd said to him.

She made her excuses and hung up, then stared down at her left hand—her chord hand—turning it this way and that, examining her long fingers, the creases at her knuckles, the callouses built up on the pads of her fingers from pressing on the guitar strings, and the criss-cross of lines that marked her palms. Those lines were supposed to hold all the secrets of one's life, so she'd heard.

How did her life become so full of secrets?

And what was she going to do now? She had no band, no shows, no manager as of Monday at noon, and if she defaulted on her contract with him, she would be out this apartment, too. Stan subleased a few of the apartments in this building to his clients, and he'd highlighted the part in the contract that stated she had one week from the termination date to vacate the property.

Abby groaned as a thought drifted through her mind. Would Stena Holder make this her home after Abby moved out? Would she become Stan's next new young thing?

ELEVEN

The sun wouldn't set for a few more hours when Jed climbed out of his truck after the afternoon spent across the way at the old ranch house with his daughters and their families for Sunday dinner. He ambled toward the new pole barn beyond his home, the sight of it filling him with guilty pleasure. How he loved his daughters, but for the first time, he was living in a world that he didn't have to share with anything more feminine than the cows in his pasture.

The day he'd signed the deed to Seven Virtues Ranch over to the girls had been bittersweet. It marked the fact that they were all truly grown, adults who no longer needed him to parent them, and although he was so proud of each one of them, he grieved a little, too. They had filled every moment of his life with their chatter, their joys and sorrows, their tears and laughter, their failures and accomplishments. There had been days over the years when he didn't know if he'd had it in him to shoulder one more moment of fatherhood without his sweet Caroline, but somehow, whether she was helping from heaven or not, he'd managed to get them all to this moment in time.

Sure, he'd had a lot of help, much of it from the girls, themselves. The Church of God parishioners had come alongside him after Caroline's death, and the Flanners from next door had been a godsend with Abby, who'd been only a few months old when Caroline had taken her last breath in the bed she and Jed had shared for nearly eighteen years. Over the years, he'd made it his duty to repay the kindness of the good folks of his community in any way he could. If a neighbor needed help getting crops in before a storm, if unforeseen disaster struck—a fire, broken water pipes, fallen trees, illness—Jed was there to offer shelter, food, tools, prayer, and friendship. The community had come to depend on him as much as he depended on them. That was how it was supposed to be, he told his daughters. And it made his heart swell to see them following in his footsteps, knowing that he had led them by example.

Even Abby, off pursuing her dreams in Nashville, never skipped an opportunity to say thank you in her own way—with her music, in particular—every time she came home.

He missed her. It had been almost three months since she'd last been in Plumwood Hollow for one of her too-short visits, and although her phone call last Friday had eased his mind somewhat, his spirit remained a bit unsettled over her situation. He pulled his phone out and glanced at the time. He was anxious to get her regular Sunday call; it should come any minute now. He'd make her stay on the line long enough to set his mind at ease.

When Abby had first gone to Nashville two years earlier, she'd been under the protective wing of the renown Remington Sounder, a man who had a reputation for finding talent in unlikely places and putting them on the map. He'd discovered Abby at The Smokehouse during one of her regular Friday night shows and had offered to take her back to Nashville, where he would produce her first album with her. Once the year was up, she'd be on her own—it was his way of giving back in honor of those who had helped him out when he'd first arrived on the scene.

As far as Jed could tell, Abby was well on the road toward making a name for herself, thanks to leg up Mr. Sounder had given her. Jed didn't like or dislike Stan Wallenberg, the man who'd become Abby's manager after her year with Sounder, but he was confident that his daughter had a good head on her shoulders when it came to people, and if she trusted Stan, Jed would, too.

That said, he'd made a point to introduce himself to Stan shortly after Abby signed with him. He'd exchanged contact information with the manager, not caring how clumsy he looked while tapping the guy's number into his phone with his gnarled rancher's fingers, and he'd made it clear that he expected Stan to answer if ever he called. "I won't abuse this information," Jed had assured the man. "But I want there to be someone on the other end if ever a real need arises."

He'd only had to call Stan twice. Once when his daughter had called home in tears because she'd left her guitar in the back of a taxi. Stan had been on the case in minutes, and the guitar had been rescued and returned to Abby in short order, along with the assurance that she should call Stan directly if anything like that ever happened again. Hopefully, there wouldn't be a next time; Abby's guitar was an extension of herself, and losing it would be like losing a limb.

Then there was Friday morning's call. Stan hadn't been very forthcoming about what was going on in Abby's life. He'd explained in as few words as possible—something Jed actually appreciated about the man—that the contract he had with Abby was just that: with Abby. Not Jed. He couldn't divulge any information without Abby's permission. But Stan had assured him that Abby was fine and had promised to check on her and deliver the message that she needed to call home.

And that was what had stuck in Jed's craw, what had him furrowing his brow every time his thoughts landed on his youngest daughter. Oh, Jed had fully expected Stan to refuse to discuss Abby with him. She was a legal adult and the contract she'd signed didn't have Jed's name on it.

But he'd also expected Stan to refuse his second request to deliver his message to Abby. He'd been so prepared for a response along the lines of, *I'm her manager, not her messenger boy.*

The fact that he'd agreed to talk to Abby on Jed's behalf was completely out of character for Mr. Wallenberg, and that didn't sit well with Jed.

The conversation he'd had earlier in the week with Prudence still rankled him, too. His daughters all had good men in their lives, men they could talk to, pour out their hearts, their hopes and dreams, their worries and concerns to. All except for Abby. Who did she have in her life? Certainly not Stan Wallenberg. It hadn't skipped Jed's attention that Abby and her guitar player, Bucky—and what the Sam Hill kind of name was that?—had a little thing for each other, but he could also tell right off that it wasn't going to last long. His daughter was smarter than that. Bucky wasn't the kind of guy to listen attentively to anyone but himself. No, she wouldn't be leaning on him for support, not for long, anyway.

Did she have any girlfriends yet? Surely, she'd made friends with some of the women she worked with at the diner. Granted, Abby had complained about Betty, the owner, on more than one occasion, and Jed was fairly certain the woman wasn't a motherly sort.

He reached up and rubbed the back of his neck where his hair clung, damp with sweat from the heat of the midday sun. He was overdue for a haircut. How was it that none of his girls had gotten on him about it?

The day had started out beautifully, the dew so heavy on the grass that Jed thought it might have rained the night before. The early morning sunlight had set everything aglow as he'd made his way out to tend to the animals in his care, and he'd paused on his back porch to gaze out over the property he now called his own. He'd offered up a prayer of gratitude for all that the Almighty had granted him in this life. The church service that followed reminded him, again, of how much he had—two pews filled with his loved ones, his offspring, and theirs. In another few years, they could make up well over a quarter of the congregation if they kept having children at the rate they were going.

Sunday dinners, still a tradition in the Goodacre family, now took place in different locations each week. Last Sunday, they'd all gathered at Joe and Courage's home for the meal. Sarah didn't enjoy cooking, and although Courage didn't love it, either, she was more than capable of whipping up a pan of homemade macaroni and cheese or spaghetti and a few side dishes. Fortunately, Joe not only loved to cook, but he was good at it, too. Even now, Jed's mouth watered at the memory of the roast chicken he'd eaten at the Lynxwilder home.

Especially since today's meal had not quite measured up. Prudence and Collin had commandeered the kitchen at the Seven Virtues ranch house, and the result of their unfortunate ability to distract each other, the pot roast had required an excessive amount of gravy just to get down, and the green beans were so thoroughly boiled that they wouldn't even stay on a fork. The newlyweds had been appropriately apologetic, of course, but

Justice, ever the brassiest of the lot, had suggested that the Stewarts not do any more of the cooking until they'd been married for at least another year.

Charity had saved the day with a peach cobbler that had all but melted in his mouth, and not in the way the green beans had. He'd brought an extra piece home to enjoy after supper tonight. He might even eat it *before* supper; who was there to stop him?

An hour later, when his phone still hadn't rung, he settled into one of the rockers on his porch and called her instead. It rang and rang until it finally went to her voice mail. He hated leaving messages—he always stumbled over his words at the thought of talking to a machine. But he didn't like that she wasn't answering her phone. "It's Jed—it's your father, Abby. Call me back." He pulled the phone from his ear and stared at the screen, forgetting for just a moment that he couldn't just set the thing down to hang up. He had to pretend to push a fake button on the glass screen to end the call, like he was in some kind of sci-fi movie.

He gave her a minute or two to call back, but when she didn't, he set the device face up on a small table beside his chair. He checked his ringer once again to make sure he'd switched the volume button to the on position after church and turned the volume was up as loud as it could go. He didn't want to miss her if he dozed. The late afternoon sun warmed the air, but a slight breeze had picked up, hinting at cooler evening temperatures to come. Insects thrummed a hypnotic song, and as he took in the peaceful setting, his shoulders relaxed, his breathing came easier, and his jaw unclenched.

"Lord," he murmured, overcome by a wave of gratitude. "Thank you for all that you have entrusted into my care. Help me do right by this land, by my daughters, by my precious Caroline, and most of all, by You."

Jed's eyelids were drifting closed when his phone rang, startling him enough to knock his hat askew. He muttered senseless syllables under his breath, waited a few seconds for his pounding heart to slow, then snatched the phone up. Abby.

"Hey, Daddy, it's me," she said in a voice so bright, Jed found himself squinting. "I'm so sorry I didn't call you earlier. This week has been crazy busy, and time just got away from me. I hope you didn't worry too much. I'm fine. But how are you?"

Jed didn't like the undertone in her voice. He didn't recognize it, and that worried him. She sounded almost afraid. He'd heard her nervous before. When she'd first told him about Mr. Sounder's offer, Abby's voice had trembled so badly that she'd stumbled over her words repeatedly. But not in fear. Not like this.

"Abby," he began, wondering how best to approach her. The fact that she was insisting she was fine even before he asked told him she had her defenses up. But defenses about what? "I'll be honest, child." What else could he be? "I am worried about you. You don't sound like yourself right now."

"Oh, Daddy, stop." She practically cut him off. "I'm fine," she repeated. "I'm pretty worn out, that's for sure, but it's just because I've had a lot on my plate. My bass player—you remember Gregor, right? Well, he decided he wanted to play with a different group who can pay him more. Needless to say, finding a replacement for him on such short notice has been a bit of a challenge. I interviewed a couple of players this last week. One of them, a girl named Stena, is really good, so I offered her the job."

What wasn't she telling him? He felt like he was getting half the story.

Or was he just being paranoid now? Prudence's words drifted through his mind again.

"Maybe you should come home for a few days, Abby. Take a break and get some rest. Can you do that? Will your schedule allow it?"

There was a pause at the other end of the line, and for a moment, Jed thought the connection might have been lost.

"I don't know if I can do that," Abby finally said. "Now that things are sorted out, I'm not sure it's a good idea to take a break. I want to give Stena the time she needs to feel comfortable with our music, you know?"

Jed nodded slowly, but kept silent. There was definitely more to the story, he was certain, and with Abby, the best way to get more details out of her was to wait her out.

This time, however, nothing more was forthcoming. The silence on the line started to sound obnoxious.

Finally, Jed cleared his throat and said, "Maybe I should come see you, then. Things are quiet around my place these days. Faith can keep an eye on my cows. It's been a while since I heard you sing, and—"

"Oh, Daddy," Abby said, cutting him off. "You *are* worrying. Everything is okay, I mean it. Our playing schedule is a little chaotic because of the band changes, so I'm not even sure what things are going to look like for the next few weeks. Stan is taking care of getting us booked again; I'll know more by the end of the month. If you come out now, you'll just be wasting your gas. Wait until things have settled a little, then come, okay? Maybe you can bring Jasmine and Yvette along. They love coming to Nashville."

Jed wasn't sure how to argue with that. She was definitely putting him off, but her reasons seemed legitimate. After pondering another moment, he said, "Abby-girl, you'd tell me if you were in trouble." It came out as a statement, but he needed her to assure him it was true.

He heard it; there was no denying that briefest hesitation before she said, "Of course, Daddy. I don't want you to worry about me, okay?"

Why were his girls so bothered by the idea of him worrying about them?

But he understood his youngest well enough to know that if he kept prying, she'd clam up even tighter. He'd have to trust her, it seemed. At least, for now. "You have enough money for food? Your bills?"

"Yes, Daddy." There was a smile in her voice when she answered, and that made him feel immeasurably better.

"You going to answer the phone when I call on Wednesday morning?"

"Yes, I'll answer the phone." She chuckled on her end of the line. "And if you don't call me, I'll call you. I promise."

"Good girl."

"I love you, Daddy."

"I love you, Abby-girl." He pressed an open palm over his heart. "Make me proud out there, you hear me now?"

"I—I hear you."

TWELVE

Saturday morning had brought Abby more bad news. She'd been certain Betty would cave and have her come into work during the busy weekend day shifts, but when Julie, one of the other wait staff, had given her Betty's message that she wasn't needed, Abby had understood it for what it was. There was no job for her at the diner; someone else had been hired to fill her shoes.

The rest of the weekend crept by on legs of molasses, and other than the trip she'd made to the convenience store on Saturday afternoon for cheap junk food and a bottle of something strong enough to help her forget her dire circumstances, Abby didn't leave her apartment until Monday morning. She somehow managed to make herself presentable for her meeting with Stan—she'd debated about whether she should even bother showing up—and over strong black coffee and a cranberry scone, she and Stan made the termination of the contract official. Thank goodness Stan was buying; Abby wasn't sure if she even had enough in her bank account to cover staples like sugar and caffeine.

Monday night, as she stood at her single window staring up at the strip of dark sky just visible above the back alley, she wondered what on earth she was doing, lingering in Nashville. No band, no shows, no day job... so why was she prolonging the inevitable? This tiny space she'd called home for the last eleven months wasn't hers, either.

With the remainder of the Jack Daniels she still had left from the weekend's binge, Abby pulled out the battered canvas duffel bag she'd stashed at the back of her closet and started throwing her things into it. Next to it, she made a pile of things she'd leave in the trash bin out back. Accessories she'd bought to make her look more like all the other musicians on the strip, including the terribly uncomfortable and even pricier snake skin boots Bucky had talked her into buying, boots that now she absolutely loathed, and the ridiculous studded bracelets, chokers, and belts her manager—*ex* manager—had insisted she wear to put an edge on her small-town girl-next-door look. Statement pieces, all of them, and she was no longer interested in making any statements.

The little kitchenette took no time at all—most of the cheap dishware and utensils were from the local Dollar Store or Walmart. She'd leave them in the cupboards. If Stena—or whoever ended up in here next—didn't want them, she could throw them away herself.

Within an hour of starting, she was finished. She'd even pulled the sheets and the plastic protective liner off the bed that had come with the furnished apartment, and had them balled up in a trash bag, ready to toss into the back of her truck before it occurred to her she was in no condition to drive. She glared at the bottle on the counter and cursed Jack Daniels for the delay in her escape. To add insult to injury, her red plastic cup was empty, so she couldn't even offer him a sardonic toast.

Besides, it was almost the middle of the night. She should get some sleep and head out in the morning. Maybe then she wouldn't feel so much like a coward, ducking out of town after dark. "Tomorrow, then," she said aloud. "With my head held high. At least until I get out of town."

Then, and only then, Abby could pull over and have a good cry. Alone.

With a dramatic sigh, she tugged the crumpled top sheet from the trash bag, spread it haphazardly over the mattress, and flopped spread eagle on top of it, not caring that she didn't even have a pillow under her head. If only her family could see her now. "Wouldn't they be proud?"

THIRTEEN

ABBY AWOKE THE NEXT morning, not at all surprised by the misery she found herself in. "That's it," she muttered. "I have got to be done with all of this. This town. This apartment. Even you, Jackie boy." She eyed the square amber bottle through slitted lids. "This is goodbye, and this time, I mean it."

It took her another hour to get her head clear enough to head out. It was a startlingly beautiful Tuesday morning, especially for someone with a lingering hangover, and Abby wondered if the furrows in her brow might become permanent after this whole ordeal. Despite the sun being out and already high in the sky, it was uncharacteristically brisk for a late July day. By mid-afternoon, the humidity would take its toll, and folks would be ducking into their favorite spots along Broadway Avenue for respite and shade, a cool drink, and a bit of the local entertainment. But now, just before noon, the sidewalks were hopping with tourists and locals alike. Abby drove slowly down the busy street lined with bars and restaurants, their doors and windows thrown open to passersby. It took her the opposite direction of the freeway home, but she felt the urge to see it once more.

"Closure," she said to herself, but the word clanged hollowly inside her head. There was no closure in what she was doing. She was leaving her dreams behind, ducking out like a coward, not telling anyone.

With a last look in her rear-view mirror, she mentally waved goodbye, and headed toward the nearest freeway on ramp.

Plumwood Hollow. Seven Virtues Ranch. Home. But was it?

Justice and Brandon still lived with Prudence and Collin at the ranch house, but Daddy had moved out, and his comforting, solid presence wouldn't be there for her to sink into. As much as she loved the house where she'd grown up, it was the people who'd made it home, and Abby was struggling to reconcile home without her father.

But she couldn't show up on the doorstep of his new place, either. He'd built his man cave cabin for himself, not for him and his daughters. He'd left them the Seven Virtues Ranch; how much harder could he hint at wanting to be on his own now that all the girls were able to fend for themselves?

"Except for this girl," Abby said mournfully. She couldn't do that to him. She wouldn't do that to him.

Nor did she want to move back into her old bedroom at Seven Virtues. The room positioned right between Prudence and Collin in the master bedroom and Justice and Brandon in the twins' old bedroom? No, thank you very much. That would be intolerable for everyone.

Maybe Faith and Cord had an empty cowboy cabin at Whispering Hills, the ranch next door. Or Charity might have a free room in the bed-and-breakfast she and Frank operated in the old Whispering Hills ranch house. Maybe they'd let her work off her room and board until she could find a job in town, since there was no way she'd be able to afford to pay for one.

None of those options were viable, though. "Because then, I'd have to tell them what happened." And she was nowhere near ready to do that. "Maybe I should just drive until I run out of gas; see where I end up." She patted her guitar case in the seat next to her. "You and I could sing for our supper."

Her truck pointed itself toward home, nonetheless, and three hours later, she was slipping into Plumwood Hollow by way of a back street, through the side of town where folks were less likely to recognize her or her truck. She still hadn't worked up the courage to head out to the ranch.

Her stomach growled angrily—she'd skipped lunch because of her queasiness, and she'd also skipped dinner the night before. There hadn't been anything in her fridge worth salvaging, and she'd only managed to scrape out maybe a tablespoon of peanut butter from the small jar she found at the back of the cupboard while cleaning the place out.

Abby pulled up to a pump at a gas station, then shoved a baseball cap down on her head, threading her long braid out through the hole at the back of it. She hoped the hairstyle would give her a soccer-mom vibe and would make her all but invisible to anyone who might see her. She was a bit of a local celebrity in the hollow, but most people knew her from the stage at The Smokehouse, where she looked the part of a country music singer. The baggy jeans and sweatshirt she wore had been an intentional choice; she couldn't bear the thought of plastering on her show smile today.

Inside the little food mart, Abby found a package of Chile and lime peanuts, a cheese Danish pastry—she was sure the ancient Danes rolled over in their graves every time the disgusting plastic-wrapped junk food was attributed to them—and a bottle of Mountain Dew. She knew the stuff was toxic—all of it, not just the fluorescent yellow-green soda—but she didn't care. "My life is over anyway," she said under her breath.

"What was that, sweetie?"

Abby froze. She'd recognize that voice anywhere. Cass Whitehouse.

She didn't turn around, but pretended to study the row of feminine hygiene products she happened to be standing in front of. Did people actually buy this stuff at gas stations? Her eyes widened at the inflated prices. Surely not.

"Nothing," she said with a swift glance over her shoulder in Cass's general direction. She pitched her voice higher than usual, letting the scratchiness from her rough night disguise it even more.

"Abby?" There was no fooling Cass, apparently. "I didn't know you were home, girl!" The woman sidled up beside her and threw an arm around Abby's shoulders in a quick hug. Then, leaning back so she could see under the brim of the baseball cap, her expression grew serious. Her warm smile didn't fade completely, but before she even said a word, Abby saw Cass knew all was not well in the world where Abby lived. When she took in what Abby was holding, she clucked—there was no other way to describe the sound. She actually clucked like a mother hen and shook her head. "Oh, dear."

With that, she snatched the things out of Abby's arms, dumped them unceremoniously on the counter, and told the man at the register, "You'll have to put these back, Dan. We have an emergency. Sorry." Then she took Abby's hand and headed out of the mart and around the building to the side parking lot where Cass had parked.

Abby, both taken aback by the unexpected encounter with someone she knew and greatly relieved that it was someone like Cass Whitehouse, followed meekly, not saying a word, until they were inside the woman's truck, the air conditioner blowing cool, refreshing air over Abby's flushed cheeks.

"Badger fixed my air conditioner just last month," Cass said as though the situation wasn't unusual in the least. "Isn't it lovely?"

"You—you and Badger are an item, then?" Abby asked in the same vein. She liked Badger, the bartender at The Smokehouse. The man didn't drink, which made him a great asset to the bar and grill. As big as the side of a barn, he doubled as a bouncer whenever the need arose, but his intimidating presence and booming voice was usually enough to keep the clientèle in line.

Despite his appearance, Badger was a lot like his namesake, and it wasn't just because of the prominent gray streaks at his temples. The man was protective of the ones he thought of as his own, and that protection had covered Abby a time or two. Once, she'd been cornered in the hallway that led to the restrooms by a guy claiming to be her biggest fan. Another time, a couple of college kids from nearby Muldoon had followed her out to her truck after a late Friday night gig. Both times, Badger had magically appeared at her side, set the errant idiots straight, and henceforth, had made sure she had an escort out to the well-lit parking lot. He also put a brighter bulb in the hallway light fixture, put up a camera in the corner with a feed to the monitors behind the bar, and completed the upgrade with a large sign mounted on the corridor wall that read, "Smile. You're on camera."

Over the years of playing at The Smokehouse, Abby had noticed the big guy's eyes on Cass, and how his expression softened around the edges just the tiniest bit whenever the buxom woman ponied up to the bar with a smile just for him. Abby had been around folks falling in and out of love her whole life, and she thought she recognized the look on Badger's face for what it was. It baffled her that Cass somehow missed it.

But if she was reading the vibes right today, maybe good ol' Badger had finally made his intentions known.

"Well, not exactly," Cass said, shaking her head quickly. Her cheeks flushed prettily, and Abby frowned at the contradictory response. "He'd never—not someone like me. I mean, he's a great guy, you know?"

"And you're a great gal," Abby shot back. "And yes, he would. *Because* you're someone like you. You're awesome, Cass."

Cass cocked her head prettily. She pulled her bottom lip between her teeth and shrugged. "Thank you, sweetie. You just made my day. We're friends, Badger and I. We're getting to know each other outside of work, anyway. Good friends, I'd like to think."

"Cass, seriously?" Abby shifted in her seat and pulled off her cap so she could look at the woman behind the wheel. "That man can't take his eyes off you."

The older woman's cheeks grew pink again, but with a saucy wink, she countered, "Which is why I dress the way I do. Making the most of the assets I have. I may not have blue blood running through these veins, but I know how to make a man look twice, right?" She shimmied her shoulders a few times, causing her full breasts to jiggle suggestively under the tight t-shirt she wore.

Abby knew the woman better than that. Cass wasn't afraid to show off her feminine curves, but that's where she drew the line. It was common knowledge that the pastry queen of Plumwood Hollow was selective about who she dated. She had been the victim of two terrible relationships with men she'd fallen for—one who abused substances and one who abused Cass—and she had no intention of ending up with the wrong kind of guy again. Cass was one of those "full of life" women, the kind who cheered others on, who took the downtrodden under her wing, who showed up whenever there was a need to be met.

Badger, Abby thought, would be the perfect man for Cass, and if she wasn't mistaken, Cass thought so, too. The problem was that Cass didn't think of herself highly enough to recognize that she could very well be the perfect woman for Badger.

"Besides, young lady," Cass said, giving Abby a stern look. "I didn't haul your skinny little butt out here to talk about me and Badger. Tell me."

Abby's stomach churned uncomfortably, then growled again. She opened her mouth to make some flippant remark about there being nothing to tell, but Cass reached over and laid a hand on her shoulder, stilling the words that were still trying to form in Abby's mouth.

"Listen. I don't need to know the details. Are you hurt?"

Abby swallowed hard at the kindness in Cass's voice. The excuses formed a lump in the back of her throat and she could only shake her head, afraid that if she tried to speak, nothing would come out anyway.

"Okay. That's a good start." Cass squeezed her shoulder gently. "Are you hiding from anyone in particular? You *are* hiding, right?" She dipped her head so she could see Abby's averted face. Then she asked the question that Abby had been dreading. "Does your family know you're in town, sweetie?"

After a moment of indecision, Abby shook her head. She swallowed hard. "No," she whispered. "I haven't talked to—to anyone. I can't, Cass. I don't know what to say," she admitted with a soft sob. The sudden well of tears filled her next words. "I've made a mess of things, and I didn't know where else to go."

"So, you came here to the Thrifty Gas and Food Mart?" Cass gently teased. "Come here, you silly thing." And with that, she pulled Abby toward her across the bench seat and enveloped her in a tight, vanilla-scented embrace.

It reminded Abby a tad too much of the flavored bourbon she'd had last night. But the hug was worth it, so she just held her breath as long as she could.

"There's nothing that can't be fixed in this world, you hear?" Cass said, stroking Abby's back soothingly. "It might take a whole tray of my cinnamon rolls and a few gallons of strong coffee, but I'm a firm believer that when folks work together, problems get solved."

"I don't think coffee and pastries are going to fix my mess," Abby breathed out.

Cass released her hold on Abby and reached up to cup her chin. "Well, I'm not about to stand by and let you go on believing that. You're still in one piece, at least on the outside, you're still as pretty as a peach, and you've got a family who thinks the world of you."

Abby wanted to say, "Exactly! That's the problem!" but bit back the words, knowing they sounded petty, churlish. No one could possibly understand the pressure she felt as the youngest daughter of the iconic Jedediah Goodacre of Plumwood Hollow. She was the last one in line to go out and make something of herself just like every one of her older sisters, his last hurrah.

Except the weight of her dreams had become too much for her to carry all alone. How on earth could she admit that to anyone? To her family. Or even to Cass, who had endured so much and had done so alone because she had no family to stand by her, behind her, around her.

Instead, Abby said, "I know. And I'm grateful for all of that. I really am." She swiped at her tears with the heels of her hands. "But I just don't think I can face them right now. Especially not my dad."

"Okay," Cass said, interrupting her gently. "You and I are going to head over to my place right now. I simply cannot allow you to ingest pastry from a food mart, you hear? I may not have a cheese danish at home, but I do have a few cinnamon rolls in my breadbox. And I make killer coffee, as you well know. Come on." She leaned across Abby and pushed open the passenger door. "Go get your truck and follow me home."

When Abby started to argue, Cass gave her a little shove toward the open door. "I'm so glad I needed gas today. And that Dan's card machine at the pump never works, so I had to go inside the food mart." She winked at Abby. "I will not take 'no' for an answer."

Abby finally conceded, shoved her cap down low, and headed back around to where her own truck still waited at the pump. She didn't really need any gas yet. She'd stopped here to buy herself some time. And some junk food.

Just as she climbed in behind the wheel, a bucket of bolts—or what some might call a motorcycle—veered into position directly behind her, pulling up way too close to her back bumper, apparently anxious for her to pull away so he could have her pump. As she turned the key in her ignition, she glared at the guy in her side-view mirror.

Until he lowered the kickstand and removed his helmet.

Abby's heart seemed to jerk to a standstill. For one endless moment, her eyes met those of the man behind her.

Recognition registered all over his face.

FOURTEEN

"Listen," Cass said as she unlocked her front door. "I was doing a little thinking on my way over here."

"Uh-oh."

Cass smacked Abby's arm lightly. "Don't get all sassy with me, young lady. I'm your knight in shining armor today." She pushed open the door and stood back to let Abby through.

They were met with a blast of cool air and the thick and heady aroma of vanilla, spice markets, and florals, a combination of scents that always surrounded Cass everywhere she went. The room was surprisingly uncluttered for someone who accessorized her body the way Cass did, but the palette was a delight to the senses. Bold, black-framed artwork filled the wall behind her butter yellow sofa with its jewel tone throw cushions in ruby, sapphire, emerald, and amethyst hues. Two mismatched Queen Anne style slipper chairs flanked the sofa, and an old steamer trunk sporting a glass top acted as a coffee table. Beside one of the chairs, a floor lamp with a beaded Victorian shade let off a soft amber light, and the sheers at the windows were just the slightest bit iridescent gold. An enormous hand-braided rag rug covered the old oak flooring and somehow seemed to pull all the eclectic elements of the room together.

"Wow. It's so..." Abby waved an arm to encompass the space, but she couldn't quite come up with the right word.

"Bizarre? Thrift store? I know," Cass said, shrugging self-consciously. "I take what I can get and I try to make it work. It's not really my strong suit—"

"Cass." Abby reached out and took her friend's hand, interrupting her. "That isn't what I was going to say at all." She frowned when Cass shrugged again. "No, listen to me. It's beautiful. It's so warm and welcoming. And it's so you. I love it." She looked around the room again and repeated more emphatically, "I *love* it."

"Well, thank you," Cass replied. With a shy smile, she said, "I do, too. I know it's not everyone's taste, but I hate matchy-matchy stuff and I'm really selective. I mean, I have to fall in love with something before I bring it home. And I don't let myself buy stuff I don't need, so everything I have has a place and a purpose."

"You need to stop tearing yourself down, woman. You are amazing! All the things you've accomplished, this absolutely adorable place you have here, and Serendipity's, too?"

Cass blushed with pleasure and headed to the kitchenette, where she dropped her enormous purse on the counter. "It's not an easy habit to break, I have to admit. Want that coffee now? Or something else with your pastry?" Clearly uncomfortable with the compliments, she changed the subject and began rooting around in a bread box on her counter. "I have a chocolate chip and banana whole grain muffin here, a couple cinnamon rolls—I made them Sunday, but they're still nice and soft. A quick warm up in the toaster oven and they'll be gooey and sticky and perfect."

Abby let the subject drop and opted for coffee and one of the rolls. While Cass puttered around her kitchen, Abby dropped into one of the chairs at the small dining table.

"So, here's the deal," Cass started, picking up on what she'd begun to say at the front door. "I've got to get back to the shop—it's being manned by Jill Sanders and Rhonda Whittaker right now. Jill, I kinda-sorta trust to leave on her own. Rhonda, I absolutely don't. This is the first time I've left the two of them alone, and I'm a little worried about what I'm going to find upon my return."

Abby snickered. She knew the Whittaker family well—Rhonda's older sister, Rita, had been in her class in high school, and if Rhonda was anything like her older sister, Cass was seriously tempting fate in trusting the girl. "Hopefully, you'll still have a shop to return *to*," Abby said, only half-kidding.

Cass rapped her knuckles on a wooden cutting board beside the oven. "Lord, have mercy," she muttered. She brought Abby a cup of coffee and the pastry, then poured a travel cup for herself. "I want to know what's going on with you, you hear? But since I can't linger here, I'm going to ask that you do. Stay here, okay? I'll bring supper home and we can eat something together while you spill your guts to me. Take a nap, watch some television," she insisted, fluttering her fingers at the living room. "Take a shower if you want, or soak in the tub. It's a super deep clawfoot; I found it in pristine condition at an auction several years back. I paid way too much for it, but I didn't care. I wanted it. Believe me, it was not a fun project, tearing out the old crappy shower and tub combo and replacing it with the clawfoot and goose neck showerhead, but it was worth every drop of blood, sweat, and tears." She chortled and shook her head. "And believe me, there was a lot of all three."

Abby hesitated, feeling guilty at the rush of relief that washed over her at Cass's offer, but then asked, "Are you sure? That would be great if I could just chill here for a couple of hours. You know, get my head on straight before I head home and face the music." She smiled wryly at the accidental play on words.

Cass slung the straps of her purse up over her shoulder. "Stay," she commanded. "We will talk when I get back after we close at seven. That's not too late for you to eat, is it? Anything you don't like? Onions? Tomatoes? Spinach?"

Abby waved her hands to make Cass stop. "I eat just about anything and everything, I assure you."

Cass made a snarky expression. "That's right. I saw what you were going to buy at Thriftys."

Abby lifted her plate with what was left of the cinnamon roll. "This is so much better for me," she said dryly.

"Hey now," Cass shot back, her free hand planted on her hip. "I'll have you know that dough is made with whole grain, unbleached non-GMO flour, Himalayan sea salt, cultured butter, and local honey. The cream cheese comes from Charleston Farms and it's sweetened with real maple syrup. It's all high-quality stuff, and there isn't a single preservative in it."

Abby's eyes widened in surprise. "Wow. I'll have another, please, since they're so good for me." She was only half-joking. The thing was absolutely divine. "Seriously, Cass. These are outstanding. I'm just going to sit here all afternoon and eat my way through your breadbox, if that's okay with you."

Cass laughed and headed out with the promise to bring home something irresistible for supper. "Save some room!" she called as she closed the front door behind her.

In the silence that followed, Abby finished her pastry, then poured herself another cup of coffee and took it into the living room. She didn't feel like watching daytime television, but she couldn't just sit there and think, either. She'd thought of nothing else but what she was going to say to her father all the way home from Nashville, and she wasn't any closer to a solution now.

She pulled out her phone and found an audiobook to listen to, one about a girl who ran away to Italy after some two-timing man had broken her heart. "Maybe I should just go to Italy," she murmured as she slouched low into one of the slipper chairs and stretched her legs out in front of her.

She was just getting caught up in the story of the young woman trying to traverse the cobbled streets of a little Tuscan town on her own when someone knocked on the front door. At first, she wasn't sure she'd heard correctly, that it might have just been some background noise in the audiobook recording, but then it came again, louder this time.

Abby ripped off her headphones and straightened in the chair. Who would be here looking for Cass at this time of day? Maybe it was the mail delivery leaving a package or something.

Should she answer the door? She shook her head in answer to her own question. No way. The whole point of her hiding out here was, well, to hide out. She waited, breath held, afraid to move lest she give her presence away.

"Cass?" The voice was muffled through the door, but there was something familiar about it. Abby strained to hear, hoping he'd speak again. Was it Badger? But surely, he'd know Cass was at work. "You here?"

After an interminable silence, Abby rose and tiptoed to the kitchen window over the sink. It didn't look directly out front, but she could see the road from it, and whoever it was would have to walk or drive past it. She'd have to be ready to duck her head if he was watching the house.

Moments later, the low rumble of an engine came to life. How she hadn't heard it baffled her until she remembered she'd been listening to the audiobook. Then the same motorcycle that had practically parked itself in her truck bed at the gas station came into view as the driver pulled away from Cass's house.

Surely, he hadn't followed them here, had he?

FIFTEEN

By the time Cass got home, it was almost eight o'clock. She apologized profusely for her tardiness. "Gina, from across the street at the hair salon, stopped in right at seven and needed a little bolstering. One of her favorite clients came in for her last haircut this afternoon. Mrs. Bensen. Do you remember her? She's been old for as long as I can remember," Cass continued without waiting for Abby's response. "I think she's worn her pretty white hair in that same elegant puffy cloud as far back as I can remember, too." She swirled a hand around her own head, then pressed her palm flat to her chest. "Anyway, apparently, Gina has been the artist behind that iconic do this whole time, and she says she's going to miss her something awful. Mrs. Bensen is moving to Louisville this week to be close to her daughter."

Abby thought of her father doing just the opposite, moving away from his family in his old age. Okay, so he wasn't moving that far—just across the road—but home wasn't home without him there.

"So poor Gina needed a shoulder to cry on. And one of my éclairs to drown her sorrows in, too, of course," Cass added with a wink. "I couldn't just shove her out the door. You understand, right?"

"Of course," Abby assured her. It was just like Cass to offer her generous kindness to everyone in need. Knowing her, she hadn't charged Gina for the éclair, either.

Abby had been ravenous about an hour ago, as if her body knew that it had been promised a real meal at that time, but she'd found an apple in the fruit drawer of the refrigerator, and the cool, crisp sweetness had staved off the worst of it. But to occupy herself, she'd already set the table in preparation for Cass and the food's arrival.

"Have you ever been to Mrs. Bensen's little cottage?" Cass asked as she unloaded the paper bag of food on the counter. "She lives over on Mulberry Court. It's near your sister's place, near the animal hospital."

"I haven't." Abby busied herself filling their glasses with ice and setting napkins at each place.

"Oh, Abby." Cass sighed dramatically and turned around to lean her hip against the counter while she talked. "It's absolutely adorable. It's a little bigger on the inside than my place here—still only two bedrooms, though, I think—but it looks like a little fairy house. It has a porch that stretches the length of the front of the house, and the garden beds all around it are just filled with beautiful flowers almost year round. It's this pale blue color with white trim, and the door is painted this deep cobalt blue with a small window in it. One with those hatches you slide back to see who's knocking."

Abby cocked her head. "Actually, I do know that place. I've driven by it a zillion times, but I've never been inside it. In fact, when I was a little girl," Abby added with a smile, "I used to think that's where the Tooth Fairy lived. I think Prudence told me that once, and I just believed her."

"That Prudence," Cass said with a chuckle. "She sees fairies and unicorns everywhere."

"That's my sister," Abby agreed, eying the food still in cartons behind Cass. Her stomach rumbled loudly, and to cover it up, she asked, "I wonder what's going to happen to the house now. Do you know who bought it?"

"Oh, she's not selling it," Cass told her, turning back to finish unpacking her goods. "I guess she has some friends whom she insists she's going to come back to see on a regular basis and wants to have her own place to stay."

Over chicken primavera and tossed green salad, Abby unloaded everything on Cass's shoulders. As she'd expected, the older woman had been nothing but kind and understanding. It was common knowledge that Cass had had more than her fair share of disappointment and failure in her life, and if anyone could understand how Abby felt, it was Cass Whitehouse.

"Your daddy is a good man, Abby," her friend said. They'd moved to the living room and sat at either end of the sofa facing each other, a pile of colorful cushions between them like a treasure trove of jewels. "He loves all of you girls more than life itself."

Abby pressed the heels of her hands to her stinging eyes. She was not going to cry about this anymore. Crying did not solve any problems. At least not the ones in her life. "I'm a big fat liar, Cass," she moaned as she flopped back against the thickly padded arm of the couch. "My dad thinks I'm still living in Nashville performing with my band." She punched the throw cushion in her lap. "In my nonexistent apartment with my nonexistent band."

Cass nodded consolingly, but didn't offer any advice. For which Abby was grateful. In her heart, she knew she needed to come clean to her family, to let them know how desperate her situation had become... to confess her failure to them, but she wasn't ready to do that. Not yet. She needed some time to lick her wounds. To come up with some kind of a solution to the situation she was in before she admitted how badly she'd screwed up. She needed a plan to get herself back on track.

"I can't tell him the truth of things yet," Abby said, her voice catching. "I just can't bear to see his face when I tell him what a screw up I am."

"You're *not* a screwup," Cass shot back, her tone firm. "Some of us trust people who don't deserve to be trusted, but that doesn't make us screw ups, Abby. It means we see the best in people. I truly believe that. Which is why it hurts so much when we get betrayed."

"Yes, well, I may have trusted the wrong person, but my whole family trusts me, Cass. And I've betrayed them all. You don't think that's going to hurt them?"

Cass shook her head. "Stop it. I won't have that kind of negativity in my home. Look at me and listen." She waited until Abby lifted her gaze to meet hers. "I'm going to make you an offer that I don't think you're in any condition to refuse."

Abby frowned. "What kind of offer?"

Cass held up a hand. "But before I do, I'm going to preface it with this. I disagree with you, Abby. I do not, for one moment, believe that your daddy—or your sisters, for that matter—would feel betrayed by you in any way. At the worst, they'd be disappointed *for* you, not in you. But I don't even think that's giving them the credit they deserve."

Abby looked away, squirming at the certainty in Cass's eyes, in her words.

"That said, I know what it's like to feel like you've let everyone down. I get it, Abby, I really do. So I'm going to make you a deal. Stay here with me for a week or two. Get some rest, and for goodness sake, eat something, girl. You're too skinny." She affectionately patted her own stomach. "Take some time to get a handle on things. Then you call your daddy and tell him what's going on. Two weeks tops, though, you hear?"

Abby straightened and turned to look at Cass. "I can't—that's too much to ask of you."

"You didn't ask, did you?" Cass shot back. "I offered."

"But what if someone finds out I'm here? Then they'll think badly of you. I can't do that to you."

Cass chortled loudly. "Everyone already thinks badly of me, darling girl."

"That's not true, and you know it." Abby shook her head. "Don't say stuff like that about yourself, Cass. I thought you said you didn't allow that kind of negativity in your house."

Cass shrugged, but nodded in agreement. "You're right. I did. But it's not me I'm worried about. I know you need some time, a little space to clear your head. I'm offering you that. I would love your company—as long as you pick up after yourself and do your dishes and stuff. I like to keep a neat house; never know when you might have company, right?" She nudged Abby's shoulder with her own. "You can have mama's old room. And don't worry," she added with a cheeky grin. "I changed the mattress."

Cass's mother had died peacefully several years ago in the little room at the end of the hall, but that fact didn't bother Abby. Her own mother had taken her last breaths in the master bedroom at Seven Virtues Ranch, and Abby had always felt that home was the best place to say goodbye to those who loved you. But she was grateful for the new mattress all the same—death wasn't always as neat and pretty as they made it look in the movies.

"And the pillows and sheets are actually new. I bought them on clearance at Bed, Bath, and Beyond last month, so you'll be the first to sleep in them. You'll have to tell me how they feel."

"I can pay you," Abby began, but then faltered as she realized that might not be true. Her bank account was teetering on empty and as far as she knew, there were no more paychecks coming in.

"I don't need your money," Cass said, her gaze understanding. "I mean, I can always use money; don't get me wrong. But I'm not about to take something from you that you clearly don't have."

"Well, I can't just leech off you, Cass. I know you don't have any extra coinage, either." She hoped Cass wouldn't take offense, but it wasn't exactly a secret that the woman didn't have much. She'd taken every penny of her mother's tiny life insurance and invested it into the purchase of the bakery she now owned and operated. The original owners, Ted and Betty Gentry, had been forced to close the little shop because of health reasons, and the place had been all but abandoned for more than three years before Cass had made an offer on it. She'd been half afraid her offer wouldn't be enough, but the Gentrys had been so pleased that someone wanted the place, that they'd not only agreed to her terms, but had given her all their recipes as well. Even so, it had taken her several years on her limited budget to get the place to where it was breaking even. Folks in Plumwood Hollow loved Serendipity's, though, and Cass worked hard to keep the place afloat. It was only recently that she'd finally been able to afford to hire help, two high school students who came in after school, and an older woman named Cathy who came in the early morning hours to get the baking started.

Cass looked like she wanted to argue, but then she narrowed her eyes and studied Abby. "You're not leeching off me, for the record. Again, I offered. But I'm not too proud to admit that I could use your help at the shop if you want to put in some time there."

"Of course," Abby said immediately, but then she frowned. "Except I don't know how I could do that without my family finding out I'm here. Someone is bound to tell Daddy—"

"I've thought of that." Cass said when Abby's words broke off. "I don't need help serving customers. I need help in the early mornings. Cathy is taking a few weeks off to help out her daughter, who just had her first baby, so I've been heading in early to do the baking prep. It's only for a few hours before the shop opens, so no one would even know you were there."

Abby nodded slowly. She wasn't a morning person, but she could certainly make it happen for a couple of weeks. Besides, beggars—and losers—couldn't be choosers, right? "Are you sure? I mean, I've been waitressing in Nashville for the last year, but I haven't done any of the cooking or baking. You'll have to show me how to do everything, but I'm a fast learner, I promise."

Cass released her full, throaty laugh. "Stop with the jabbering, girlie. Yes, I'm sure. It's easy stuff and once you get it down, you'll practically be able to do it in your sleep. I prep the dough the night before, so it's already in the bread pans and on the baking sheets."

Abby grimaced. "What if I screw it up? Burn the bread?" She dropped her voice to a whisper, as if uttering blasphemy. "Or, even worse, burn the cinnamon rolls?"

Cass shrugged. "Then the townfolk will stage an uprising with pitchforks and torches, I suppose. And yes, I'll let you take the blame." She chuckled. "But I don't foresee that happening. I have everything down to a science, and since essentially all you're doing is moving things in and out of fridge units and ovens—all timed down to the minute—you're going to have to try really hard to burn anything. I promise."

"If you're sure," Abby said, nodding quickly, not wanting Cass to have any second thoughts. "I'm totally down for it. Yes. Please."

"Good." Cass said just as quickly. "Then you can start tomorrow. Which means I will get to sleep in again—woo-hoo!" She thrust a victorious fist into the air. But when she saw Abby's nervous expression, she said, "Well, not tomorrow, I won't. I'll get up with you the next couple of days to make sure you feel comfortable manning the ovens, of course. By Friday, you should have it down."

"Okay," Abby said slowly, still not so sure herself. "But you'll keep your phone near your bed, so if I freak out and need help, I'll be able to reach you, right?"

"You won't freak out and you won't need help," Cass countered confidently. She snatched up one of the cushions and hugged it fiercely. "I can't wait to be able to sleep in again. It's really hard to party all night when you have to get up at three in the morning. A girl can't live on only a few hours of sleep, let me tell you."

"Partying all night, are you?" Abby teased. "With Badger?"

Cass shrugged, making her ample bosom swell provocatively. "Well, I don't want the other dames of this little town thinking he's fair game, you know? So I just show up, stake my claim when I catch anyone eyeing him, then mosey on home when I can't keep my eyes open any longer."

"A girl's gotta do what a girl's gotta do," Abby said with a slow nod. She wasn't sure how healthy Cass's behavior was, but at least she was forthright about it.

"Seriously, though," Cass told her. "It's not that at all. Badger takes an hour break at around nine, and he likes it when I can be there to spend it with him. It's like a mini date night every night he's working," she added with a pretty blush.

"Ha! I knew it," Abby said with a knowing chuckle, pointing a finger at Cass. "So the truth is that he's the one staking his claim on you, not the other way around. I'm so glad he finally found the light!"

Cass grinned back at her. "Well, he's definitely coming around, and I'm definitely showing him the light, if you know what I mean."

Actually, Abby didn't know what Cass meant—not exactly—but she wasn't about to ask for clarification. As long as Badger didn't come around for some light while Abby was staying with Cass, she'd be happy to stay ignorant about the woman's double entendres.

"Wait. Does that mean—" Abby pulled her cell from her back pocket and checked the time. "Cass! It's almost ten o'clock!"

But Cass was batting away her words before she finished her statement. "It's all good, honey. I told him I needed to catch up on my beauty sleep tonight."

"I'm so sorry, Cass. I didn't even think to ask you if you had plans before I showed up."

"You know what they say," Cass said with a wink. "Absence makes the heart grow fonder. It's good for people to miss each other." She sighed dramatically and hugged her cushion again. "And let me tell you, young Abstinence Goodacre. I miss that man all the time. I swear, even when I'm with him, I miss him, because I know I'll be heading for home on my own at the end of the night. I'd like to wrap him up and put him in my pocket so I'd never have to be without him."

"Okay. That's not weird at all," Abby said dryly. "Besides, I don't think there are any pockets in the world big enough to squeeze that man into."

"I'll give you that. It is pretty weird now that I say it out loud." Cass agreed with a nod. Her smile turning dreamy. "That man, though. He's just so big and quiet, you know? Sometimes I wish I could squeeze the words out of him."

Abby nodded. Badger, the brawny bartender at The Smokehouse, was exactly as Cass had described. An ox of a man with a thick but neatly trimmed beard, dark hair with silver-white streaks at his temples, and shoulders as wide as a barn door, he kept a tight-fisted control over The Smokehouse. To strangers, the man was nothing if not intimidating, but to those who knew him, who'd spent time at his bar, Badger was a gentle giant with a heart that took up every square inch of the inside of his chest.

And there was no man in the world better suited to someone like Cass. She, too, was larger than life, with her voluptuous curves, her flamboyant style, and her own enormous heart, and Abby was sure she wouldn't be the only one in Plumwood Hollow who was glad to see Badger and Cass finding their way to each other.

"But enough about Badger for now." Cass set the cushion aside and leaned forward toward Abby, taking one of her hands and squeezing it hard. "I need to be clear about one thing, though, sweetie. If your father gets word of you being here, I'm not going to lie for you. He won't hear it from me, but I won't turn him away if he comes asking after you, you hear?"

Abby nodded slowly. That was more than fair. Cass was bending over backward to give Abby sanctuary right now.

"Your sisters, either. And mind you, that Prudence is way too intuitive for her own good. I swear she's got super powers." Cass released Abby and stood. "Two weeks tops, Abby. If you haven't come clean by then, I'm calling your daddy for you and handing you the phone. That man has always been kind to me, and I won't repay him with secrets and lies."

"I understand," Abby assured her. "You're offering me far more than I could have hoped for."

"And you're going to call him in the morning, you hear? Even if he doesn't know *where* you are, he needs to hear *how* you are, that you're all right. And he needs to hear it from you. No texting."

"Got it. He hates texting, anyway." Abby gave Cass a serious look. "Thank you, Cass. I don't know what I would have done today if you hadn't appeared on the scene. I can't begin to tell you how much I appreciate this."

Cass chuckled and held out a hand to help Abby up. "We'll see how grateful you are at three o'clock in the morning. Come on. Let's get your stuff out of your truck and get you settled into Mama's room."

Less than an hour later, Abby lay in bed trying in vain to fall asleep before midnight, a ridiculously early hour for the nocturnal schedule she'd been keeping for the last two years. In the dark stillness, she allowed her mind to pull her back to the moment at the gas station when she'd watched that motorcycle pull up too close behind her, when he took off his helmet and they'd made eye contact.

Surely, she'd misread his expression. He couldn't have recognized her, not with her ball cap pulled low, not that tiny little strip of her reflection. He would only have seen her eyes, and even then, from too far a distance to be certain of anything.

But he'd shown up at Cass's front door not even an hour later.

"My truck," she moaned, smacking her forehead with her palm and squeezing her eyes shut. "Oh, help me, Rhonda. He'd know my truck anywhere."

SIXTEEN

Three o'clock in the morning came far too soon for Abby. She'd had a tough time falling asleep, even as exhausted as she was. Thoughts of her family plagued her, the deception she was feeding them, that she was forcing Cass to be a co-conspirator, and the knowledge that she was living a lie.

It had all weighed on her like a lead blanket pressing her down into the mattress beneath her. Her mind reeled over events of the last several weeks as she wrestled with what went wrong, what she could have done to prevent the collapse of her dreams, especially considering the multitude of opportunities that had been handed to her. She wondered if Remington Sounder had heard that she'd abandoned ship, and the thought had her curling in on herself, clutching her stomach as misery tore through her, making it difficult to catch her breath.

Not to mention the certainty that she might be on a collision course with Mr. Motorcycle, especially if he really had recognized her. She'd all but talked herself into believing he hadn't, that he'd come by Cass's place for some other reason entirely, but in the light of day—actually, in the darkness before dawn—her gut told her otherwise.

There'd been a good hour or so when she'd debated whether or not to go hunting through Cass's cupboards for something with a little kick that might make sleep come easier. She'd stood her ground, though, and had eventually drifted off into a fitful slumber, tossing and turning with dreams of falling over cliff edges, of sinking into quicksand, of getting blown off her feet by fierce winds.

But Abby was upright and dressed when Cass tapped on her bedroom door, and although she didn't have a whole lot to say, she made a solid attempt to smile as brightly as she could muster.

"Good morning," Cass offered with a puffy-eyed wink. "But I'll wager there's not much good about this hour of the day, am I right?"

Abby nodded, accepted the steaming mug of creamy, sweet coffee Cass handed her, and followed her hostess into the cute little kitchen.

"I hope you don't mind me doctoring up your Java," Cass said as she bustled around the small space. "I figured this first morning you'd need the extra boost. If you don't drink it that way, I won't be offended if you dump it and start fresh."

Abby shook her head. "No, it's good. I usually drink it black because I never have any real cream or sugar in my apartment, but I like it this way. Dessert in a cup. Breakfast for champions, right?"

"It's my rocket fuel, that's for sure." Cass picked up her enormous handbag from the counter and looped it over her shoulder. "It's healthier than a soda, I guarantee, and it sure goes down easier. I use raw cane sugar and real cream, so at least there aren't the chemicals you find in soda."

Abby nodded and lifted the mug to her lips. "Smells better, too," she said when she came up for air. "Thank you for this." Her stomach rumbled in agreement as the drink warmed her from the inside out.

Cass paused at the front door and cocked her head at Abby. "I'm sorry. I didn't even ask. Are you hungry? I usually eat from my day-old stock when I get there, but if you want me to whip up a batch of scrambled eggs or—"

"No, no. I'm fine. I'm not a big breakfast person." Abby scooped up her own purse. "Although I might become one if I get access to your pastry counter every morning."

They arrived at Serendipity's shortly, and once Cass had shown Abby how to disarm the alarm and adjust the thermostat, she immediately began pulling sheet pans and loaf pans from the refrigeration unit and sliding them into tall shelving units. "These have to sit out for about an hour to get to room temperature, which is why we turn the heat up so high first thing in the morning. Sorry; you'll have to sweat it out."

"It feels good right now," Abby said truthfully. It was still early enough to be chilly, even in the middle of summer, but she had no doubt she'd be peeling off layers in no time.

"While you're waiting for those, you'll prep the shop for opening. The pastry counters need to be sanitized every morning, the tables and chairs set out and wiped down, and the display cases made ready for the specials for the day. You don't have to put anything in them; I'll do that when I get in. Half the time, I base the day's specials on my mood, and believe me, that can change on the drive over."

Abby followed Cass into the little shop and eyed the windows, relieved to see there were blinds on every one of them. The glass door was frosted, too, a large 'S' etched into it.

As if reading her mind, Cass continued. "The blinds stay closed until we open, so no one will be able to see you at work." She paused and pressed a hand to her chest. "I don't mind working here alone in the middle of the night, but I don't like the idea of anyone else knowing I'm here by myself. We girls have to take every precaution, right?"

By the time Cass had walked Abby through all the tasks she'd be responsible for performing, the first of the pastries were ready to go into the oven. "The bread loaves will need another forty-five minutes before they're at the right temperature," Cass explained, "so you'll just rotate them into the ovens after the second round of pastries."

Cass then took her into the pantry where she stocked the non-perishable ingredients. "I try to stay on top of all of this, but if I have any extra time in the morning, I come in here and take stock of what I have, what's running low, and make a list so I can put in an order before I run out of supplies." She pointed to a clipboard hanging from an S-hook on the end of one of the shelves. "That's my master list. Old school, I know. Who uses clipboards anymore, right?"

"I love clipboards," Abby said with a grin. "Whenever I use one, I feel smarter."

"They're sassy, aren't they?" Cass shot back. She pulled the clipboard off the wall and flipped it around so Abby could see the enormous hot pink lipstick kiss sticker on the back of it.

They worked together for the next few hours, Cass pleased with how quickly Abby picked up the tasks needing done. "I think you're ready to do this on your own already, but for your peace of mind, I'll come with you tomorrow. But I'm going to make you do everything without my help."

"I don't know if that's wise, Cass," Abby hedged.

"Pfft. I'm confident you can do this on your own, girlie. It's the same stuff every morning. Piece of cake. I'll be here one more day, but then, Friday morning, you're on your own."

"Really?" Abby agreed to a certain extent—the tasks were pretty basic—but she was hesitant to take on the responsibility by herself so soon. "What if I mess something up?"

Cass shook her head, the warmth of the kitchen giving the woman's skin a peachy glow. "You won't," she said firmly.

"But what if—"

"You won't," Cass said again. She reached over and laid a hand on Abby's arm. "I don't doubt you one iota, Abby, so stop doubting yourself."

Abby hated the lump that rose in her throat, blocking any words she might say. She nodded instead.

"Good girl," Cass said, patting Abby's cheek before turning back to the last of the bread loaves that were still cooling on the racks.

Good girl. Her father had spoken those same words to her just yesterday.

"I'll take you home now," Cass said, dusting her hands off on her apron before untying it and hanging it up on a hook by the pantry door. "Then I'll come back and open up the shop at seven. I'll be home for a nap right after the lunch rush. Betty Gentry still covers for me when I'm desperate; isn't that sweet? I think her old customers like seeing her here now and then, too."

"That's great that she's willing to step in when you need her."

"Yep, and best of all, she insists I pay her only in pastries, so it's a win-win for everyone."

"That's a sweet deal, indeed."

"One last thing," Cass said as she gestured at the refrigeration unit again. "Getting rid of yesterday's leftovers. Have you had enough to eat this morning?"

"Getting rid of them? You just throw them all away?" Abby was appalled at the idea of throwing away all the delicious day-old pastries and loaves of bread that took up a whole shelf and a half in the cooler.

"Oh no," Cass corrected her. "Whatever doesn't get sold or eaten, I take over to the homeless shelter on Pinehurst Ave. Joseph's Storehouse—do you know it?" Cass paused in her task to wait for Abby's nod. "That's something I'd like for you to do, too, if you're willing. We'll stop by there on the way home to drop this stuff off."

They drove in behind the shelter and pulled up to a back door that stood open, light and conversation spilling out into the shadowed alley. Inside, Abby found the kitchen equipped with dated but sturdy stainless steel equipment and appliances. The place was already bustling with staff prepping huge trays of scrambled eggs, oatmeal, and sausage links for folks who needed a good breakfast.

She and Cass were greeted warmly—Cass hugged everyone, of course—and the bread and pastries they'd brought were made quick work of by a woman named Petra who laid them out on enormous trays and set them on a buffet counter beside the other serving trays.

"Do you always have that many leftovers?" Abby asked when they'd said their goodbyes and were back in the truck.

Cass grinned and shrugged, the gesture telling Abby much more than her words did. "Usually, yes."

"So why don't you just make less?" Abby thought she already knew the answer, but she asked anyway.

After a moment's hesitation, Cass said, "I can't afford to run out of goods at the shop—paying customers keep my doors open—but I *can* afford to give away my extras to folks who can't afford to pay. And everyone wins."

"You've got a lot of win-win situations in your life, don't you?" Abby asked.

Cass chuckled softly. "Well, for someone who has experienced a few too many lose-lose situations, it's about time that I figured out how to turn things around, don't you think? So yes, you're right. I love it when everybody wins."

"How do you do it?" Abby asked in all seriousness. "How do you just keep going with your head up all the time? You're my hero, woman."

Back at the apartment, Cass gave Abby a quick tour of the small, but well-stocked kitchen. "Feel free to eat whatever you can find in the fridge or pantry, okay? If you need anything that I don't already have on hand, Nesbits Grocery delivers for super cheap. And they're fast, too. Sometimes I get my order within the hour, depending on how busy they are. They like me better than their other customers, of course." She propped a hand on her hip and wiggled her eyebrows suggestively, although Abby knew it was just for show. "I tip really well, too, so that probably motivates them to hustle."

Well, Abby wouldn't be tipping anyone anytime soon. She didn't have more than a few dollars to rub together. But she didn't say so to Cass; she just nodded and thanked her for everything.

Nor did she plan to go through Cass's food for free, either. She'd only use what she could pay for, even if it meant she had to go without. She could fill up on the day-old stuff at the shop, she supposed.

Then again, knowing what became of Serendipity's leftovers, whatever she ate would be taken from the mouth of someone who probably needed sustenance a whole lot more than she did.

"I'll think about it later," Abby declared as she made her way to the pretty little bathroom in the hallway. She'd take a quick shower to wash away the grit of flour and stickiness of sweet dough and sugary glazes she'd been working with, then she'd crawl into bed and get some more sleep. "I'll think about everything later," she added when thoughts of her family reared their heads.

She'd call her father when she woke up. She'd tell him she was fine, but busy, and keep it short and sweet so she wouldn't feel pressure to come up with anymore lies.

SEVENTEEN

Jed mopped his brow with the handkerchief he always had on hand. It was going to be a toasty Wednesday, that was for sure. But he intended to get as many of his morning chores done before the worst of the heat set in.

He'd slept fitfully the night before, plagued by dreams he couldn't recall and the gnawing ache in his thigh bone that had never quite gone away after they'd put him back together. He still couldn't recall most of the events of the day he'd had his tractor accident, but between his doctors and nurses, his daughters—Faith, in particular, who'd discovered him torn up underneath the thing—and his own understanding, he'd pieced together what he believed had happened.

Jed had backed up a little too aggressively that late afternoon, wanting to be finished with his task for the day, and had rolled a back tire up a young sapling that had wound itself around the axle. The tractor had flipped onto its side with Jed pinned beneath the back wheel well, shattering his thigh bone and snapping the ball joint of his hip. He'd endured multiple reconstructive surgeries and countless hours of therapy to get him to the point where he could get around without the aid of a walker. He still used a cane now and then, but only in the privacy of his own home on the coldest of days when the bone-deep ache was at its worst.

He was anxious to hear from Abby today. In spite of her assurances that she was all right, he couldn't shake the notion that she wasn't telling it the way it was. He was still considering making a trip down to Nashville to visit her, but he hated the thought of surprising her that way, especially if she didn't want him there. So he planned to bring it up again today. This weekend would be as good as any to drive out to see her. He enjoyed her music, not because it was his style, but because she was his daughter, and watching her come alive on stage made him ache to reach for Caroline's hand so they could bask in parental pride together. But even if she wasn't playing anywhere while the band got things sorted out, he'd like to see her, to see with his own eyes that all was well in her world.

His phone rang just after nine AM, and he frowned as he pulled it from his back pocket. She was up already?

But it wasn't Abby.

Nope, it was that Ransome woman again. What did she want now?

He debated whether to answer her call or not—what if Abby called while they were on the phone? His girls insisted he could put someone on hold to answer an incoming call, but no matter how he tried, he always managed to hang up on one or the other.

Abby rarely called before noon, though, and on the fourth ring, he finally answered with a gruff, "Hello?"

"Good morning, Jedediah Goodacre," came the husky greeting on the other end of the line.

"Good morning, Ms. Ransome," he replied, then wished he could take it back. It sounded, even to his own ears, like he was flirting with her.

Was he flirting with her? His neck grew warm, and he reached up and cupped his hand around the base of his skull, the damp strands of hair reminding him once again that he was overdue for that haircut. He cleared his throat. "What can I do for you?" he asked, suddenly anxious to get this conversation over with.

"Well, I'm glad you asked," she said, and he could hear her wide smile in her voice. "I'm calling to let you know that I'm coming out to Plumwood Hollow earlier than I'd thought. I'll be there for several days next week. In fact, I'll be arriving this Sunday." She sounded ridiculously excited about the prospect. "Another place has just gone on the market—a small ranch house and two outbuildings on nine acres. Doesn't that sound perfect?" She didn't wait for him to respond. "I must get out there to stake my claim on it before anyone else does. My realtor insists it won't last long. Not in this market."

Jed stayed silent, a little afraid to ask the question that danced on his tongue. And she'd be staying... where?

"Sarah Lynxwilder said she can pick me up from the airport and that she's happy to put me up Sunday night, but as you might already know, they've got family visiting next week."

Charlotte fell silent, and Jed found that he was holding his breath. He let it out slowly and softly through his nose, but still didn't speak. Instead, he prayed she wouldn't bring up the one thing he was certain she would. *Almighty God, protect me.*

"Are you still there?"

"I am," he said. For a moment, he'd considered hanging up on her again, maybe feigning a bad connection. But his pride and manners wouldn't allow him to do so.

"Good. I'm calling to ask if you'll let me stay at your place like we talked about last time. I can't wait to see what you've done with it."

Jed frowned. *We* hadn't talked about it. She had. And he'd disagreed with the idea whole-heartedly. He cleared his throat, preparing to tell her once again, in no uncertain terms, that she could *not* stay with him.

"I wouldn't ask, Jedediah, knowing as I do about your old-school sensibilities," she said, her tone cajoling, but not quite condescending. "But I'm running out of good options. I spoke to Justice yesterday, hoping for an empty room at Seven Virtues, but she tells me Prudence has a group coming in for a week-long course she's teaching out there. That girl of yours. She is something else."

"She is," he concurred, the words coming out brusque. He wasn't sure if she was speaking of Justice or Prudence, but they were both something else in his opinion, so his agreement was apropos, regardless.

"All of your girls are," Charlotte said, echoing his thoughts, her voice suddenly serious. "I hope you know that."

Jed held the phone away from his ear and glared at the screen. She didn't think he knew that? "I do," he said into the mouthpiece, wondering if he sounded as angry to her as he did to himself.

Not angry, no. Unsettled. Uncomfortable.

Nervous? Did she really make him nervous?

Why, yes. Yes, she did.

Charlotte Ransome reminded him of an unpredictable mare. A fine-looking, sleek-lined, long-nosed mare with a personality that kept him on his toes. Indeed, she did make him nervous.

"Anyway," she went on, apparently not put off by his tone. "There are empty rooms at Charity's Whispering Hills B&B, of course, but it's a little out of my price range. Don't you dare tell your daughter that, though, my friend. They're charging far less than they should for the services they provide. It's just more than I can comfortably pay, that's all. Especially with the looming expenses of a cross-country move."

Jed understood. When he'd first heard how much folks were paying to stay at the new bed-and-breakfast Charity and her husband were operating at Whispering Hills Ranch, he'd nearly had a coronary. A two-night stay there cost more than most people's monthly mortgage payments.

Even so, he knew what was coming next.

"So I'm counting on your good graces, kind sir. Will you have me? Can I stay in your spare bedroom? I clean up after myself, I can cook for us both while I'm there. I'll even pay for the week's groceries as a token of my gratitude."

No. No, you can't stay with me. No, I will not have you. No, you cannot cook for me. Jed opened his mouth to say those things, but nothing came out.

"Besides, I'm counting on you to come check out the properties with me, anyway, so it kinda makes sense that I stay there, right?"

Makes sense to whom? But when he opened his mouth to turn her away, instead, the words that came out had him rocking back on his heels in disbelief. "I suppose if I'm escorting you around town anyway, it does."

Over the phone, he heard what sounded like Charlotte clapping her hands. How she managed to do so while still hanging onto her cell was beyond him. Maybe she had one of those infernal "hands-free" contraptions his girls were always trying to get him to use shoved into her ears. He hated those things—one could never tell if the person wearing it was talking to someone on the phone or just plain loony.

"Thank you, thank you! I am so relieved. I was starting to feel like a third wheel nobody wanted."

I didn't say I wanted you. The childish thought marched across his tongue, but he bit it back.

"And don't you dare say 'If the shoe fits.' Even though I can practically hear the words dancing in your head."

"Those were your words, not mine," Jed declared, a reluctant smile tugging at the corners of his mouth. She'd practically read his mind.

"Maybe," she said. "But you can't deny that you're not exactly excited about having me stay with you."

"On the contrary," he shot back sarcastically. "I'm absolutely giddy about it."

Charlotte guffawed in that deep, almost masculine way of hers. "I'm having a hard time picturing you giddy about anything, Jedediah Goodacre. But the way I see it, you owe me a few nights."

"I what?" he sputtered, his words vibrating with surprise. "How on earth do you figure that?"

"Well, my darling man, I opened my home to your flesh and blood, didn't I? Took in your Justice and her man in their hour of desperate need?"

Jed rolled his eyes before he remembered she couldn't see him. He cleared his throat—loudly—instead. "And here I thought you'd acted out of the goodness of your heart." He tried to sound affronted, but the back-and-forth bantering was starting to wear him down, and the grin that had threatened earlier turned into a quiet chuckle.

"Well, well, Jedediah Goodacre. Do my ears deceive me, or are you actually admitting that I have a good heart?"

Jed lowered himself onto the top step of his back porch. "Yes, Ms. Ransome. You have a good heart. That has never been a question. A good head on your shoulders, though? After seeing some of the properties you've considered purchasing, I'm going to have to reserve judgment for now."

Charlotte snorted appreciatively, but had an immediate response. "Then it's a good thing I've got you along for the ride, isn't it? I'll be the heart, you be the head, and together, we'll make an indomitable team, won't we?"

"I thought I was going to be Peace, and you were going to be Quiet," he countered, recalling their last conversation.

Charlotte hooted so loudly that Jed winced and had to hold the phone away from his ear.

As loathe as he was to admit it, at least out loud, Jed wasn't exactly averse to the idea of teaming up with Charlotte Ransome. In fact, something else he was reticent to admit: he wasn't exactly averse to the idea of spending one-on-one time with Charlotte Ransom, of her being a guest in his home.

He'd have to let everyone know about it before she showed up on his doorstep, that was for certain. He wouldn't allow the gossips to have a field day with this situation. The woman was staying in his guest room for a valid reason, and if folks didn't like it, they could keep it to themselves.

"How about I have Sarah bring me over on Monday around noon? Will that work for you?"

"That'll be fine," he said, nodding slowly, his mind busy reworking his daily schedule to accommodate her in his routine. "Would you like to join me for lunch on Monday, or will you be eating with the Lynxwilders?"

"Lunch with you would be lovely. Does that mean you're cooking?" He could hear her smiling again.

"I'll make us a couple of bologna sandwiches," he teased.

Charlotte let out a sound of pleasure into the phone, one that made Jed's pulse react unexpectedly. "I haven't had a bologna sandwich in far too long. That sounds terrific."

Jed couldn't tell if she was kidding or not, but he grinned at her response anyway. "It's a date, then." The moment the words were out, Jed regretted them. Neither of them could afford to think of their upcoming cohabitation that way.

"It's a date, then," Charlotte echoed softly, and Jed realized with great trepidation that it might already be too late.

EIGHTEEN

By the end of her morning shift on Thursday, Abby was fairly certain she could manage the prep work on her own, just as Cass had said. Cass insisted on having Abby do everything herself while she just watched—or rather, she sat in one of the two cushy armchairs near the gas fireplace in the front of the shop and drifted in and out of sleep while Abby worked. By the time they made it home, Cass was refreshed and bright-eyed and ready to start her day, while Abby wanted nothing more than to hose off and crawl back into bed.

Friday morning found Abby coming awake even before her alarm clock went off. Her eyes burned from fatigue, but she was too nervous to sleep. Despite how comfortable she'd felt with her tasks yesterday, she was now scared to death she'd do something to screw things up. Why on earth had she let the woman convince her she was ready to do the prep work on her own?

Abby dressed and brushed her teeth, then slipped out the front door as quietly as she could, hoping Cass wouldn't wake up. The woman deserved to be able to sleep in a few more hours.

It took her three attempts to get the alarm code punched in correctly, and by the time she cranked up the thermostat, she was already sweating bullets. "Calm down, chickie," she told herself, afraid that if she didn't get her head on straight, she'd for sure do something catastrophic. She was several minutes early, but she pulled everything from the coolers, then headed through the two-way doors into the front of the diner, where it was still dark and still.

By the time she'd disinfected the tables and chairs and all the various surfaces customers might come in contact with, she had her confidence back. She started singing, softly at first, then with more feeling, the empty, high-ceilinged room creating lovely resonance.

But I don't think that I'm sad now,
I'm not anything more than I was when I left.
But maybe that's my problem,
I'd sooner crack in two than let myself forget.

Ten minutes later, the first batch of pastries was in the oven—Danishes, of all things, and Cass's looked and smelled like something the Danes would be proud to claim—and Abby went back to work prepping the glass display cases. She could do this. And in spite of the inhuman hour, it was kind of peaceful. There was space to breathe, to think, to just be herself again.

All I can do right now is take a breath...

As she worked, the mouthwatering aroma of butter and cream cheese, the tang of lemon zest, and a hint of almond extract practically exploded from the kitchen, and Abby lifted her voice in appreciation.

The moon has fallen from that old, familiar sky
In both of my hometowns
It's in the puddles on the pavement from the rain
That never really came
The empty day's as blue as the dried up flowers
In front of my old house.
And yet here I am, still wondering if maybe
I'm the one who's changed.

Just as she was returning the last of the empty cake platters to the top shelf of the display case, a loud banging startled her, and she broke off with a shriek. The abrupt silence that followed reverberated loudly in the room after her heartfelt crooning.

It came again. Someone was knocking on the front door. At four o'clock in the morning?

In one swift, albeit rather clumsy move—she banged her elbow into the corner of the case, sending tingling pain shooting down her arm and out the tips of her fingers—she spun around, hit the panel of light switches on the wall behind her, and snatched up the phone that was charging in its cradle beside the cash register.

The room went dark, and sure enough, the street lamps outside silhouetted a shadowy form on the other side of the front door, arms akimbo, feet planted wide. Abby glanced down at the phone in her hand, her thumb poised over the 9, at the ready, then back to the door.

He—it had to be a *he*—was huge. Enormous. Towering. Menacing.

"It could be just the angle the light is shining on him," Abby countered in a whisper, cringing at how loud her voice sounded in the empty room. No human was that tall.

She pressed the 9, then a 1.

Could he see her, too? The lights were all on in the kitchen, shining through the square window panes in the swinging doors that separated the front of the shop from the back. "It's not like he doesn't already know I'm here," she muttered, forcing a note of bravado into her voice. In fact, turning off the lights felt a little like hiding under her covers when she was a kid. Like a monster wouldn't know what that lump in the bed was? Like he couldn't grab her right through her comforter?

Okay, now she was starting to freak herself out. She should not be thinking about childhood monsters right now. Not when there was potentially something—some*one*—a whole lot scarier on the sidewalk out front wanting to get inside Serendipity's.

Wanting to get to her.

Abby backed stealthily into the kitchen, her gaze fixed on the frosted glass door with the 'S' etched into it, praying whoever it was out there wouldn't attempt to break through it with a brick, or a tire iron, or whatever else they guy might have on him. She kept her hands on the swinging doors so they wouldn't flap closed after her—they made a surprisingly loud sound when the rubber seals slapped together.

She ducked down, not wanting her head to be outlined in the windows for the intruder to see. Was he actually an intruder, though? Anyone could walk on the sidewalk at any hour of the day or night. In fact, anyone could knock on the front door; that wasn't a crime.

"Hush your mind, Abs," she muttered to herself.

A firm rap on the back door of the kitchen made her jump, and she let out a terrified shriek and dropped the phone. It skittered across the tiled floor and slid under one of the shelving units that held the loaves of bread that were still warming to room temperature. "Oh, no, no, no, no, no!" she moaned softly, crouching down to peer under the unit. She'd need something with a long handle to get the stupid handset out.

She froze on her hands and knees when yet another knock sounded on the back door. Had the person come around the building? Was it even the same guy? Or were they like those velociraptors in the Jurassic Park movie, the ones who worked as a team... in the empty kitchen... tap-tap-tapping their sharp claws on the windows... pushing down on the door handle....

"Daddy," Abby whimpered, shrinking into an even tighter crouch. "Help me."

Why hadn't she just gone home? Why had she thought hiding out from her family was such a great plan? None of this would be happening right now if she'd just done the right thing. And now Cass would have to suffer yet another trauma in her life because she'd be the one to find Abby—or what was left of her—when she came to open her shop in a few hours.

At least the ovens were all set on timers, so the place would probably still be standing.

Her thighs were starting to tremble, both from the position she was in and from the adrenaline coursing through her. Fight or flight?

Flight. All. The. Way.

Except that she'd left her cell phone and her truck keys in her bag and it was hanging on a row of coat hooks by the door. The door outside of which the dinosaur-alien-no-way-it's-human creature stood knocking. The door that led out to the alley where she'd parked her truck. Her mode of flight—there was no way she could outrun a velociraptor alien creature on foot. Besides, it was still an alley. She'd seen enough movies to know that alleys were where terrible, terrible things happened.

Maybe if she didn't move, didn't breathe, then whoever it was would just go away.

Wait. What if it was the police come to check on the place? She could have set off the alarm after all before she'd gotten the code entered right. "What should I do? What should I do?" Surely if it was the police, they'd have announced themselves, though, wouldn't they?

The knock came again. Not louder or harder, but more persistent. She covered her mouth with a sweaty palm to keep back another shriek.

"Abby?"

Who on earth? Had she somehow conjured up her father, and he'd come to her rescue? Or had he found out where she was, after all, and had come to confront her about her poor life choices?

But no, that was not Jed's voice, she was certain, and Abby didn't know whether to be relieved or freaked out even more. Who knew she was back in the hollow? And how in the world had they—he… it—tracked her down here and at this time of the day?

Unless her benefactress had broken her promise and told someone. Cass wouldn't, would she? Abby couldn't think of anyone else who would know where to find her. Or that she needed to be found in the first place. *Oh, Jesus, please send someone to help me.*

"Abby? Are you in there? Open up."

Clearly, the person knew her.

Clearly, the person expected her to be there.

Clearly, the person assumed she'd let him in. "Stop being such a coward," she admonished herself under her breath. "Stand up and face whatever it is like a real country girl."

She straightened to her full height and crept forward, careful not to bump against anything, trying to remember if she'd actually locked the door behind her when she came in.

"I locked it. I know I did." Of course she had.

Hadn't she?

The door handle rattled—just like it had in that stupid, stupid Jurassic Park movie—and Abby froze again. Then, to her utter dismay, the door began to open. "No, no, no, no!" She spun on her heels, reached for the closest thing she could use as a weapon—a heavy maple rolling pin—and ducked behind one of the counters. If only Cass had given her keys to the front door of the shop, she would have made a run for it out that way.

NINETEEN

The idea of having a guest in his home—his first official guest, in fact—had Jed viewing the place from a different perspective and with a very keen eye. Not only would it be a guest, but a lady guest, and after more than thirty years of living with females of all ages, Jed was no stranger to the way women saw things.

But as he perused the different rooms, he found himself nodding with satisfaction. "You'd be proud of me, Caroline," he said. "A place for everything and everything in its place." She and the girls used to say that together when they'd go around the house and pick up at the end of the day. Jed was always the basket carrier—she'd hand him one of their largest laundry baskets and have him walk from room to room while the girls loaded and unloaded it as they picked up and put away their various toys and belongings. He still found himself gathering things at the end of the day, even living by himself, and making sure everything was where it belonged. It sure made it easier to greet the start of a new day when he wasn't faced, first thing, with his messes from yesterday.

"You make all things new," Jed said, lifting his gaze heavenward. "Thank you, Almighty God, for new beginnings, fresh starts, and second chances."

He'd furnished his guest room with a rustic bed, nightstand, and a tall dresser he'd tried to purchase from Charity and Frank when they were still in the process of converting Frank's old family home into their bed-and-breakfast, but Charity had threatened to stop cooking his favorite apple crumb pie if he tried pulling out his wallet one more time. He'd conceded, accepted the set of furniture—which she insisted was a perfect fit for his log house—and spent a little extra on a really nice mattress, instead. Charity had ordered him a sheet and comforter set from her favorite online store and had helped him set the room up so that it looked warm and welcoming, but still manly enough that he didn't have to apologize for it.

Of course, he'd expected his first guests would likely be Caroline's parents up visiting from Florida, or perhaps some rodeo personnel who needed a place to stay because the B&B was full when the rodeo came to the hollow. Never in a million years would he have guessed that his first guest would be a woman he found he had a bit of a hankering for.

Jed was an honest man, and if he was being honest, he had to admit that he had trouble *not* thinking about that Ransome woman, about her long, lean lines, those legs that went on forever, blue jeans slung low on her slim hips. So different from his petite, buxom wife, whose full curves had filled his hands and warmed his body in ways that made him feel ravenous and sated at the same time. When Ms. Ransome spoke to him on the phone in that husky, pushy voice, he could close his eyes and picture her, clear as day. The shooting spark of anticipation in her storm cloud gray eyes, the way her thick silver hair fell in heavy loose waves down her back. He wanted to touch that hair—did it feel like his own? Or was it soft and silky, the way his daughters' hair felt after they'd brushed it out?

"Stop your foolishness," Jed admonished himself. "She's off limits."

And she was. For a variety of reasons. One, the woman lived in Colorado, and he had no inclination to take up with someone who lived so far away. Granted, the whole reason she was paying Plumwood Hollow a visit was because she intended to move her and her flock of sheep out here to God's favorite part of the country. But she'd been threatening to do so for almost a year now, and nothing had come of it.

Half the time, Jed figured she just used it as an excuse to visit their little piece of paradise.

Not that he could blame her. As far as he was concerned, there wasn't a prettier patch of earth on the planet than Plumwood Hollow.

Even after she moved, though—*if* she ever did—Jed still had no interest in starting anything up with her. He'd finally gotten *away* from all the womenfolk in his life. He wasn't about to surrender his freedom so quickly, especially not to a woman who was so bullheaded about the way she wanted things.

How she'd wedged her way into his life over the last year, for example. He hadn't asked to be her tour guide, that was for sure. Why couldn't that realtor she'd hired help her out more? Do his job? What good was he if he didn't know anything about the properties he was showing her? Anyone could look up the details about a property—square footage, number of rooms, number of outbuildings, number of acres—just head down to the county register and ask the right people the right questions. A real estate agent, a person who made their living shuffling land deeds, should at least have the inside scoop on things, shouldn't he or she? When Jed had learned of some of the properties the woman was considering, there'd simply been nothing to do but step in and help.

Had he asked for that job? No, sirree, Bob. But nor could he just stand by and let her get blindsided by men who might take one look at those swaying hips and silver hair and do wrong by her.

Not that Ms. Ransome could be easily cowed. But then, she'd likely never dealt with some of the stubborn old coots who lived in the local hills and hollows. Jed was well aware that there were many folks in these parts, especially the farther away from town you got, who still regarded their women as little more than chattel.

Jed didn't stand for men who treated their women as such, nor did he have any desire to see a woman cow to her man, but marriage was a partnership, after all, a coming together of two equal parts to make a whole. He was old school—just ask his daughters—when it came to the roles men and women played in a marriage, however, and he wasn't so sure the rancher woman had any inkling of the kind of give and take that made for a working relationship. By her own admission, she'd been single for more than sixty years, never having anyone but herself to consider in her decision-making, her plans, in how she lived her life. No, he wasn't interested in sharing a life with someone whose world centered around herself.

Granted, he hadn't been in a marriage relationship in over thirty years, either, at least not with a living, breathing, perfectly imperfect woman. He still thought of himself as married to his sweet Caroline, but he knew he'd quite likely elevated her to sainthood in his mind. Which had made it easier to resist the attention of other women over the years; no one could compare to his beloved dead wife.

There'd been a nice woman in Muldoon more than ten years back now. She and Jed had been seeing each other once or twice a week for a few months. He'd been on the verge of asking her to meet the family over Sunday dinner when Faith, accompanied by Hope and Charity, had come to him with the revelation that she was pregnant, and that there would be no father involved in raising the baby.

That there would be yet another child to raise in the Goodacre household.

Jed had beaten himself up, convincing himself that he'd missed the signs of trouble brewing in his home because of his divided attention, and he had immediately broken things off with Lora Lee. She'd been lovely, someone he'd thought he might be able to share the front porch swing with someday, and it had broken his heart to see how badly he'd broken hers.

But he had renewed his commitment to put his girls first, and they'd needed him, each one of them in their own way over the years. He decided that if the Almighty intended for him to be the husband of another woman, then God would have to hand-deliver her to his front porch.

The Ransome woman, it seemed, was bent on hand-delivering herself to his front porch, but Jed wasn't so sure the Almighty had anything to do with it. And for that very reason, he wasn't so sure he should be entertaining thoughts of offering her anything more than a place to lay her head and a seat at his dining room table while she was in town.

Sure, he was grateful that she'd been on the road the night of Justice and Brandon's accident, that she'd been so instrumental in helping those two besotted kids figure things out between them. But did that gratitude have to extend to anything more than that?

"What do you think?" he asked the thin air, knowing Caroline had a whole lot better things to do than discuss his mixed emotions about the Ransome woman.

He had to stop calling her that.

Jed pulled the door of the guest room closed behind him and headed out to the kitchen to put away the last of his supper dishes before calling it a night. The light over the deep farm sink glowed soft and golden, making the copper basin gleam. It had been a luxury, that sink, but he'd found it at a massive discount at one of the local hardware stores; it had been returned by a customer who'd been unhappy with some cosmetic damage it had sustained in shipping. Jed had taken one look at the small dinged up spot, decided it looked to him like something that would give the sink character, and had bought it for a song.

He rinsed out his coffee cup and hung it on the mug rack tucked up under the cabinet next to the sink, then put away his plate and silverware and the pot he'd used to warm up the leftover chicken pot pie Courage had brought him over that morning.

"Don't worry," she'd said after a quick hug. "Joe made it, not Sarah or me." She'd also brought a box of fresh produce he'd ordered from Joe. "You're not paying for this, Daddy," she said, pushing away the money he tried to thrust into her hand. "Don't be ridiculous."

His girls wouldn't let him buy much of anything for himself these days.

"They must think I'm just a helpless old man," he muttered with a shake of his head. "Wouldn't it shock the Bo Jangles out of them if I took up with some woman after all these years?" The thought made him chuckle softly, but then he shook his head at the idea. It would shock the Bo Jangles out of the whole community. It might even shock the Bo Jangles out of himself if he actually did more than just toy with the idea.

"Besides," he admonished. "That woman hasn't really given you any reason to believe she might be interested in taking up with you. Maybe that's why she's not afraid to stay here alone. Maybe she thinks you're nothing but a helpless old man, too."

The notion had him standing up straighter, squaring his shoulders—in spite of the twinge that shot down his spine into his leg—and lifting his chin as he set off down the hall to get ready for bed. His limp suddenly felt more pronounced, and he consciously made an effort to keep his bum leg from dragging the way it often did by the end of the day.

In the bathroom, he stared at his reflection in the mirror over the sink. Yes, indeed, he needed his mop trimmed. At least it still grew in thick all over his head. Abby told him he had Sam Elliott hair, and Jed didn't mind the comparison. Any actor who could do justice by bringing a Louis L'amour Western to life on the big screen was fine by him.

There were deeply etched lines at the corners of his gray eyes, the clean-shaved flesh under his jaw hung a little loose, and there were defined creases in his neck that made it look like his skin was having a hard time holding itself up.

Upon closer inspection, several extra-long white hairs sprouted at odd angles from his already bushy brows. "Ouch!" he grunted when he unsuccessfully tried to rip one out with his fingers. He'd have to dig out the personal groomer thingy Justice had given him as a housewarming gift.

"Since we won't be around to pluck those things for you," she'd teased.

Supposedly, it took care of rogue eyebrow, nose, and ear hairs, and although Jed wasn't often inclined to try all the latest newfangled gadgets advertised as must-haves these days, after turning his head to the side and examining his ears, he thought it might be high time to take the motorized device on a trial run.

Not quite an hour later, he forced himself to put the dangerous little buzzers down. His right eyebrow was noticeably closer cropped than his left, he'd accidentally swiped a divot out of one of his sideburns when he got a bit too aggressive on his left ear hairs, and he was still a little too unsure of himself to risk shoving the hungry little thing up his nose. He'd stick to the pair of embroidery scissors Caroline had suggested he use shortly after they'd married.

"Oh, that's okay," she'd told him after he'd snipped off the offending nostril hairs and tried to return the tiny scissors to her. "You keep them. For next time."

"Why do I care, anyway?" Jed asked his scowling reflection. "As long as I can see, hear, and smell, and eat, who cares how long my facial hair grows?"

Actually, Jed cared. He didn't want anyone to look at him and see nothing but a helpless old man, especially not his girls. He wasn't a prideful man, but he did have his dignity to uphold, something he'd fought hard to do while raising seven daughters on his own. He had an enormous soft spot for single parents, and although he'd never want to be accused of bragging, he liked to think Caroline would be proud of him for the way he'd fathered their children, and for his part, however big or small, in the way each one of the girls was growing up into such lovely young women.

He wanted them to be proud of him, too. He wanted them to see him not as some haggard hairy has-been, but as a viable contributing member of society, as a man who still had a purpose on this earth, as someone they wanted in their lives.

And, truth be told, he wouldn't mind if that Ransome woman—Charlotte—looked at him that way, too.

TWENTY

"Abby?"

Wait. There was something familiar about that voice. She lifted her head so she could just barely see over the top of the counter she was hiding behind. Her fingers gripping the rolling pin were squeezed so tightly they were beginning to cramp. The door opened wider, and a very large person—there were no tentacles or dinosaur claws, but then again, he was still facing away from her—into the kitchen before turning around to scan the room.

"Abs, it's me. Mike. You in here?"

Mike Nesbit? What? How? And holy schmoly. What had happened to him since she'd last seen him? He'd been a big guy before he'd left for college—he'd played linebacker his senior year—but he must have grown another several inches, and he'd bulked up considerably since then. He hadn't looked quite so beefy when she'd seen him at the gas pump... but then, he'd been wearing riding gear and was still straddling his bike when she'd pulled away.

Abby rose slowly, still wielding the rolling pin like a club. "I'm here," she said in a tight voice, at a loss for anything more clever to say.

"Well, hey there." He grinned at her from across the room, then eyed the rolling pin in her hand. One brow lifted. "Should I get ready to duck?"

She heard the teasing in his voice, but she didn't smile back.

"Hey," he said again, gentler this time, when she didn't respond. His expression grew serious. "It's just me. It's okay."

"What—what are you doing here?" Abby asked, a little breathless now. It was the adrenaline from the shock pumping through her system.

Because it couldn't be the way his shirt stretched taut over his broad chest, or the curve of his biceps under the short sleeves. Or the fact that she could very clearly recall the way his strong arms felt wrapped almost too tightly around her... leaving her just as breathless as she was now.

"Cass didn't tell you I was coming." It wasn't a question.

"No." She was going to kill the woman. Not only had Cass *not* told Abby about Mike showing up this morning, but she'd clearly told Mike that Abby was back in town and would be here at Serendipity's alone.

If she knew Cass, Abby was certain that the woman—Abby wasn't going to call her 'friend' anymore, not after this—was trying to set her up with Mike Nesbit. Everyone knew they'd been a thing back in high school, but that didn't give Cass the right to throw them together like this. Especially after promising not to tell anyone about Abby's presence.

Abby reached a hand up to touch the messy bun on top of her head. Great. She hadn't bothered to even brush her hair, she wore no makeup, and she had on saggy leggings and a ratty tee under the apron she wore. Not exactly the way she'd have liked to look upon seeing Mike for the first time in over a year.

The second time, if you count the food mart on Tuesday. But she wasn't counting it. He'd only seen her eyes in her rear-view mirror and the back of her head through her truck window.

"That woman did not tell me you were coming," she reiterated.

"I'm dropping off the supplies she ordered. She said you needed sugar first thing this morning...." His voice trailed off as though he might be coming to the exact same conclusion about Cass's shenanigans.

Only then did she notice the two-wheeled dolly stacked with boxes that he'd dragged in with him. And that the too tight shirt he wore had the Nesbits Grocery logo emblazoned across the front of it.

"Sorry," Mike said, a frown tugging down the corners of his mouth. "Clearly, you really weren't expecting me. I didn't mean to scare you—just doing my morning deliveries." He glanced at the rolling pin she still clutched at her side, then met her gaze again. "You should lock the door when you're here alone."

Abby grimaced and practically dropped the rolling pin on the counter in front of her, the weight of it clattering loudly against the stainless steel surface. "I—I know," she stammered. "I guess I was so nervous about doing everything right this morning that I forgot to lock it behind me."

"Then I'm glad it was just me," he said, still serious. "At least I'm one of the good guys."

Abby was glad it was just Mike, too, but she wasn't about to admit it. She'd never been more relieved to see a familiar face, but of all faces, it had to be his? Besides, she wasn't so sure she'd put him in "the good guys" camp.

"I'll be more careful from now on," she finally managed to say. "Oh, and um, was that you at the front door a minute ago?" She had to ask. The idea that there might be some weirdo—although, probably not an alien-dinosaur—lurking out on the sidewalk in front of the shop still had her buzzing. When Mike didn't respond right away, she added, "Someone was out there." She sounded like a scared little kid.

She felt like a scared little kid.

"Yeah, that was me. I knocked back here first, and when no one answered, I went around to the front because I'd seen the light on. Then I heard you singing, and I realized why you hadn't heard me at the back door." One side of his mouth hitched up and... yep, there was that dimple again. "You sound pretty amazing for three o'clock in the morning, Abs. Especially that last note."

Abby resisted the urge to press her hands to her cheeks to cover the rush of color she knew was there. She'd screeched like a banshee when he'd knocked, and she knew it. "Well, you scared the living daylights out of me. I wasn't expecting anyone to break down the door, okay?"

Mike rolled his eyes. "I hardly broke down the door."

"But how was I to know you wouldn't? Again, I wasn't expecting you. Or anyone, for that matter."

"Sorry," he said, but his smirk said he wasn't very recalcitrant. "I honestly didn't mean to scare you."

"Well, you did," she retorted, then capitulated. "But I forgive you."

After a moment of awkward silence between them, he turned back to the load of boxes he'd brought in. "Where do you want this?"

"Um, I honestly don't know. Is it all sugar?" Was it possible Cass hadn't meant it as an innuendo, and that there really was something Abby was forgetting she needed to do with fifty pounds of sugar? "I mean, I thought that all I was supposed to do was take things in and out of the oven and set up the front of the shop. I don't actually make any of this stuff myself."

Mike nodded slowly, his lips pursed, eyes narrowed as he studied her. Finally, he said, "It's not all sugar. There's flour, and butter, too, and a couple pounds of apples. I can just put these in the pantry myself. I'm pretty sure I know where everything goes. Want to check this stuff off her list while I unload it?" He lifted his chin toward the clipboard.

"Okay," Abby said, still flummoxed by the whole situation. "I can do that." As if she wasn't stressed out enough already, just making sure she got her first morning alone right.

She waited to let Mike pass by her, then made a concerted effort not to stare at his broad shoulders, the play of muscles under his shirt as he wheeled the heavy load ahead of him, and she definitely didn't notice how nicely his worn jeans fit him in all the right places.

At the pantry door, Mike turned around, catching her by surprise—and catching her checking him out, too. She quickly averted her gaze, but the only indication that he'd noticed her perusal was the one eyebrow that shot up like a question mark. He reached up and took the clipboard from the wall, then held it out toward her. "Here you go."

Abby hurried over and snatched it a little too aggressively out of his hand. "Thanks," she said, trying to cover for her behavior. "I'm still—I just wasn't expecting anyone else here this morning."

"Got it," Mike said, nodding slowly, then went about the task of tearing open one box at a time and loading things onto the neatly ordered shelves, listing each item as he did so.

He seemed to be taking his sweet time, Abby thought, wishing one of the oven timers would go off so she could have something to keep her busy. She stared at the walls, the ceilings, the labeled pantry shelves, anything but at Mike bending and lifting and, well, using those guns he'd been so proud of back in high school. When he finally unpacked the last box, he straightened and rested one arm on the handle of the dolly. Abby held her breath and clutched the clipboard to her chest.

"How long are you in town for?" he finally asked, and the question caught her off guard enough that she answered it truthfully. He hadn't asked her why she was working for Cass, why she wasn't playing some gig in Nashville, or even why she was back in the hollow.

"I—I honestly don't know." She lowered her gaze, but then brought it right back up. She didn't want him to think she was ashamed or embarrassed about being here. Even though she was. "I'm taking a break, that's all."

Mike nodded, looked toward the stack of ovens, lifted his nose in the air, and said, "Danishes. They're my favorite."

"Cass knows how to do right by the Danes with them, that's for sure," Abby said, her shoulders relaxing a little at the change of subject. This was Mike, after all. He might not be one of the good guys exactly, but he wasn't one of the bad guys, either. Even she had to admit that.

"Got any of those in the day-old stash?"

Abby's eyes narrowed. "Maybe I do. Maybe I don't." In her trepidation over her first day alone on the job, she'd forgotten about the day old goodies. In the aftermath of the adrenaline rush, she was suddenly ravenous, and a cheese Danish sounded like just the thing. "I haven't looked yet."

"I can help you with that, too," Mike offered with a grin. He had the nicest teeth, Abby thought. Not quite straight, exactly, but they matched his crooked smile perfectly.

She rolled her eyes at him. "I'm sure you can. You could probably 'help out' with everything in the day-old box." She lifted one hand to make air quotes. "Cass lets you have access to the stash, does she?"

Mike shrugged, his eyes bright with something more than just humor. "I've learned a little self-control over the years. I've even been known to stop at just one these days."

The words hit Abby in the middle of her chest, and she had to look away. "Well, aren't we all grown up now?" Oh, why couldn't she just hold her tongue when she didn't have anything nice to say?

"I'd like to think so," came Mike's quiet response. The room suddenly felt cavernous in the silence that followed his statement, and Abby jumped when the first of the oven timers went off.

"I—I need to get those," she said, setting the clipboard on a counter nearby. She wasn't going to get any closer to him. She'd hang it up after he left. She bustled over to the first of the ovens and reached for the door.

"Don't forget these." Mike had crossed the room right behind her and held out a pair of oven mitts. He had a second pair in the other hand. "I'll get this batch if you want to get another round put in."

Abby took the black oven mitts from him with a mumbled "Thanks," and shoved her hands into them before sliding the three trays of pastries out of the first oven and moving them to the cooling racks close by. "But I—I'll be okay with all of this. You don't have to stay and help. I mean, don't you have more deliveries to make?"

Mike slipped his hands into the other set of oven mitts—his were purple with yellow polka dots and red trim at the wrist—and held them up for her approval. "And miss out on the chance to wear these beauties?" He opened a second oven and began unloading it. "I only had two deliveries this morning," he went on to say. "I already took the mother load over to Lola's, that new 24-hour truck stop over off County Line Road. You been there?" Abby just shook her head, and Mike continued. "Well, you should try it. They have the best roast beef sandwiches. Lola's husband, Herman, slow roasts it on the spit out back himself, and it's amazing. Anyway, this is my second and final stop." He straightened and held his decorated hands out at his sides. "I'm all yours for as long as you need me. As long as you pay me in day-old pastries, that is."

Abby felt the smile tugging at her lips and she turned away, not quite ready to give in to the notion of spending time with him.

"Although," Mike hedged in a tone that obviously meant to draw her attention back to him. "These hot out of the oven Danishes sure look good. Maybe I'll just take one—"

"Don't you dare!" Abby squawked, whirling on him. "I have to account for every single one of them, or Cass will take it out of my paycheck." Not exactly true, since there was no paycheck involved. But she knew that Cass had a quota she made each day, and Abby wanted to make sure Cass knew she could trust her from the get-go.

Mike jumped back with his hands up as though she might hit him, but his eyes crinkled with humor. "Will you let me stay and help, then?" he asked, lowering his hands slowly. "I don't have to be back at the store for another two hours."

Abby chewed on her bottom lip and studied him, still undecided. Should she ask Cass first? Wouldn't that be the best thing to do? But she couldn't just call her now, not at this hour of the morning.

"I'll be on my best behavior," Mike cajoled. "I promise."

"Why do you want to?" Abby asked. She couldn't let him endear himself to her this way, not while she was feeling so vulnerable. "I mean, why not go home and go back to bed? Get a little more beauty sleep. Not that you look like you need any, standing there all bright-eyed and bushy-tailed like that." She headed to the racks to grab the first couple of bread loaf pans.

"So you think I'm beautiful?" Mike asked, crossing his polka dot mitts over his chest.

"I didn't say that," Abby shot back, no longer able to bite back her smile. "Open that oven door for me, will you? Since you insist on standing right in my way." She slid the perfectly rounded loaves of bread inside. "What I said, in so many words, Mike Nesbit, is that you look like a squirrel."

"A beautiful squirrel," he countered. "In so many words."

Abby shook her head and playfully poked him in the shoulder. "You keep telling yourself that, big guy."

Mike grinned down at her, and she suddenly realized just how close they stood. Abby straightened her shoulders and spun away from him, heading back for another batch of bread. She couldn't let him stay, even if the company might be nice.

"I'm serious, Mike. You don't need to stick around; I've got this." When she turned back to him, his expression had her faltering. "Don't look at me like that," she said, laughing nervously. "I'll still let you have a day-old Danish, if there are any. I haven't looked in the box yet. I might even let you have two for not being a dinosaur alien serial killer."

"A what?" Mike laughed as he worked the pretty oven mitts off his hands and laid them next to hers on the counter.

"Nothing. Never mind."

"You thought an dinosaur alien serial killer was knocking politely at the front door?"

Abby rolled her eyes. "Shut up."

He leaned against the counter and crossed his arms, watching her casually as she stayed busy. She put a few more loaves in the ovens, set the timers, and then started scooping the freshly baked Danishes off the cooling trays and lining them up on parchment paper lined trays that she slid into one of the refrigeration units.

Finally, she stopped and faced him, her hands on her hips. "What?"

"What, what?" Mike shot back.

"Why are you still standing there? Go." She pointed at the door. "I have work to do. You're in my way."

Mike glanced over his shoulder at the empty counter top behind him, then back at her, that dumb eyebrow raised again.

"I just mean that you're here, disrupting my focus. I need to make sure I don't screw things up on my first solo day on the job."

For a moment, Abby thought he might argue with her, but finally, he straightened and crossed to where he'd stood the dolly with the empty boxes stacked on it. He tipped the cart handle back toward him, but paused and eyed her once again. "I get the impression I might be the only who knows you're here," he said.

Abby frowned and shook her head. "You're not." It wasn't a lie. Cass knew she was in town, too.

"Who else knows?" he pressed.

"Lots of people." Well, that was a stupid answer. It was a total lie. "I mean, the people who need to know. They know, okay?"

"Like your dad? Your sisters?" Mike asked. "Because I had a nice conversation with Charity just yesterday afternoon, and she didn't mention a thing about you being back in the hollow. You'd think she'd have said something, you know? Seeing as how you're a local celebrity and all."

Abby couldn't tell if he was being sarcastic or just factual. "Well, maybe it's *because* I'm a local celebrity. Ever think of that? Maybe she was trying to protect me by not blowing my cover. Like I said, I needed a break."

"Maybe?" He narrowed his eyes and cocked his head at her, propping one big foot on the support bar of his cart. "So your family *does* know you're here?"

Abby clenched her teeth together, trying to force the falsehood out of her mouth. She couldn't do it. "No, Charity doesn't know I'm here, okay? Are you happy?"

"So?"

"So what?" Abby was really getting irritated now. "I have work to do, Mike. Can you just leave now?"

His eyebrows drew together in consternation. "Fine. Just tell me this. Do I need to keep it a secret that you're here?"

Abby's shoulders drooped at the question. One more person she was forcing to let her hide behind. She closed her eyes and bowed her head. When she lifted her gaze to meet his again, he was still frowning, but the edge of frustration that had tightened the corners of his mouth was gone. He looked concerned more than anything.

"You don't have to lie for me," she finally conceded. "But it would be really nice if you wouldn't offer any information about me, either. Cass—and now you—are the only people who know I'm in town." She made an apologetic face at him. "I know it's not fair to put you in this position, especially since I'm not going to tell you why, but I'd rather my family not know. At least not yet."

Mike nodded slowly, but his gaze never left her face. "One condition."

Great. He wanted to bargain with her and she had nothing to bargain with. "What?"

"You don't have to explain anything to me today. Or even tomorrow. But I do want to know what's going on, Abs."

"Why?" she asked, feeling the flush of her shame burn its way up her neck to color her cheeks. "Why does it matter why?"

Mike set the dolly upright again and took a few steps toward her. Abby backed up a pace, and he stopped. "I'm not going to hurt you," he murmured, almost like he was talking to a scared animal. He reached out a hand toward her, palm up. "It matters because I care about you." He kept his hand out, even though she didn't take it. "We're friends, aren't we? Things between us weren't so great two years ago, but I'd like to hope that we can be friends again. What do you say?"

Abby studied his long blunt-tipped fingers, the broad square of his palm, the thick mound at the base of his thumb, the oddly pale skin of the underside of his wrist. How long would he wait for her to take it—how long would he, quite literally, extend the hand of friendship—before he gave up and let it fall back to his side?

Finally, she stepped toward him and covered his palm with her own. His fingers curled gently around her wrist and he pulled her ever so slowly a little closer until there were less than two feet between them.

"I've missed you, Abstinence Eve Goodacre," Mike said, his river rock blue eyes locked with hers. "I'll keep your secret for you."

For a moment, Abby thought she'd lost her voice. "Thank you," she forced out, unable to look away.

Mike's gaze flicked to her mouth, then back up again. It was only for a moment, but Abby thought her heart was going to stop at the sudden flare of heat in his expression. She pulled her hand from his grasp and crossed her arms tightly, forcing herself not to step back. He wasn't intimidating her—and not for one moment did she believe he intended to. No, the pressure she was feeling at that moment was something building inside of her.

"Thank you," she said again. Then, even though he hadn't asked again, she offered, "And I will tell you why, okay? Not yet, but soon."

Mike nodded slowly as he lowered his hand to his side, his fist clenched loosely. "I'll see you around, then," he said. Without another word, he wheeled the dolly to the door, but paused there and turned back to look at her. "In case Cass hasn't told you, Abby, I do regular deliveries here Monday, Thursday, and Saturday mornings."

"Today's Friday," she said, frowning in confusion. She glanced at the calendar on the wall near the pantry, suddenly uncertain about a lot of things. "Isn't it?"

Mike nodded. "Yeah. I came today because you needed sugar, remember?"

"I didn't—"

"I know. We've already established that. It was just Cass, up to some of her usual shenanigans."

"Right," Abby replied, feeling the burn in her cheeks again.

"So..." He drew the word out until Abby met his gaze. "That means I'll be back tomorrow morning around the same time with her usual weekend supplies. Just giving you a heads up. It'll be me and a few of my alien-dinosaur serial killer buddies."

"Jerk." She threw one of the oven mitts at his head.

Mike dodged it, then bent to pick it up before saying, "So if you actually do need anything at all, just give me a holler, okay? My cell hasn't changed." He paused and cocked a brow at her. Did he want her to admit that she hadn't removed his number from her phone?

"Okay." She wouldn't acknowledge it one way or the other.

"Or you can call into the store, too, of course," he told her. "That number hasn't changed, either."

"Got it."

"Good."

"Good," she echoed, then made a shooing gesture. "Now go."

Mike grinned, saluted her, then pushed open the door. "See you in the morning, then," he said. He backed out of the kitchen, pulling the dolly along, and let the door swing shut behind him.

Abby hurried across the room, but just as she was reaching for the deadbolt, Mike poked his head and shoulders back inside. "Don't forget to lock up after me."

Abby reached up like she was going to flick him in the forehead, but he laughed and ducked out too quickly, leaving her standing in the quiet room, shaking her head and grinning like an idiot.

Mike would be back tomorrow morning. Great.

She needed to have a little chat with Cass. "You won't tell anyone, my great aunt Jessamine," Abby muttered under her breath. "Who else have you already let it slip to?"

TWENTY-ONE

"Oh, Abby," Cass insisted, clasping her hands in her lap, her expression imploring. "Please forgive me. I was going to tell you Mike would be showing up so you wouldn't freak out. Then I completely forgot. I'm so sorry."

"Yeah, well, I freaked out." Abby told her. She waved her arms around like a catty wampus windmill. "Like, crazy woman freaked out. I screamed like a prepubescent boy."

Cass cackled gleefully, then covered her mouth with her hand. "I'm sorry. I shouldn't laugh, but I can just picture that whole scene playing out in my head. So? Was it nice to connect with Mike again?"

"Connect with him? Seriously, Cass? Of all people in the world, why on earth did you tell him I was here?"

"Why are you so upset? You two have been friends since you were in diapers and I thought it would be nice to see a familiar face. One who wanted to see yours, too," Cass said. She'd taken a midday break and come back by the apartment to check on how Abby's first day alone had gone. "I mean, I did tell him you'd be there, but only because he specifically asked. I didn't offer him the information, I promise."

"He asked?" Abby said, dubiously. "Like, he asked you if I'd be working this morning when he brought the delivery of sugar you told him I needed?"

"No, no, no," Cass replied, shaking her head vehemently. "It looks bad, I admit, but it's not like that at all."

"Look, Cass," Abby said, lifting her hands in surrender. "I honestly don't care now. Please know that I am super grateful to you for what you're doing for me, okay? It's okay. I mean, it's just Mike, and he's willing to keep things under wraps, at least for now. But please don't let it slip to anyone else that I'm here. Or at least let me know if you do before I find out from that person."

"I didn't let it slip," Cass insisted, something in her expression making Abby think she was starting to get a little offended. "He asked me about you, Abby. He came up to me and asked about you."

"But, how? Why would he even think that you would know anything about me being—"

The gas station. He'd seen her—she shivered at the memory of that moment their eyes met and held—and then he'd watched her follow Cass out of the parking lot. "He saw me leave with you."

"Yeah," Cass said with a slow nod. "And he came into the shop yesterday afternoon and asked where he could find you."

"So you told him I was working for you."

"Not exactly." Cass stood and crossed into the little kitchen. From the cupboard, she pulled out two wineglasses. "Want something to drink? I have—"

"No, thanks." Abby cut her off, waving both hands in the air. "I'm not—I can't—" She knew that was a road better left untraveled for now.

Cass chuckled good-naturedly. "I don't have anything alcoholic in the house," she told Abby. "I just like pretty glasses. I was going to offer you water, lemonade—the powdered, make-it-yourself stuff—or some homemade sweet tea."

"Oh. Sorry." Abby grimaced. "I've had a little trouble with this guy with the initials Jack and Daniels lately, so I cut myself off."

"Good for you," Cass declared. "If you're anything like me, that might just be the best decision you've ever made. I can get in enough trouble on my own without the help of any mind-altering substance. Don't get me wrong; I love a Midori sour every now and then." She puckered her lips and made a loud, kissy sound. "Makes my mouth water just thinking about it. But I'm telling you, I'm good for one mixed drink and that's it. Even then, I'm glad I'm friends with the bartender, girl. Badger looks out for me, and I let him know just how much I appreciate it."

"TMI, Cass. TMI." Abby covered her ears. "I'd love some of your sweet tea, though."

Cass returned to the table with two goblets of iced tea topped off with thick lemon wedges. "Listen, Abby. About Mike." She leaned forward, her ample cleavage threatening to spill over the top of her scoop-necked shirt.

Abby had to force herself not to look at the mounded flesh on display. "I'm listening."

"That boy did see you at the gas station and he did ask about you. But he asked because he thought it was strange that when he asked one of your sisters how you were doing—Charity, I think—she made it sound like you were still in Nashville making a big splash on music row, or whatever they call it. He had the good sense not to correct her, but it was obvious to him that something was up with you. When he stopped in at my shop, he wouldn't accept my evasive responses. And believe me, honey, I tried to feed him all kinds of nonsense without making a liar of myself."

"Take a breath, Cass." Abby said crabbily. She already knew this part of the story. "So he coerced you into telling him where I was?"

Cass narrowed her eyes and swatted a red-nailed hand in the air between them. "Don't be that way, Abby. He didn't manipulate or coerce me. I don't fall for that kind of thing anymore, anyway."

Abby had the good sense to recognize for what it was, the quick flash of shame that washed over her. She sighed and apologized quickly and sincerely. "Ugh. I'm sorry. That was a low blow, and I know you're smarter than that."

"You got that right, girlie." Cass winked at her to show there were no hard feelings. "No, Mike insisted on knowing if you were okay. And if I know anything, Abby, other than puff pastry and yeast dough, I know people. Men, especially. He was like a dog with a bone, not because he wanted the scoop on your secrets, but because he was genuinely worried about you."

"Worried? But why?"

"You really have to ask?" Cass rolled her eyes as if Abby's question was the most ridiculous thing she'd ever heard. "That boy has never stopped pining for you; you must know that. It's no secret in these parts, anyway."

Abby dropped her gaze to her goblet and ran her fingertips up and down the stem of it. She'd seen it there in his eyes that morning.

"He's as strong and steady on the inside as he is on the outside, you know," Cass said softly. "He's a good guy, Abby."

Abby took a deep breath and nodded. "So I've been told." Straight from the horse's mouth, in fact. "It's not that I really mind him knowing I'm here, Cass. I was just surprised to see him this morning, especially since he knew I'd be there like it was no big deal. It freaked me out for one, but also, what was all that about me needing a sugar delivery? I was so confused. On top of being freaked out."

Cass scrunched up her nose and smiled sheepishly. "Now that…" She drew out the word, then took a long sip of her tea. "That was just me trying to be cute," she said when she finally lowered her glass. "I thought you'd appreciate the sweet, sweet sight of that handsome face… that strapping young body—"

"Cass! Ew! You're old enough to be his mother."

"I beg your pardon!" Cass gasped dramatically and pressed a palm to her bosom. "His slightly older sister, maybe, but his mother?" She managed to laugh and look aghast at the same time.

"Being his slightly older sister wouldn't make you ogling him any better," Abby retorted.

Cass shrugged. "You're right, you're right. Which is why I had no qualms about sending him your way. You, my dear, are free to appreciate him to your heart's content."

Abby shook her head emphatically. "I did not come here to 'appreciate'—" she said, lifting her fingers to make air quotes around the word—"anyone. I came here to lick my wounds and figure out what I'm going to do with my life."

"Well, can't that include figuring out who you're going to do your life with?"

Abby pushed back from the table. "You are insatiable, Cass. Stop trying to play Cupid with me. I'm a loser, a failure, a flop, and a waste of a life right now, okay? I will not become anyone else's burden. It's bad enough I've foisted myself on you."

"Uh, uh, uh." Cass shook a finger at her. "Leave that negative talk at the door, girlfriend. Now you have to tell me four wonderful things about yourself."

"What? Why?" Abby made a disgruntled face at her. "And four? Why four?"

"You must," Cass insisted. "To counteract the four ugly things you just said."

Abby shook her head. "I can't think of any."

"Fine. I'll start," Cass said, undeterred. "You sing like an angel. Your turn."

"No."

"Okay. I'll go again." Cass cocked her head and narrowed her eyes at Abby. "You are lucky enough to be part of one of the finest families in the hollow. Your turn."

"Cass, come on." Abby couldn't meet her gaze. Her cheeks were warm. It was difficult to sit there and listen to someone list good things about her, especially knowing what a mess she'd made of everything.

"Your turn," Cass prodded in a sing-song voice. She nudged Abby's foot under the table. "And if you don't come up with something, I'll keep going. But just so you know, the rule is that no matter how many I list, you still need to come up with four on your own."

"What a stupid rule," Abby said, rather waspishly.

"Four things," Cass repeated. She wiggled four fingers in the air.

"Fine. I have good hair."

"Oh, yes!" Cass agreed with a quick clap of her hands. "You do have the most glorious hair. Want me to go again?"

"No. I have a pretty guitar."

"Doesn't count. That's not you."

"Yes, she is. Blossom's as much a part of me as my right arm." Abby insisted, holding up the said arm and wiggling her fingers the way Cass had.

"Nope. Doesn't count." Cass gave a firm shake of her head. "It's against the rules."

"Are you just making these rules up as you go?"

"My house. My rules." Cass bobbed her head in a sassy gesture. "I'll go again while you think. You are kind and you treat everyone with respect, whether they deserve it or not."

Abby was shaking her head in shame before Cass had finished her sentence. She certainly wasn't treating her hostess very kindly or with much respect at the moment. "You obviously don't know me very well," she said.

"Oh, psht. I know you just fine. And don't even try to tell me that you've changed as much as all that. According to what you said happened in Nashville, it's your kindness and your belief in other people—especially in those who don't deserve it—that landed you back here in the hollow so unexpectedly."

Abby was still shaking her head, but slower now. She hadn't really looked at it from that perspective before. "But I got careless, Cass, and that's the opposite of respect. I got careless with Bucky's heart, with my own in the process, and by extension, with my band."

"This Bucky fellow," Cass said with a snort. "Are you sure he even has a heart? Sounds like he's got a tiny little gravestone inside his ribcage where his heart withered up and died." She held her thumb and finger about a centimeter apart. "And it's inscribed with the letters M E."

Abby snorted in appreciation, then said, "I'm sorry I'm so cranky today."

"You only got a few hours of sleep, girlie. I can hardly expect you to be anything else." Cass stood and carried her glass to the sink. "I've got to get to get back to the shop now, but you take the rest of the day to come up with at least three more things you like about yourself, you hear? I'll be expecting a recitation over supper."

"Recitation, hm?" Abby raised her eyebrows at Cass. "That's too big of a word for someone going on three hours of sleep."

"Enjoy your afternoon. I should be home around seven this evening, and I'll bring something home for our dinner theater—starring Ms. Abstinence Goodacre of The Abstinence Goodacre Band—tonight." She gave Abby a way too boisterous hug and sashayed out of the room.

"Great," Abby muttered. "Just great." She was so tired she wasn't even sure what she was 'so greating' about. She headed for one of the overstuffed armchairs and turned on the television. At least Cass had Netflix, Hulu, and a few other streaming channels. She'd find something interesting to binge watch; take her mind off her worries for a while.

When she awoke to the sound of her phone alarm chiming right beside her head, it took her a few moments to orient herself. The room was dimly lit by a night light, a beaded lampshade plugged into the socket in the corner of the room. Her phone told her it was 2:30 in the morning, and taped to the back of it was a note from Cass. She must have somehow set her alarm for her, too.

I used your thumb to unlock your phone. There's spaghetti in the fridge and garlic bread in tinfoil in the breadbox. If you're one of those people who have to eat something green with every meal, there's half a cucumber in the produce drawer, too. See you in the morning—and no, you're not off the hook.

TWENTY-TWO

It had taken every ounce of willpower not to go back to bed when she returned to the apartment after her early morning shift. She'd gotten plenty of sleep, having passed out on the sofa yesterday afternoon sometime and sleeping straight through until her alarm. But she still felt drained and out of sorts. On edge.

Mike had made his regularly scheduled Saturday morning delivery consisting of twice as many boxes of supplies as he'd brought the day before. But his morning was packed with grocery deliveries to places, just like Serendipity's, that were prepping for their busy weekends. So although he'd greeted her warmly and asked for her help with checking things off Cass's clipboard again, he hadn't stayed any longer than it took to collapse the boxes and wheel them out to the recycle bin in the alley for her.

She thanked him and sent him on his way with a *pain au chocolat* she'd pulled out of the day-old box for him, relieved to be able to hurry him along. She was having enough trouble concentrating on the tasks at hand, and his presence only distracted her more. But after he was gone, she found herself feeling a little bereft with only herself for company, and she kinda wished he'd stuck around a bit.

Back at the condo, she found a note Cass had left on the refrigerator door telling Abby she'd gone out to breakfast with a friend and would go straight to work from there, and it didn't help that the house was quiet and still shadowy in the early morning.

She poured herself an enormous glass of Cass's strong, sweet tea from the fridge, and somehow, Abby managed to stay upright the rest of the day. By the time Cass got home, though, Abby was well into her second wind, and had decided to show her appreciation to her friend by setting the table and making a new batch of tea for the meal.

"Well, look at you being all sweet," Cass said as she bustled into the kitchen carrying a large paper bag in each hand. They were both stamped with Serendipity's logo, and Abby's mouth started watering as her mind conjured up all of her favorite menu items.

"And look at you bringing home the bacon." Abby could give as good as she got.

"How did you know?" Cass asked over her shoulder as she began emptying the bags out onto the counter. "I brought us some of my famous avocado BLTs. I remember how much you love them."

Abby's eyes widened in surprise. "You're right. They're one of my all-time favorites. Your bread is to die for, Cass. Every single kind, but that rustic stuff that's soft and chewy in the middle with the crisp, buttery crust?" Abby sighed dreamily, then lifted a hand to her mouth to check for drool. "I'm starving."

"Good. So am I." Cass quickly plated up the sandwiches, scooped an enormous helping of potato salad from another container onto each plate, then brought them both to the table. "There are two more little containers in one of those bags, one with baby dills and one with Greek olives. Grab them, will you, and bring them to the table."

They bowed their heads in a quick prayer of thanks for the food, then dug in. Between bites, they made small talk about how the day at Serendipity's had gone, what Abby had done to keep herself busy and awake. Then, as if on cue, as Abby put the last bite of her sandwich into her mouth, Cass gave her a prodding look. "Well?"

"Well, what?" Abby said around the mouthful of one of the best sandwiches she'd ever had. Had they always been this good? But she knew exactly what Cass was getting to.

Cass rolled her eyes and stabbed a fork in Abby's direction. A small chunk of potato salad clung to the utensil, and Abby leaned away, just in case. "Okay, fine," Cass said. "I'll start again. You have a good head on your shoulders. You're a thinker."

Abby sighed and reached for her glass. "You're not going to drop this, are you?" she asked after taking a long sip of tea. "Fine." She held up one finger. "I can sing."

"Nope. Doesn't count," Cass said with a shake of her head. The motion set other body parts to jiggling, too. "I already said that one."

Abby rolled her eyes. "Right. So number one: I have good hair."

Cass nodded encouragingly.

"Two. I have good skin." And she did. She'd always had good skin, something her friends had coveted back in high school. But she'd always taken good care of it, too. She wasn't obsessive about it, but she never went to bed without washing and moisturizing her face and hands, and she liked to think that her skin stayed clear out of gratitude.

"Three. I am brave. Or at least I've been known to be brave."

"You *are* brave, girlie. You're the only one who seems to think otherwise. Look at what you did, running off to Nashville to follow your dreams."

"And now I've run back home with my tail between my legs."

"It's temporary. Think of this as a hospital stay. Even the bravest soldiers get wounded now and then, and they can't just stay on the battleground and keep fighting. They need to get their wounds taken care of, to heal up before they can pick up their swords—or in your case, your axe—again and get back out there. Doesn't make them—or you—any less brave, does it?"

Abby nodded slowly. "I guess I can see that." She shot Cass a sheepish look. "How'd you get to be so wise, woman?"

Cass laughed gently. "Counseling. Good friends. Helping other people. I'm telling you what, that's the key, Abby. Helping other people takes the focus off of me and suddenly, my problems don't seem quite so insurmountable."

"Well, then, you're welcome."

Cass gave her a puzzled frown. "For what?"

"For helping you see that your own problems aren't quite so insurmountable," Abby quipped. She tossed a crumpled up napkin at Cass, whose hand shot out and caught it. "Wow," Abby said, her eyes widening in surprise.

Cass shrugged and threw the napkin right back. "Don't forget. I spent a few years of my life dodging things flying at me. You and your wimpy little napkin are no match for this warrior woman."

For a moment, Abby wondered if she should apologize, but the look on Cass's face made her hold her tongue. It was obvious that the woman across from her was proud of how far she'd come, of the chains she'd broken, of the victories in her life, and Abby didn't want to belittle that with a 'sorry.' "You're my hero, Cass," she said instead. "I mean it. And not just because you make the best BLTs in the whole world, either." She lifted what was left of her sandwich in a salute.

Cass smiled and shrugged. "We can't all be country superstars, you know."

"I'm not—"

"You are," Cass interrupted. "Tell me one more fantastic thing about yourself."

But Abby was tired of playing the game. Insisting she was something she wasn't didn't make it true, and saying nice things about herself out loud didn't solve anything. "No, I'm not, Cass. At best, I'm a country superstar wannabe. At best," she reiterated firmly. "And even then, only on my good days. And today is not a good day. In fact, this whole month is not a good day."

Cass shrugged. "Maybe today isn't, but there's always tomorrow—"

"Why did I know you were going to say that, Little Orphan Annie?" She didn't mean it to be cruel, but it kinda sounded spiteful and mean, anyway. "Look, you and I deal with our problems differently, Cass," she said, trying to soften her words. "And honestly, right now, I don't think I'm in the right frame of mind to deal with much of anything. I'm sorry I snapped at you."

"All is forgiven." Cass waved off her apology. "Did you like the sandwich?"

Abby smiled sincerely and pointed at her plate, where nothing of the meal remained except for a few crumbs and the stem end of a pickle spear. "I can't remember ever having a better BLT."

Cass beamed under the praise. "I'm glad. I only buy a specific kind of avocado now; to me, it makes all the difference in the world flavor-wise."

"I'm sure the right produce helps, but it's your bread that does it for me," Abby told her. "It's even better than I remembered." She began gathering her dishes and pushed back her chair. "I'll clean up tonight, okay? You've been working all day, so you go put your feet up and watch your favorite show or something."

Cass didn't argue, but instead of going into the living room, she pointed at one more paper bag on the counter. "I brought home chocolate croissants, either for dessert or for your breakfast, if you'd prefer. I figured since you made them, you should definitely have one. They turned out perfectly, by the way."

"Well, thank you," Abby said, reaching for the bag and unrolling the top. The aroma that burst from inside it had her mouth watering. "I'm so full right now, but how can I resist?"

"Why don't we watch a movie and have them with some hot tea in about half an hour?" Cass suggested. "That will give me time to take a quick shower and get comfy. You pick a movie, okay?"

Although the thought of a chill night in front of a girlie movie sounded rather attractive, Abby hesitated, knowing she should be in bed in another hour if she was going to have to haul herself out of bed by three in the morning.

"Tomorrow is Sunday," Cass reminded her, as if reading her mind. "I don't open until eleven, which means you don't have to get there to do the prep until seven. So you get to sleep in a little—I'm assuming you're not interested in going to church with me in the morning, right?"

Abby glanced at the clock on the stove. If she went to bed right after the movie, she'd still get at least a full eight hours of sleep. "Sounds like a plan. What do you feel like watching? And please don't say 'The Bachelor.' I just can't."

Cass laughed and got up from the table, too. "Ha! You and me, both, girlie. How about Captain America? The first one. Yum."

Abby rolled her eyes at the dreamy look on her friend's face. "Are you objectifying Chris Evans, Cass Whitehouse?"

"Never!" Cass declared. I think that Red Skull guy is hot-hot-hot!"

Just before Cass disappeared into her bedroom, she called back over her shoulder, "By the way, you still owe me one!"

Abby knew better than to ask what she meant. She owed Cass a lot more than just one of anything.

She sighed, her shoulders drooping as she held her hands under the stream of water from the kitchen faucet and waited for it to get hot. She owed a whole lot of people a whole lot, period.

TWENTY-THREE

"Daddy, you need a haircut," Faith whispered into his ear from her seat directly behind him. The family had grown too large to all squeeze into one pew. Faith and Cord and their youngsters had been the first to migrate, then Courage and Joe and his mother, Sarah, had moved to sit next to them, leaving just enough room for Justice and Brandon at the end of the pew. If either of the twins started having babies, the Goodacre clan would have to commandeer yet another row in their small church.

Not that Jed minded. There was nothing that did his heart so good as to look around and see his family gathered to worship the Almighty together. A full quiver; God had truly blessed him.

Although there was one arrow missing, and Jed felt that empty spot in the pew beside him like a missing limb. He was looking forward to Abby's call this afternoon, but not with the pleasant anticipation he usually felt. No, he was anxiously awaiting word from her, his spirit unsettled inside him whenever he let himself dwell on all that she was facing out there in the wild world alone.

How he wished that woman hadn't planted those thoughts in his head.

Ms. Ransome said she was coming into town this morning, but she wasn't at church with the Lynxwilders. Either her trip had exhausted her, or she would be arriving after the service was over. Maybe she was driving this time. Was it safe for her to be on the road all that time alone? It wasn't just a day trip from her home in Colorado to Plumwood Hollow. He knew she had a cellphone with a hands-free device, but was she diligent about keeping the contraption charged....

Why am I getting so worked up about her? He had to stop letting her take up so much space in his head.

Jed reached up and smoothed down the hair at the back of his neck in acknowledgment of Faith's observation. She squeezed his shoulder affectionately in turn.

Reverend Treadwell greeted the parishioners warmly, opened the service with a prayer, then Trudy Huckster, the church secretary *and* pianist, pounded out the opening chords of an old hymn. It was one of Jed's favorites, and he joined in, his rich husky voice filling out the bottom end of the melody carried by his daughters around him. Sometimes it still surprised him to hear other male voices in the fold, although Levi Valiente, they'd all discovered, might be able to wield a blade with the precision of a neurosurgeon, but couldn't carry a tune in a bucket. But between Cord, Frank, Joe, Brandon, and now Prudence's husband, Collin, Jed found himself in good company, pleased that the men his daughter's had chosen all enjoyed lifting their voices in song, too. Other than Abby, the Goodacres weren't necessarily a musical family, but the whole gang appreciated a good singalong, whether it be to worship music in church, campfire songs around the backyard bonfires, or caroling with friends at Christmas during the annual lighting of the Christmas tree downtown.

After the first song, the pastor invited folks to take a few minutes to greet those around them. Jed had gotten ready a little earlier that morning, leaving extra time for him to even out his eyebrows. Every time he caught a glimpse of himself in the mirror, he did a double-take. How could changing the shape—and thickness—of one's eyebrows make such a difference in an old man's appearance?

He'd done his best to even them out at least, although he could swear he'd seen women with thicker brows than his were now. He just hoped to high heaven that his girls wouldn't make a fuss over his awful DIY trim job, at least not in church. He'd hear about it over the Goodacre Sunday Family Dinner, for certain, but they'd better keep their opinions to themselves in the house of God. Respect. That's what he'd taught them, and he hoped they'd do right by him today.

"Well, Jedediah Goodacre. Look at you!"

Charlotte Ransome.

Taken by surprise, Jed forced himself not to take a step backward. Where had she come from? He could have sworn she hadn't been there where the service started.

He lifted his chin just the smallest bit and took her proffered hand. "Ms. Ransome," he said by way of greeting. "Nice to see you." And it was, he realized. She looked cool and fresh in a pretty white top and a red calf-length skirt over a pair of black snakeskin cowboy boots with silver accents at the toes. Her long hair was swept up in some kind of a loose hairdo that softened the angular lines of her face. Her eyes sparkled warmly as she shook his hand, her gaze perusing his face like she was drinking him in.

At least, that's the way it felt... until she spoke.

"Doing a little manscaping these days?" she asked, waving a finger at his eyebrows.

So much for respect in the house of God. He could feel the eyes of every one of his family members turning toward him.

Jed started to withdraw his hand, but Charlotte brought her other one up and caught his between both of hers. "I like it," she told him, nodding slowly, deliberately. And I really like the longer hair," she added, tipping her head sideways as if to try to see around to the back of his head. "The bachelor life suits you, it seems."

"Daddy!" Justice cut in from the far end of the pew. "You used the kit!" She brought both her thumbs up and nodded encouragingly.

"Nice," Brandon echoed, nodding the same way Charlotte had.

Jed felt and intense flush creep up his neck. He turned around and sat back down. He'd forego greeting anyone else that morning. In fact, he might just forego the family dinner, too. Because it had just occurred to him that if Charlotte Ransome was in town and staying with the Lynxwilders, then she might be attending the Goodacre Sunday Family Dinner, too.

TWENTY-FOUR

By the time the service was over, Jed had gathered his wits about him and determined that no one—not his daughters or their husbands or their children *or* that outspoken woman—would keep him from his—*his*—Goodacre Sunday Family Dinner.

Especially since they would all be eating at Whispering Hills. Charity's weekend guests had all checked out early for the day, and she'd promised him a pot roast, something he hadn't had in far too long. Along with the main course, she would have an array of side dishes that would rival the roast in excellence, he was certain, and there was also a rumor that one of his favorite desserts was on the menu: Charity's strawberry rhubarb pie.

But Jed made a point to head over at the last minute, deciding he didn't want to deal with any cordial banter—or teasing—until he had something more substantial in his stomach than just the bowl of quick oats he'd made for himself before church. He usually enjoyed his oats, doctoring them up with blueberries or other dried fruit, butter, and a dollop of real maple syrup or honey, but he'd been in such a hurry that morning, that he'd only had time to add butter and honey and a little cream before having to scarf it down to get out of the house on time for church.

He was ravenous when he pulled up around the back of the Whispering Hills Bed & Breakfast. The family would be gathering in the cowboy mess hall out back. They'd all fit around the enormous dining table inside the converted ranch house, but Cord paid Charity to provide a Sunday meal to his employees, so whenever she hosted the Goodacre Sunday Dinner, she included all the cowhands, too.

Thankfully, Charlotte was engaged in a conversation with old Binks, Cord's aged foreman, and Jed got roped into an animated debate about electrical fencing products with Faith and a few of the other ranch hands. By the time they all sat down for the meal, he'd somehow avoided even catching the woman's eye.

Although, truth be told, he'd found himself watching her often, wondering why she didn't look his way.

It didn't matter whose house the meal was held at, Jed always took the patriarchal seat at the head of the table. He'd offered to step down on multiple occasions, but no one seemed to think that was an option but him. As he settled into the comfortable chair, he found himself gazing over the large gathering with a swell of both pride and gratitude in his heart. He was truly a blessed man. The young men and women who worked for Cord may not be part of his immediate family circle, but all those who were gathered at their table that day knew him by name and treated him with great admiration and respect.

I miss my Abby-girl.

The thought lodged under his skin like a thorn, and for a moment, he had to hold his breath to keep the words from pouring out of him. Then he caught himself. Why couldn't he say so out loud? Shouldn't they all be missing her, too?

"I miss our Abby-girl," he said, reaching for the hands of his two eldest granddaughters, Jasmine and Yvette, who sat on either side of him.

"I do, too," Jasmine bemoaned, her shoulders slumping dramatically. Yvette nodded her agreement, always the quieter of the two.

"We all do, sweetie," Faith said, leaning over to kiss her daughter's head. "This is tourist season, though, and she's playing almost every night."

"She already missed the 4th of July," Jasmine said with a sigh. "She missed the town picnic and the fireworks, too."

"That lady who sang the National Anthem wasn't a very good singer," Yvette contributed loyally. "Abby would have done it so much better."

They'd all hoped she'd consider coming home for the event earlier in the month, but as they were learning, holidays and special events were performance artists' busiest times.

"Let's ask the good Lord to bless our food," Jed said, squeezing the girls' hands gently. "Looks like a lot of hungry people at this table today."

There were several nods and grunts of agreement, and just before he bowed his head, Jed caught Charlotte's eye at the other end of the long table. She winked at him—*winked!*—and then bowed her head, causing the loose tendrils of hair to brush against the long column of her neck.

Jed swallowed the lump that had risen in his throat and squeezed his eyes shut, forcing his mind to focus on his gratitude for God's provision instead of on wondering if Ms. Ransome's neck was as soft to the touch as it looked.

Fortunately for him, Charlotte was seated so far away from him that conversation with her was pretty much impossible. Which meant that although he couldn't seem to keep his gaze from drifting in her direction more often than it should, he was able to enjoy the good food and company without the added pressure of wondering what on earth would come out of her mouth next.

The girls did, indeed, rib him mercilessly about the terrible trim job. "It would look better if you got a haircut," Faith told him with a kind smile. "At least it would look intentional."

"I like it long!" Charlotte called out from her end of the table, and Sarah beside her nodded in agreement.

"I don't," Jasmine said, wrinkling her nose. "It makes you look like one of those old guy models in those cowboy magazines."

Old guy models? Was that good or bad? Either way, if his granddaughter didn't like it, then it pretty much didn't matter what anyone else thought. "I'll get it cut this week," he told her, sticking out his pinky finger toward her. "I promise."

Jasmine linked pinkies with him, and they shook on it. A glance at the other end of the table found Charlotte grinning at him, like she knew something he didn't.

Jed didn't like that one bit.

Although he had to admit she was really quite lovely with all that silver hair and those silver eyes and the upward curve of her smiling lips. From afar, he decided. She was quite lovely from afar.

Up close? He still hadn't made up his mind about that.

He made it home with plenty of time before Abby called to rest his eyes while he read one of the cowboy magazines Jasmine had referred to, then got up and put on some coffee. Right at four on the button, his phone rang.

"Hey, Daddy," Abby said by way of greeting. "How's it hanging?"

"Why do you ask me that?" he said admonishingly. "Do you even know what that means?"

"Yes," she responded, but she sounded a little sheepish to him.

Good. She should. The question was uncouth. *Show some respect, child,* he wanted to remind her. But he held his tongue, letting his silence speak for him.

"Sorry. How are you?" she amended.

"I'm fine. Had a nice meal at Whispering Hills today. We missed you, Abby-girl." He thought he heard her sigh, and he immediately felt remorseful. She didn't need to feel guilty about going after her dreams. "We prayed for you," he added. "And everyone says to tell you hello. Especially Jasmine and Yvette, of course. Those two are your biggest fans, I'll have you know."

Abby chuckled on the other end of the phone, but to Jed's ears, the mirth seemed a little hollow. "I know. They're awesome. They text me almost every day, usually just to say hi and that they miss me, but it almost always includes goofy selfies of them, too."

Selfies. Pictures people take of themselves. He had yet to take one of himself, and if he had it his way, he never would. Oh, he'd been subject to many pictures taken with someone's phone held at arms length—usually with his offspring or their offspring—of course, but no one was going to catch him posing in front of his own camera, that was for certain.

"How are you, child?" Jed asked, part of him wanting to hear that she was just fine, doing her thing.

"I'm fine, Daddy. Busy, as usual. In fact, I can't talk long," she told him, a hint of apology in her voice. "I've got to get ready to go soon."

"Where are you playing tonight?" he asked. He knew her schedule had gotten rearranged, but he still wanted to know where she was when she was out late at night.

There was a weighty pause down the line before Abby answered his question. "Um, tonight, the band is playing at Legend's Corner." She didn't expound, even though he waited for more information.

Finally, he asked, "What time are you on?"

"The gig starts at eight."

"Well, I'll be sure and pray for you at eight tonight, then," he said, wishing he could keep her on the phone longer. This check-in hadn't set his mind at ease much, other than that he knew she was still alive, at least. "Have fun getting ready. I love you, Abby. Go make us proud."

"I love you, too, Daddy," she said brightly. "I—I have to go. Bye!" And with that, she hung up.

Jed stared down at the phone. Something was definitely up. He should just call her and ask her right out what was wrong.

His thumb hovered over the green call button, but then he shook his head. He'd spoken to her manager just a week ago. He'd heard from Abby three times since. He needed to trust her, to let her grow up without him being a helicopter parent. He'd heard Jasmine used the term about Faith a time or two, accusing her mother of hovering, of being too protective. "I'm thirteen, mom. You have to let me grow up at some point, okay?"

Thirteen. He remembered when Abby was thirteen. She'd had that same sassy spirit, always ready to spar, quick with a comeback or a dry-humored retort, and desperate, even back then, to prove her worth at the end of a long line of sisters.

Jed didn't envy Abby's position, but he thought she'd done a fine job of holding her own in the Goodacre household.

"And now look at her," he said to himself as he shoved his phone into his back pocket. "Singing on stage in front of all her adoring fans. My baby girl is following her dreams, just like the rest of her sisters." He headed out into the late afternoon sunshine, refusing to allow himself another moment's worry over Abby.

TWENTY-FIVE

SLEEP HAD COME AGONIZINGLY slow that night as her phone call with her father played over and over in her mind. She hadn't lied, not exactly, but she'd certainly led him to believe something that was as far from the truth as it could possibly be. She wasn't fine. Sure, she was safe and fed—*well* fed, in fact—and had a roof over her head and a super comfy bed to sleep in. But that wasn't what he'd been asking. She wasn't in Nashville; she hadn't been for almost a week now. She wasn't gigging anywhere; unless you called singing in the empty front room of Serendipity's at three in the morning gigging.

She hated lying to her father. And the longer she went without telling him the truth, the harder it was going to be to come clean. She knew that, but she still couldn't bring herself to do it.

When her alarm startled her awake, Abby felt like she hadn't slept for more than a minute. She must have gotten several hours under her belt, though, because the sun had made an appearance, and it had been just after midnight the last time she'd checked the clock on her phone. Grateful that the shop would be closed to customers for the day—which meant she didn't have to get up before dawn—she dragged herself to sit on the side of her bed, hands on her knees as she tried to work up the energy to get up and get dressed.

"And of course, Mike is going to be there today," she reminded herself with a weary sigh. Not that she needed reminding. She wanted to see him again, far more than she was willing to admit out loud, and up until her conversation with her father yesterday, she'd been looking forward to the early hours of Monday morning. She'd even planned what she'd wear—her favorite jeans with the rip in one knee, the scoop neck tee in Mike's favorite color, turquoise, and her red Chuck Taylors. Because she worked in a kitchen, she couldn't wear her hair down, but she thought it looked pretty cute in a messy bun on top of her head, anyway. No jewelry except for the diamond studs her father had given her, just like her sisters before her, for graduation from high school.

But now, the thought of doing her makeup and trying to put on a happy face had her feeling rather overwhelmed. Why was she even bothering? It wasn't like she and Mike had any kind of a future together. He wouldn't leave the hollow and his family's business, and she wouldn't—*couldn't* —stay. Nothing hadn't changed. Sure, she was hiding out here in town, but it was only temporary until she figured something out.

Maybe it was better that she'd look as crappy as she felt. Maybe he'd take one look at her this morning and unload as quickly as he could, then take off, relieved that there was no longer anything tying him to her.

There was a knock on her bedroom door.

"Come in," she called.

Her bedroom door opened slowly, and Cass stuck her head around it. "Good morning," she said in an unusually hushed voice. "I should have caught you last night, but I didn't really think about it until the morning. Why don't you sleep in, Abby? Take the day off. I'm not on any set schedule today, so there's no need for you to get up and do all my prep work for me. I have nothing else going on today, so I've got everything covered, okay?"

"I take it Badger isn't going to be back in town today?" Abby asked, half-grinning, half-squinting up at her hostess.

"You take it right," Cass said with a little shimmy of her shoulders and a wink. "So heads up, darling girl. I'll bring food home tonight, but then you'll be on your own for supper the next few days, okay?"

"That's fine," Abby said brightly. The last thing she wanted to do was cramp Cass's style, especially when it came to whatever was going on between the woman and Badger. Abby wanted that relationship to work out, and not just for Cass's sake. Badger had often seemed so alone to her. Not lonely, but alone, nonetheless, and although he seemed perfectly content with it, Abby couldn't help but wonder how his world might change for the better if he were to find someone who looked at him the way her sisters looked at their husbands.

The way Cass had looked at him for the past several years, almost as far back as Abby could remember.

"But I will make sure there are plenty of eggs and bacon and meal fixings here so that you won't starve," Cass added.

Abby patted her stomach, and despite the contradictory hollow sound it made when she did, she said, "I do not think there is any fear of that. I think I've gained a dozen pounds in the last week."

"Good," Cass said without candor. "You needed a little fattening up. Now go back to bed. You look like something the cat dragged in. If I didn't know any better, I'd think you'd been out partying all night."

"That's me," Abby said, lifting a hand and spinning it around in circles above her head. "Party girl. Right here."

"Bed," Cass reiterated firmly, then pulled the door shut behind her again.

Abby lay back on the pillow and closed her eyes, tugging at the crumpled linens beneath her until she was burrowed back in bed, the blankets tucked up under her chin. She sighed gratefully, then again with a wave of disappointment.

She wouldn't see Mike today, after all.

"It's for the better this way," she muttered to herself as sleep began tugging her down, down, down into the blissful comfort of slumber.

Abby woke up again a couple of hours later to a quiet, cool house. She felt surprisingly well-rested, thanks to Cass's kindness. She decided to wear what she'd picked out after all—who cared if Mike saw her or not? She dressed to please herself; she reminded herself sternly.

In the bathroom, she brushed out her hair and pulled it up into the messy bun. Her face was still a little puffy from sleep, so after washing it and brushing her teeth, she decided to go without any makeup for the day. An hour later, after she'd eaten some scrambled eggs and toast, she poured herself a second cup of coffee and had settled into one corner of the sofa with Blossom. She'd had an idea for a song that morning while waiting for her toast to pop up, and she needed to get it out of her system before she forgot it.

A lyric popped into her head, followed immediately by a melody that grabbed the words by the tail and wrangled them into submission. Abby let the two parts of the song duke it out in her mind while she strummed softly, laying down chords in the background. Then she began to hum, the tune drifting out of her like a soft summer breeze.

This was, to her surprise and delight, the fourth song to come to her in so many days. And that was after weeks—no, months!—of a dry spell where there had been nothing left in her well. She hadn't written a new song, at least not anything worth keeping, since the last time she'd been home a few months ago. She was reticent to entertain the notion, but she couldn't help acknowledging the simple fact that her best work seemed to come out of her when she was closest to home.

Except there was no real home for her here in the hollow anymore, was there? Sure, she had a share in the family ranch, and she'd always have a place to lay her head there, regardless of what else was going on at the property. But that didn't mean she *belonged* there anymore. She wasn't naïve enough to believe that.

And besides, she'd taken her music as far as she could in this little town. If she could be satisfied with playing The Smokehouse for the rest of her life, then there would be nothing wrong with that. *If* that's what she wanted.

But that wasn't what Abby wanted, and she'd tasted what she wanted when she'd toured with Remington. She'd never felt anything so exhilarating, so satisfying, so alluring as listening to the chords of her guitar reverberating back to her through the enormous monitors on the stage in front of her and the speaker towers behind her. She'd thrilled every time her voice rang out into the crowded arenas, thousands of voices singing her lyrics along with her, the uproar of cheers and applause when her name was announced.

That's what she wanted. She was more than willing to earn it, too, if she could just figure out how.

Although, she was fairly certain it didn't mean hiding out in Plumwood Hollow and writing secret songs she couldn't tell anyone about.

TWENTY-SIX

JED FELT AS JUMPY as a long-tailed cat in a room full of rocking chairs. He could hardly believe it himself, but that woman made him ridiculously nervous. The women in his life were all unique individuals, but he knew them, and very little they did ever surprised him. Charlotte, on the other hand, was the most unpredictable creature he'd ever met, and that's what made him so nervous. He was allowing her into his personal space, into his sanctuary, and he had no idea what to expect to come of the next several days with her.

Yes, indeed, he was nervous.

Charlotte would be knocking on his door at any minute now, and although he had no doubt that the lunch he'd made—*not* bologna sandwiches—was top-notch, if he did say so himself, it was what came after they were finished eating that had him so rattled. He'd show her to the guest room, of course, and then leave her alone to unpack or whatever it was that women did to make a space their own, even for such a short time. But they didn't have plans to go visit the first of three properties until the next day, after he was done with his morning chores.

Which meant that between lunch and dinner, he might have to find ways to entertain the lady, and he honestly had no idea what that might look like.

Or maybe not. For all he knew, she already had plans for the afternoon, and being the independent woman she was, hadn't thought to tell him what they were.

Not that they were any of his business, anyway. She really wasn't his guest so much as that she was simply using his guest room to stay in while doing her business in the hollow. No, it wasn't any of his business what she did with her time when it didn't directly involve him. And for now, she'd only asked him to accompany her to see properties for sale in the area.

Even though he was expecting it, her knock made him jump, and he dropped the mug he'd been rinsing so that it clattered loudly in the deep sink.

"Hello?" she called out, and he could tell by the clarity of her voice that she'd already come through the front door without waiting to be asked in. "My goodness, Jedediah Goodacre. This place is fantastic!" Her exclamations reverberated off the walls of his little home as he hurried from the short hallway and out to the front room of the house. She stood in the middle of the main room, the combined living room/dining room/kitchen, turning in a slow circle, taking everything in as she did. "I mean, you could use a little art on your walls and maybe some better lighting in here, but other than that, it's really quite charming." She stopped spinning when her gaze landed on him.

"Can't you give a straight compliment without offsetting it with a barb, woman?" he asked. She had complimented him, he was pretty sure, but maybe she was just patronizing him? "I *have* artwork on my walls, by the way, but it takes a discerning eye to see it."

Charlotte shot him a skeptical look. "Hmmm. Is it made out of the same material the emperor's tailors use?"

Jed crossed the room and ran a palm along the smooth, polished curve of a log. "I am not duplicitous, Ms. Ransome."

"Nor am I," she interrupted. "And you can call me Charlotte, you know. That's what all my friends call me."

"Fine. Charlotte," Jed said with a quick nod. The name felt soft and feminine on his tongue and he had to resist the impulse to say it again. "The art on my walls is the walls themselves. Look at this striated grain, and the burled knots." Like an art docent, he pointed out the unique markings of the different wood he'd used in his construction. "The trim around the doors and windows is made from flame maple or curly maple; see the tiger strip pattern, how it undulates in wavy lines? Why on earth would I want to cover any of this stuff up?"

Charlotte was nodding in agreement by the time he finished his diatribe. "You are so right, Jedediah Goodacre."

"Jed," he said, more sharply than he'd intended. "You can call me Jed." Although, now that he said it out loud, he wasn't so sure he wanted that after all. He found he liked hearing his full given name on her lips.

She continued as if he hadn't spoken. "Why on earth, indeed?"

For a moment, he thought she wanted to know why on earth she should call him Jed, but then he realized she was echoing him. They stood there, staring at the wall behind the new sofa he'd picked up at the furniture warehouse in Muldoon a few days ago. The coffee-brown leather suited the rustic log house well, but it still seemed a little obtrusive to Jed, who had grown accustomed to the sparseness of the front room. He probably wouldn't have bought the thing if it hadn't been for Charlotte. He wasn't about to give up his easy chair to her, and the only other chairs he had to offer guests—besides the rocker out on the front porch—were his dining table chairs with their high straight backs. He kept two at the table, one by the front door so he could sit down to don or doff his footwear, and the fourth one set against a wall near the hallway where it had become a catchall for items he rounded up to take to his room at the end of the day. But they wouldn't do to offer a guest to sit on. At least not one who planned to stay for more than a minute or two. The couch was really quite comfortable, he had to admit, but then, he'd paid a pretty penny for it, even with the significant "summer clearout sale" discount, so it had better be.

"Are you hungry?" Jed finally asked, still not looking at her. "I made barbecue pulled pork in the slow-cooker. Started it last night."

"Wow. Really? For me?" She pointed at her sternum, a gesture that might have seemed insincere on anyone else, but Jed could tell Charlotte was genuinely surprised.

He cleared his throat. "Well, I did invite you over for lunch, didn't I? Did you really think I'd serve you emulsified meat scrap patties, did you?"

Charlotte laughed at his dry retort, then surprised him by slipping her arm through his. "Then yes, I'm famished. And excited to try your cooking," she added. "I've had Charity's, so you've got your work cut out for you." She bumped his ribs with her elbow and laughed again. "Actually,

I've sampled some of the twins' cooking, too, and now that I think of it, Charity might just be a fluke."

"I think you might be surprised, then," Jed said as he led her to the table where two place settings were already put out.

"I don't know. I'm a hard woman to surprise, Jed," she cajoled.

His abbreviated name sounded odd in her voice, giving him second thoughts about her switching to it. But he was enjoying the feel of her standing so close to him, too much to be bothered by her good-natured ribbing. Other than his daughters with their affectionate hugs, it had been a long time since anyone had held onto him the way Charlotte was now, and he found that he rather liked it.

In fact, he rather liked a lot of things about this woman, he had to admit. Yes, she was unpredictable, and that still made him nervous. But she was also forthright, bold, and spirited, and Jed found those traits in her to be refreshing. He liked nothing about a coy woman, a lady who played games and kept men guessing, and Charlotte Ransome was anything but coy.

He pulled out a chair for her at the small dinette set and waited until she was seated before he circled the table to his own place. "We'll ask the Lord's blessing, then I'll serve up the food."

Charlotte reached across the table toward him with both hands. "Works for me."

For a few moments too long, Jed stared at her long fingers with their pronounced knuckles, her short, working woman's nails, the chunky silver and turquoise rings, the collection of jangling bracelets encircling her bony wrists, the raised veins and mottled age spots. Her hands bore the evidence of a long life being lived to the fullest.

Even on her deathbed, Caroline's hands had been delicate and soft, the skin almost transparent, her only jewelry their wedding set on the ring finger.

To his amusement, he found beauty in both. In truth, Charlotte's hands looked a whole lot more like his own than Caroline's ever had.

"Take my hands, Jedediah Goodacre," Charlotte prodded gently, beckoning with her outstretched fingers. The smile on her face told him she had an inkling of what was going through his mind.

He did, and after he said the blessing, he removed the lids from the serving dishes and watched with satisfaction as she loaded her plate with generous helpings of his food.

Charlotte waited for him to dish up his own plate before digging in, then picked up her sandwich with both hands and leaned forward over her plate to take a bite. He watched her, waiting for her reaction, and couldn't hold back the smile when she closed her eyes, nodded, and made a long appreciative sound. "Oh my lands, that's good," she exclaimed when she'd swallowed. "I must know your secret; mine never turns out this tender and juicy. It practically melts in my mouth." She waved at his plate, her bracelets clinking prettily. "You must try it. I mean, I know you made it and all, but you can't just sit there watching me eat. I might scare you off."

"Scare me off?" he asked, picking up his own sandwich the way she had, in lieu of using the silverware he'd set out, just in case.

"Because I'm going to chow down on this thing," she expounded with a throaty chuckle. "And I'm not going to be responsible for how messy it gets. This is not a knife and fork kind of sandwich, my friend. It's a face-first feast."

Jed had been afraid that the conversation would be stilted, but Charlotte dove into everything, it seemed, with great gusto. They compared summers in the arid part of the country where Charlotte lived to the humidity and abundance of water in the hill country of the Midwest. They talked about raising sheep versus cattle, spaying and neutering methods, ear tags versus nose tags. Charlotte wanted to know how each of his girls was doing, how they were handling his abdication of his place in the family home, as she called it. She expressed her excitement at all the new ventures taking place at Seven Virtues Ranch—the twins' trick riding school, Prudence's botanical education center and gardens, and Justice and Brandon's new home.

"I'm so happy for those kids," she declared, a hint of ownership in her voice that made Jed smile. The woman had, indeed, played a big role in getting them hitched. "For their sake, and for mine," she continued. "If not for them, you and I wouldn't be sitting here today, and wouldn't that have been a tragic loss for both of us?" She said it so matter-of-factly that Jed found himself nodding in agreement.

But the truth of it was that she was right. He had enjoyed getting to know the woman sitting across his table from him over the last several months that she'd been coming to the hollow. The sparring, the teasing, the flirting—the *flirting*—and the conversations like this one. Even the challenges she threw his way, the ones that made him think about his life choices, about the decisions he'd made for himself and his girls, right down to Abstinence's name. Yes, even the hard stuff he found he appreciated.

Maybe she wasn't exactly unpredictable after all. Maybe she was just different and unique and it was the change taking place in himself—and his feelings toward Ms. Ransome—that was unsettling him.

Before he knew it, they were both pushing away their empty plates. "Coffee and pie?" he asked, although he wasn't sure if he had room for anything else at the moment. He didn't usually eat so much at the noon hour, especially if he had to head back outdoors in the summer heat. But today, he'd gotten as much done early so he could be available to his guest.

"Oh, goodness," Charlotte exclaimed, shaking her head slowly. "I think I'll have to pass, at least on the pie right now. I am at capacity." She cocked her head and raised one brow in question. "But maybe we could revisit the idea in a couple of hours? A mid-afternoon break?"

"Sounds like a plan," Jed agreed whole-heartedly.

"So, what are your plans for this afternoon?" Charlotte asked, standing and gathering the dishes together.

Jed almost told her to stop, that he would handle the clean-up, but when he opened his mouth to say so, she shot him a quelling look.

"And don't treat me like a guest, Jedediah Goodacre. You cooked, I'll clean up. When I cook, you can do the dishes. Deal?"

Jed chuckled and nodded. "Deal." He relaxed back into his chair and watched as she made herself comfortable in his kitchen. She seemed to know intuitively where the soap and dish towels were, where the clean dishes went after she dried them, and when she asked if he had any empty Mason jars to store the leftover pork in, he had to admit that she fit into his life just fine. He crossed to the pantry and took a clean quart jar from a top shelf and handed it to her, then propped a hip against the counter so they wouldn't have to raise their voices over the running water and clanking dishes.

"I don't have anything lined up to look at today," she told him, picking up the conversation from before. "But I'd love a tour of your place. What do you have here? Thirty acres, right?"

"Thirty-two," he said with a nod. "There was an old barn already here, but it wasn't in good enough shape to put to use right away. It's going to be a long-term project; there's a lot of great wood worth keeping and most of the support framework is salvageable. In the meantime, I've put up a new pole barn. It's got electricity and plumbing, so eventually, once the old barn is restored, I plan to convert about a third of the new one into my workshop. I'm still not sure about the rest of it," he said with a shrug. "But I'll figure something out, I'm certain."

"I've seen your beautiful woodwork," Charlotte said, shooting him an appreciative smile. "It's really artwork, you know? And not just here on your walls, either," she added with a chuckle. "The beds at the old house, the fireplace mantle, the kitchen cabinetry. Charity told me you'd done a minor remodel for her when she started her catering business, particularly redesigning the pantry. Not just functional, but beautiful, too. And yes," she said, drying their plates and handing them to Jed to put away. "I snooped around the place and saw it all. You're quite gifted, Jedediah Goodacre."

He was glad she was using his full name again. "Thank you. That means a lot coming from you. My daughter tells me you are quite the artist yourself. I saw the wall hanging you made for their wedding gift. It's remarkable. I've never seen anything like it."

"My wool art. From my pretty little sheep," she confirmed. "That's what I do." She dried her hands on a towel, then wiped up the water splatter from around the sink before hanging the towel to dry. "You know, I'd love to talk to you about making some custom frames for me. I worked with a guy in Colorado for years, but he passed away not long ago, and I've had a difficult time finding anyone who was willing to accommodate the odd sizes and shapes of my wool work without charging me an arm and a leg."

She held both hands up and wiggled her fingers. "And I can't do what I do without both my arms and at least one leg to work my loom, you know?"

Jed nodded slowly, pondering the idea. He liked challenging projects, which was why he'd made the decision to build his own log house and restore the old barn. He'd been impressed with the frame around Charlotte's artwork; Justice had asked for his help in mounting it in their new home, giving him the opportunity to really study the piece. He was certain it was something he'd enjoy creating himself.

"I especially love the garden fence you and Prudence built," Charlotte continued. "That gate? It's fantastic. Otherworldly. I'd love to create something to go with a frame like that." She closed her eyes briefly like she was picturing it, then she waved a hand as if to bat the thought away. "Anyway, think about it. Once you get your workshop up and running, of course. I've got this whole move thing on my plate right now, so it's not a pressing need. At least not yet."

"I'll definitely consider it. It seems like something I could sink my teeth into." He shot her a sheepish grin. "My daughters tell me I'm becoming a gentleman rancher, and I think that means they think I'm not much good for anything these days. They don't even need me for my money, anymore. Can you imagine?"

Charlotte laughed along with him, but he could see in her eyes something that was both compassionate and calculating at the same time. "A gentleman rancher is one thing, but not good for much?" she finally said. "Maybe it's about time you set them straight on that."

AT THE SUPPER TABLE Monday night, Abby toyed with the spaghetti on her plate. She was hungry, but she was also heavily burdened by the things weighing on her heart.

"What is it?" Cass finally prompted after several attempts at more casual conversation. "Is there something wrong with my meat sauce?"

"No, no," Abby assured her, grimacing in apology. "It's delicious. Of course." But she set down her fork, anyway, and settled back in her chair. "I know what Number Four is." She was glad when Cass didn't speak; she just studied her quietly and waited for Abby to expound. "I'm honest. I mean, at the heart of hearts, I am. I hate lying, and I hate being lied to. And because of that, I don't like what I'm doing right now. The way I'm hiding out like this."

Cass nodded slowly, but still said nothing.

Abby sighed long and slow, fighting back the tingle of tears behind her eyes. "All day, today, I wandered around your apartment, thinking about what I should be doing instead. I hate that I'm lying to my dad, to my family. I hate that you—and Mike, too—have to cover for me." She lifted her eyes to Cass's and said, "But do you know what I hate even more than that?"

"What, sweetie?" Cass was too kind; that was all there was to it. Abby had to look away from her gentle expression.

"I hate that I am not living up to everyone's expectations of me, that I'm letting them down and they don't even know it."

"Who are you letting down?" Cass asked, concern furrowing her brow.

"My dad, my sisters, this whole town." Abby pointed at Cass. "You."

"You're not letting me down," Cass countered, sitting forward and resting a forearm on the table.

"You pitched in a ton of cash on my GoFundMe, Cass."

"That wasn't just me, girlie. That came straight out of the jar on the counter with your name on it. Lots of people donated to your cause."

Abby rolled her eyes. "I don't know whether to feel better or worse. That just means there are that many more people who put their money on me."

Cass toyed with her spoon while she studied Abby for a few moments. "You know, I'd heard tell that the youngest child is the most selfish. Up until now, I'd always thought that was some silly old wives tale. I mean, I'm the youngest in my family, and I'm not selfish at all." She winked at Abby and added, "I'm the oldest child, too, by the way, and I'm also an only child. And yet, I'm still perfect in every way. Just ask me; I'll tell you."

Abby ignored Cass's attempt to lighten the mood with her self-deprecating sarcasm and tried not to take offense. "What do you mean? I'm not selfish; that's why I feel so terrible that people have invested in me and I've ruined everything."

Cass was shaking her head before Abby finished her sentence. "That's just it. Listen to yourself. Me. I. *I* have ruined everything. *I* feel terrible. People invested in *me*. It sounds like it's all about you." She tapped her chest over her heart. "Maybe you and that stone-hearted Bucky fellow have more in common than I thought."

Affronted for real now, Abby scowled, but she ignored the Bucky jab. "Well, it is kinda all about me," she insisted. "I mean, I'm the one who let everyone down. I'm the one who took their money and squandered it. I'm the one who has to—to—"

"To what? To humble yourself and tell folks you're not perfect? To come down off your stage and admit that you didn't give them their money's worth?" Cass finished for her. "That's really the root of all of this, don't you see? Our pride. It's what makes us selfish."

Abby couldn't meet Cass's gaze. She fidgeted with the crumpled napkin in her lap and chewed on her lip. What could she say? Cass was right. Everything she said was right. Abby was embarrassed. Wounded, yes, but mostly just embarrassed and ashamed.

"You know, I thought it would take a little longer before we got to this conversation," Cass said quietly from across the table. "I figured it would take you at least another week of wallowing before you finally pulled your head out of your butt and decided to do something about it."

"Nice visual," Abby muttered, her skin practically blistering at the truth of it all.

"It is what it is." The words might have been flippant, but Cass's tone wasn't. "Abby, listen. Like I said, you've got a good head on your shoulders. Open your eyes and see this for what it is; I know you can do that. Maybe you're so miserable because you already do see it. So maybe it's time to put on your big girl panties and come clean to all those folks you're sitting here feeling so bad about. You might be pleasantly surprised to find that you're the only one who thinks that way."

Abby did look up then, no longer caring if her stupid tears overflowed. She crossed her arms around her middle against the vulnerability she was experiencing. "I don't know how to go about doing that."

"Then ask for help. Or are you too proud to do that, too?"

"Don't be a jerk, Cass." Abby's arms tightened in defense. "This is a lot for me to deal with, okay?"

"Okay." The woman gestured at Abby's plate. "You going to eat that? Because I'm not about to let any of that divine pasta end up in my trash."

Abby glared across the table at her hostess. "You know, I'm having a little crisis right now."

"I know. I'm not stopping you," Cass said, shrugging one shoulder. "I just want that pile of goodness on your plate if you're not going to eat it."

Abby grabbed her plate in both hands and pulled it toward her, almost dumping it into her lap. "Yes, I want it. I want the Parmesan toast crust, too." She pointed at a small green glob on her plate. "And I want that dollop of pesto, as well, thank you very much."

Cass picked up her own piece of toast and took a big, crunchy bite, holding Abby's gaze the whole time. "I don't want your cheese toast," she said after she'd swallowed.

"Good. Because you can't have it. It's mine."

The corners of Cass's mouth started to twitch. The bridge of her nose crinkled, and the laugh lines around her eyes deepened. Then she was laughing.

"Seriously?" Abby asked, trying hard to stay ticked off, but suddenly aware of how ridiculous the whole situation was. "You know, woman, I think you might just be a little crazy."

"A little?" Cass squeaked, her eyes watering now.

"Stop it," Abby demanded, but to her consternation, she too was beginning to feel the pull of laughter in the pit of her stomach. "I'm not done wallowing. I still have another six days to go before my two weeks are up."

"Fine," Cass managed to get out. "I'll laugh. You wallow. Again, I'm not stopping you."

This time when Abby threw the napkin at her, Cass was too caught up in her merriment to deflect it, and the thing bounced off the middle of her forehead right into her glass of tea.

Which set both women off.

Several minutes later, Cass was sprawled like a drunken sailor in her seat, and Abby was bent over the table, her head in her hands, her stomach aching from the hilarity. "You're right, Cass," she said without lifting her head, her words muffled against her palms. "Help me, crazy woman. What do I do now?"

"First," Cass said, straightening slowly while clutching her stomach. "Oh, goodness, but I haven't laughed that hard in way too long. First, dear girl, eat up." She nudged the plate Abby had pushed aside in the middle of the laugh-fest. "Then, get some sleep. Tomorrow morning is going to come way too early as it is."

"But—"

Cass held up a hand, cutting her off. "I'm working on a plan. Do you trust me?"

"Not in a million years. You're mean and you can't keep secrets and you laugh at me."

"Good. Eat up. I've got a few folks to see." Cass scooted her chair back and started to rise.

"Wait. Who are you going to see?" Abby asked, suddenly cautious.

"The right people. The right *person*," she amended. "And no, I'm not going to tell anyone you're here. That's your responsibility."

"Okay." Abby drew the last syllable out, lacing it heavily with doubt.

"Trust me. I got this."

"But I don't trust you. I just said that."

Cass stood and reached across the table to tweak Abby's nose. "I love you, too."

TWENTY-EIGHT

Charlotte was duly impressed by the design and construction of his log home, his barns, both the old and the new, and the precision of his fence lines that broke up his grazing land. There was nothing that stirred a man up, Jed was discovering, more than a woman who found great pleasure in a man's handiwork.

After pie and coffee, they headed out on horseback and walked the property line that was demarcated by a wide creek that started at a natural spring at one corner of the property. The water was high for summer; they'd had a wet spring, and the shades of emerald and sage that covered the fields and filled out the trees was more evidence of such. Wild roses fell in white lace drifts at edge of the woods, like petticoats peeking out from beneath lifted skirt hems, and the breeze that buffeted Jed and Charlotte along carried scents of moss and earth, the perfume of honeysuckle, and the sweet tang of wild grasses.

Jed rode his faithful companion, Admiral, an American Paint whose dam Jed had brought with him from Texas. Admiral had been born seven months later and he and Jed had been inseparable since. The horse was technically now in his senior years, but like Jed, age was simply a state of mind, not a number, and neither man nor horse gave a hoot about the senior label. There was a whole lot of living left in both of them.

Charlotte was on Abby's horse, a middle-aged Quarter with black socks and a black smudge between his ears that looked like it had been pressed there with a giant thumb. Although his papered name was Finnegan Flyer, Abby had irreverently dubbed him Ash, and it had stuck.

Jed had a hard time keeping his eyes off the woman who rode alongside him. She sat astride the russet gelding with the ease of someone who'd spent a lifetime riding. She moved with the horse, letting the animal beneath her set the rhythm for both of them, her touch light on the reins, her body shifting to accommodate uneven surfaces and rough places. Ash, too, seemed more attentive than usual to his rider, following Charlotte's gentle lead as though they were old companions. "You ride like you're hearing music," he said aloud, wondering if she'd understand what he meant. "It's a pleasure to watch. You're a pleasure to watch."

"Why, thank you, Jedediah Goodacre." She beamed over at him and her eyes sparkled from under the brim of her hat. "It's funny you say that," she said. "I don't always hear music, exactly, but there's a sense of rhythm out here, nonetheless. Do you hear it? Or maybe, can you sense it? Not just the horse hooves, although that does set the pace somewhat."

Jed studied her as she spoke and smiled when she gave him a self-conscious look. He wasn't about to patronize her with a nod when he wasn't sure what she meant, so he waited for her to expound.

Charlotte lifted one hand and waved it in front of her, almost like she was calling an orchestra to order. "I don't know. I guess I'm just a silly old woman with an overactive imagination, but in my mind, I can hear it, like a heartbeat, like the whole earth is breathing, sighing, swaying, in and out, back and forth, always back to center." She turned to him and shrugged, her demonstrative hands stilling as she rested them on the pommel in front of her, the reins hanging loose in her fingers. "I suppose I listen for it, and because I want it to be there so badly, I hear it."

Jed nodded slowly, contemplating her ideas. "I think I know what you mean," he finally said, "although I've never thought of it as music before. But there is definitely a rhythm to this life, the seasons, the cycles, the patterns that help us make sense of things."

Charlotte dipped her head so he could no longer see her eyes under her hat brim, but the soft smile that tugged at her lips made him believe he'd said the right thing. "Making sense of things, always moving back to center, the cycles, the seasons, the patterns." She spoke quietly, perhaps reverently. "It's like every living—and maybe even non-living—thing has this inner sense alignment, this unquenchable yearning for balance. And I think," she said after a brief pause. "I think we know when we hit that sweet spot. We may not stay in that sweet spot all the time, but I think we recognize it the moment we're there. That center mark. That place where we belong."

"Home," Jed said. That, he understood. That feeling of coming home. Of belonging. "That's what I thought when I first moved to Plumwood Hollow with my family twenty years ago now. A place we could call home. A place where we could belong." He pulled to a slow stop and lifted his gaze to the horizon where the sky was just beginning to turn shades of apricot. "I found that at Seven Virtues, and again here on this small piece of land. I'm a blessed man, Ms. Ransome, to have found home not once, but twice in my years here."

"I feel it, too, you know," Charlotte said after a long stretch of silence. She had come to a standstill beside him, her eyes on the glowing colors of the sunset. "In this hollow. It feels like home to me, too."

Jed studied her. "What about your place in Colorado? You've been there awhile, haven't you?" He tugged on Admiral's lead, turning his head toward home, and Charlotte followed suit, walking along beside him as they continued the conversation.

"I love my place in Colorado," she told him. "But I *made* it home. I turned it into a place I could love, but it took a while. I put down roots there, and eventually, I found my footing, but I always felt like a transplant, like I'd come from somewhere else. Does that make sense?"

"Perfect sense." He didn't say so, not wanting to take over her story, but he'd felt the same way about Texas and the wide open spaces that were so different from the hills and hollows of western Kentucky.

"When your kids started talking about your ranch, this town, and then showed me pictures from home, I swear my heart started pounding, Jed. It was like I could taste it. Like I could hear this place calling my name."

Jed felt like he hadn't stopped nodding the whole afternoon. Everything she said resonated with him, even the woo-woo stuff about the music all around them. Now that he was listening for it, he thought he could hear it, too, or perhaps just the echo of what she was hearing. Charlotte's rich, throaty voice flowed in and around him as she spoke, and—perhaps it was just the magic hour—when he looked at her, she seemed to glow, like she was lit up from inside.

"Fireflies!" Charlotte exclaimed, her voice a little breathless as she pulled up short and gestured ahead of them. "They're everywhere!"

"We call them lightning bugs in this part of the world, you know," he teased, entertained by her childlike delight at the sight of the flickering insects drifting up out of the tall grasses. He brought Admiral around to stand beside her. "You don't have them in Colorado, then?"

"Not where I live," she told him. "Although I hear the little critters are making a comeback in different parts of the state again. But no, I've never seen them like this out there. In fact, I haven't seen them like this since I was a young woman and traveling around the country." She reached across the space between them and touched his arm. "My goodness, Jedediah. I'd forgotten how magical they are."

Jed took her hand in his and just held it while she watched the light show as the sky darkened around them. They weren't so far from the house that they couldn't find their way in the dark, and if they needed to, they'd get off the horses and walk them back. But he'd been out on Admiral around the property enough in the last year, and Jed was certain his horse would head straight for home if given his head. They could afford to linger.

They made it back under the light of a three-quarter moon, and both of them agreed that a second round of pork sandwiches was called for so they could forego cooking. "You're an easy woman to please," Jed teased her as they sat down to the table to the same meal they'd shared earlier in the day.

"Or maybe I'm just easily pleased by you, in particular, Jedediah Goodacre," Charlotte said with a husky laugh just before she headed down the short hall to the bathroom. "I'm going to wash up and I'll be right out to help warm things up!"

Jed began pulling things from the refrigerator. The smile on his face seemed to have become a permanent fixture, and he wondered if his cheeks would ache in the morning. That Ransome woman surprised him at every turn. Her delight in the lightning bugs, her appreciation for his little homestead, the music of nature she moved to. And yes, statements like that one. She surprised him because, not, as he'd first thought, because she was unpredictable, but because she was so transparent. There was no guessing needed to know what was going on in her head—she appeared not to have a disingenuous bone in her body.

Jed could count on maybe one hand how many people he knew whom he could say the same thing about.

As he scooped the meat into a saucepan to warm it up, it occurred to him that she no longer made him nervous, not after the afternoon they'd just spent together. His pulse picked up the pace, his chest tightened, and his palms tingled at the thought of being around her, but it wasn't nervousness that had his ears tuned to hear her voice and his eyes darting over his shoulder at the sound of her footsteps in another part of his home.

No, indeed.

That was anticipation.

"I'm too old for this," he muttered through the grin he couldn't wipe off his face. He took a deep breath and peered through the window over his kitchen sink out into the velvet sky, where the twinkling stars now danced with the lightning bugs. "*Am* I too old for this?" he asked quietly. Was it silly to hope for some kind of an answer, or a sign, something to let him know that Caroline would understand?

TWENTY-NINE

J ED AWOKE WITH THE sun, still wrapped in the sense of euphoria he'd gone to bed with. It was both disquieting and invigorating, and he found that he was looking forward with great anticipation to a whole day spent with Charlotte.

She'd insisted on getting up with him so she could help with the morning chores around the property, and although it was still early, even for him, he wondered if she was already up, too.

Jed propped a pillow up behind his head and reached for his reading glasses on his bedside table. Then he picked up his Bible and opened it to his place marked with the threadbare red ribbon. "Good morning, Lord," he murmured, giving his eyes time to adjust to the shadowy morning light in his room. "Thank you for giving me another day here on earth. Use me for your kingdom, Father, and let me make a difference in someone's life today." It was the same prayer he started every morning with, and today was no different.

Several minutes later, just as he was tucking the ribbon into a new place and closing the Bible, he heard sounds of life in the kitchen. He stilled and listened, wondering if he should go out there and check on her, see if there was anything she needed.

But it wasn't cupboard doors opening and closing like she was looking for things. No, Charlotte was making coffee in the fancy coffee maker Faith had given him for Christmas. It had taken Jed nearly a month to master the thing with all its push-button options, but after showing his guest how to operate it just once last night, she'd assured him that she thought she'd be able to work it just fine. Apparently, she'd been right, because in moments, the aroma of rich roasted coffee beans wafted under his door. He breathed in the fragrance and held his Bible to his chest, crossing his arms over it. "Thank you, Almighty God, for coffee," he said, his eyes lifted heavenward. "And for the woman who is out there making it for me."

He went on to ask God for his help in finding the perfect place for Charlotte and her sheep, and that it would be abundantly clear when they found it, based on things like property size, functionality, location, and, of course, price.

He said, "Amen!" and swung his legs out from under the covers and over the side of his bed, then pushed to his feet. His right hip ached a little, but it always did in the mornings, especially after a long ride on horseback. Nothing that a little walking off wouldn't help. He dressed methodically, the way he always did. He didn't trust his leg to hold him when he first got up each day, so putting on his pants and socks meant sitting down to do so. He would not be a fall victim, not if he could help it. He had no desire whatsoever to end up anywhere near a hospital with something as senseless as a broken bone from a fall he could have prevented. He wasn't an idiot—he'd seen what broken hips did to folks his age. More often than he liked to acknowledge, a fall for folks his age turned into a death sentence, and was usually a slow and painful one.

After making his bed and using the bathroom where he brushed both his teeth and his hair—it really was too long to just run his fingers through it in the mornings the way he often did—he headed out into the short hallway.

He passed by the open door of the guest room and paused, just for a moment, at the sight of her unmade bed, her suitcase open and spilling its contents out onto the storage bench at the foot of the bed. Was it a sign? Caroline had always said that the best thing one could do to start a day with their best foot forward was to make their bed. If nothing else went right the rest of the day, then at least one would know that they had a neatly made bed waiting for them at the end of it all. All of his daughters but Abby still followed the same practice, but he figured she'd eventually just hire someone else to do it for her.

"Don't look in there!" Charlotte called out, leaning back from where she stood at the counter so she could peer down the hall at him. "I went on a mad search this morning for something and haven't tidied up after myself."

Jed's face warmed in embarrassment over being caught sneaking a peek, but he lifted both hands in surrender. "Eyes closed," he said, ducking his head and heading out to the kitchen to join her.

"I hope I didn't wake you," she said as she poured a cup of coffee and handed it to him. "You like it black, right?"

He nodded and thanked her, pleased that she'd remembered. One sip told him the woman knew how to brew it right. "Ahh," he said when he lowered the cup. "Delicious."

Charlotte wore a pair of light gray, wide-legged pajama pants that were a little long, even on her. Her feet were bare, and he noticed her toenails were painted a deep orange; the color reminded him of the sunset they'd shared last night. She also had on some kind of short robe or wrap-around shirt, and although she was covered from collarbones to toes, he knew they were still her bedclothes, and he suddenly felt a bit like an intruder, even in his own home.

Something in his expression must have given away his thoughts, and Charlotte said, "I tried to be quiet, but I awoke early this morning and couldn't fall back to sleep. So I thought I'd make coffee for us, then crawl back in bed with my first cup of the morning and spend a few minutes with God." She gestured down at her getup. "I didn't plan on greeting you in my jammies. That might be making myself a little too comfortable around here, especially since I had to practically force your hand to let me stay here."

Jed frowned, not liking the way that sounded. "Charlotte, you are welcome in my home. I want you to feel comfortable here."

She nodded quickly. "I know, I know. But I want *you* to feel comfortable here, too, Jedediah Goodacre, and this isn't the way to do it." She grimaced in frustration. "And now that I've made such a big deal about it, neither of us is comfortable, and now it's going to be awkward for the next hour or two until we find our rhythm again." She set down her coffee cup. "I'm going to go get dressed. I'll be right back, okay?"

"Hold up, Ms. Ransome," he said, lifting a hand to stop her. "I thought you were going to spend some time with the Almighty. I wouldn't want you to miss out on that."

Charlotte rolled her eyes and sighed deeply. "Yeah. That. Which is why all my stuff is tossed around the room." She met his look with a sheepish expression. "I can't seem to find my Bible. I never leave the house without it, but it seems that this time, I've done just that. I have a Bible app on my phone, so I suppose I could use that, but it's not the same as holding one open in your lap, is it? The crinkly pages, the scribbled notes in the margins, the stuff tucked between the pages that's forever falling out."

Once again, Jed was nodding. "Would you like to borrow mine?" he asked before he could talk himself out of it. He wasn't a big notes-in-the-margins kind of guy, nor did he stuff things in the pages of his leather-bound Holy Book, but he agreed whole-heartedly with her that there was nothing better than holding that weighty tome in his hands. "You're more than welcome to use it; it's on my bedside table." He picked up her coffee cup and handed it to her. "Go. I'll get breakfast going. You like scrambled eggs and bacon? Or would you prefer pancakes and sausage?"

Charlotte took the mug and held it between both hands, the rings on her fingers—apparently, she slept in the things—clinked against the ceramic. "You aren't supposed to cook for me, remember?" she said, and Jed thought he heard a slight tremor in her voice. Was she nervous now? Or excited in the same way that he was? She watched him with wide eyes, and Jed felt compelled to reassure her.

"I'm cooking for myself. I'm just making enough to share with you, too. Go." He shooed her away with one hand.

"Thank you," Charlotte said, the tremor still there. "I mean it, Jedediah. For letting me stay here, for sharing this wonderful place—your home, your land, your food, your Bible—with me." She held up the coffee cup. "For this divine elixir."

"It's my pleasure," he said, opening the fridge and pulling out a carton of eggs. He paused in his task and turned to face her. "I mean it, too, Ms. Ransome."

"And your Bible?" she began again after a short pause. "Are you sure? That's not too personal?"

"Go," he repeated firmly. "Now. Or your eggs will be cold before you get back."

Charlotte giggled—she actually giggled, to his amusement—and hurried from the room, the aroma of her coffee mingling with the scent of something sweet and clean, like freshly mowed hay and wildflowers. It reminded him of something Prudence might whip up under Pixie Cut Botanicals hair and body care line of products.

"You know, I could get used to that smell greeting me every morning, Lord," he said, as he began to form patties out of the fresh sausage he'd bought from Levi's butcher shop earlier in the week. "Especially if it comes with a woman who starts her day out conversing with you," he added.

Jed could put up with an unmade bed and a little mess in exchange for a god-fearing woman. The thought of his Bible in her hands made his heart swell. Yes, indeed. He could get used to mornings like this more often.

They didn't finish the chores any faster than if he'd done them alone. Charlotte was more of a distraction than anything else, regaling him with stories about working with sheep, many of them anecdotes that made him glad he was a cattleman and not a shepherd. They sounded like a lot of work, but he could hear the affection for them in the tone of Charlotte's voice.

"They really are just fluffy little lumps of stupid," she said at one point. "But they all know me and come running to me whenever they see me, and it just melts my heart. But I need them for their wool for my livelihood, and they need me to keep them alive. If I do a lackluster job caring for them, they give me lackluster wool for my work. So you see? We have a lovely little symbiotic relationship, one that has worked for us for some time."

"Do you ever get lonely out there by yourself? Justice tells me your nearest neighbor is about a mile away."

"Yes," was all she said.

"Yes, your neighbor is a mile away? Or yes, you get lonely?" Jed prodded.

"Yes to both," Charlotte said frankly. "The one isn't so bad—the old coot is about the least neighborly fellow you'll ever find. But the loneliness?" She shrugged. "Some days, I think, if it weren't for the sheep...." She let the sentence hang for just a second, then reached up to scratch Admiral's neck.

They were finishing up in the barn feeding the horses—Jed kept Abby's horse to keep Admiral company—and mucking out the stalls. Jed stopped raking through the straw in Ash's stall and straightened to study Charlotte. Her words didn't sit well with him. He didn't like imagining her on those days, the ones she was referring to.

She let out a choppy laugh. "Whew!" she said. "That got deep, didn't it? But you should know that's why I'm doing something about it. That's why I'm moving. I'm not about to just let myself sink into depression or wander out into the prairie and get lost. I'm lonely, and that can be fixed. So I am to fix it by spending less time alone." Her voice grew stronger as she spoke, and Jed released the breath he didn't realize he'd been holding.

"I'm glad to hear that, Charlotte." He laid the pitch fork tine-down into a wheelbarrow and headed down to the door at the far end of the barn and out to the compost heap where he tossed the straw and manure he'd just picked up from the stalls. She walked alongside him. "Lets find you the perfect place so you can make that happen sooner than later, okay?"

"Sounds good to me," she agreed, and Jed was relieved to hear the lightness back in her voice again. *Almighty God, provide us—Charlotte—with the perfect property on which to raise her sheep, a place that says 'Home' to her.*

THIRTY

Thursday morning, Abby was prepared for Mike's appearance, but she still jumped when his knock sounded on the back door. She'd propped the swinging doors between the front and back of the shop open so she could hear him, but he came while she was in the middle of switching out the first batch of pastries from the ovens for bread loaves.

"Coming!" she hollered, hoping he could hear her through the heavy back door. She managed to get the last two loaves into the oven without dropping one or burning herself, shook off the purple polka-dot oven mitts she'd claimed as her favorite, and not just because Mike had worn them that first day he'd shown up, and hurried to the door to let him in.

"Morning," he said over his shoulder as he backed in with his loaded cart. Although his smile was wide and warm, Abby still noticed his puffy, sleep eyes and his tousled bed head.

"Morning, Mike," she replied, not trying to hide her smile.

"What?" he asked, standing the dolly upright just inside the door. He reached up and patted the back of his head, then shrugged one big shoulder. "And this is brushed, too. You should have seen it an hour ago when I first crawled out of bed."

Abby felt her cheeks grow warm at the thought of Mike crawling out of bed. She turned away quickly. There was something inexplicably intimate about being alone with someone in the pre-dawn hours. Especially someone who had once held her and kissed her the way Mike had.

"Want to grab the clipboard?" he asked, and she wondered if he sensed her disquiet. "There's this and another load out in the truck, but we can make quick work of this together."

"Why so much?" Abby asked, pulling the clipboard from its hook and following him into the pantry.

"The weekend is coming, and she starts stocking up early. My Saturday deliveries are about this size, remember? She's only open from just before noon until five on Sundays, but she still moves so much stuff over the weekends." He turned and tossed her a look over his shoulder. "How long did you say you were going to be here?"

"I didn't," Abby said, the change in subject catching her by surprise. "I'm not exactly sure." All week she'd been waiting impatiently for Cass to give her even a hint at what she had up her sleeve, but Cass had spent every evening with Badger, who'd gotten back to town Tuesday afternoon. Abby had seen very little of her hostess since then. She steered the conversation back away from her again. "So why do you bring stuff on Mondays? Isn't Serendipity's closed for the day? Why not Tuesday, Thursday, and Saturday? Seems like it would make more sense."

Mike grinned up at her as he bent to open up a box packed tight with cartons of heavy cream. The look in his eyes told her he'd picked up on her redirection. "That's right. You slept in on Monday," he teased.

"Cass made me," she said, a little more defensively than she'd intended. "I got up to come in with her, but she insisted she didn't need my help."

"I'm just giving you a hard time, Abs," Mike said, straightening up to line several cartons of oat milk on a high shelf. "Cass usually starts Mondays with an inventory check, then I bring her what she needs to get the week started. She spends the majority of her afternoon deep cleaning and catching up on her bookkeeping. Stuff like that."

"You sure know a lot about what goes on here," Abby commented.

"I used to work for her, don't you remember? I did what you're doing now, and I also helped her with her bookkeeping on Mondays."

"I'd forgotten," Abby admitted. She'd thought he was crazy to get up so early before school, especially during football season, but Mike had insisted he liked the work.

"I don't officially work for her," Abby started to say. "I mean, I'm working for her, but she's not paying me. Well, she's paying me in room and board." Ugh. She was nervous-rambling.

"She didn't pay me, either," Mike stated casually.

"She—she didn't? You worked for free?" Abby was startled by that revelation.

He handed her an empty box. "Collapse that, will you, and start a stack of them against the wall by the door. I'll take them out when I go. And no, I didn't work for free."

"But—"

"My dad paid me." He hefted an enormous bag of bread flour up off the floor and set it gently into an empty food-grade bin lined up next to several others with a variety of labels. Abby stared in appreciation at the bulging muscles in his arms and back as he did, then snapped her bottom jaw shut before he turned around... or before she started drooling. What was wrong with her?

"Why?" The question came out sounding a little breathless. "I mean, why did he pay you and not Cass?"

Mike leaned against one of the shelves and shoved his hands in the front pockets of his jeans. He looked like an oversize kid, and she had to bite back a smile. He eyed her questioningly. "You don't remember any of this, do you?"

"I—I guess not." She was doing a lot of stammering this morning. "I mean, did you tell me? Am I just forgetting?"

Mike shrugged. "Maybe it wasn't public knowledge. I guess I just assumed everyone knew what was going on."

"Well, tell me," Abby insisted, stepping a little closer, the clipboard pressed to her chest. "Maybe I'll remember if you give me a hint."

"Cass was struggling back then, big time. You remember her boyfriend? That guy who beat the crap out of her?"

Abby nodded. Of course, she remembered. The night he'd been arrested had left an impact on the whole town. There wasn't much violence in a place like Plumwood Hollow, and word of Cass's assault had spread like wildfire. There'd been a fair share of folks who weren't embarrassed to say they thought she'd gotten what she deserved, living in sin with him the way she was, but most of the community had been rightly appalled and had shown their love and support to one of their own with well-wishes, cards and flowers, and a renewed commitment to keep the hollow safe. A contingent of folks had gone to her home while Cass was in the hospital, thoroughly clean and straighten up the place so that she wouldn't have to come home to the horrific crime scene left in the monster's wake. Others had helped man Serendipity's while she recovered, including the Gentrys, and although the baking wasn't quite on par with Cass's normal fare, she hadn't gone without customers the whole time.

But Abby wasn't sure what that awful time had to do with anything. "That was like five or six years ago. You weren't working for her then."

"Not back then, no. But not only did he beat her up, Abs, he drained her savings account, too, what little she had left from her mom's life insurance after she bought this place. So on top of getting stuck with a medical bill she couldn't pay, the money he took was to keep this place in the red while she was still getting the business profitable."

"Whoa," Abby said, still not quite sure what the terrible story had to do with Mike and his dad. But she had an inkling she'd soon find out.

"So she swallowed her pride and asked for help. She borrowed enough money from her customers to cover her expenses over the rest of the year, hoping she could earn enough over the holidays to pay everyone back what she owed them. She had a great plan, one that everyone foresaw as profitable."

"Don't tell me," Abby murmured, lowering her gaze to the floor, her heart sinking, too. "The plan fell through."

Mike waited for her to meet his eyes again. "Not Cass's plan. Her's was practically fool-proof. But that was the year that the Blodgetts Savings and Loan collapsed. The CEO had been skimming from their customers for years and finally got caught."

Abby's eyes widened, and she groaned softly. "I remember that," she said, nodding slowly. "It left a lot of people in dire straits."

"Yeah. And Cass was one of them. Not her fault she trusted the wrong bank, but it became her problem, anyway."

"Oh, Mike. This is a terrible story. Why do you know all these details?"

Mike shrugged. "I've always been interested in finances, you know that. I've been doing my parents' books for years—I'm much better equipped to do it than Dad is, I can tell you that much. I mean, he's great at handling the customers, but the books, not so much."

"He must be very proud of you," Abby said, trying to ignore the twinge of jealousy in her stomach.

"He's definitely grateful for what I bring to the table." Mike tapped his temple. "And not just for my math skills, either, you know."

Abby heard the suggestive tone and she should have known better than to ask. But hindsight, as they say... "Oh yeah? What else do you bring to the table?"

Both of Mike's dimples showed up and in his eyes was that same ember she'd seen sparking to life last week. He lifted both arms into bicep curls and flexed. "I come packing," he said, and there went that one eyebrow again. "Wanna touch my guns?"

Abby suddenly found it difficult to breathe, and the spacious storage pantry shrank about ten sizes. He had definitely been working out over the last couple of years. Or lifting a lot of heavy boxes. And she *definitely* wanted to touch his guns, truth be told. She managed a shaky smile. "That's all right," she said, drawing on every ounce of self-control she had left in her arsenal. She tapped her own temple a little too aggressively and tried not to wince. "I remember your guns just fine."

"Ah, come on," he cajoled, pushing away from the wall where he'd been leaning and taking a step toward her, one arm still flexed. "For old time's sake?" He made the muscle jump up and down like there was some creature dancing just under his skin.

"Ew, no!" She scrunched up her nose in mock disgust and tried not to laugh at his antics. When he started doing the whole alternating pectoral flex that had once so impressed her back in high school, she squeezed her eyes shut in desperation. "Stop it, Mike!" she snorted, reaching one hand behind her to feel for the pantry door. She didn't remember closing it behind her. "You're such a freak," she added, going for friendly jabbing to diffuse the rising tension in the air. But her voice came out husky, laden with a raw emotion that sounded a little too much like desire.

Something shifted in the air around her, and Abby slowly opened her eyes... her gaze landing smack dab in the middle of Mike's chest. He'd stopped a foot in front of her, and his body was no longer doing its circus act.

He held one hand out to her in an invitation. Not to touch his guns, not to feel his chest muscles jumping under her palms, but an invitation to remember what had once been between them. She could practically see the memories spilling over the edges of his slightly cupped palm.

Abby lifted her eyes slowly, up the strong column of his neck, along the smooth curve of his jaw—Mike had never been able to grow much facial hair—to his mouth. His bottom lip, fuller than his perfectly defined upper lip, the corners tipped up just the tiniest bit, even when he wasn't smiling. Like he always kept one cocked and ready to fire at any moment.

She stood there awash in the memory of that smiling mouth, the warmth of it pressed to hers, both soft and firm at the same time, gentle and assertive, giving and taking. She had to look away; she had to resist the pull of him, of her ache for him. They'd been in this place before, and it hadn't ended well.

If she placed her hand in his, he would pull her close, wrap those amazing arms around her... and this time, he might never let her go.

She couldn't do that to him again.

She couldn't do that to herself again.

Abby's hand landed on the door handle behind her, the clipboard in her other hand still clutched to her chest, like it was the last thin barrier keeping them apart. Summoning every ounce of willpower she had in her, she took a deep breath and pushed the door open, then backed out of the pantry, holding the door wide for him to follow.

Mike slowly lowered his hand, and although she could still feel his heated gaze on her, she couldn't meet his eyes. From her peripheral view, she saw him reach back for his dolly. Then he, too, moved out of the storage pantry past her toward the alley door. "I'll be back in a minute with the next load," he said, his voice as wrecked as hers.

They made quick work of stocking the rest of the supplies, their limited conversation awkward and stilted, sticking to the task at hand as though none of the intimacy of the last few moments had passed between them.

It wasn't until after Abby had locked the alley door behind him that she realized Mike hadn't finished telling her Cass's tragic tale.

She leaned her forehead against the cool surface of the heavy steel door and closed her eyes in misery. She was exactly what her friend had said she was. She pressed the heel of one hand to her chest. "My selfish stone heart is engraved with a big, fat, capital M-E."

THIRTY-ONE

THEY'D LOOKED AT THREE places over the last two days, and although she hadn't fallen madly in love with any one of them, she wanted to go back to the Gallups' homestead again. The acreage was a little more than what Charlotte was looking for, but the ranch house, although not large, was well-built and had been properly maintained over the years, with large, north-facing windows in the living room.

"I could set up my looms and frames in there," Charlotte told Jed. "It's got great natural lighting."

But she sounded more resigned than hopeful to Jed, and although he didn't say so, he worried that she might be settling. The small nine-acre place she'd moved up her trip for already had an offer pending. They'd driven by the place, and what they could see of the property from the road had been promising, but without seeing inside the home and outbuildings, there was no way to really know if it would work or not. Jed had promised that he'd keep an eye on the place, and if it went back on the market, he'd take a look at it for her. He had a good idea what she was looking for, having spent so much time with her searching for the right one.

"I think maybe I just need to step away from all of this," Charlotte said, Thursday afternoon as the two of them sat across from each other at his table with their coffee, sharing a plate of Charlotte's cinnamon scones that were still warm from the oven. "Get a more objective perspective." She snorted at his hurt expression. "Not a break from you, my friend. You have been the best part about this trip, in fact."

"Well, thank you," he said, not quite sure how else to respond to such a warm compliment, especially since it made him feel downright giddy as a schoolgirl to hear her say it. "It has been a pleasure having you in my home these last few days."

"Don't sound so surprised," she teased. "I told you I was a good guest, didn't I?"

"You're a lovely woman, Charlotte Ransome." He spoke softly, gently, because he meant the words.

"Why, Jedediah Goodacre." Charlotte pressed a hand to her chest and blinked owlishly at him. "I think that is the nicest thing you have ever said to me."

It was easy to banter with this woman. It was easy to get up each morning and step into the dance they performed around the kitchen as they started their days together.

"It helps that you can cook like this." He held up the scone he was eating. Was it his second? Or third?

"All part of my ploy to make you let me stay with you again."

"Ha! I knew you had ulterior motives."

"Seriously, though," she said, pointing a long finger at him. "This place, Jedediah. It's so peaceful and serene here, and yet you're only a hop, skip and a jump away from your family across the road." Justice and Brandon had been over for supper on Tuesday night so they could spend some time with Charlotte, and the four of them had enjoyed a long visit out on the front porch, Jed and Charlotte in the matching rocking chairs, Justice and Brandon nestled together on the front porch steps. A few other family members had been by to say 'hello', and Charlotte had popped over to Seven Virtues to meet Prudence's husband and to tour the education center, and had been ridiculously impressed by it all. "You are a blessed man, my friend."

"And I am a grateful man, Ms. Ransome."

"I know," she said. "I can see how much you cherish what the good Lord has given you."

They sat in comfortable silence for a few moments, then Charlotte picked up from her earlier comment. "Anyway, I think I'm going to take tomorrow off. Go shopping downtown or maybe see if Prudence can use an extra pair of hands in her gardens. And no," she said, waving a hand at him when he opened his mouth to speak. "You don't need to take any more time away from your life to look after me. I'm perfectly capable of entertaining myself for a few hours. Besides, tomorrow night is Ladies Night at The Smokehouse, and Sarah has invited me to join her and her sister and maybe a few other friends. Sounds like fun, don't you think?"

Jed shook his head emphatically. "No, it does not sound fun at all. In fact, you couldn't pay me to step foot in that joint on Ladies Night. I've heard the stories," he added dramatically.

Charlotte's eyes twinkled as she said, "You know, Mr. Goodacre, I think you might be surprised at how much fun you'd have in a roomful of ladies. Are you sure you don't want to come with us?"

"I'll be sitting right out there in one of those rockers for the evening, thank you very much," he said, pointing toward his front porch. "And no, I will not wait up for you."

That was an outright lie. He would most certainly wait up for her, and they both knew it. He knew she knew it by the look in her eyes.

"And what are you going to do with all your free time tomorrow now that you don't have to be my tour guide?" she asked him.

Jed reached up to cup the back of his neck, suddenly self-conscious about his hair. "I promised my granddaughters I'd get my mop trimmed this week," he said. "I think I'll head into the barber shop in the morning."

Charlotte cocked her head to one side as if to try to see around to the back of his head. "That's right. You did, didn't you? But I do like it this length," she told him, repeating the sentiment from last Sunday. "Especially the way the ends curl just a little behind your ears."

"I do not have curls," Jed declared, frowning fiercely at her.

Charlotte held up her thumb and forefinger about half a centimeter apart. "Just little ones," she teased. "But a promise to your granddaughters is a promise to your granddaughters, and I will not stand in the way of that."

"Good call," he said with a chuckle. "Those two are a formidable force to go up against." He finished his coffee and made to rise. "Well, then, I suppose I'd better get back to work. Any thoughts on supper?"

Charlotte made a shooing gesture. "I've got tonight's meal covered. I'm making my special homemade lasagna, so I have to run to the store for ingredients. I might even stop by that delicious pastry shop, the one with the amazing cinnamon rolls, and pick up some dessert. Serendipity's, I think it's called?"

"Can't go wrong with Serendipity's. Everything Cass makes is worth every penny."

"Perfect. You go do your thing this afternoon, and I'll do mine, and we'll meet back here in about two hours. Deal?"

"Deal."

"Oh, and I'll call the Gallups in a bit, too," Charlotte said, toying with the handle of her coffee cup. She still had a half-eaten scone on her plate. "Maybe I can go back over there on Saturday."

"I can go with you, if you'd like," Jed offered.

"I'd like," she said with a warm smile.

Jed felt his insides melt at her words.

THIRTY-TWO

Jed removed his hat and laid it on the passenger seat beside him, then straightened the collar of his clean shirt in the rearview mirror. It was just a haircut, sure, but he wasn't about to show up with greasy hair and a dirty neck. It was something his wife had drilled into his head right from the very beginning of their marriage. Back when she'd been the one to cut his hair for him. "I'm not going to touch that head of yours if you can't respect me enough to come to me washed up and ready."

He hadn't bothered calling Ed to schedule an appointment, even though he knew Faith always did back when she was keeping tabs on his hair. But Jed figured if he had to wait for a few minutes, he was fine with that. Charlotte would be out and about all day and had no need of him, so other than his chores, that left his day pretty flexible.

Besides, the barbershop was a good spot to catch up on the local news with the guys, where facts didn't get muddied by emotions.

Unless Pete Zeller was there, of course. Justice had once rightly called the old coot a gossip-mongering drama queen. Pete drove an early morning route for the Plumwood Courier and Press, so he actually did, in effect, get a handle on the local news before anyone else. The man, however, liked to embellish the facts just enough to make the legitimate paper sound like a gossip rag, which in turn kept the readership high. Even though folks knew to take everything Pete said with a grain of salt, his truth-stretching did make people curious to know what the real stories were. Especially now that his son, Pete Jr., had moved away and was no longer around to contradict everything his father said. The father-son duo had been like a local comedy act, and Jed found that he kind of missed the non-stop bickerfest—one of Abby's coined terms, if he recalled correctly—between the two.

For a Friday morning, Ed's Barber Shop was hopping. There were several cars parked out front, most of which Jed immediately recognized, and through the large plate-glass window with the red, white, and blue old school barber shop pole logo on it, he could see that all the chairs were filled.

Jed placed his hat back on his head and climbed out of his truck, not bothering to lock it behind him. No one locked their vehicle doors in this town. At least not in the daylight. In spite of the fact that Officer Gunther regularly advised folks to do so. "Times, they are a-changing, my friends," he'd say. "And so should your habits." Gunther was a good man, if a bit overzealous in his role as Chief of Police, but there were some things that just stuck in a man's craw. Not trusting his fellow man—his friends and neighbors whom he'd grown up with—was one of them. Jed wasn't sure he wanted to live in a world where folks like Ed's customers had to start locking their cars just to come inside for a haircut and a shave.

Inside the shop, Jed was greeted with nods, chin thrusts, and a few guttural noises that passed for greetings. "It'll be about fifteen minutes," Ed said over his shoulder at Jed, his hands not stopping as he ran a humming trimmer around the hairline of a middle-aged man Jed didn't recognize. He must be the owner of the five-year-old white GMC parked at the far end of the lot, Jed decided, grudgingly acknowledging that there were, indeed, unfamiliar faces in his hometown. But a man who frequented the neighborhood barbershop wasn't likely to be the wrong sort, not in Jed's estimation.

Jed didn't bother responding to Ed; instead, he took a seat in one of the four ancient armchairs by the window. The leather seats were cracked and peeling at the edges, and the wooden arm rests were discolored with age, but in spite of the hundreds, perhaps thousands, of men's backsides that had sat in them, the old chairs were still surprisingly comfortable.

Phineas Thacker sat opposite Jed. He looked up from his newspaper and said, "Ever since those girls of yours got all married up, things haven't been the same around Schooners. Oh, they work a shift now and then, but it's not like the old days, that's for sure."

Phineas had a special place in his heart for diner lingo, and Courage and Justice had made it a point to learn as many of the old-school catchphrases as they could while working at Schooners. Folks loved trying to stump them and the cooks, but the girls—especially Courage—had a real knack for remembering all the hilarious terms.

Jed smiled and nodded in agreement at Phineas's statement. Then the man went back to his paper.

Things weren't like the old days these days. And not just because men couldn't leave their doors unlocked and all of his daughters were 'getting all married up' as Phineas put it. Not all of it was bad, he had to admit. He liked the men his girls had married. Granted, he hadn't always liked them—especially that Cordell Overman. The kid had gotten Faith pregnant, then gone off in pursuit of his own life. Sure, he'd come shuffling back several months later and asked if Jed would give him his blessing to ask Faith to marry him, but back then, Jed had believed it was too little too late. He'd sent the boy running scared, and had later had to eat his words when Cord showed up again a decade later, determined to win back Faith's trust. And Jed's. And he had done just that.

Young Frank Flanner, the boy from next door? Well, who could have anything but the greatest respect for a man who was willing to give his life for his country, his countrymen, and his fellow soldiers? Frank had nearly done just that—he'd barely survived a terrible ambush, returning home with only one leg and some horrific scars, physically, mentally, and emotionally. And although he was still a work in progress, the man also ended up with Charity, who had lost her first husband to a similar fate. His battle-weary daughter had initially railed against the notion of loving another soldier, but she'd fallen just as hard for Frank as he had for her.

Then there was Prudence's husband, Collin Stewart. Jed knew the two of them still got censorious looks from some folks in town, but fortunately, no one ever deigned to do so in front of Jed. He'd have a thing or two to say about that. Mr. Stewart had been Prudence's high school literature teacher her senior year, and the two of them had started falling for each other even then. Being honorable, however, the young man had taken a teaching job elsewhere, returning years later when he believed Prudence's reputation would be above reproach by his interest in her. Unbeknownst to him, he'd broken her heart when he first left—Prudence had seen it as an outright rejection of the heart that she'd offered him—and it had taken the poor fellow a fair amount of effort to win back her trust. Jed could understand why Collin had done what he'd done, why he'd left town for all those years, even if there might have been a better way to do things. But wasn't hindsight always twenty-twenty? Now, though, the two of them were as happy and hopelessly in love as any two dreamers could ever be.

Jed knew Levi, the local butcher, Hope's husband, long before his second eldest daughter had fallen for him. Jed thanked the good Lord every day that his gentle Hope, who had been abandoned by her first husband, a snake of a man, and had found a deep, abiding, lifetime love in the arms of a man like Levi Valiente.

The twins—he always thought of them together, even though they were as different as night and day—had both married men Jed knew and respected, too. Joe Lynxwilder, a local organic produce farmer, had quietly courted Courage, in spite of their age difference, and every time Jed saw the couple with their heads bent together over a plant, a garden plan, or a new seed catalog, his heart swelled in his chest. And Justice. Stubborn, brilliant, black-and-white Justice. He still didn't know all the details of what had happened between her and Brandon a couple years ago, but when they returned from their last rodeo circuit with their relationship patched up and a ring on her finger, Jed had known all was right in the world again.

Then there was Abby. From the time his youngest daughter was just a wee thing, it had been obvious that the girl had wings. He'd watched her flit from one guy to another during her teenage years, never landing on any one person for long enough to make things official. It was almost like she knew instinctively not to form any concrete attachments to the hollow, to keep herself unattached so that when the right wind came along, she'd be free to spread her wings and soar right on out of town on it.

Except for the Nesbit boy. There had definitely been something serious there, at least for a time during their senior year of high school. Jed had seen the two of them together, the young buck standing a little too close for a father's comfort, Abby's fingers brushing possessively along the slope of his shoulder, their eyes finding each other from across a room, or across a football field. But they'd graduated high school and gone their separate ways, Mike off to business school in preparation of taking over the family business one day, and Abby to Nashville under the tutelage of Remington Sounder.

His youngest had a good head on her shoulders, Jed often found himself thinking, and although he wanted to see her as happy and settled as the rest of her sisters were, maybe her happiness would come from something—or someone—else altogether. Maybe for Abby, being settled was not what would make her happy.

"The heart needs to know that it belongs somewhere to someone, Jed," his sweet Caroline used to say. Then she'd rest her palm on his chest directly over his heart and say, "My heart belongs right here with you."

How Jed missed his beloved wife. She'd been gone more than twenty years, and yet there were times when it seemed like she'd left just yesterday.

Today, though, Jed had gotten up with a new pep in his step. He'd had trouble falling asleep the night before, concern for Charlotte's search for a new home keeping his mind active as he contemplated all the places they'd visited together. He'd finally drifted off while discussing the situation with the good Lord, and although he hadn't figured out a good solution, he had awakened feeling much more at peace about God's faithfulness. When Jed had stepped out of his room to face the new day, he'd ended up face-to-face with Charlotte instead, coming out of her room across the hall from him.

"Good morning, Jedediah Goodacre," she'd said, her voice husky from sleep. The sound of it sent a rush of sensation down his spine, and for a moment, he wasn't sure if his voice would work at all.

"Good morning, to you, Ms. Ransome," he'd finally returned with a nod. "Are you hungry?"

Charlotte had stepped forward, linked her arm through his, and planted a quick, friendly kiss on his cheek, still rough with morning stubble. "I'm always hungry, my friend. Let's go start this day together right, shall we?"

Charlotte had headed out shortly after breakfast, but her words kept repeating themselves all morning as he went about his chores, then showered and readied himself for a trip into town. The last few days spent with her had been full to the brim, not with activities and events that wore him out, but with long-forgotten emotions, and changing perspectives, and like-mindedness... with age-appropriate female companionship.

It was something he hadn't even known he was missing in his life. His daughters were wonderful company, and they'd filled almost all the hollow places for the last two decades. But they could never offer him the kind of companionship Ms. Ransome did.

Had he moved to his own place to finally get some solitude? Or had he subconsciously moved to his own place so he could find someone else to share it with, now that his girls no longer needed him?

Indeed, the last few days with Charlotte had him rethinking a lot of things.

"Howdy, folks!" Pete Zellar pushed through the front door of the barbershop, disrupting Jed's train of thought with his boisterous greeting. "It's a fine day for a haircut, isn't it?"

Jed put a finger to the front of his hat, but didn't say anything. Zellar didn't notice; he was rooting through the newspapers and car magazines stuffed haphazardly into the racks on the wall.

A few moments later, he lowered himself into the seat next to Jed, and in a voice loud enough to stop almost all the other conversations in the room, said, "I drove by Serendipity's early this morning on my way home from work. And guess what I saw." He paused to flip open a magazine and turn a few pages before glancing around the room to assess his audience. Finally, he said, "I saw a blue pickup truck parked down the alley. One that looked an awful lot like your youngest girl's, Jed."

Jed straightened in his seat. Disinclined to believe every word out of the man's mouth or not, if anyone would know Abby's truck, it would be Pete Zellar. Abby had bought it from Pete's son a couple months before Pete Jr. left town.

THIRTY-THREE

ABBY'S HEART POUNDED WITH anxiety as she waited for Mike's knock early Saturday morning. She propped open the swinging doors between the front of the shop and the kitchen just to make sure she didn't miss him, and hurried through the task of setting up the front of the shop so that she could get to the door quickly when he finally showed.

By four-thirty, the sun was just starting to lift the veil of night, and Mike still hadn't made an appearance. Abby only had another hour of work to do—if she took her sweet time—before she was finished for the morning. He had said he brought supplies on Saturday mornings, too, hadn't he?

Forty-five minutes later, the kitchen was ship-shape, the floors swept and mopped. The counters were sterilized and gleaming, and the shelves were stocked with almost twice the supply of breads and pastries for the weekend customers who would start filling the tables as soon as Cass opened Serendipity's doors at seven A.M. She'd even gone so far as to put pretty paper doilies under the condiment caddies on each table, just for something else to do.

Still no Mike.

She looked around and found no excuse to stay. With a sigh, she headed for the panel of light switches, but rather than swiping them all down with one hand the way she usually did, she methodically turned each one off, one at a time, until the whole kitchen was bathed in darkness, the only gleam of light coming from the windows in the swinging doors where the morning light that was flooding the front of the shop spilled through.

Then she pushed open the alley door... and screeched like a barn owl, nearly dropping the box of day-old baked goods she would drop off at Joseph's Storehouse on her way back to Cass's place.

Mike stood just outside on the cracked pavement, his loaded cart behind him, one fist still raised in preparation to knock. "Hey," he said, his serious expression breaking into a wide grin. "Just me."

"Gah!" Abby exclaimed, pressing one hand to her pounding heart. "I almost started swinging," she said, narrowing her eyes at him. "Stop laughing. You could be lying on the ground clutching your family jewels, you know."

"Nice." Mike's tone was slightly censorious, but he was still struggling not to laugh. "Nashville classed you up, did it?"

"Don't be a jerk." That was the best comeback she could muster? Sheesh. "You're late."

"I'm right on time."

"I've been waiting for you for the last two hours."

Mike's eyebrow rose slowly. "I've had a busy morning, Abby. You're not the only customer on my Saturday route, remember?"

Okay. So he was mad about her shutting him down earlier in the week. Or hurt. Or both.

Well, so was she. "Yeah, well, now I'm going to have to put in overtime. I was just getting ready to leave, as you might have noticed." She glanced over her shoulder into the dark dining room behind her.

"I don't need you to stick around. I did this job before you did."

Angry *and* hurt, apparently.

Without a word, Abby stepped aside, propping the door open for him.

"Thank you," Mike said as he passed her with his dolly. When she didn't follow him, he paused to turn on a few of the lights, then said, "It'll go quicker if you want to help."

The sky was growing lighter with every passing minute, and she did need to get out of the alley before anyone recognized her truck. There were already signs of life on the street as the local businesses began prepping for their Saturday morning customers. Abby stepped back inside the kitchen.

Mike had the first box already unpacked and shelved by the time she snatched the clipboard off its hook by the pantry door. "That was oat milk?" she asked. "A dozen cartons?"

"Yep." He tore into another box. "And this is brown sugar."

There were seven boxes altogether, and they were through them in less than five minutes. "Wow," Abby commented dryly. "That didn't take nearly as long as it usually does. You have your Wheaties this morning?"

Mike didn't scowl or frown; he just met her gaze without any emotion at all. "You said you had to leave. I was trying to be sensitive to your needs."

Ouch. The words reverberated inside her head like a clanging gong, the weight of them making her shoulders droop. She suddenly wanted to cry, remembering the last time he'd said pretty much the same thing to her.

She shook her head and looked away, hoping he wouldn't notice the tears that were gathering in her eyes. This was not the way she'd planned for things to go with Mike. She heard him move right before she felt the careful weight of his hand on her shoulder.

"Abs," he said gently. "I'm sorry. I *am* being a jerk. I'm—" He broke off when she lifted her teary gaze to his.

And then she was in his embrace, cradled against his big, solid chest, those lovely, lovely arms wrapped oh-so-tenderly around her. He held her like she was something fragile, breakable, and perhaps in that moment, she was.

Breakable, perhaps, but safe right where she was. Protected by this man—he was no longer the boy she'd once loved. That Mike Nesbit would not have apologized so quickly. That Mike Nesbit would not have held her so carefully. That Mike Nesbit would have continued to make her pay for rejecting him.

No, the boy had become a man, and he stood before her now, offering her only what she needed, and not demanding what he wanted in return.

"I'm the one who should be apologizing, Mike," she murmured, her voice muffled against the fabric of his shirt.

He didn't contradict her, but one of his large hands moved up and down her back in a calming motion, and Abby found the tension draining from her body. She rested her head against his shoulder, her ear subconsciously tuning into the steady rhythm of his heart beating inside his chest, and she slowly let her arms circle his waist.

Suddenly, the door from the alley opened. They both stiffened in surprise and turned to see who had intruded on their tender moment.

"Daddy?" Abby gasped as she tore herself from Mike's embrace and took a few staggering steps away. "What—What are you—?"

Mike froze for only a moment, then moved close to her side, resting a hand on her back. She wasn't sure if she appreciated his show of support or not, but the look on her father's face at the gesture told her in no uncertain terms that Jedediah Goodacre was not a happy man.

"Sir," Mike began.

"Don't 'sir' me, young man. Not while your hands are all over my daughter."

Mike stiffened beside her; she felt the tension of his body vibrate through the hand at her back. Jed hadn't moved. He just stood in the open doorway, his eyes fixed on her.

He didn't look angry, not exactly, and Abby was at a bit of a loss. She took a tentative step forward, then glanced back at Mike with an apologetic grimace before turning to face her father again. "I'm—" Should she apologize? But for what? For the fact that she was back in Plumwood Hollow? For not being in Nashville like she'd led him to believe? For walking in on her and Mike in what must look to her father like a rather compromising situation? Where did she even begin?

"It's true, then," Jed finally said. "It is your truck out there." His expression told her he hadn't needed to see her face to confirm what he already knew was true.

Still at a loss for what to say, Abby just nodded.

"And you've been keeping company with her." Those words were directed at Mike. The look in Jed's eyes when he swung his gaze to the guy behind her could have sliced through titanium.

"We've been working together, sir," Mike said.

Jed's brows rose slowly, and even in the soft morning light, Abby could see the flush coloring his neck and cheeks. "That's what they're calling it these days?"

Abby couldn't decide whether to take cover behind Mike or step between the two of them to stop the impending brawl. "Daddy," she began. "I—I was going to—I was planning to come talk to you this weekend."

Jed's glare shifted back to her, but as far as she could discern, he'd hardly moved a muscle since pushing open the door. He seemed somehow bigger than he had the last time she'd seen him. Taller. Straighter. Definitely more formidable.

Except for his eyebrows. They were definitely *less* formidable.

Wait. *Is he—is Daddy manscaping?*

The ridiculous and inopportune thought caught her off guard, and she slapped a hand over her mouth, even though she hadn't said a word out loud.

Daddy's eyebrows were indeed no longer bushy. Not only had they obviously been trimmed—hacked back might be a better term for it—but the left one was decidedly less bushy than the right. What had he done? He reminded her a little of a kid who hadn't gotten caught with the hair clippers in time.

And he'd gotten a haircut, too. His hair, however, looked great. Stylish, in fact.

But the eyebrows! There was simply no way the hair and the brows could have been done by the same person.

Suddenly, Abby couldn't *not* look at them. They were so bad.

"The weekend is here." Jed must have noticed something not quite right in her expression, because he lifted his chin just a notch so that he was practically glaring down his nose at her.

"I—I know," she choked out, moving her hand away from her mouth just long enough to say the words. "Can I come by the house—I mean, your place tonight?" she stammered, completely rattled. Even though she'd been to his log house a few times over the last year, it still felt strange to not have him living at the Seven Virtues Ranch house. "Whatever time works best for you," she added. She hadn't planned on him even knowing she was in town for at least another day or two, and she certainly hadn't prepared what she'd say to him yet. But then, a lot of things that had happened today had not gone according to her plans.

Jed cleared his throat. "That won't work for me. I'm busy this evening."

Abby's eyes widened a little. She couldn't decide whether to be hurt by his dismissal or relieved. "Oh. Okay. Can we talk sometime tomorrow afternoon, then?" Cass didn't open until the lunch hour, but while Abby was staying with her, she'd committed to working her two or three hours every day except Monday when Serendipity's was closed.

"You won't be at church, I presume." It wasn't a question.

"Um, no. Probably not. I—I have to do the prep work for Cass in the morning."

"Prep work," Jed repeated wryly, his eyes moving from Abby to Mike. "Right. Will you be doing prep work with her, Mr. Nesbit?" he asked Mike pointedly.

"No, sir. I'll be at church with my folks."

Jed harrumphed, and his gaze returned to Abby. "That won't work, either. I'm busy after church."

What game was he playing? Did he or did he not want her to come talk to him? And busy doing what? Sunday dinner with the family? And why not just say so?

"I've got company," Jed said, and for a moment, Abby wondered if she'd asked her questions out loud.

"Okay." She shifted from one foot to the other, realizing she was out of options. "Do—do you want to talk now? Since you're here?" It was the last thing she wanted to do. She was having a difficult time adjusting to the odd hours she was keeping, and last night, sleep had come slowly because her mind wouldn't stop spinning around the circumstances in which she found herself. On top of that, the emotional roller coaster of the morning spent first waiting for Mike, then the ugly sparring with him, followed by what might have been the start of a tentative truce between them, had her reeling emotionally.

Jed eyed them both for a long moment. "Here's what I want from you, young lady," he finally said. The way he said 'young lady' had a coil of unease knotting her belly. Then he shook his head. "No, here's what I *expect* from you."

Abby felt Mike step up beside her again, although this time, he didn't touch her.

Jed pointed at Mike. "And this goes for you, too, young man, if you're going to be in cahoots with my daughter."

"Daddy," Abby began, a wave of guilt washing over her. It was her fault Mike was in the line of fire.

"It's okay," Mike murmured beside her. To Jed, he said, "I'm not in cahoots with Abby, sir. I'm only respecting her wishes."

"Respect?" Her father's no-longer-bushy brows shot up again, but Abby didn't find them nearly so comical now. "I'm not so sure you understand the meaning of the word, Mr. Nesbit."

Mike drew up straighter beside her, but he didn't argue.

"What I expect is honesty from you. I expect an explanation for this—" He broke off and made a circular motion with his hand that encompassed the kitchen, the two of them, and quite possibly, Cass and Serendipity's, too. "And I expect it to be the truth."

"I know, Daddy."

"I'm not finished."

"Sorry." She felt like she was three years old and had been caught with her hands in the cookie jar.

As though he'd read her mind, Jed said, "You are no longer a child, Abby, and because you are an adult, I expect you to behave like one. Because you are an adult, it is no longer my place to require that you tell me where you are at every given moment, nor do I require you tell me who you're consorting with these days."

"We're not consorting," Abby murmured, trying to keep her tone respectful. First they were in cahoots, now they were consorting? This all felt a little bizarre, especially on so little sleep. She crossed her arms and said, "This isn't about Mike, Daddy. It's between you and me, okay?"

"Far as I'm concerned, Mike being here makes this about Mike, too," Jed countered, his gaze still moving back and forth between them.

"It's okay, Abs," Mike said again beside her, briefly brushing her elbow with his fingertips.

"We're not consorting," Abby repeated stubbornly.

Her father picked up where he'd left off, not even acknowledging her irritation. "But if you're going to tell me something, I expect it to be the truth. That, daughter of mine, is something I have always expected of you, no matter how young or old you are. Honesty. Truth."

"I know," Abby acknowledged on a sigh. "I know, Daddy, okay?" She toyed with the hem of her shirt, both relieved and nervous at the same time. Relieved that the truth was out to her father, and nervous at what the fallout was going to look like.

"So here's what I want. I want you to come to me. When you're ready, Abby. Not because I've found you out. And not because I've interrupted this little... interlude here." He jutted his chin at Mike in a gesture that was less than polite. It hurt Abby's pride nearly as much as it must have hurt Mike's. "Then I want you to come clean to me about why you felt it necessary to lie to me. To your whole family. To this whole town. Why I had to find out from Pete Zellar, of all people, that you're back in the hollow. Lying low, apparently. Taking advantage of the good graces of someone like Miss Whitehouse, it seems."

Oh, geez. Pete Zellar? There'd be no keeping her presence in Plumwood Hollow a secret now that Pete knew she was here, that was for sure. "How did he—?"

"He recognized your truck." Then he added unnecessarily, "The truck that used to be his son's."

"Oh."

"Oh, indeed," Jed echoed, but something in his tone had shifted, and Abby braved looking at him. She couldn't be a hundred percent certain, but she didn't think he seemed quite so angry anymore. In fact, he almost looked a little relieved.

"Honesty," he said, lifting his hand and ticking things off on his fingers. "Truth. Respect."

"Okay," Abby said, just barely above a whisper. She was beginning to feel a deep well of shame opening up beneath her, now that the shock of the unexpected encounter was wearing off. It wasn't the first time she'd been reprimanded by her father in front of Mike, but that didn't make this any less embarrassing.

"When you're ready to come to me on your own accord, that's what I want from you." He pointed at Mike, but kept his eyes locked with hers. "Come without him."

"Okay," she said again, mortification making her cheeks burn.

"You and I, Mr. Nesbit, will talk later."

"Sir." Mike nodded.

"You, at least, I know where to find," Jed stated, shooting one last withering glower at his daughter, intended to do exactly what it did: put her in her place. With that, he turned on his heel and headed back out into the alley, pulling the heavy door closed firmly behind him.

"Well." The word came out of her in a wobbly whoosh.

Beside her, Mike chuckled softly. "Yeah. Well." Then he reached for her hand. "Abby?"

She didn't turn toward him, but neither did she pull her hand away. "What?"

"I meant what I said." He gestured at the door. "Before your dad dropped in. I'm sorry for the way I acted this morning." He tugged on her hand gently. "Forgive me?"

Abby did look at him, then. She squeezed his fingers and said, "There's nothing to forgive, Mike. You've been a lot nicer to me than I deserve, that's for sure."

Mike didn't reply right away, but when Abby started to pull away from him, he said, "Listen. I know we're traveling on two different paths." Those were her words from two years ago; she remembered them clearly. "I know we can't be anything more than friends, like you said. I know that," he reiterated. "But if I'm being honest, and apparently, that's the flavor of the day, then I have to tell you that you're too important to me to let our past keep us apart."

Abby swallowed hard, wishing things could be different, but not knowing how to bridge the divide they'd carved out between them. "So are you," she managed to say around the lump in her throat. "Too important to me," she clarified.

Mike took her other hand so that they stood facing each other. "I want to be your friend, Abby. And correct me if I'm wrong," he added, cocking his head and giving her a teasing grin. "But I get the feeling you could really use one right about now. You seem to be on a lot of folks' black list...."

Abby tried to look offended, but he wouldn't let go of her hands when she tried to pull away.

"I'm just giving you a hard time, woman," he said.

"Except that it's true, and you know it." She looked up at him through her lashes before dropping her gaze to their clasped hands. It felt nice to be touched by him this way. It was just physical contact, maybe the first of the building blocks that would eventually become a bridge between them, and for now, it was exactly what she needed. "I've missed you, too, Mike," she admitted, speaking so softly she wondered if he'd heard her. She raised her volume a little and said, "Your offer of friendship means a lot to me right now."

Abby was sure he would pull her into a hug again, and when he did, she was also sure that she'd go willingly. But instead, Mike lifted each of her hands to his lips, pressed a kiss to each one, then released his grip on her.

"You hungry?" he asked, eying the box of day-old pastries she'd left by the door. "And I don't mean for those."

"Maybe," she said, her curiosity piqued. "Why?"

He pulled his dolly after him as he headed for the door, then scooped up the box. "Let's get out of here. I'm going to cook for you."

"Cook for me?" That was the last thing she'd expected him to say.

"Cook for you," he repeated, chuckling at her surprised response. "My place."

"Your place?" Again, not what she'd been expecting. "You have your own place now?" she asked, still not wholly convinced his offer was legit.

"I do," he said with a magnanimous nod. "I'm living in the apartment over the store for the rest of the summer."

"The summer." She was starting to sound like a deranged parrot.

"You going to copy everything I say?" he asked with a dubious look, clearly thinking the same thing as she was.

"But why just for the summer?" she wanted to know. "When did you move out of your folks' house?"

"Not sure if you heard, but my dad had a long bout with pneumonia in the spring last year. He ended up having to take a chunk of time off, so I switched schools to be closer to home so I could help with the store."

"Is he okay? Your dad?" Abby asked, reaching out to rest her fingers on his forearm. How had she not heard about this?

"He's fine now, yes," Mike assured her. "But with my full class load and working here whenever I wasn't in school or sleeping, my schedule got a little crazy. No one was living in the apartment at that time, and it just made sense for me to move in there."

"Only for the rest of the summer, you said. What then? Back home?"

"Actually, I'm buying a house in a few months," he said, nudging one of the wheels of the dolly with his booted toe.

"A house?" Abby exclaimed. "Mike, that's great. Wow. I'm kinda jealous, said the homeless kitchen maid." She stuck out her bottom lip at him, then had to pull back quickly when he reached out to grab it. "So? Are you going to tell me about this house you're buying?"

"I'll give you all the details over scrambled eggs and bacon." When she still waffled, he rolled his eyes and gestured toward the door with his chin. "Get a move on, woman."

"Well, aren't you still just as demanding as ever," she retorted. "Some things never change."

He shrugged. "We can't all be perfect like you."

Abby let out a scathing snort. "Ha. I'm about as far from perfect as a girl from Plumwood Hollow can get. Just ask my father. And my band."

"You'll always be perfect to me, Abs," Mike countered, holding the door wide for her. "Come on. Let me feed you."

Abby hesitated only a moment longer as she assessed her state of wellbeing. She was still exhausted, there was no doubt about it, but the rush she'd just experienced, first at being gathered close to Mike's body, then at the sudden appearance of her father, had her feeling agitated and unsettled, points of adrenaline-fueled energy ping-ponging through her system. In another hour, she might be crashed out, face down on her bed, but right now?

"Why not?" she finally said, trying to pretend she didn't notice the elated smile that spread across Mike's face. "We'll have a spill-all fest, shall we? I mean, I owe you an explanation for all of this, anyway. Besides," she added sheepishly. "I could use the practice for when I have to come clean to Daddy."

"Whatever excuse you need, Miss Goodacre," Mike said, tossing the cocky comment over his shoulder as he headed toward his delivery van with its enormous apple green and turquoise logo splashed down both sides. "I know you just want to spend a little more time with my handsome mug this morning."

Abby was glad he couldn't see the blush that colored her cheeks as she ran her hand across the light switches on the electrical panel, turning them all off in one fell swoop. She double-checked them to make sure the door was locked, then turned to find Mike waiting at the narrow curb, holding the box of pastries she still needed to deliver to Joseph's Storehouse.

"Shall we drop these off together?" he asked, lifting them a little higher. "We can head to my place first, then walk these over since it's just down the block from me."

That would mean walking in public with Mike. Where anyone could see her. Granted, it wasn't even six o'clock in the morning on a Saturday, so it wasn't likely there'd be that many people out and about. And Daddy obviously already knew she was in town. But still... "That's all right. I'll just swing these by on my way."

He studied her for a moment, a flicker of doubt crossing his features. "You won't ditch me, will you?" he finally asked, and the mixture of hope and uncertainty in his voice made Abby go all soft inside.

"I won't ditch you, Mike. I'll be there. I promise."

He still didn't look a hundred percent sure, but when she unlocked her truck door, he circled the hood and slid the box of baked goods into the passenger seat while she climbed in behind the wheel. "Just come up the outside steps out back. You know the ones."

She did, indeed, remember those steps that led up to the apartment above the grocery store. The last time she'd been on them, the little one-bedroom place had been rented by a part-time employee who also attended college in Muldoon. Patrick Something-or-other, she thought. He'd hosted what started out as a small party for a few close friends that quickly got out of hand. No one had been seriously hurt, but a fight had broken out between a couple of guys over one checking out the other's ex-girlfriend. There had been tears—the girl's—and punches thrown—the guys'—and the three of them had been forced to take it outside where they soon attracted the attention of someone passing by who then called the police. Mike's parents had been called, of course, not just because Mike had been at the party and they'd been underage drinking, but because the Nesbits owned the building. Jed had also arrived on the scene, and although he'd said very little to her on the car ride home, she'd decided then and there that partying with a bunch of older college kids wasn't nearly as cool as it sounded.

"I remember," was all she said. Because she also remembered the kiss she and Mike had shared on those stairs, her standing one step higher so they were better matched in height. She hadn't even had to tip her head up to press her lips to his, to wrap her arms around his neck as she leaned into him.

"Just come on up," he said, a knowing spark in his gaze. "I'll leave the door open for you."

THIRTY-FOUR

J ED WANTED TO STRANGLE that kid of his.

Except that she wasn't a kid anymore. He had to remember that.

He'd taken one look at her in the arms of that Nesbit boy—not a boy anymore, either, but a man—and he'd been struck in the chest with a one-two punch of awareness. His baby had grown up.

Sure, he'd seen her sashaying her way across the stage in bars and clubs in Nashville. He'd watched her wow her audiences and fend off romantic advances from men twice her age. He'd sent her out into the wild world, as Charlotte Ransome called it, confident in her ability to take care of herself.

In his head, he'd known that she was, indeed, an adult, a young woman.

But his heart had clung to the child she'd been, and finding her hiding out in some back alley—okay, so it wasn't a back alley. Hiding out in Cass's kitchen in the early hours before dawn, though.

And it was in a room off the side alley.... He cleared his throat and gripped his steering wheel a little tighter.

Despite his Papa Bear reaction to seeing Mike's hands on his little girl, Jed had recognized Abby's posture for what it was. She'd been holding onto the young buck for dear life, if he'd read her right. There'd been nothing truly inappropriate about the scene he'd walked in on....

Well, maybe not nothing. He'd seen the way Mike looked at his daughter. He knew that look; for Pete's sake, he'd seen it on the faces of all the young men who'd recently become his sons by marriage to his other daughters.

But what scared him most about what he saw... what wounded his heart more deeply than he could ever have imagined, was the fact that his

Abby-girl was looking to and leaning on another man for the comfort and security and stability she'd always sought out in Jed.

His Abby-girl. He could still remember the fragile weight of her tiny body when the midwife had handed her to him so that she could tend to Caroline. How pale and listless his beautiful wife had seemed, yet how animated the light in her eyes had been when she looked at him holding their seventh daughter.

He'd made the decision then and there that he'd never let Caroline go through that again. No matter what she said, no matter how hard she begged. They'd been told they shouldn't have more children, that Caroline was too weak to go through yet another pregnancy. That had been three pregnancies and four babies ago, and his wife had insisted each time that she wanted to try one more time to give him a son. One more time. And then one more time again.

No more. Not after the seventh daughter.

"Seven is the number of completion in the Bible," he'd told her, although she'd said that very thing several times throughout her pregnancy. She'd been so certain the Lord would give them a son for their seventh child. "This perfect little girl is our completer, my love."

He'd seen the light within her dim for a moment, but she hadn't argued. She'd either been too weak to argue, or, as he hoped, she'd realized the truth in his statement.

For whatever reason, every time she gave him another daughter, his wife had felt more and more like she'd somehow failed him. He'd assured her in every way that he could think of that she was everything he could ever imagine a wife could be, that she was all that was good in his life, that having her by his side made the truly difficult times bearable. He'd insisted time and time again that she had not ever and that she never would fail him... and then she went and did exactly that.

By abandoning him.

It had happened so quickly, so violently, so horrifically, that even now, the memory of that terrible night flooded him with agony.

She'd been sick the last few months of her pregnancy, but she'd assured him that once she delivered, she'd regain her strength, that having a new baby to hold—"A son, Jeddy!" she'd say, her face aglow with a beatific smile—to love, to care for, would energize her.

But she hadn't recovered. She'd continued to fade before his eyes, and no matter how hard he prayed, no matter how much he begged God to let her live, he'd stood by, helpless, as she had slipped out of his grasp.

He'd awakened to her sharp cry for help in the middle of the night, her face twisted in agony, her left arm clenched tightly to her chest. By the time he'd lurched up in bed and was crouched over her, she was unable to speak clearly, her eyes glazing over. Jed had dialed 9-1-1 and was speaking to a dispatcher when Caroline arched up in bed, her back stiff, her jaw clenched, her right arm flung out, reaching for something, for *someone* to help her.

He'd dropped the phone as he grabbed for her to keep her from hurting herself, wrapping his arms around her from behind as she stiffened backwards into him, at one point, her skull smashing into his mouth and splitting his lip. It was then that he saw the blood pooling between her legs, and his desperate pleas turned to angry wails.

By the time the paramedics had arrived, she was gone. And in all the chaos, he hadn't said goodbye. He hadn't told her he loved her. He'd only raged at God... when all along, he knew it was his fault.

He could have put his foot down and insisted they stop having more children. He could have gone in and gotten the surgery that would have prevented all of this.

He could have said no to her.

He *should* have said no to her.

Because by not saying no to her, he was, in essence, silently agreeing that they should keep trying for that elusive boy. His sweet Caroline was dead because Jed couldn't say no to her.

The baby she'd left behind, the tiny girl they still hadn't officially named because they'd been so sure she was going to be a boy... and then as Caroline grew sicker postpartum, they'd kept putting off naming...

What better name to give her than the seventh virtue, Abstinence?

Even back then, he'd known it would be a heavy name for anyone to carry, but under the shroud of grief and anguish where he found himself, he convinced himself that the name was beautiful. Tragic, bittersweet, yes, but beautiful.

"But Daddy," the twelve-year-old Faith had said to him when he told the girls the name he'd chosen for their baby sister. "Doesn't that just mean not having sex? I mean, it's kind of a weird thing to name someone. I don't know how she's going to feel about that name, especially once she gets to high school. Being a teenager is already brutal enough." She had been mother-henning the family her whole life.

He'd explained to her and her sisters that the name was much more noble than that, that it was an old-fashioned word that meant the opposite of over-indulgence in things that would cause trouble in life. The more he explained to them, the more it rang true in his heart, and the more determined he became not to be talked out of the name.

Faith had finally capitulated, albeit under great duress. She'd stood in the kitchen doorway as he sat at the table putting on his boots early one morning, and told him that he could name her baby sister Abstinence if he was going to be pigheaded about it, but she would call her Abby, and that was final.

He still saw the surprise on people's faces when they found out his Abby-girl's full name, and he was proud of the way his youngest daughter had embraced it and made it her own. Sometimes, it even seemed like she flaunted it, practically dared people to make something of it.

She'd even used it in the name of her band—against her agent's recommendations, in fact.

Yes, the girl-now-a-woman could look after herself.

His Abby-girl no longer needed him the way she once had.

Although, he mused with a spark of something like hope, if it was Mike Nesbit his Abby-girl found herself needing...

Part of him worried that he'd done the wrong thing in not sticking around to talk to her at Serendipity's, but a bigger part of him had perked up at the scene he'd come upon. If there was anything or anyone that might bring his daughter home to the hollow, it was Mike Nesbit. Jed had always known Abby had wings she needed to spread, that her musical ability couldn't be contained in a place like Plumwood Hollow where the most appreciative audience divided their attention between Abby's songs, their barbecued ribs, and whatever foaming liquid was in their mugs at the Smokehouse. But maybe young Mike, if not Jed and her sisters, would be a tether to home for Abby.

When she'd ended the romance with him, it hadn't been just Mike's heart she'd broken. No, she'd broken Jed's, too. Because without that boy on the other end of the line, Jed wasn't sure he'd have been enough to bring the girl home again for more than anything but a quick visit every now and then around the holidays.

In fact, last year, she hadn't even come home for Thanksgiving. That had been a first in the Goodacre home, the first time it hadn't been the whole family gathered around the table for the big meal.

But if what he'd seen this morning was any indication, there might be hope after all. And Jed, even with his emotions in such a turmoil, hadn't wanted to douse the spark he'd seen between them by demanding Abby come talk to him at that precise moment.

No, he'd opted to leave them to each other, to let that little scene play out a little longer.

And now, there he sat, parked in another breezeway just out of sight of Serendipity's back door, watching the two of them head off in the same direction.

Not toward Cass's house.

Toward Nesbit's Grocery store.

In the direction of Mike Nesbit's upstairs apartment.

He'd have to trust the two of them from there, trust that they did, indeed, know what the word 'respect' meant, in spite of what Jed had said to Mike earlier.

As he started his engine and eased out onto the street after they'd disappeared around the corner, Jed had to admit that he felt like a meddling, manipulative helicopter dad, as Jasmine would have called him. He'd heard the term often from his eldest granddaughter when she thought her mother was too overbearing.

When he pulled up in front of his home, he realized he wasn't nearly as upset as circumstances called for. He sat in his driveway and pondered that for just a moment before a movement caught his eye in the early morning light.

Charlotte Ransome sat in one of the rocking chairs, a cup of coffee in one hand, a woven blanket draped around her shoulders. Her long silver hair was piled in a messy heap on top of her head, one leg tucked under her, the other she used to keep her chair rocking. He could make out her bare toes under the hem of her pajama pants. She waved at him and held up her mug, her wide smile beckoning to him.

"I could get used to this, Lord," Jed said softly, not taking his eyes off the woman on his front porch. He found that he was looking forward to telling Charlotte everything that had happened since Pete Zellar had mentioned seeing Abby's truck the morning before.

Charlotte had come home late last night after her evening spent with Sarah, and although he'd waited up for her, he'd only done so to make sure she returned safe. He hadn't wanted to burden her with his plans to hunt for Abby in the pre-dawn hours; Charlotte had clearly been exhausted, but she'd looked restored in spirit, and he hadn't wanted to burst that bubble she'd brought in with her. They'd both gone straight to bed, then. Jed had known that four o'clock would come far too soon... and not nearly soon enough. He hadn't bothered calling or even texting Abby; if she was in town, then she'd been lying to him over the phone. No, he needed to see for himself what was going on.

THIRTY-FIVE

In spite of her promise to Mike, Abby had waffled after all. After her stop at the homeless shelter, she'd actually turned out of the driveway and started in the direction of Cass's place. It wasn't that she didn't want to spend more time with Mike.

In fact, it was that she *did* want to spend more time with him that had her running scared. She couldn't stop thinking about how nice it had felt to be held by him again, that the way he looked at her felt nothing like the way Bucky used to look at her. Sure, the hunger was there—she knew it for what it was because she recognized it in herself—but it was a hunger for more than just a quick satiation.

Right now, Abby couldn't give anyone anything. And she wouldn't compromise either of them by offering Mike something temporary. Not only was it not in her to do such—"I am Abstinence" she declared under her breath—but she knew without a shadow of a doubt that Mike wouldn't accept that from her, either.

Which was why, in the end, she turned around and headed back to Nesbits, to the parking lot behind the grocery store. She didn't give herself time to rethink her decision yet again, but got out of her truck, closed the door firmly behind her, and climbed the stairs to the second-story apartment where, sure enough, the door was standing ajar.

"Come in," Mike called out before she could knock. When she ducked inside the cool interior, she did a quick perusal of the place before her gaze landed on him. He stood on the other side of a short breakfast bar with a whisk in one hand and a glass bowl of what appeared to be batter ingredients in the other. He wore an apron that had once said *Kiss the Cook* across the front. The dark blue fabric looked like it had seen better days, and the letters were faded from too many washings so that it actually read *iss the Coo*. A Belgium waffle maker steamed hotly on the counter beside him.

He'd remembered. He'd worn the apron and was making her waffles.

"Still love Belgians?" he asked, like he could read her mind. "Want to help? You can man the waffles."

Abby cocked her head at him and grinned. "I thought you said you were going to cook for me. If I'd known you were going to put me to work, I'd have gone back to bed."

"I'll let you wear my apron," he cajoled. "And no one, Abstinence Eve Goodacre, and I mean, *no one* ever gets to wear my apron except me."

She made a show of reading the words on his chest, then giving him a knowing shake of the head. She pointed at the thigh-length apron. "I know what you're trying to do here, Michael Theophilus Nesbit."

It wasn't his middle name—he was Michael John Nesbit, just like the four generations of Nesbit firstborn sons before him—but he'd agreed that if he could call her Abstinence, then she could call him something old-school and vintagey, too. She'd chosen Theophilus—"It means loved by God, so you can't complain," she'd told him. And although he'd made a big show of cringing the first several times she used it, she hadn't been fooled.

He gave her a wide-eyed, innocent look. In a pompous, albeit terrible, British accent, he declared, "I know naught of which you speak."

But he did know. She'd given him the apron for a birthday present, telling him that he'd have to learn to cook, because the only way they were going to eat once they got married was if he figured out how to feed them. But she'd promised to be there to encourage him with kisses.

Mike had convinced her to model the apron for him, then he'd grabbed her around the middle and showered her with kisses instead.

"Ha. You think I'm falling for that again?" She chuckled sardonically, still shaking her head. "You know, you don't have to trick a girl into letting you kiss her. You could just ask nicely." The moment the words were out, she wanted to round them up and shove them back down her throat.

Mike's eyes went dark, and he lowered the hand holding the whisk. But instead of doing just that, asking her if he could kiss her, he nodded slowly, swallowed hard—she could see the motion of his Adam's apple at his throat—and said, "I'll have to remember that. For when the girl I want to kiss is ready to say 'yes'," he added, then lowered his gaze to the bowl in front of him, picked up the whisk, and started mixing the batter.

Abby dropped her bag on the floor just inside the front door. "Um, so seriously, how can I help?" she asked, wondering if this hadn't been a terrible idea after all. "Want me to take over for you with those?"

"Nah," he said, only a telltale rasp in his demand to indicate how affected he was by her words. "Too many cooks in the kitchen and all that. How about you get out our dishes out? We'll sit right here at the bar if you're okay with that. The plates are in the cupboard next to the sink and the silverware is in that drawer." He pointed behind him with his elbow.

"Sure. I can do that." Abby was glad he wasn't looking at her, glad he couldn't see the heat that must have turned her cheeks crimson. She went about her task while the room became infused with the delicious aroma of sweet vanilla and cinnamon—Mike always added cinnamon just for her—as the waffles puffed up and browned to perfection.

"You'll be proud of me," Mike said after a bit. His teasing grin was back. "I have graduated to real maple syrup, I'll have you know. No more Mrs. Butterworth. Although I do miss that buttery flavor at times."

"Just add more butter to your waffles, then," Abby said with a laugh, glad he was steering the conversation back to safe territory.

"It's not the same, and you know it. There's nothing quite like that fake butter flavor, Abs."

She rolled her eyes, then pulled out one of the two stools opposite where he stood. "That smells amazing. I didn't think I was hungry until now."

"Beats day-old pastries, hm?"

"Well," she hedged. "I don't know about that. I guess I'll have to try them to find out."

"How do you want your eggs?" he asked. "Scrambled or fried? Yolks broken, of course."

He remembered that, too.

"Scrambled would be easier, wouldn't they?"

"Scrambled, it is, then." He lifted the first waffle out and set it on a cookie rack inside the pre-warmed oven, then while the second waffle cooked, he whipped up half a dozen eggs and dumped them into a cast-iron skillet on the stovetop. From the fridge, he pulled out a little bin of blueberries and handed them to her. "These are already washed and ready to eat. Sorry—no whipping cream."

"You don't have to be sorry, Mike," she insisted with a shake of her head. "This is amazing. Far more than I expected."

A few minutes later, Mike had cleared the counter of the waffle paraphernalia, hung his apron on a hook inside the narrow broom cupboard, and had moved the second stool around to the other side of the bar so that he could sit facing her while they ate. Abby closed her eyes and made an involuntary moan at her first bite of her perfect waffle. Finally, she could hold her appreciation no longer.

"Mike," she gushed. "How on earth did you make these even better than Charity's? I didn't think that was possible, but apparently, I was wrong. And I am never wrong. Or at least I wasn't before this." She waved her fork at him, then snatched it back when a drop of maple syrup plopped onto the counter between them. "Oops."

Mike shrugged like it was no big deal, but the satisfied smile on his face told her he was quite pleased by her response. "I've been working on them for a while now. I'm glad you approve."

"I do," she agreed, nodding with gusto before shoving another bite into her mouth.

It wasn't long before they'd fallen into something that at least looked and sounded like comfortable conversation, even though Abby felt like her skin was buzzing with awareness of his every move, of being so close to him, of the way the timbre of his voice washed over her with every word he spoke. She wanted to chalk it up to her lack of sleep, but she knew it was more than that. It was like her senses had awakened from an amnesic trance and every nerve ending was firing at the memories this day was evoking.

"So?" Mike said after a lull in the conversation. Then he went straight for the jugular. "Want to tell me what's brought you home to the hollow?"

Abby looked down at her nearly empty plate. It had been so nice to sit here with him and pretend that everything was normal, that there were no elephants in the room, no old wounds that hadn't quite healed over, no empty promises, no broken dreams. But wasn't that why she was here, across the counter from him?

So, she told him. She started back to her first trip out to Nashville under the protective wing of Remington Sounder, of the idealistic bubble she'd lived in during that remarkable year of working with the superstar.

"I bought your album the day it went up for preorder," Mike told her. He pointed at his phone on its charger across the room. "If it had been an actual record or even a CD, it would have already worn out. It was amazing, Abs. I couldn't stop listening to it."

"Thanks," she said, shy in the warmth of his praise. "I was really proud of it, too." She wanted to say more, but she didn't want to sound ungrateful.

Mike heard the hesitance in her voice, though. "But..." he prompted.

"But." She chuckled softly. "But it didn't really feel like me, you know? Or sound like me. It was like an amalgamation of me and a dozen other groups Rem worked with. It's like he brings out a particular sound. It's not a bad thing, and it sells really well. Very mainstream, pop-country stuff that's easy to sing along to."

Mike nodded, but said, "It was still you, Abs. It was just a different version of you." He winked at her. "I guess I just like all the versions of you, so it worked for me."

"Mike," she said, a soft warning in the single word.

He took another sip of his coffee—the guy even made ridiculously good coffee—and nodded for her to continue.

"So when it came time for me to go out on my own, I guess I was a little confused by how popular that poppier, upbeat version of me had become. I guess I got swept up in it. When we formed the band, it was around those songs, and even though I wanted to inject more of my own style into the songs we were performing, I kept getting push backs from the group, from the audience, and especially from my manager. The guy had come highly recommended, and honestly, he wasn't a bad guy. In fact, he's really good at what he does, and that's getting his bands out there on stage, getting them heard, getting them openings."

She paused to refill her coffee cup from the carafe Mike had set between them. With so much caffeine in her system, she could kiss her morning nap goodbye. Maybe she'd sleep better tonight, especially since she didn't have to get up quite so early in the morning.

"So I started playing what the crowds wanted. Giving in. Selling out. And once I started compromising, it just got easier and easier to do." She stared down into her mug, a band of shame tightening around her chest. "And it wasn't just with the music, either. That compromise started seeping into other parts of my life, too, you know? The people I spent time with. The way I performed my day job. I even—" She broke off, suddenly uncertain of how much she should tell Mike. She didn't want to hurt him unnecessarily, but she didn't know how to tell her story without bringing up Bucky. She opened her mouth, closed it, then sighed, unsure where to pick up her story again.

Mike didn't interrupt or try to fill the silence. He seemed prepared to give her all the time she needed to find the right words.

"I ruined everything, Mike," she finally said. "In the last three weeks, my bass player defected to a better-paying band—or at least a band with hotter chicks in it—and even though I found a great replacement in record time, it wasn't fast enough. All our gigs got canceled, my guitar player hates me, my agent dumped me, I lost my day job, and I got served an eviction notice saying I had seven days to be out of my apartment. Oh, and I left my drummer high and dry—I have no idea what he's doing now, but he's out of that income because of me, and he's got a wife and kids to feed."

"Wow."

"Yeah, wow," she agreed sardonically. They sat in contemplative silence for a few minutes, and then Mike took a deep breath and in and let it out slowly. Abby braced herself for whatever he was going to say.

"I came to see you. It was a couple months back."

Abby's head snapped up. No amount of bracing could have prepared her for that. "You—you did?"

Mike nodded, but didn't expound.

"Why didn't you tell me? I mean, how did I not know? Why didn't you—"

The look on his face told her everything his silence didn't. A couple months back. Then Mike already knew about Bucky.

"Oh." She closed her eyes and nodded slowly, her heart sinking inside her. What could she say? How could she make him see that she hadn't traded Mike for someone like Bucky? That she'd been caught up in living the lifestyle, the adrenaline of an audience, and that poor Bucky had essentially been the ultimate compromise. Yes, she'd used him, and as hurt as she was by his cruel behavior toward her in the last few weeks, she wasn't going to shirk the part that was her responsibility. She'd known what she was doing that first time she'd let him kiss her after a heady show. She'd recognized that acquiescence for what it was... yet another compromise. She'd known what she was doing that first time she'd let him kiss her on stage after she sang "Friends to Lovers," and she'd been right. The crowd *had* indeed gone wild. Everyone loved a country song come to life, right?

Bucky had known the song wasn't about him. She'd written it long before she'd ever met him. But she'd known what she was doing when she let him pretend that it was.

And Mike had seen it play out—that country song come to life—right in front of his eyes.

He'd come to see her perform, and he'd gotten far more than he'd bargained for.

"I take it things didn't work out between you."

Abby watched Mike's strong fingers as he toyed with the handle on his coffee cup. "They never worked out for us," she stated dully. "Not from day one. He was just another compromise, Mike."

He shrugged one shoulder. "Bummer for him."

Mortification coursed through her and she nodded, not meeting his gaze. "He deserved better from me."

"Really?" His response was quick and sharp. "From what I saw, he didn't deserve squat. Especially not from you."

Abby winced. She certainly hadn't expected that kind of response. "What—what did you see?" Although, she wasn't sure she wanted to know. In fact, she wasn't sure she wanted to discuss Bucky—or any other guy, for that matter—with Mike at all. But the question was out, and there was no taking it back.

Mike slouched a little on the stool, sliding his empty mug away. "I saw him kiss you on stage. He looked...."

When he didn't finish the sentence, Abby finally lifted her eyes to his. And wished she hadn't, not when she saw his pained expression.

But Mike grinned then, even though the smile didn't quite reach his eyes. "He looked like he couldn't decide whether he wanted to kiss you or shove you off the stage."

Abby's eyes went round, and although a slightly hysterical sound tried to explode out of her mouth, she somehow held it back and slowly nodded instead. When she could speak, she said, "You know, you pretty much nailed it on the head."

Mike grew serious again. "Then I saw him with another woman at the bar after you left."

Abby cringed. "Right."

"He seemed to be enjoying himself a little more with her."

Abby nodded. No surprise there.

"She seemed to be enjoying herself, too."

"Got it."

"In fact, it wasn't just his kisses she seemed to be enjoying." Mike moved his hands in a provocative manner, like he was sliding them down the body of a voluptuous woman. "Apparently, that guy is good with his hands. Knows how to play more than just his guitar."

"Got it, Mike." Now he was just punishing her.

After a moment of silence, he got in one more shot to the gut. "They left together. And when I say together, I mean, they were pretty much fused into one unit."

Abby pushed her stool back and stood. She gathered her dirty dishes into a stack in front of her. "I already know I screwed things up, okay? With you, with Bucky, with my band, my career, my dreams, now with my dad. All of it. I'm a royal screw up and I'm sorry. You don't need to rub it in, okay?"

THIRTY-SIX

"Do you want my opinion or advice?" Charlotte asked him when he'd finished pouring out his woes. "Or do you just need a listening ear and a shoulder to cry on?"

"I appreciate the listening ear, absolutely. But if you have advice, then please." Jed gazed out over his lawn toward the barn and the pasture beyond. He'd fed the horses before he left, but he'd need to go move the cows to a new pasture before too long. "Especially if it's a woman thing. I don't mean to pull the man card, as my daughter's often accuse me of doing, but if you understand what's going on because you are a woman?" He took another sip of his coffee. "Then, yes. I would greatly appreciate your advice."

Charlotte nodded contemplatively and ran her fingertip around the rim of her empty coffee cup several times before speaking. "Your daughter, bless her heart, has a whole lot to live up to. Between being the youngest of seven—and not just seven children, but seven girls, mind you?—and all six of them having apparently figured out what they want out of life, *and* how to get it? Well." She spoke emphatically, waving one hand around like she was preaching. "She doesn't have *one* tough act to follow, my friend. She's got six. And she has to prove herself worthy of you on top of that."

"She knows she doesn't need to prove anything to me," Jed countered. "And Abby has more musical talent in her little finger than all of her sisters combined. She's not following in any of their footsteps. She knows exactly what she wants. Always has." He didn't intend to argue with her, but her observation prodded at his insides, making his defenses rise.

"She may know what she wants," Charlotte said, but he couldn't tell if she agreed with him or not. "But could it be possible that she knows what you want her to want?"

Jed shook his head abruptly, sloshing his coffee a little with the forceful action. The liquid had cooled significantly, but he set his mug on the little rustic table between them and shook the moisture from his fingers. "No, Ms. Ransome. You're off base there. A country music star has always been Abby's dream. That child has been singing her whole life, even back before she could walk. I'd hear her in her crib at night, cooing and jabbering, lullabying herself back to sleep. You know how little boys can turn just about anything into a gun? Well, my Abby turned just about everything into a microphone. By the time she was in school, she was telling everyone she knew that she wanted a guitar for her birthday. She'd never played on in her life, but that was all she wanted."

"She sounds like a very determined little girl," Charlotte interjected. "My kinda girl."

Jed nodded. "Very determined. She never wanted to do anything else, either. It's always been music, Charlotte. Always."

Charlotte smiled tenderly. "I understand. I've heard her, too. I can't imagine why she'd want to do anything else but sing and play that guitar of hers."

Jed waited. So did she agree with him or not?

"That's not really what I'm asking, though." She frowned down into her empty cup before speaking again. "Is it possible that her goal isn't to become a country music star, but to please you? To make you proud? Just like all her other sisters have done?"

"Wait a minute." Jed held both hands up in front of him, palms out. "I'm having a hard time trying to connect the dots here. The last time I saw my daughter two months ago, she had just finished up playing the stage at one of the most popular Nashville clubs." He sat forward in his rocking chair and gripped the armrests with both hands. "She and her band got two standing ovations that night. Two, Ms. Ransome. From what her manager tells me, that's not very common. A year with that Sounder fellow, too. Also not common. She did all that on her own, not for me. Not because

I pushed her into it. In fact, she dropped the Sounder thing on me out of the blue, and believe me when I tell you that I had to all but swallow my tongue when she did. Some big music man wanted to take my little girl on the road with him? What father in his right mind would think that's a good idea?"

Charlotte just watched him as he railed. In some ways, it felt good to spill all of this out unfiltered. But it wasn't something he was accustomed to doing, and he couldn't help wondering what she must think of him. But, of course, Charlotte remained silent now.

"But I smiled and nodded and gave her my blessing. Why?" He didn't wait for her to answer. "Because I knew it was something she'd always dreamed of doing. I knew it was a wish come true for her. I knew that Sounder fellow could help her pursue her dreams in ways I never could." He swallowed hard and added, "It hurt like hot coals in my gut to hand over my position as her caretaker to some Nashville bigwig, Ms. Ransome. But I did it. For her. Not for me."

She still took her sweet time in responding, but finally, Charlotte stuck out her foot and poked him in the knee with her bare toes. "I'm sorry. That must have been incredibly painful for you."

A lump the size of a summer tomato rose in his throat, and Jed had to swallow hard just to breathe. "She's my baby girl, Charlotte," he said, as if that explained everything. "And the last time I saw her, she was doing just fine. She was making it happen. She was living her adventure in a big, big way." Frustration spurred him up out of his seat and he crossed to the porch rail and leaned his hips against it, unable to sit any longer. "So what is she doing back here in the hollow, hiding out in Cass Whitehouse's kitchen, necking with that Nesbit kid at five o'clock in the morning?"

Charlotte chuckled at his summary of things. "Which part bothers you most? That she's here in the hollow hiding out, or that she's here in the hollow playing kissy-face with 'that Nesbit kid'?" she asked, making air quotes around the last three words.

"This isn't a joking matter," Jed scoffed. "And the part that bothers me most is the lying part. The secrets. The misleading and omissions. Why on God's green earth wouldn't she just tell me if something was wrong?

Because something must be wrong for her to be here, lying about it. But what did she think I'd do? Send her to her room?"

"Maybe she thought you'd be disappointed in her for not succeeding at something she loves and is supposed to be so good at." She held up her hands and started listing things one finger at a time. "I mean, there's Faith and ranching. From what I hear, she single-handedly saved Seven Virtues from the brink of disaster when she was still just a kid herself. Younger than Abby is now, right? Success—check. Doctor Hope and her animal hospital. Success—check. Charity and her catering business, and now the bed-and-breakfast, too? Success—check. Courage and Justice, trick riding stars, and now a school with a two-year waiting list. Prudence and her education center. Do you see where I'm going with this?" She paused and studied him, her fingers still up in the air.

Jed frowned, narrowing his eyes at her wiggling fingers. Could it be that simple?

"And think about this," Charlotte said. "Here you are all nestled into your bachelor pad, all your girls grown and flown the coop." She slapped her hands together like she was dusting off the dirt of a long, dusty trail ride. "Your job is done where they're concerned."

"Well, I wouldn't go that far," he countered, frowning contemplatively. "My daughters know they can come to me anytime, for anything. They know I'm here for them." Even as he said the words, he realized he had no confidence that they were true.

"Do they, though?" Charlotte prodded, none too gently, either. "And are you?"

"Am I what?" He felt himself bristling, not caring for her straightforward assessment. Even though he'd asked for it.

Charlotte made a sound that might have been a chuckle, but a very sarcastic one. "Are you here for them? Do you want them here in your home?" She waved at the porch, their two rockers, then pointed at the front door of the log house. "You have two chairs out here. Two chairs at your kitchen table. And your recliner and a brand new loveseat in there. A couch for only two, my friend. And correct me if I'm wrong, but I have a gut feeling that you bought that sofa and the bedroom furniture in the guestroom because I insisted on coming."

"The bedroom furniture isn't new," Jed stated defensively.

Charlotte raised her brows. "When did you get it?"

"I got it from Charity, if you must know. Stuff she was getting rid of up at Whispering Hills when they did the bed-and-breakfast remodel."

"Okay, but when? When did you bring it over here and set it up?" Charlotte pushed.

"What are you getting at, woman?" Jed snapped, his temper getting the best of him. Her challenging expression didn't change, but there was a flicker of something in her eyes that made him feel about two inches tall. Censure? Disappointment? "Sorry. That was uncalled for."

"Forgiven," she said with a kind smile. "I know I can rub folks the wrong way." She leaned forward, planting her bare feet squarely on the floor, her eyes never leaving his face. "But Jedediah, think about it from Abby's perspective. Clearly, as you say, something has gone wrong in Nashville, right? And your daughter comes running home with her tail between her legs, except that home is no longer home. It's now not one, but two schools full of strangers coming and going on her old stomping grounds. Her bedroom has been taken over, and her daddy—the heart of the home—has moved on to newer pastures. Literally."

Jed didn't like what he was hearing, that was for certain, but it was starting to sink in, to make sense.

"I'm only guessing, Jed, but if I had a dollar on me, I'd bet that she didn't come to you because one, she didn't want to disappoint you, and two, because she didn't want to mess up your new manly-man man cave here." She made a sweeping gesture to encompass the house, the barns, and the rest of the property. "I think she probably feels a little like she has no home left to come back to."

Jed sighed deeply, then returned to the rocking chair and dropped into it. "So what do I do now?" He wanted to be done talking about it. He needed an action plan. Something to *do*.

THIRTY-SEVEN

MIKE WAS ON HIS feet, too, but he stayed on his side of the counter. "Sorry, Abs. That was too far, I know." His words were still laced with pain, but his eyes had softened and she could tell his apology was sincere. "Don't go. I was out of line."

Abby shook her head, but remained standing, like she still wasn't sure if she was going to stay or flee. She hugged herself, her arms crossed like a shield, her fists clenched tightly at her ribs. She still held her crumpled napkin in one hand. "It's okay," she muttered. "I deserve it."

"No, you don't." Mike reached for her plate, stacked it on his, and put them in the sink behind him. He ran some hot water over the sticky dishes, but left them there to circle the counter so there was no longer that barrier between them.

Abby felt too vulnerable, and she took a step back, darting a glance over her shoulder to judge the distance between her and the front door.

Mike clearly sensed her unease, and he leaned his hip against the counter, bracing his hands on either side of him. She could tell he was doing his best to remain calm, to act like this conversation wasn't tearing them both up, but she knew him better than that. His knuckles were white from gripping the edge of the counter, and the muscles of his jaw twitched as he said, "It's obvious that things didn't go quite the way you'd planned," he began.

"Understatement of the decade," Abby interrupted.

Mike gave her a sympathetic half-smile. "Because you're here and not there."

"Amazing powers of deduction, Mr. Nesbit." She rolled her eyes and took another step back. She should just go. This wasn't doing either of them any good.

"Which means that you're already beating yourself up pretty badly. Probably worse than anyone else would, if I know you. And I like to think that I do know you, Abby."

"People change, Mike," Abby murmured, unable to hold his gaze. Hadn't she just been priding herself on knowing him well enough to be able to read him? Why wouldn't the same go for him? "Stuff happens and people change," she insisted, not sure which of them she was trying to convince.

He paused, as if considering the notion, then countered, "You can't have changed that much since you left town."

Geez. Hadn't Cass said something pretty similar? *But I have changed,* she wanted to argue. *I'm not the hometown hopeful I was back then.*

"Regardless, you don't need me beating you up, too." Mike fell silent until she looked over at him. "Besides," he added, the corners of his mouth turning up again. "You still have to face your dad with this. I'm sure whatever he doles out will leave marks."

If they'd been sitting at a table, Abby would have kicked him in the shins. Instead, she threw her napkin at him, and just like Cass, he caught it midair. She was going to have to stop throwing things at people; it never worked out the way she planned, either. "Yeah, now that's one conversation I'm not looking forward to."

Mike's brows drew together like he was pondering something he couldn't parcel out. Finally, he asked, "Why didn't you tell him, Abs? Why hide out in the first place? You don't think he'd understand all of this?"

Abby's shoulders drooped, and suddenly she was overwhelmed by exhaustion. "Don't you get it, Mike?" she asked plaintively. "I didn't just leave a path of destruction behind me in Nashville. I've let my family down, I've let my friends down. I've let my whole hometown down. I couldn't bear it, facing everyone after the mess I've made of things."

Mike was shaking his head, a confused look on his face. "Wait. Hold up. I may not be the sharpest tool in the shed, Abs, but in what way have you let everyone in this whole town down? Isn't that a little dramatic?"

"No!" she declared, a little louder than she'd intended. She forced herself to remain calm. "No, Mike, you don't understand. Either that, or you just don't remember."

He studied her like he wanted to contradict her, but he kept his mouth closed and just waited for her to continue.

"This town? The people here who know me, or at least know who I am? I couldn't have gone to Nashville without their help, Mike. Remington Sounder—whom I have also let down, by the way. After all that he did for me to get me launched out there? I'll never be able to face that man again." She rubbed a hand over her eyes before continuing. "He didn't give me a free ride, you know. I had to come armed with more than just my voice and my guitar. I had to come with funds of my own, funds I didn't have. Funds I wasn't about to ask my daddy for, either. That man has sacrificed enough for all of us girls."

"I was here. I remember all of this. That was back when you and I were still... talking."

"Then why are you asking? All those fund raisers? The garage sales and car washes? The money jars on every check-out counter in town? Even Pastor Treadwell took up that love offering for me; don't forget that."

Mike was nodding along with each item she listed.

She scowled at him. "And yet, you still have that condescending look on your face."

Mike furrowed his brow and said, "So let me get this straight. You are hiding out in Cass's kitchen, not telling anyone, including your dad and sisters, who all love you and think you're still singing on some stage in Nashville. At least up until yesterday when Pete Tell-All Zellar squealed on you, that is. You're hiding out because you're too embarrassed to tell people things went south on you in country music stardom?"

She couldn't quite read his expression now. Was he angry? Appalled? "I'm not just embarrassed, Mike," she corrected. "I'm ashamed. I owe everyone so much money. They believed in me, they supported me financially. This town paid my way into Nashville, and how to I thank them? By running back here with my tail between my legs, having drunk the country music stardom Kool-aid, as you so aptly put it. Penniless, reputation shot to hell, and my dreams nothing but a shredded tangle of trash in the gutter. I've let everyone down, and I have no one to blame but myself."

"And Remington Sounder. And your agent. And your bass player. And your guitar player." He was nice enough not to call Bucky any names, although Abby didn't miss the tension in his jaw as he included him on the list.

"All of them, yes," she said, nodding vehemently. "I've let them all down."

But Mike held up a hand to stop her. "That's not what I meant. You are not an island, Abby, no matter how much you try to convince yourself—and those around you—of it. You aren't the savior of all of humankind, or even of Nashville, and not even your band. You didn't get to where you are all on your own—you even said so, yourself, right?" He didn't wait for her answer. "You can take the blame for your part in things, but that's just it. Your part. All those other people had roles in the way things have played out, too. And I'm sure that's just scraping the top of the pile." He made a vague gesture in the general direction of Nashville. "And isn't a lot of this just the nature of this industry? I mean, sometimes thing just happen beyond your control, don't they?"

Abby wanted to argue, she wanted to bear the burden of the troubles that had befallen her. She did feel responsible for all the people she'd let down.

"Think about it. You didn't intentionally go out and spend all that money on fancy shoes and new guitars, right? You didn't squander it away on booze and boys, did you?"

Her cheeks grew warm at the inadvertent mention of her relationship with Jack Daniels and she ducked her head, hoping he hadn't noticed.

"You have a great album, one that seems to be selling well—"

"One that I make only a pittance in royalties on." She sounded like the spoiled little girl Cass had accused her of being.

"You poor thing." Apparently, Mike thought so, too. "People all over the country, maybe all over the world, are learning your name—"

"Oh, please," she muttered.

"Will you stop interrupting me?" He was beginning to sound impatient, and she really didn't blame him.

"Sorry."

"You still have your voice. And Blossom, too, right? Didn't I see her in the passenger seat of your truck at Thrifty's?"

Abby nodded, pleased that he not only remembered her guitar's name, but that he actually used it.

"And you can still write songs." It wasn't a question. "I heard you that first morning at Serendipity's. You were singing too loud to hear me, but I heard you."

Abby lowered her gaze. He was starting to sound like Cass now, pointing out the good things in her life.

"You know, it seems to me that you, Abby, are the one with the memory problem, not me. Don't you remember the hours and hours we spent together with you writing songs while I stocked shelves in the back rooms downstairs? Or you writing songs while I worked on my car? And your truck? Side note: Please tell me you have changed the oil in that thing since the last time I did it for you."

"I have. I mean, I paid someone to do it for me, but yes, it's been changed," she said defensively. Granted, her father had to remind her three or four times before she finally did it.

"Good." Mike went back to the previous topic. "How about the hours we spent together on the lawn mower? No, wait." He held up a finger and shook his head. "That was me on the lawn mower, and you, sitting in the shade writing songs."

"You couldn't hear me while you were mowing the lawn," she argued.

"Maybe not, but I could still tell what you were doing."

"Fine," she said with a huff. "Yes. Yes, to all of the above. I still have those things. But I have no band. I have no stage. My reputation is still shot to hell, and I don't have enough pride left to hitch up my suspenders and figure out how to face everyone. So I'm hiding." She grimaced, recalling the look of disappointment on her father's face. "Or, I was. Until today."

"Maybe that's your problem, Abs."

She frowned at him, not sure what he meant.

"Maybe your problem is that you've got too much pride left. Maybe it's your pride that's keeping you from coming clean with everyone. You say you've let everyone down, but maybe, just maybe, do you think you're really just upset at letting yourself down? That you thought you were better than this?"

"Stop," Abby said, holding up both hands. Now he *really* sounded like Cass. She didn't need this from him. She'd come over for breakfast, not for a lecture. "No. You don't understand, Mike." She fought the surge of tears that wanted to well up and spill over. She crossed the room, scooped up her purse and keys off the floor, and pushed open the door.

But she found that she couldn't just leave. She hated the way things always got so messy between them. She wanted him to understand the position she was in, but just like in the past, Mike simply didn't get it. She took a deep breath of the already muggy morning outside Mike's air-conditioned apartment, eying her truck and the escape so close at hand. But she stopped and turned to face him, desperate for him to see her perspective. "You don't know the pressure I live under day in and day out. Look at my sisters, Mike. Every one of them has turned out perfect. They all have frighteningly handsome husbands, the most beautiful and amazing children, fantastic jobs that will provide financial security for generations to come, and they all look after Daddy like he's Plumwood Hollow royalty. Then here I am, the baby of the family. The dreamer. The girl with her head in the clouds. The one everyone indulges, pats, and coddles."

Mike's response was *not* what she'd been expecting. "Wow. Your life sucks. Must be rough to have a family like yours. To have all those opportunities handed to you."

Abby sputtered wordlessly at his cruel sarcasm. She'd had enough. She pushed the door wider and started through it, but her purse strap caught on the doorknob and jerked her backward. Mortified and seething, she wrestled with the stupid thing for far too long. That would teach her to use a purse. She missed her backpack.

Mike took advantage of her momentary stay. "I mean, a whole town, Abs?" He was goading her, and when she dared to scowl over her shoulder at him, he was standing there in the middle of his little living room, feet braced apart, arms crossed. Apparently, he'd had just about enough, too. "It's pretty bad when you have a whole town rooting for you. To have so many people who love you and believe in you? What on earth do you have to feel sorry for yourself about, huh? You're right, it seems. You have changed. You never used to sing this sad country tune about how rotten your life is."

"Oh, yeah?" Abby shot back, all the emotional turmoil inside her boiling up. "Well, the song goes from bad to worse. Let me read you the lyrics." She held her arms out at her sides, as if daring him to size her up. Her voice rose in frustration and hurt. "Here she is, Abstinence Eve Goodacre, the youngest of Jedediah Goodacre's seven—count 'em, folks—*seven* motherless daughters. Ain't she a peach?" She lifted a finger to her lips and said, "Shhhh. We're not going to discuss it in front of her, y'all, but do you know why Jedediah Goodacre named his daughter Abstinence? I'll tell you why. Because he felt guilty for knocking up his invalid wife to try yet again to have that elusive son to carry on the Goodacre name. Not only did he get another girl—number seven, I'm telling you—but birthing that little thing is what killed her mama."

The words came out like vomit, and the moment they were out, Abby wanted to get out the bleach and scour them out of existence. Where was it all coming from? She'd never admitted these things to anyone before, not even out loud to herself. She loved her father more than life itself, so why was she so intent on raging against him? Now that she'd started, though, she couldn't seem to hold back the rest of the torrent.

"Abstinence. What kind of dad names his daughter Abstinence, Mike?" She wasn't asking for an answer; she had one of her own already spewing out. "I'll tell you. The kind of dad who labels his daughter as—" Her voice broke, but she sucked in another lungful of air and forced the words out. "As his deepest regret. Not only was I not a boy," she railed, squeezing the door handle so tightly she thought she might break it off. "But I lived." She said each word emphatically, scathingly. "I lived when his beloved wife didn't, and for the last twenty years, I have been nothing but a glaring reminder of his deepest regret. Abstinence. If only he'd practiced abstinence, then I wouldn't be here and *she* would. So excuse me if I worry about being a disappointment to people, okay?" Abby swiped angrily at the hot tears that had dared to break free and were now streaming down her cheeks. She took a deep breath and let out an angry, dry laugh. "You want to know the best part about all of this? I don't even have a home to come back to, now that Daddy's tossed me out of the nest and flown the coop himself. So I'm stuck sleeping on Cass's dead mom's bed. How about them apples, huh, Mike?"

"Ah, Abs," Mike began, his voice rough, but not with anger now. The look on his face was one of shock and misery, regret.

Abby wanted nothing to do with anymore regret from anyone. She lifted her chin and glared at him through her tears. "Go ahead. Mock me now, Mike. Kick me while I'm down. You can't hurt me any worse than he has."

THIRTY-EIGHT

"DID ABBY SAY WHEN she would come talk to you?" Charlotte finally asked.

Jed shook his head. "I screwed that up, too. She offered to come over this evening and I told her I had plans. She also said she could come over tomorrow after church, but that's our family dinnertime." He sighed wearily. "I basically told her I had too much going on in my life to make time for her, didn't I?"

Charlotte nodded slowly. "Seems so."

He dropped his head in his hands, his elbows on his knees. "You'd think after more than thirty years of being a father, I'd be a whole lot better at it than this."

She reached over and laid a hand on his shoulder. "Why don't you go back? Now. Go find her and tell her you want to talk to her right now."

He didn't lift his head. "But what about Gallup's place? Aren't we going over there this morning?"

Charlotte snorted dismissively. "I'm a big girl, Jedediah Goodacre, and your daughter needs you a lot worse than I do right now. Besides, I'm not going back there this morning."

He straightened in his chair and looked over at her. "You're not?"

She smiled at him, her eyes twinkling, like she had a secret she was just bursting to tell. "Nope. And do you know why not?"

Instead of answering, he just cocked one no-longer-bushy-old-man eyebrow at her.

"Because I have already found the perfect place for me and my sheep. The place I want to call home."

"You have?" A wave of something new and unsettling washed over him. She'd found a place... without his help? Without his feedback? His stamp of approval? "Where—when did you find it? If not the Gallup's, then...?" He left the question unfinished when he saw the look on her face.

Charlotte beamed as she said, "It came to me yesterday while talking to Sarah. I was telling her how hard I've looked for the last—what is it now? Eight months? Nine? How many different places have you and I gone to look at since last fall? And that doesn't include the first few I went to on my own, either."

Jed held his breath. Why did she have to talk so much? Couldn't she cut to the chase and tell him the important details? The most important detail of them all being *where.*

"I told her how much I love your wonderful place—*this* wonderful place—and that none of the properties we looked at felt like this one does. Like home to me."

He stiffened, her words suddenly making a different kind of sense to him. "You—you want *my* place?" Jed stared at her like she'd grown a second head. "But I'm not selling. It's not for sale."

Charlotte's smile didn't even falter. "I know," she said, nodding. "I'm not asking you to sell me your place. I realized yesterday as Sarah and I were talking, that you, Jedediah Goodacre, are a big part of the reason this place feels like home to me.."

He reared back in his chair, his eyes widening at her inference. "Well, you can't just move in here with me," he blustered. "I know I let you stay here this last week, against my better judgment, mind you, but I'm not looking for a roommate. Or a housemate, or whatever they call it." He shook his head vehemently. "Besides, as you just said a minute ago, I need to make a place for my daughters in my new life—at least my youngest one, who is now apparently homeless—a place she can still call home. And that would be in my guestroom. Where you're sleeping now."

Charlotte shrugged one shoulder. The grin on her face had turned almost mischievous, the sparkle in her eyes leading him to believe that she was goading him. "I wouldn't want to stay in the guest room if I moved in here, you know."

Jed rose so quickly, the rocker scooted backward to knock against the wall behind them. "What are you proposing, Ms. Ransome? What kind of man do you take me for?"

Charlotte laughed. She *laughed*. That rich, throaty sound rolled out of her like he'd just said the funniest thing in the world. "I'm not propositioning you, okay?" she insisted, a hand pressed to her chest.

She gestured for him to sit back down, and after a ferocious internal debate, Jed lowered himself to the edge of the rocking chair again.

"I know exactly what kind of man you are, my friend. A respectable, upright, honorable, honest, hardworking, passionate—"

Jed held up a hand to halt her flow of words. "Please get to the part where you tell me what designs you have on my property."

Charlotte pushed up out of her own chair, set her empty cup on the little table beside his, then moved to stand right in front of him. No, not stand. She lowered lithely to her knees right in front of him and reached for both his hands. "It's not really your property I have designs on, you must know. It's you, Jed, that my heart is set on. Although the package deal is pretty sweet."

"What—what are you doing?" His gaze darted back and forth between their clasped hands, the large, shiny rings on almost every one of her fingers, the single gold band on his wedding ring finger, and then at her sincere expression.

"I'm not propositioning you, my friend. I'm proposing to you. Marry me, Jedediah Goodacre. Let's share the rest of our lives together. You and me—and Abby, of course, for as long as she needs us—here in this place that we can both call home."

Jed gaped at her, not certain that he'd heard her correctly. But there she was, on bended knee, his hands in hers, saying the words that were coming out of her mouth. There was nothing wrong with his ears.

"Marry me," she repeated, this time more earnestly. "Be my husband. Let me be your wife."

"Stop!" he demanded, his mind scrambling to make sense of it all. "Hold up, now, you hear? This is not the way these things are done." He pulled free of her hands and gripped the arms of the chair so hard he thought his fingers would cramp.

Charlotte sat back on her heels. "I didn't know there were rules when it came to love."

"Love? Love?" he sputtered. "Who said anything about love?"

A flicker of hurt flashed in her eyes, but she squared her shoulders and lifted her chin a little higher. "I'm saying it. I love you, Jedediah Goodacre." She reached out and rested her hand on his knee. He flinched under her touch, but she continued speaking as if she hadn't noticed his response. "I think I have loved you from the first moment I saw your scowling face at Justice and Courage's wedding."

"That's not possible," he muttered, at a complete loss as to how to proceed.

"And I think you might just feel the same way about me."

"Wait. Wait just a minute." Jed pushed the chair back again, not caring that it bumped loudly against the wall. He needed to put some distance between them. He needed to think clearly, and he couldn't do that with her so close. On her knees, no less. "Is this some kind of game?" he asked, his tone harsh. Because he was starting to put two and two together, and he wasn't liking the way things were adding up. "Was this your plan all along, Ms. Ransome? To come out here, waste my time looking at properties you knew you'd never buy because you've had your heart set on this one—mine—all along?" It sounded ridiculous even as he said it, but what other explanation was there?

"No," Charlotte insisted, shaking her head slowly. "Jed, no. That's not the way it is."

"Then what is it? Did you and Sarah cook up this scheme together? I suppose you've spent the last week here sizing things up, taking stock of what I have, of what could be yours, hm?" Why were all the women in his life so deceptive? Manipulative. Secretive. Even his friend, Sarah Lynxwilder. It made his chest ache.

The flicker of hurt became a dark shadow of pain. "I am not taking stock, Jed, and I'm not playing any kind of game with you. What kind of woman do *you* take *me* for?" she said, echoing his words back to him. She rose slowly, carefully, almost like she was afraid she might break. "I proposed to you. That's all. Plain and simple."

"That's all?" he barked. "Simple? Do you have any idea how big a deal marriage is, how complicated it can be, *Miss* Charlotte?" He cruelly emphasized the Miss. "It's not something to go lightly into."

Charlotte held up both hands in surrender. "I don't need a lecture, Jed. And I don't need you to remind me that I've never been able to find a man willing to take me on. You're just the last one in a long line of them, okay? I get it. Not marriage material here."

"That's not—that's not what I meant," he stammered, ashamed of his condescension toward her.

Charlotte moved to the little table and picked up both coffee cups, then grabbed the blanket that had slipped from her shoulders when she'd moved to kneel in front of Jed. "It's okay," she told him. "I'm sorry I put you in such a difficult position. I honestly thought this would go much differently, and I feel terrible about this whole thing." She turned to look up at him, and her eyes glistened with unshed tears. "I'm going to spend tonight at Sarah's place. I hope you'll understand." And with that, she circled the rocking chairs, brushed past him, and headed inside.

The fragrance of sweet wildflowers and sage lingered in the air behind her. Jed remained frozen in place, listening in vain for her returning footsteps.

He had to get out of there. He couldn't stay while she packed up her belongings and cleared out of his home. He made his way clumsily down the porch steps and climbed back behind the wheel of his truck.

"Time to talk to Abby," he muttered after several moments. "Might as well deal with all the crises at once. How can it possibly get any worse than this?"

He started the engine, not so wrapped up in his thoughts that he couldn't appreciate the low rumble of his truck, and headed back into town to find his daughter. Relieved to find her truck still parked behind Nesbit's Grocery store, he pulled in beside her and got out.

From upstairs, he could hear raised voices. The front door of the apartment overhead was open, and all he heard was Abby's harsh shouting.

At a loss for what to do, he started up the steps, slowly, quietly, not wanting to eavesdrop, but intent on making sure she wasn't in any trouble, either.

When he heard his name—"... the youngest of Jedediah Goodacre's seven—count 'em, folks—*seven* motherless daughters. Ain't she a peach?"—Jed stopped and held his breath. He couldn't recall ever hearing Abby speak in such a bitter snarl before.

It only got worse. "... do you know why Jedediah Goodacre named his daughter Abstinence? I'll tell you why. Because he felt guilty for knocking up his invalid wife to try yet again to have that elusive son to carry on the Goodacre name. Not only did he get yet another girl, but birthing that little thing is what killed her mama."

Jed recoiled like he'd been struck. Is that what his precious baby girl believed? About him? About herself? Did she blame herself for Caroline's death? Had he never taken the time to make sure she didn't take that burden onto her shoulders? How could he have been so remiss?

He didn't know whether to charge up the remaining steps and beg her forgiveness or turn tail and run.

"Abstinence. What kind of dad names his daughter Abstinence?" she demanded, her words bludgeoning him now. "I'll tell you. The kind of dad who labels his daughter as his deepest regret. Not only was I not a boy." Jed heard a sharp, wrenching sob tear out of her. "But I lived. I lived when his beloved wife didn't, and now I am nothing but a reminder of his deepest regret. Abstinence. If only he'd practiced abstinence, then I wouldn't be here and *she* would."

He couldn't stand there and listen for another moment.

How had he failed his child so badly?

But it was what she said next that sucker punched him. "Go ahead. Mock me now, Mike. Kick me while I'm down. You can't hurt me any worse than he has."

Jed's stomach churned and roiled, and he wasn't sure he was going to make it to his truck without being sick. He slid clumsily in behind the wheel and covered his face with his hands. "Oh, Lord Almighty," he murmured, his words muffled against his palms. "Help me. How can I mend her broken heart?"

He needed to go. The door was most likely standing open because Abby had been preparing to leave. She could come down those steps at any moment and find him there. That wouldn't help matters at all. He had to get out of there.

He fumbled the key into the ignition, his hands shaking with the flood of emotions and adrenaline coursing through his system. Just as he was turning out of the back parking lot, he glanced back in his large side-view mirror to see Abby, halfway down the steps, staring after him.

She'd seen him. And surely, she must have guessed that he'd heard her.

THIRTY-NINE

"It's better this way," Abby said to Cass that night at the supper table. Cass had cooked up a pot of aromatic Thai chicken curry served over sticky Jasmine rice. Abby hadn't eaten much all day, not since her breakfast with Mike, and although her stomach was still in knots, she couldn't resist the delicious food her hostess had prepared. Cass wouldn't be meeting Badger at The Smokehouse until later on that night; he wouldn't have a break until ten.

"How is it better?" Cass challenged her gently. "Being at odds with those you love is never a better way."

"But I don't love Mike," Abby insisted.

"I wasn't referring to Mike." Cass studied her with raised eyebrows. "Methinks the lady doth protest too much."

Abby shook her head. "I'm not protesting anything. I'm just stating a fact. I don't love Mike—"

"Except that you do," Cass contradicted. "And he loves you."

"You don't know that," Abby started to say, but Cass cut her off again.

"Actually, I do. I have watched you two grow up together, go from friends to lovers, then lovers to enemies. And honey, it breaks my heart because I can see that it's also broken your hearts, too. What happened between you two?" she asked.

Abby rested her elbows on the table and hunched forward, grimacing. She didn't know if she had the energy to dredge up that memory, but the look in Cass's eyes told her that her friend wasn't going to let the matter drop. "It's a tale as old as time," she began. It may have sounded silly, but it was true. There was nothing new and unusual about their story. "We had two different paths to take, that's all. We were both super supportive of each other's dreams, you know? He was going to go get his business degree and come back to the hollow to take over Nesbits one day, and I was going to Nashville or California, or wherever the music took me. At least, Mike was super supportive until he realized my dreams weren't going to stay dreams, that I was actually going to pursue them." She sighed deeply, the memories still painful. "Right before I left, he asked me to stay here. With him."

"Oh, wow. That's a big ask," Cass acknowledged.

"Yeah. And when I didn't give him the answer he wanted, he got—well, he got a little aggressive. Kinda mean."

Cass leaned forward, clearly shocked and concerned by the revelation. As well, she would be with her history with abusive men. "What does aggressive mean? Did he hurt you?" she asked, reaching across the table to lay her hand over Abby's. "Honey, this is important. I thrust the two of you alone together in the wee hours before morning. I've never had any doubts about Mike's character, but if I did something that endangered you in any way, then I am so sorry. Are you—he hasn't—"

"He hasn't," Abby assured her. "And you're right to trust him. Mike is and always was one of the good guys, as you said. I was just hurt, you know? Betrayed by the guy I loved, one I thought loved me as much as I loved him."

"He didn't assault you or do anything against your wishes," Cass added for clarification.

"No, it wasn't like that." Abby shook her head quickly. "He was just desperate, I guess. He didn't want to take no for an answer because he knew I loved him, and he couldn't understand why that wasn't enough for me." Abby took a sip of her sweet tea before continuing. "He basically gave me an ultimatum, that if I wasn't going to stay with him, then he wasn't going to stick around waiting for me to come crawling back to him."

"Oh, wow," Cass said again, this time in a hushed tone. "Yikes."

"So I told him I understood how he felt, because I did, Cass. Even though I thought I was going to puke all over him, I knew going off on our separate paths was going to be brutal on our relationship. So, I agreed that long-distance relationships were hard, and that maybe it would be best if we just made a clean break. I think he thought I was calling his bluff or something, because he looked at me like I was the one breaking up with him. But he said I was right, that he'd been thinking the same thing, anyway, and that he didn't really want to be with someone who was always going to have one foot out the door."

"Oh, Abby, how dreadful."

"Yeah," she said with a nod, toying with a sliver of red pepper left on her plate. "Then he asked for one last kiss. His exact words were, 'A goodbye kiss. Just one more for the road.' I reluctantly agreed, not because I didn't want to kiss him, mind you. I was just so afraid that if he kissed me, I'd capitulate and stay home after all." Abby pushed her empty plate away and set her fork face down on it. "I think he knew it, too. And it almost worked. One kiss turned into two, then we were getting all hot and heavy. His kisses always were hypnotic, like a drug to me, making me go weak at the knees and all that stupid stuff, and he made sure that was the best kissing we'd ever done. When his hand slid up under my shirt, Cass, I almost surrendered everything. My mouth, my body, my dreams. Almost."

"But you didn't."

"I didn't." It wasn't really a question, but Abby confirmed it anyway. "Although there have been times over the last two years when I wish I had," she said ruefully. "But no, I stopped him when he started unbuttoning my shirt. Looking back, I don't think he had really planned to coerce me that way. I truly believe he didn't think I'd stand my ground about leaving. That's what I mean by saying he was desperate. He was out of options, you know? So, when I pushed him away, it was like the straw that broke the camel's back. The rejection that sealed the deal. He gave it one last college try and went in for one more kiss, but I turned my head away and wouldn't let him. He released me and stepped back, and he didn't try anything else. That night, anyway."

"Not that night..." Cass prodded. "But another night?"

Abby nodded. "Remember the night of my party at the Smokehouse?"

Cass chuckled. "Of course I do. I planned most of it."

"Duh. Right." Abby rolled her eyes. "The shirts were amazing, by the way."

"Some of my best work," Cass said, breathing on her fingertips and rubbing them on her shoulder.

"Yeah, well, that night Mike showed up with another girl. I don't know if you know the family, but her name was Stephanie Bernard. I think she's still in town." Abby hadn't thought to even ask Mike if he was seeing anyone. Was that why he hadn't tried anything yet? Why he hadn't attempted to offer her anymore than a comforting hug or two? Surely, Mike would have said something, though, wouldn't he? "Well, Stephanie'd had a crush on him all through high school, and I can only imagine how thrilled she must have been to finally have his attention."

Cass sat back, her jaw dropped in shock. "Mike Nesbit had the nerve to show up to your goodbye party with another girl on his arm?"

"Yep." Her response was short, clipped. She marveled at how much the memory still hurt. "I could tell he didn't give a fig's fiddle about her; I mean, he hardly paid her any attention all night, which was pretty rotten for her, if you ask me."

"That must have been the case, because I don't remember this stuff happening at all," Cass said with a slow shake of her head. "And I pride myself on being pretty aware of any soap opera shenanigans going on around me. But, Abby, every time I saw him, Mike seemed to have eyes only for you. I figured he was giving you a little extra space so you could mingle. I thought he was being a gentleman and sharing you with the rest of us."

"I know," Abby said. "I think that was his intention. I swear there were times it seemed he forgot he'd brought her. He'd walk away from her, then eventually make his way back to her side. At one point, he bought her a drink and set her up at a table by herself, then he went to the bathroom. When he came back—because, yes, I admit to paying close attention to every move he made that night—he went straight to the pool tables and jumped in a game with a couple of his friends. I swear he completely forgot he'd brought her, because all of a sudden, he spun around and stared over at the table where the poor girl still sat waiting for his return. Then he hurried over and practically dragged her back to the game with him, directing her to a seat closer to them. I felt really bad for her, Cass. He was being so awful to both of us."

"He was trying to make you jealous."

Abby shook her head. "I don't think so. I think he was hurt, and he was trying to make me hurt even worse. Do you remember that song I wrote, 'Friends to Lovers'?"

"I do," Cass told her. "I love that song. Oh!" Her eyes went wide. "It was about Mike?"

"Yes. It was no secret, at least not to him. But that night when I played that song, he led Stephanie over to our corner. You know the one over by the jukebox where that support beam creates a little nook? I think he took her there for the same reason he took me there—so most people wouldn't be able to see what he was up to. Except for me. I had a clear shot of them, and he had a clear shot of me."

"Oh no," Cass murmured. "I think I already know where this is going."

"The last line of the last chorus is, '*And we'll seal our forever with a kiss.*' I knew what he was going to do, so I closed my eyes as I sang those words. I didn't see it actually happen, but when I opened my eyes, I could tell by the look on Stephanie's face that she'd gotten one of Mike Nesbit's heavenly kisses. I swear she had stars in her eyes. And Mike." She swallowed hard. "He wouldn't meet my eyes after that. Knowing him, I think he probably felt ashamed of what he was doing. But back then, it was just another kick to my already battered and bruised heart. That was pretty much the last interaction we'd had until last week when he showed up at Serendipity's and scared the living daylights out of me."

"Has he kissed you since you've been home?"

"What? No!" Abby frowned. "We can't stop arguing long enough to even think about that."

"Love and hate are typically two sides of the same coin, as they say," she singsonged. "I have a feeling kissing you is something Mike has given a whole lot of thought to. And I daresay the same goes for you, too, if that blush is any indication." Cass wagged a finger at Abby and chortled.

"But none of that really matters," Abby countered. "That's what I meant when I said it's better this way. Nothing's changed about our circumstances, Cass. I'm not going to stay in the hollow, and he's not going to leave the hollow, so there's no reason for us to be any more than just friends."

"But what if—"

Abby cut her off. "It's not going to happen, okay? I have to figure out what I'm going to do now. How I'm going to get back on the horse and ride out of town again. My two weeks is up in another day or two, right?"

"And your dad?"

"My dad." Abby deflated in her seat and let out a long sigh. "My poor dad. I've tried calling him several times today, but he isn't answering. He told me this morning that I couldn't come over to talk to him this evening because he had plans. Or tomorrow after church. So I suppose he's doing whatever those plans are. I left two voice messages and one text. I'm just praying he can forgive me so we can talk. I'm the worst daughter ever, Cass."

Cass took several long moments to respond. "You know, Abby, your delivery might not have been ideal, but your complaints are legitimate. I mean, sure, you could have gone to your daddy and had a nice, cozy conversation about how much pressure you're under being seventh in line of near-perfect girls who get all the good men..." she said in mock disgust, but Abby knew there was some truth behind the words. Cass had carried a torch for Joe Lynxwilder for years, only to have Courage steal his heart. "And I can totally see that having a name like Abstinence can't have been easy, especially growing up," she continued. "Naming you that was a risky move, but not on his part. It was all your risk, wasn't it?"

Abby shrugged one shoulder. "I never really minded my name, and now it's grown on me, and I like it. It's unique, and it's easy to remember, so it actually works to my advantage." She furrowed her brow and tried to put into words what had been going through her mind since spilling her guts with Mike that morning. "What's always bothered me is the fact that no one wants to talk about why I ended up with it. So, of course, I've harbored a lot of my own assumptions about it. I mean, sometimes I can even convince myself that all of this—Mom dying, Dad hating me—"

"Don't say such things. Your daddy does *not* hate you," Cass reprimanded.

"I know that in here," Abby said, tapping her temple. "But there are times when I'm ready to believe otherwise. Which proves my point. Because I don't know the whole truth, I fill it in with my emotional imaginings, and that's—I don't know—dangerous, you know? Destructive."

"You bet it is," Cass agreed. "It's time for you and your people to start talking; you know that, right? And it might have to start with you, girlie."

"Meaning?"

"You need to go see your daddy."

"But when? He said he had plans for the next two days."

"Right now," Cass declared. "Get in that little truck of yours and scoot on out to his place. His social plans—I think Charlotte Ransome is back in town and staying with him this week—are not more—"

"Wait. Hold up. What?" Abby sat straight in her chair and held both hands out in a stop gesture in front of her. "Did you just say Charlotte Ransome is staying with my dad? In his new place?"

Cass's eyes grew wide, and she made an O with her mouth. "That's right," she exclaimed. "You wouldn't know about it."

"Uh, yeah," Abby said sarcastically. "But you'd think *someone* would have thought to mention such a thing to me before now. How long has this been going on? And you're sure this is my father we're talking about?"

Cass chuckled and shimmied her shoulders like an excited little girl. "I know, right? They've got the whole town a-buzz-buzz-buzzing with speculation. Jedediah Goodacre shacking up with an out-of-towner." Cass winked at Abby. "No one really believes there's any hanky-panky going on, of course. I mean, it's your father. There's not a more upstanding man this side of the Ohio River, but that's what makes it such juicy gossip."

"I still can't believe it. You're absolutely sure?"

"Oh, yes, I'm sure. I heard it from the horse's mouth. Not that I'm calling Charlotte Ransome a horse, or anything. Although she does have that long nose and all that silver mane of hair—"

"Charlotte!" Abby interrupted. "Let's not get off track here."

"Sorry. Right. Anyway, Charlotte and Sarah Lynxwilder stopped in at Serendipity's yesterday afternoon for a cup of coffee and some shopping fuel, as they called it. I overheard them talking about how the week was going. She's in town looking for property—still hasn't found the perfect one, I guess. So your dad's been going to different places with her since he knows this area like the back of his hand."

"And you just happened to overhear all of this?" Abby narrowed her eyes at Cass.

"Fine. I *may* have found a section of the wall that needed some major scrubbing, okay? And it just happened to be close enough to their table for me to be able to hear some of what they were saying." She lifted her hands in a gesture of innocence. "Anyway, Charlotte went on and on about how wonderful Jed's place is, and that she really wanted one just like his. I didn't hear Sarah's response, but the two of them started giggling like teenagers, their heads bent together and whispering away."

"I'm still having a hard time imagining all of this is going on. My dad and Charlotte Ransome?" She furrowed her brow in thought. "You know, she did kinda get him worked up a few times back at the twins' wedding. I wondered if there'd been a spark there, but I'd forgotten about it. Hmm."

"Oh, there's definitely a spark there," Cass declared. "It's snap, crackle, pop between them every time they're together. She's been out to Plumwood Hollow several times since the wedding, you know. The two of them act like they just get on each other's nerves, but if you ask me, that's their version of a courtship."

"Oh, wow." She sounded like Cass now, but the idea of her father dating again, and someone like the independent fireball of a woman that was Charlotte Ransome, was a bit mind-blowing at the moment. "I mean, go, Daddy, but wow."

"Right?" Cass asked again.

"The manscaping!" Abby exclaimed, smacking her hand on the table hard enough to make the silverware jangle. "I noticed his haircut—that hasn't changed in forever—but he'd definitely done something to his eyebrows."

"A sure sign of true love," Cass gushed, pressing her hands together in suppressed glee. "He wanted to look good for his lady friend."

"Wow-wow-wow," Abby breathed.

Cass cleared her throat dramatically and drew out her next word. "Anyway..., what I was starting to say before I was so rudely interrupted," she teased, "was that your father's social plans should not be more important than his relationship with you, so don't let what he said push you away. He was just hurt by the deception, I'm sure, and caught by surprise."

"Not to mention the cray-cray he overheard me yelling about him at Mike's place when he came back. I have a feeling he'd come back to talk to me, after all. Then when he heard all those awful things I said about him, he split."

"Again, only because he got caught by surprise. Give the man a little space to find his dignity again, girlie. He's just been handed his dad-card on a silver platter by his baby girl." She reached over and squeezed Abby's hand again. "In the meantime, you need to start believing in yourself again, honey. You need to start believing that you're worth it, you're worth him setting aside his stuff so that you two can patch things up. And not just with a bandage, mind you. Get out the scalpels and start carving away at all the bad stuff until you get to the bottom of things."

"I don't know," Abby waffled.

"Fine. I'll do the knowing for you. Go see your father. It's an order." Cass rose and started gathering the dishes. When Abby stood up to help, Cass tut-tutted her. "Nope. I got this." Then she grew serious when Abby sank back into her chair, still undecided. "I mean it, Abby. I want you to go talk to Jed tonight. It's past time. You two need to set things right between you; you can't move on to your next adventure until you do. And besides, I have an ulterior motive for making you do it, too."

Abby frowned at her. "What does that mean? What's your ulterior motive?"

"Remember that plan I told you I was working on?"

Abby had forgotten all about it. "Yes." She drew the word out with great trepidation.

"How would you like to a do a Friday night at the Smokehouse next week? Badger just gave me the thumbs up on it this afternoon, and I wanted to tell you about it tonight."

Abby shook her head as panic rose up in her at the thought of getting on a stage again. And not just any stage, but her hometown stage, where everyone would want to know how things were going in Nashville. "No. I—I can't do that."

"Yes, you can. And do you remember why I started working on that plan?"

"No one knows why you do the things you do," Abby retorted, but she was just giving her friend a hard time to deflect the question a little longer. Of course, she remembered.

"You wanted a way to come clean to all these people you've let down, right?"

She didn't let Abby respond, but that was probably a good thing, because her heart was racing at just the thought of having to face all the people in this town who'd sent her off with such fanfare.

"Well, *I*..." she said emphatically, pressing a hand to her chest. "I wanted a way for you to see that you haven't let anyone down, that they're all still rooting for you. That people in this town want to help their own, through thick and thin, Abby. I know this personally."

Abby met her eyes. "Mike told me about you and Serendipity's and what that guy did to you."

"I hope he told you what this town did for me, too," she said sagely. "Without the good people of Plumwood Hollow, I may not be alive today, and certainly, Serendipity's wouldn't be around. And I hope he told you that his family—" Cass broke off, and she swallowed audibly, her eyes glistening with emotion. She started again. "I hope he told you how much his family, in particular, did to help me. His parents gave me a month's worth of supplies at no charge and Mike came to work for me for free. He wouldn't take a penny from me, Abby. I found out later that his dad was giving him a paycheck, and when I tried to settle that debt, Mr. Nesbit wouldn't hear of it."

Abby nodded. "Mike told me."

"By the way, Mike was willing to do the work for free. His dad only started paying after he found out his kid was getting up before school to come help me out."

"I know. He's one of the good guys. He always has been."

"So are you, Abby. Do you know that? You are one of the good guys, too. And forgive me for beating a dead horse here." She held up a hand to stop Abby from interrupting. "Just hear me out, okay? I think you and Mike need to see this through to the other side. You two belong on the same team in whatever capacity you can manage; I believe that with every fiber of my being. You don't have to be married with kids in a small town to prove that you love each other. People do what you do, honey. They go on the road for days, weeks, sometimes months. Not just musicians, either. Truckers, traveling health care providers, fight attendants and pilots, just to name a few. Do you think none of those people have loved ones waiting for them back home?"

"I know what you're saying," Abby cut in when Cass paused to take a breath. "I'm not arguing with you. I'd be okay with that; honestly, I would. In fact, back when we were dating, that's where I thought we would end up. With me traveling around with my music, and Mike keeping the home fires burning. I didn't love the idea, but I loved Mike, and if that was the only way to make it work, then I thought it was worth it to both of us. Boy, was I delusional. Because it was Mike who couldn't accept it." She toyed with the hem of her t-shirt, tugging on a loose string until it snapped off. "And I respect that, Cass. He deserves to be loved the way he wants. Someone who will always be there waiting for him at the end of the day. He wants someone he can take care of the way his father has taken care of his mother."

"Did he say that to you?"

"In so many words. He always tells me how much he looks up to his parents and their marriage, that he wants what they have."

"Well, what they have is pretty amazing."

"I know!" Abby declared, a little louder than she'd intended. "I know that, Cass. But it doesn't change the fact that I want something different. I don't want to the demure little wife keeping house and playing with the kids and cooking big family meals for Sunday dinner." She made a dismissive sound. "Not that there's anything wrong with that. It's a calling for some people, but not for me, just like my music is a calling for me, but it's not for others." She sighed loudly. "I would love to be loved as much as Mike's dad loves Mike's mom; don't get me wrong. Just not in the same way."

"And you're sure that's not also what Mike wants?"

Abby shook her head in frustration. "Cass, please. Can we not talk about this anymore? I honestly don't know what Mike wants these days, but I can tell you this. He doesn't want anything to do with me right now. So again, please, let the whole Mike thing go for now, okay?"

"Okay," Cass said, obviously biting her tongue to keep from saying what was on her mind. "So what about The Smokehouse?"

"You are relentless," Abby groaned.

"Is that a yes?" Cass asked brightly, ignoring Abby's tone. "Because I know you can do this. I know you have it in you to get up on that stage and face your friends and family. Think of it as an opportunity to thank them for believing in you, even when you struggle to believe in yourself. A little gratitude goes a long way in this town, honey. A *lot* of gratitude? Well, that will get you fans for life with these folks."

Could she do it? Was she brave enough to be truthful about her shortcomings, her failures, to the good people of Plumwood Hollow? The more she thought about it, the more she wondered if maybe it was the only way to set things right. Maybe then she could start over. From scratch. Make a new plan. A better plan. A plan she was a little more prepared for, now that she knew how things worked out there beyond the safe little bubble of their hollow.

"But," Cass said, drawing Abby's attention back to her. "I don't want you doing it until you clear the air with your dad. Mainly because I don't think it would be cool to go public at The Smokehouse, about you being in town, I mean, if you haven't come clean with your daddy first."

Abby nodded slowly. In the end, his opinion of her mattered the most of anyone. "Probably a good call."

"There's nothing probably about it. It's a good call and I'm making it. So scoot. Skedaddle. But take your key with you." Cass wiggled her eyebrows suggestively. "Not sure when I'll be home."

Abby played along and stuck her fingers in her ears. "La-la-la-la-la," she sing-songed as she headed toward her room to find something to wear besides her pajama pants and a t-shirt. Having lived with Cass for almost two weeks now, her suspicions had been confirmed that Cass's hedonistic behavior was all for show. Underneath her strut and swagger, behind the flashy cleavage and jingle-jangle jewelry, Cass was all heart.

FORTY

J ED WAS SURPRISED, BUT grateful to find the church doors open so late on a Saturday night. He slipped inside the sanctuary and slid onto a bench near the back. The building was simply constructed, a rectangular room with classrooms running up each side, and the pastor's offices behind the dais with its old-fashioned podium, the small choir loft, and the row of padded chairs designated for the pastor, the choir director, or anyone else that might be involved with the service.

He didn't speak, not wanting to disrupt the reverential silence that shrouded the large room. There was something intimate about an empty house of God, as if after everyone had gone home, the Holy Spirit lingered in the aisles to pick up the burdens that had been laid down. Jed had a whole lot of burdens to lay down on this night, and he certainly didn't want to hurry the Holy Spirit out of the room anytime soon.

At the end of the day, Jed had gone to the one place he could think of to find solace for his battered pride and his bruised heart. He felt like he'd just gone twelve rounds, not once, but twice, with hardly any breathing room in between.

The thing that bothered him the most about Charlotte's offer of marriage, he'd come to realize, was that she'd been the one brave enough to make the move. It was as simple as that. He'd spent the last nine months essentially trying to convince himself that he didn't deserve another chance at love, that he'd had his one and only with Caroline, and that he was just fine with the gray-and-grizzly bachelor life, because from the moment that woman—Charlotte Ransome—had walked up an introduced herself to him at Courage and Justice's wedding, he hadn't been able to get her off his mind. Or out of his heart.

But he'd been afraid to move on.

And because Ms. Ransome was fearless, she'd taken the bull by the horns and emasculated him by doing his job for him.

Then there were his daughter's words, the last ones he'd heard her throw at Mike. They had taken him out at the knees.

"You can't hurt me any worse than he has." They'd ricocheted off the walls of that second-floor apartment and crashed into him, sending him stumbling backwards down those stairs. It was a miracle he'd managed to get to the bottom without his legs giving out from under him.

How had he been so blind to her pain for all these years? Did she truly believe he thought of her as his greatest regret? But then, how could she not? He now saw things from her perspective, *why* she'd been so driven to succeed with her music, with something so different from the rest of the family. His Abby had spent the entirety of her young life so far doing everything she could to prove that she was worthy of his love.

He must have been sitting there in prayerful silence for a good ten minutes before he heard the voices. By the time he realized they were coming his way, it was too late to slip out the back door.

"Jed?" Reverend Treadwell.

"Well, Mr. Goodacre! What a surprise to see you here!" And Trudy Huckster. They had both entered the sanctuary from one of the side doors that led to their offices. Trudy, Pastor Treadwell's devoted secretary, had her enormous purse tucked under one plump arm, and appeared to have been shooing the pastor out ahead of her.

"My apologies for coming in unannounced," Jed said, standing quickly, willing his bum leg not to wobble. "The doors were open, so I made myself at home. You getting ready to lock up for the night?" He stepped out into the aisle, not sure whether he should exit the building immediately or wait for them to make their way down the aisle so he could walk out with them.

"Well, I don't know now," Pastor Treadwell said as he stepped off the stage. He studied Jed's face as he drew closer. "Seems to me we've all ended up here right now for a reason. Maybe we should linger a bit and see what the Holy Spirit has to tell us."

Part of Jed wished he'd hightailed it out of there the moment the two of them stepped on stage. But hearing the reverend say, in so many words, something so similar to Jed's own thoughts about the Holy Spirit had him sliding back into the pew. "I would be open to that," he said, simply.

"Would you like me to stay or go?" Trudy asked, her voice kind as she hesitated behind the pastor. "But one of you will have to walk me out to my car so I don't get mugged."

Jed had to duck his head to hide a smile. Trudy wasn't joking. If he'd heard her say it once, he'd heard it a thousand times. It seemed to be her greatest fear in all the world; to get mugged. "No, stay. I could use a woman's advice."

Trudy and Pastor Treadwell exchanged a quick glance, one that made Jed's antenna perk up. Had they been talking about him? *Don't be paranoid, old boy,* Jed admonished himself. *Not everyone in Plumwood Hollow spends all their time talking about you.* "Unless you need to be somewhere else, of course," Jed added.

She didn't even hesitate, but side-stepped into a pew on the other side of the aisle and settled in. When she set her purse in the empty spot beside her, it thunked loudly, and Jed wondered what on earth she hauled around in that thing.

The reverend sat in the row in front of Jed, but he draped an arm over the back of the bench in order to see him.

It took him almost another ten minutes before Jed began. "I could use some godly advice."

For the next half an hour, he spoke more words in one sitting than ever before in his life. He poured out his soul to his friends and to the Holy Spirit. He told them about his burgeoning feelings toward Charlotte, his longstanding guilt over his part in Caroline's death, and the inexcusable burden he'd put on Abby's shoulders all the way up to the battles he'd fought—and lost—this morning with both Charlotte and Abby.

"Ms. Ransome was gone when I returned home just before noon. I drove by the Lynxwilder's to be sure her car was parked there, safe and sound. My daughter, too, is being tended to by someone other than me. She's holed up at Cass Whitehouse's condo. And yes, I drove by there as well, to make sure she made it back safely after her visit with Mike Nesbit."

"And then what did you do?" Trudy asked from across the aisle.

"I went back home and did my chores, then sat outside on my porch and stewed," he admitted.

She shook her head and tut-tutted under her breath.

"But I couldn't sit there for very long, doing nothing. How is it that I have been extremely busy every single day just doing my own thing, then that woman disrupts my world and turns it on its head, and now that she's gone, I suddenly have far too much time on my hands?"

Reverend Treadwell chuckled at the wry humor.

Trudy, however, frowned and gave her pastor a stern look before saying to Jed, "You know, Jed, I have been replaying that woman's words in my head and it seems to me to make perfect sense. She spoke to you openly and plainly, and you accused her of playing games. She told you she loves you, she told you she felt at home in your place, that she'd thought things through and believed joining your households together would be a good fit. The way I see it, you're the one being stubborn and playing games here, taking offense at her transparency and then denying your true feelings for her. Call it what you want, my good man, but you've got the look of love all over your face. So does she when she's in your company."

Jed didn't deny it. He'd been coming to terms with his feelings for the woman all day—truth be told, he'd been coming to terms with those feelings since the day he'd met her. He'd felt such a wave of emptiness wash over him when he'd returned home to an empty house earlier. His home, it seemed, was just a house without Charlotte Ransome in it.

"My womanly advice—and I'd like to think it's godly, too," huffed Trudy. "Is that you do right by that lovely Charlotte, Jedediah Goodacre. If you want to marry her, then accept her proposal. No one in this day and age cares a lick which one of you proposes, if that's what eating at you. Say yes to the dress," she pronounced with a robust chuckle. "Get it? She's the dress?"

"I get it," Jed said.

At the exact same time, the reverend said, "We get it, Trudy. Although I don't think that's quite what the phrase means."

"In our case, it does," Trudy shot back, brushing her hands together in satisfaction. "So that's settled."

"I'm not sure if it's exactly settled between Jed and Miss Ransome," Reverend Treadwell hedged, giving Jed a dubious look.

But Jed surprised himself almost as much as the other two when he said, "It's settled. You're right, Trudy. I sent that woman away because of my pride, and now it appears that I'm going to have to eat my words and do a whole lot of groveling."

"That's the spirit," Pastor Treadwell said, reaching back to pat Jed on the shoulder. "And I won't officially congratulate you yet, but if it makes any difference, you've already got our blessing. We like that woman a whole lot around here."

Trudy added her two cents. "She and her little flock would make a fine addition to our little Plumwood Hollow community, Jed. We think it's time you make an honest woman out of Charlotte Ransome, seeing as how she's already living with you."

Apparently, Jed had been right. They *had* been talking about him. "She's not living with me," he began, then closed his mouth. Who was he kidding? If he could figure out how to convince her of what was in his heart, then it was just a matter of time before she was.

Trudy and Pastor Treadwell waited for him to continue, but when he remained silent, Trudy spoke up again. "On to your next dilemma. Your baby girl. Hoo-ee, Jedediah, There's just something about Abby, I'm telling you."

Jed nodded. "She's more precious to me than she could ever know."

"She's precious to all of us," Trudy agreed.

"Amen," Pastor Treadwell concurred.

"Well." Trudy leaned forward in her seat, her eyes alight with a plan. "I have an idea I'd like to suggest."

FORTY-ONE

ABBY SAT IN ONE of the rocking chairs on her father's porch and stared unseeing out over his property. Of course, he wasn't home. He'd told her he had plans, hadn't he? He was probably out on a date with Charlotte Ransome, in fact.

The idea of her dad dating still sat awkwardly on her mind, but the more she thought about it, the more amenable it became. Why shouldn't he date again? It had been twenty years since his first wife had passed away. He was still a nice-looking man, and barring any tractor accidents, he could still have a good twenty years or more ahead of him. Now that he'd moved out of Seven Virtues and into his own place, why not find someone he could spend his golden years with? Someone who didn't need him to clothe and feed them, to wipe their tears or doctor their boo-boos. Someone like Miss Independence, the shepherdess wool artist from Colorado, Charlotte Ransome.

The lightning bugs danced the tango in the dark, their flashing butts sending rhythmic coded mating messages to each other, and Abby couldn't help but smile at the sight. She'd chosen the seat farthest away from the soft glow of the porch light, and when one of the little critters drifted close by her, she reached up and grabbed it out of midair. She lifted her hands and peered through the opening between her thumbs into the dark space created by her cupped palms. "One potato, two potato, three potato, four," she counted under her breath. "Five potato, six potato—oh!" The insect flashed its twinkle butt again.

When she opened her hands, the bug just sat there, nestled in the palm of her hands, flashing about every six seconds, until Abby said, "Go. Fly. Be free!" She lifted her hand high and gave it a gentle shake, and the lightning bug took off.

Abby criss-crossed her legs, her feet tucked under her, and watched the insect flit out to the porch rail, then past it. It didn't go far, though, and a few moments later, it had circled back around to land on her knee. It crawled back and forth several times, like it was lost and alone and trying to figure out which way to go. It finally stilled, perched on the bend of her knee as though looking out over the precipice, trying to work up the courage to jump.

"You and me, both," she murmured. In fact, the more she thought about it, the more she recognized herself in the lightning bug. She, too, had been released out into the great big world to test her wings. "Go. Fly. Be free!" her family had all essentially told her as they tossed her out of the nest.

Sure, it had been her idea, but no one—not even her father—had tried to talk her out of it, or at least into waiting until she was a little older. Not one of her family members had suggested she reconsider, that she might be too young, not ready.

Oh, had they done so, she still would have gone. She was nothing, if not stubborn. And they'd probably all known that and had encouraged her because they wanted to support her dreams.

But still, it would have been nice if at least Daddy had tried to talk her out of it. Even if it had only been for show.

"You're such a baby," she muttered. "You can't have it both ways, you know."

But like the lightning bug still blinking on and off on her knee, Abby, too, had come back. And although she knew she couldn't stay here indefinitely, she battled with her fear—and failure—as she faced whatever came next. She, too, felt perched on the precipice of the unknown. What was out there for her? And was it enough to keep her from flying back home again and again, head low, light snuffed out?

But the bug, she noticed, didn't have his head down, and his light hadn't even dimmed. In fact, it was happily twitching its antennae and flashing his little butt every five or six seconds.

Even the lightning bug was still brave enough to keep flashing its light. *This little light of mine. I'm gonna let it shine.*

"So you think I should do the Smokehouse gig, don't you?" Abby asked aloud. She wasn't sure whether she was talking to herself, to God, or to the insect.

Just then, a truck out on Carpenter Road slowed and pulled into the long driveway. At first, she thought it was her father, and her heart jumped into her throat. But even in the dark, she could tell it wasn't his old truck. She blew on the lightning bug and it took off into the night with great gusto, then Abby got to her feet. It was getting late, she was alone out here, and only Cass knew where she was. She felt in her back pocket for her set of keys with the pepper spray attached to it.

As the truck drew nearer, though, she realized who it was coming up the drive, and she dropped back into the chair. She wasn't sure she was ready to face the one person who had, in fact, asked her to stay. The one person who had hoped against hope that he could talk her out of going.

"Hey," Mike said as he drew closer to the porch.

Abby remained sitting, but greeted him politely. "Hi." Was he here to meet with her father? After the things they'd said to each other that morning, she couldn't imagine why else he'd be there. "Are you looking for my dad?"

Mike shook his head. "Not exactly." He put one foot on the first step and braced a hand on the rail. Was he afraid to come up to the porch? "I stopped by Cass's place tonight to see you, and she told me where you were. I figured if you were brave enough to come see your dad, then I should step up, too."

"You don't need to be kind to me, you know."

"I'm not here to be kind to you," Mike said, moving up the steps slowly, like he was approaching a scared animal. The porch light shone on his face, and what Abby saw there made her pulse pick up its frantic rhythm again.

That morning, after she'd stepped out onto the second-floor landing to find her father clambering into his truck, after she realized that he'd most likely heard everything she'd said about him, she'd started down the stairs, yelling at him to stop, to come back. Her father had ignored her shouts and drove away. She had spun around to find Mike on the landing behind her, his expression drawn with concern.

And she had turned on him with a whole new wave of pain and misery.

"Look what you made me do!" she'd raged at him as she charged back up the stairs. Mike had backed into the apartment, stepping out of her way to let her pass, then closed the door behind him. Abby stood in the middle of the room, her arms squeezed tightly around her middle in an effort to quell the urge to throw up. She hadn't seen her father's face, but when he'd ignored her and drove away, she'd felt such a sense of abandonment that it was a wonder she'd stayed upright. "He *heard* me, Mike. He heard those terrible things I said about him."

Abby had known she sounded ridiculous, blaming Mike for the situation she'd found herself, but she honestly didn't know how much more she could take on her own shoulders.

Mike had stood there and let her unload on him.

"You and I can't be friends, Mike. Don't you see that? It always turns out badly. And it's usually me hurting you. I see that look in your eyes right now. I've done it again, haven't I? Given you the wrong answer." She'd waved one hand in a circular motion to encompass the apartment. "Oh, I know what you were doing here this morning. Trying to show me everything I was missing out on. Buttering me up. But for what?" Her voice had grown louder, pitched high with tension. "What do you want from me, Mike? You think you can change my mind and convince me to stay? Didn't we dance to this song already?"

He'd shaken his head slowly, but he hadn't spoken.

"Let me set the record straight for you, once and for all. I don't belong here. I don't belong in Plumwood Hollow. I don't belong at Seven Virtues Ranch. I don't belong with you. And now," she'd said, shooting an arm out to point in the general direction Jed had gone. "Even my family may disown me." She'd dropped her chin to her chest and let out a sound of pent up frustration, something between a growl and a yell. "Why did I let you get under my skin again?"

"You know," Mike had started slowly, but there'd been no mistaking the steel edge in his voice. "You're right. I have heard this number before. In fact, I've heard this tune far too many times since you've been back in town. Write a new song, would you? This one is getting old." Then he'd pushed open his door and stepped aside, leaving no doubt in her mind that he was ushering her out the door and out of his life.

But now, here he was, standing on her daddy's porch, a look in his eyes that she'd never seen before. "Then why are you here?" she asked, not quite sure she wanted to hear his answer.

But she was that lightning bug, and it was high time to jump. If she was ever going to unfurl her wings again, she'd need to have somewhere safe to land so she wouldn't crash and burn.

She needed to start rebuilding the bridges she'd torn down between her dreams and home.

She needed to start with the heart of her home, and that meant repairing the roads between her and the people she loved most in the world.

As she looked up at the handsome Midwestern boy-turned-man standing before her, she had to admit that Michael Theophilus Nesbit the Fifth was one of those people.

FORTY-TWO

Jed waited in the foyer with Trudy while Pastor Treadwell turned off a few lights in the building. There had been a planning meeting that night in one of the larger classrooms, which was why the front doors had been unlocked when Jed arrived, and the pastor and his secretary had been making rounds to shut everything down. "Providential timing," Pastor Treadwell had assured him when he'd apologized for keeping them so late.

In fact, it was too late to see Charlotte, although he was desperate to clear the air between them. She'd spent enough nights in his home that he knew she liked to wind down her evenings soon after dark. "I love the morning light the most," she'd told him one morning as they sat side by side in the rockers. "At the end of the day, folks seem desperate to keep the darkness at bay, so they frantically turn on all the lights. But by morning, they've renounced their stance, and they try to hide from the sun until the last minute."

"Fickle folks, we humans are," Jed had agreed.

"Not me, though. The moment the sun makes itself known, I'm up and welcoming it with my arms—and eyes—wide open. And look," she'd said, gesturing at the view before them. "Isn't it glorious?"

No, she would already be in bed by now, and if she wasn't, it would only be because she was complaining about him to Sarah.

But he wouldn't think that way. He was going to hope for the best.

Abby should be in bed, too, seeing as she had to be up before dawn for her job, but knowing his daughter and the naivety of the young, she was much more likely to be awake and still going strong. It wasn't quite ten o'clock. Did he have it in him to face her tonight?

Pastor Treadwell returned to the foyer, set the security alarm, then followed Trudy and Jed out the front doors, locking the place up behind him. As if intuiting Jed's thoughts, the reverend turned around and said, "A word of advice, my friend. Having a bit of experience in this myself, I'm going to suggest that you go home and pray about all of this. Give it to the Lord tonight. Sleep on things so that your emotions aren't still right up close to the surface."

"And their emotions, too," Trudy chimed in.

The reverend nodded. "Exactly. Miss Ransome is safe with Sarah, and Abby is with Cass. They're in good hands for the night." He pointed heavenward to indicate he meant God's hands. "The Lord knows best how to care for a wounded heart and soul. Let him start the healing process without your help. Things are always a little less volatile in the light of day, I promise you."

Jed didn't love the idea of going to bed without resolving things between him and the women in his life, but he agreed to let things rest for the night. He'd likely see Charlotte at church in the morning, and he'd ask her then if she'd have lunch with him so they could talk. If she said yes, he'd have to excuse himself from the Goodacre Sunday Family Dinner at Faith's home after church.

It would be a first for him, but it was a sacrifice he was willing to make for the woman he wanted to spend the rest of his life with.

As far as Abby went, he'd thought long and hard about Trudy's suggestion, and he now had a tentative plan. He'd touch bases with Cass to make sure his daughter was all right staying with her for another twenty-four hours, but come Monday morning, he had his work cut out for him.

That night, he lay in bed praying for each of his daughters and their families, something he always did when he had trouble sleeping. He also included Charlotte Ransome in his prayer, asking for the Lord's blessing on making her his bride.

It would be a second for him, but his gray-and-grizzled bachelor card was a sacrifice he was more than willing to make for the woman he wanted to spend the rest of his life with.

FORTY-THREE

"I'M HERE BECAUSE I said some unforgivable things to you this morning, and although they were unforgivable, I'm still hoping you'll let me apologize, and that maybe you'll forgive me, anyway."

"But you were right, Mike," Abby insisted. "I have been whining and complaining about my life for so long that I've forgotten how to be grateful. Cass told me tonight that I needed to practice gratitude. That I needed to start thinking about other people more than myself, and then maybe I wouldn't be such an idiot."

"She said that?" he asked, one eyebrow raised in question, the corners of his mouth lifting slightly, too.

"Well, not those exact words." Abby wrinkled her nose and shrugged. "But, yeah."

Mike cocked his head at her and asked, "What are you doing here? Does your dad know you're out here?"

"Nah. I've been sitting here for the last half an hour or so, hoping he'd show up, but I think he might be out on a date." She couldn't help the slight flinch as she said the words out loud.

"A date?" Mike echoed, his surprise evident. "Wait. Is he really seeing Miss Ransome? I head a rumor this week, but thought that was all it was."

"Apparently it's no rumor," Abby said. "He told me he had plans tonight, remember? I was hoping he just meant there was a show on the History channel he couldn't miss. But he's not here." She gestured toward the driveway where Mike had pulled in next to her truck. "Neither is his truck, which brings me to the conclusion that he's somewhere else."

"Great powers of deduction," Mike teased in a drawl.

"I know. Brilliant, aren't I?" Abby rolled her eyes. "But the longer I sit here, the more I'm wondering if I really want to be here when my father gets home from a date. With a woman, by the way, who happens to be staying here with him."

"I'd heard that, too." Mike said with a grimace. "About her staying here, I mean. Not a rumor, I presume?"

"Not a rumor," she replied. "Do you want to sit? I mean, if you're here to see me, then using my great powers of deduction, I'm going to assume you want us to talk, and my neck is starting to hurt from having to look up at you."

"Sure," Mike said, and moved to sit in the other rocker. "Thanks."

"Actually," Abby sat forward. "Let's get out of here. The more I think about him coming home to find me sitting on his front porch, especially if the evening went well for him, the more I think this may not be such a good idea. We can talk, but follow me back to Cass's, okay? She'll be out at The Smokehouse until Badger sends her home. I can't stay up too late since I'm doing the prep work in the morning, but I don't have to be up until six tomorrow."

"Nice. You get to sleep in," Mike said, getting to his feet again, then offering her his hand. "I'm down with that. Let's go."

Abby let him help her up, but she didn't let go of his hand immediately. When she lifted her eyes to meet his, she saw it still, that vulnerability that had nearly broken her that morning. But there was something else there, too. He seemed somehow more fixed, like the North Star in the sky.

He remained silent while she studied him, but she sensed the tension pinging through him. His fingers still wrapped around her hand twitched tellingly.

"I'm sorry, too, Mike," she murmured, willing herself not to look away. "For the things I said to you. None of this is your fault. I can't believe I tried to pin this on you."

Mike blinked, then his gaze dropped to her mouth.

He was going to kiss her. Right there on her daddy's front porch, Mike Nesbit was going to kiss her.

Oh, how she wanted him to kiss her. She felt herself sway just the tiniest bit. Or was that him?

No. Wait! They couldn't do this. Not again. They'd spiral right back into chaos if he kissed her.

With every ounce of willpower she could muster, she released his hand and stepped back. "Forgive me?" she asked, hating how breathless she sounded.

Mike just nodded, and she wondered if his voice wasn't working any better than hers was.

Abby turned and started down the porch steps, pausing to glance over her shoulder at him. He hadn't moved. "Coming?"

"Cass's place. Yes," Mike finally said, and indeed, the words came out a bit strained, if Abby was hearing correctly. "See you there."

They climbed into their respective trucks, and Mike waited, ever the gentleman, to let her go ahead of him.

As Abby had predicted, Cass was already gone. There was a note propped up on the kitchen counter telling Abby not to wait up for her. *Praying things get patched up between you and your daddy. And between you and that delicious Mike, too, of course.* Abby snatched the note off the kitchen table, grateful Mike hadn't seen it. He still stood at the door, waiting to be invited in.

"Come in and sit. You choose where. Want something to drink? Cass always has good sweet tea on hand, but there's ice water, too."

"Water sounds good. Thanks." Mike headed into the living room and sat down on one end of the sofa. Great. Should she sit on the sofa with him or take the chair across from him?

She brought him his water glass, then sat in the chair across from him, the coffee table like a line drawn in the sand between them. She heard Cass's voice in her head. *You two belong on the same team.*

Mike took a sip of water.

Abby took a sip of water.

Mike set his glass down and sat forward, his elbows on his knees.

Abby tucked her feet up under her and rested her elbows on the armrests of her chair. She held onto her glass like it was her last line of defense. She groaned inwardly. *Isn't this awkward?*

"Look—," Mike began.

"So—" Abby spoke at the same time.

"You go first," they both said in unison.

Abby held up her glass. "I'm going to take a drink, so speak now or forever hold your peace."

Without preamble, he did. "I want you to stay in Plumwood Hollow."

She almost snorted her mouthful of water back into her glass, but with a short fit of convulsive coughing, she somehow managed to keep it where it was supposed to be. "I'm sorry?" It came out as a question, and she honestly wasn't sure if she was apologizing for the hacking or if she just wanted him to repeat his statement one more time.

Mike had waited until she caught her breath, then he said, "Hear me out, Abby. Please."

Why was he insisting on having this conversation yet again? Hadn't they covered this already this morning? Same old song, same old dance? But that something... that shift in his demeanor, that glint in his eyes, whatever it was that she'd seen on his face at her father's home was still there, and Abby conceded, even while preparing herself for battle. "Okay."

"If I had things my way, I'd want you here in the hollow with me. All the time. But I've learned the hard way that I can have things my way with someone else, or I can have you your way." A flush had started to creep up his neck, and he threaded his fingers together between his knees, obviously ill at ease. "But you know what else I discovered?" He kept talking, holding her gaze, his eyes pleading with her to listen, to understand. "I learned that it isn't just about what I want. The things I want to have. The people I want to have. The fact that I want to have something for myself; it's a pretty selfish motivation, don't you agree?"

Abby thought about all the things she wanted. Fame. Fortune. To be a household name. To be a superstar. Except... was that *all* she wanted?

"Remember when I said that I was one of the good guys?"

"I do," Abby responded. "Cass said the same thing about you."

"Yeah, and you used to say it about me, too, Abs."

"Because it was true. And I can see that it still is," Abby acknowledged. "But that doesn't—"

"Please." He cut her off, not rudely, but firmly. "I need to get this out before I chicken out."

"Sorry. Go ahead." She pretended to zip her lips.

"Well, that night of your party at The Smokehouse, I was the worst kind of guy. To both of us. And to Stephanie, too."

Especially to Stephanie, Abby wanted to say, but she'd essentially promised not to speak.

"Especially to Stephanie," Mike echoed, but he said it out loud.

Abby grinned and nodded.

"Shush," Mike said sternly, but his lips twitched as he tried to keep from smiling, too. "I'm sorry for that night. I'm sorry for being so cruel to you and Stephanie."

Abby unzipped her lips halfway. Out of one side of her mouth, she said, "Forgiven," before zipping it back up again.

"We never officially dated, in case you're wondering."

Abby wouldn't admit it out loud, but she almost shivered at the wave of relief that washed over her. Stephanie was a nice enough person, but it really wouldn't have mattered who she was. Abby had a hard time imagining anyone with Mike. Anyone but Abby.

"I did take her out the following week to The Smokehouse, both dreading and hoping I'd see you—and you'd see us—one more time before you left. I thought you'd be performing your final Saturday night gig, you know? I tried to be all covert about it, nonchalantly glancing at everyone who came in the front door, keeping on eye on the backstage area, chatting it up with Badger while trying to work up the courage to ask if you were going to sing."

Abby lifted her fingers to unzip her lip again, then she hesitated and asked, "Can I be done with this? I promise to let you say what you need to say, okay?"

Mike made a show of considering her request carefully, then said, "I guess I'll just have to trust you."

The way he said it made her pause, as if he was telling her something important, and not just playing along with her little game. "I guess you will. Where were we?"

"Your last Saturday in the hollow."

"Oh, yes!" Abby said, tapping her temple lightly. "That was my last night in town. I spent it with the fam."

"Yeah, I thought as much when you never showed. But Stephanie figured out the real reason we were at The Smokehouse, and she stranded me there." He chuckled dryly. "Coward that I was, I had asked her to drive that night, so when she left, she took my ride with her."

"I'm almost afraid to ask, but why did you make her drive?"

The flush that had already suffused his face got a little brighter. "Because I didn't want her riding in your seat in my truck. It was too weird for me, but I couldn't exactly tell her that. So I lied and said my battery was dead and I didn't want us to get stranded anywhere."

"How ironic," Abby mused. The conversation lulled for a moment before Mike picked up where he left off.

"I've had a lot of time to think about this," he said after a deep, fortifying breath. "And here's what it boils down to, at least from my perspective. What I asked of you back then was not a compromise. It was a sacrifice. I'm asking you now for a compromise." He cleared his throat and said, "Abby, you must know that it's always been you. I have loved you from as far back as I can remember. I don't know exactly when it changed from platonic to this, but I just know that it did, and as hard as I've tried, there's no going back."

"Oh, Mike," Abby sighed, hating the pleading in his eyes. "No, please, stop," she whimpered, dropping her face into her hands. "I can't take this, not again."

"Listen, Abby," Mike insisted, reaching out and taking her wrists, gently pulling her hands down. He had circled the coffee table and was kneeling in front of her. "This morning you said that you no longer have a home to come back to, now that your dad moved out on his own. I know the old ranch house isn't the same anymore, either, right?"

Abby nodded, but couldn't meet his eyes.

"So let's you and me make Plumwood Hollow our home together. Not so you will stay here, Abby. I want this to be the place you come home *to*." He moved his gentle hold from her wrists to her hands, twining his fingers with hers. "I want to be your home, Abstinence Eve Goodacre. Your safe place to land." He brought their clasped hands to his chest and held them together over his heart. "I want to be the place you come home to."

Abby sat in stunned silence, hardly able to believe what she was hearing. She opened her mouth to speak, but there was nothing there. She tried again. "You—you mean...." She didn't want to put words in his mouth. She didn't want to build up her hope, only to come crashing back to the ground when he pulled the rug out from under her again.

"I love you, Abby. I want us to find a way to make it work. Even more importantly, I want what you want." He shook his head, a goofy half-smile on his face. "That's not quite true. I don't want to be a country singer, that's for sure."

"Ha ha," Abby said and rolled her eyes, all while trying to blink away the tears that were threatening to spill. Happy celebration tears this time—or at least she wanted them to be more than anything in the world.

"I want for *you* what you want for you," Mike clarified, his voice gentle, his eyes searching her face.

"And I want for you what you want for you," Abby echoed, hoping against hope that he meant what he was saying. "I always have, Mike. You belong here; it's so obvious to anyone who knows you how much this town and the people here mean to you. I never wanted to take you away from the hollow—"

"And I never should have asked you to stay," he interrupted. "All this time lost." He shook his head and squeezed her hands. "Because of my stupid pride. I'm such a big lug, and I'm sorry." He leaned forward and rested his forehead against hers. "I love you, Abs, and I don't ever want to lose you again."

"I—I love you, too, you big lug," Abby managed to croak out past the tightness in her throat.

Mike let go of her hands and reached up to cup her face in his palms. "I'm going to kiss you now."

"And we'll seal our forever with a kiss," she whispered. "Finally." Then she closed her eyes as he lowered his mouth to hers.

His touch was gentle, soft, almost like a first kiss, and Abby sighed against his lips. She felt him smile at her response, and when she rested her hands on his chest so she could lean into him to deepen the kiss, she swore she could feel the thumping of his heart against her palms.

Mike wrapped his big arms around her and drew her right up to the edge of her chair, pulling her against him. One hand slid up her spine to cup the back of her head, his fingers buried in her hair, still gentle, but leaving nothing to the imagination about what kind of future he had in mind.

Abby kissed him back with equal measure, overwhelmed by the oh-so-perfectly comfortable familiarity of the man in her arms.

When Mike finally lifted his head, he smiled down at her, then pressed his lips to her forehead. "Wherever you go, whatever you do, I will be right here waiting for you," he murmured close to her ear.

Abby flinched at the well-known lyrics. "Oh. My. Gosh," she said, pushing him in the chest so that he almost fell backward. But she couldn't keep the laughter from bubbling up. "Are you quoting Richard Marx lyrics to me right now?" She chortled in delight when she saw his self-satisfied grin. "You are! You are pulling an eighties movie on me!"

"Do I know what my girl likes, or what?" he asked, pushing to his feet and reaching out both hands to her. "Besides, you started it by quoting *my* song, you know."

"Your song? What makes you think I wrote that about you?" Abby asked coyly, letting him pull her up to stand in front of her. Then she shrieked her surprise when he bent and scooped her up in his arms. "What are you doing? Put me down, you big lug!" But she threw her arms around his neck and hugged him fiercely, belying her demands.

Mike just laughed as he circled the end of the coffee table again and returned to the sofa where he sat again, this time with her in his lap. "I was hoping you were going to sit here with me," he said as he settled her more comfortably in his arms. "That's why I chose the couch. But no, you sat all prim and proper in your old lady chair over there—"

"Do *not* let Cass hear you call anything in her house 'old ladyish.' She'll ban you from Serendipity's for life." Abby shook a playful finger at him.

"And putting this silly little table between us," he continued, nudging the coffee table with his foot, completely unfazed by her dire warning. "Like that thing could stop me if I wanted to get to you."

"Oooh," Abby teased, then rested her head on his shoulder. "You showed me, didn't you?"

Mike's arms tightened around her. "I hope I did. And I plan to keep showing you for the rest of our lives."

"I think I could stick around for that," she said, listening to the steady rhythm of his heart against her ear. She hoped her next question would spoil the tender connection they were reforging. "But Mike, what does all of this look like to you?"

He was quiet for so long that she wondered if he understood her question. But he stroked her back softly and said, "Honestly, I don't know. But I think if we both agree that we're in this together, we can figure it out. I've got two more years of school, but I transferred to Muldoon so I could still live here in the hollow. I'm not going anywhere. I know you need to focus on what you're going to do with your music, but while you're home, let's make some plans, okay? You never really said how long you think you'll be in town this time."

Abby stayed nestled against him and shrugged one shoulder. "I honestly have no idea. But without a band, a manager, and a place to live in Nashville, I guess I don't plan on going anywhere soon. I need to start making phone calls, but I have a feeling I've got an uphill battle ahead of me to get back in the good graces of some important folks." She tried not to let herself get discouraged at the thought.

"So we have a little time, right?" he asked. "A couple months?"

Abby nodded. "I'd say at least a couple of months unless I get lucky and someone out in Nashville is willing to bet on me."

"It'll happen, Abs." Mike spoke the words softly, his mouth moving against her hair. "You have what it takes."

Abby pressed a soft kiss to the underside of his jaw.

"I have something for you," he said after a few moments of comfortable silence. "I got it ages ago, but I think you'll still like it."

Abby straightened, lifting her head to look at his beautiful face, his impish grin, those sparkling eyes. "What is it? Do you have it now? I mean, with you? Because if you don't, I'm going to go lock myself in Cass's dead mom's room."

Mike choked out a surprised laugh. "Do *not* let Cass hear you call her guest room her dead mom's room. That's just wrong in every way."

"I know." Abby grimaced. "Sorry. But seriously, Mike. You can't say something like that and not follow through."

"Do I need to kiss you again to get you to stop talking long enough for me to answer you?" Mike asked, pulling her close again and nuzzling her neck with his five o'clock shadow.

"Stop!" she shrieked, attempting to rear back out of reach of his chin. "You'll give me whisker burn and Cass will know we've been making out on her sofa."

"My intentions, exactly," he said with a lascivious wiggle of his eyebrows. But he relaxed his hold of her and then slid her over onto the couch beside him. "I have it with me, of course."

Abby held out both hands, palms up, and smiled up at him. "I haven't gotten a gift from my man in a long, long time," she teased, loving the way it felt to call him hers again. "This better be good."

Mike rose and reached around to his back pocket. He pulled out what looked like a plastic bubble container from a gumball machine, and Abby's smile got bigger with anticipation. Mike used to always waste his quarters on the goofiest stuff in the bank of gumball machines at Nesbits. She had a whole shoebox full of tiny, cheap trinkets he'd bought for her throughout their friendship. She wasn't sure where it was now that her father had moved out and her bedroom had been claimed for Pru's education center, but she'd worry about that later.

She lowered her hands to her lap, lacing her fingers together, as Mike knelt on the floor in front of her again, this time on only one knee. He popped open the plastic bubble and held it out for her to see. Inside the small red cup was a delicate gold band encircled by a row of tiny gems.

"They're just chips, but they're diamonds," he said a little sheepishly. "It was all I could afford in high school."

In high school? Abby looked from the ring to his sweet face. "It's beautiful." She squeezed her hands together tightly in her lap, not wanting to assume anything by this gesture, but hoping with all her being that this meant what she thought it did.

Mike cleared his throat. "I bought it as a promise ring for you before you left. I wanted you to have something you could always wear to remind you that I was here waiting for you, praying for you, loving you. I made sure it was low-profile so it wouldn't interfere with your guitar playing." His hands trembled slightly, making the ring rattle against the cheap plastic. "But then I chickened out, not because I didn't want you to take this with you, but because I didn't want you to go at all."

A promise ring. Mike had bought her a promise ring. He *had* believed in her, even back then. He'd intended to send her off into the great big world with the symbol of his love on her finger.

"Forgive me for being young and afraid, Abs. I was so afraid to let you go that I ended up losing you, anyway."

Abby's heart sang inside her chest. She reached into the tiny container and pulled it out, holding the beautiful piece of jewelry up between them. In a whisper, she said, "This is no gumball machine prize, Mike."

He shook his head slowly, his eyes locked with hers, those dimples making an appearance and turning her insides to mush. "It did not come from a gumball machine, no." Then he took the ring from her, reached for her left hand, and lifted it to his lips for a kiss. "Will you wear my ring, Abstinence Eve Goodacre? It might not be a real engagement ring, but it means the same thing to me. It's a symbol of my promise to you, Abby. I promise to love you, to be faithful to you, to support you in following your dreams. Marry me. Let me be the one you come home to."

"It's real enough to me, Michael Theophilus Nesbit the Fifth," she told him as he slid the slim band of diamonds in place. "Yes. Yes, to all of it. Yes to coming home to you."

FORTY-FOUR

To Jed's relief, Sunday morning found Charlotte sitting at the end of the pew with Sarah and Joe and Courage. He'd been half afraid she wouldn't attend church because of him. He caught her eye, and she smiled at him, but the light in her was noticeably dimmer this morning. His fault, he knew. And his responsibility to fix it, too.

Concentrating on the reverend's message was nigh unto impossible, but Jed somehow managed to retain enough of the important points to be able to discuss them with Pastor Treadwell should he be put on the spot. By the time the last notes of Trudy's piano playing filled the sanctuary and the congregation was released, Jed was coiled so tightly, he was afraid he might just spring up out of his seat.

Jed forced himself to remain his usual stoic self as he stood in the aisle at the end of the pew, hat in hand, held out of the way behind his back, and let folks pass him by. He intended to catch Charlotte before she even left the building.

"Good morning, Jed," she said as she approached. She smiled warmly at him and touched his arm in greeting, but that challenging spark was missing in her gaze. And she'd called him Jed.

"May I have a word with you, Ms. Ransome?" he asked without preamble.

Charlotte's brow furrowed, and she stepped back, presumably put off by his brusqueness. "Right now? Here?" she asked, glancing around the still full sanctuary. "Sure."

"No." He cleared his throat and tried again. "I'd like to take you to lunch somewhere. But if you already have plans, then I'm hoping you'll settle for coffee and some of Charity's pie out at my place this afternoon."

Charlotte widened her stance just the tiniest bit, then had to step back to let an enormous man pass by.

"Morning, Jed," Sherman Bench said with a dip of his chin.

"Morning, Sherman." Jed reached up to touch the brim of his hat in greeting, then remembered too late that he held it behind his back in his other hand.

Charlotte took her position again, feet planted solidly in front of him, and Jed could tell she'd taken advantage of the momentary reprieve to put on her battle face. For the life of him, he could not read her expression.

"Sorry about that," he began, then paused. What was he apologizing for? Or was he just talking to dispel the awkwardness between them? Had things ever been this complicated with Caroline? Hadn't he just been thinking—what? Two days ago?—that Charlotte was easy to read, straightforward, transparent? If there hadn't been so much riding on this moment, he might have chuckled at the irony.

"I can do lunch," Charlotte finally said. Then she crossed her arms.

That was never a good sign, a woman's crossed arms. Jed should be relieved at her response; instead, he felt a primal urge to shove his hat on his head and abandon ship. "All right. Would you like to go to—"

"At your place," she said, interrupting him. "I'm not interested in airing our personal lives to the public forum."

"All right," he said again, then had to clench his jaw and press his lips together to keep from smiling. There was the Charlotte he knew and loved. Speaking her mind and not pulling any punches.

"Of course, since we'll already be there, I am going to assume you'll stand by the offer of coffee and pie, too," she added, her chin raising just a notch.

Hoo-boy. There was that spark back in her eyes. So she was planning on spending the whole afternoon with him. He'd better not let his mouth even twitch. "Of course," he agreed with a slow nod.

"And I'm going back to Sarah's to change into something more comfortable first," she announced.

"If that's what you want to do." He glanced past her shoulder at Faith, who was watching them intently from where she still sat in the pew, her fingers laced over the mound of her growing pregnancy. There was nothing wrong with her, he could tell. She'd pulled the tired, pregnant mama excuse to stay and eavesdrop. Or to make sure he'd be okay if Charlotte refused him, he supposed. She did have something of a Mama Bear look on her face. He winked at her to reassure her, and her features softened noticeably.

Charlotte glanced over her shoulder to see who he was interacting with. She gave Faith a quick wave and a smile, then turned back to Jed. "When should I be there?"

"Give me an hour," Jed said, already formulating a plan that would kill two birds with one stone. He'd caught Cass's eye while he'd been waiting for Charlotte, but instead of coming over to say hello to his clan the way she usually did, she'd given him a quick flutter of her fingers and ducked out the back door. Clearly, she was avoiding him, probably assuming he might be upset at her for harboring Abby.

He wasn't. Not anymore, at least. He'd been pretty riled up yesterday morning, but after hearing Abby's side of things, he'd gone from resentful to grateful for her in a heartbeat. She'd given his daughter sanctuary when she didn't believe she had anywhere to go. For that, he would ever be in Cass's debt.

But he still needed to check in with her about Abby. He would swing by Serendipity's and pick up some roast beef sandwiches and a backup dessert if Charity wasn't doing pie—he hadn't confirmed that detail before he offered it to Charlotte. And while he was there, he'd let Cass in on his plans.

He hoped she'd agree that he was doing the right thing.

Charlotte glanced at the silver watch on her wrist. "I'll see you at 11:43, then."

"All right," Jed said again, willing himself not to chuckle. This was going to be fun, he decided, working his way back into her good graces. Her willingness to join him at all was probably the biggest hurdle, and he'd just cleared that one without a hitch.

"And you can stop being so smug," Charlotte added with a scowl. Was he really so easy to read? "I haven't forgiven you, Jedediah Goodacre. I'm just hungry."

"Right. Of course." He forced a stern scowl to settle on his face. Maybe she hadn't yet forgiven him, but she hadn't called him Jed, either. He could work with that.

When she'd gone, Faith rose and came to stand beside him. "I take it you're not going to be at our place for dinner today?" It was not a question. "Should I send Cord over with some food? I've got a roast in the oven and Charity said she's bringing blackberry cobbler."

Jed was relieved that Faith didn't seem too upset about him bailing on the family dinner. He hoped that soon enough, he and Charlotte both would be attending every Sunday, but today? Well, today, he needed to set the record straight, and he wasn't going to put it off a moment longer.

"I'm going to head over to Serendipity's and pick up some sandwiches. I told Charlotte I'd have pie, so I'd better grab one of her mini apple pies while I'm there."

Faith put her arm around his waist and grinned up at him. "Well, Daddy. I can't say that this is a surprise, you and Ms. Charlotte, but it still feels really, really weird. You are a dating man," she declared.

"Hush, child," he said, wrapping her shoulders in a quick hug and planting a kiss on top of her head. "Let's not count our chickens before they hatch. I've got a little groveling to do today."

Faith pulled back a little and eyed him sternly. "Daddy. What did you do?"

He chuckled and almost told her to mind her own business, but then thought better of it. He should tell her his side of the story now, because if all went well with Charlotte today, he had a strong hunch that she'd be telling the whole family *her* side of the story for years to come. "I all but accused her of being a gold-digger," he admitted, trying to keep it succinct. "Of trying to coerce me into marriage so she could get her mitts on my property."

"Daddy!" Faith took a full step backward, nearly toppling back into the pew. By now, the church was nearly empty, but he glanced around quickly, hoping they hadn't drawn any unwanted attention.

"Careful," he admonished, cupping her elbow and guiding her down the aisle toward the foyer.

"But—but—" Faith sputtered. "Why on earth would you say such things to her? What did she do to make you think that?" She was clearly aghast at his behavior, but looking for a good enough reason to take his side in spite of it.

"She said my property felt like home." He paused, wondering how much to tell Faith without giving away any confidences Charlotte might want kept between them.

"Well, that doesn't sound like a money-grubber to me. That sounds like a compliment." Faith frowned dubiously.

"She also said she wanted my place to be her place. In so many words."

Faith stopped in her tracks, her arm linked with Jed's, forcing him to come to a quick stop, too. "Wait. Are you telling me she asked to move in with you? Like, as a roommate? Or a—a girlfriend?" She stumbled over the label, and Jed couldn't blame her. It sounded as foreign to him as it obviously did to her. Then she clamped a hand over her mouth and her eyes got even bigger. "Oh, Daddy. Did she ask you to marry her?"

Jed felt heat rise up the back of his neck, and for a moment, he wished they were already outside so he could put his hat back on. Fortunately, Faith had spoken in hushed tones, so no one had heard her question. "For now, daughter, I'm going to keep the rest of our conversation to myself. Once I've settled things with Ms. Ransome, depending on how things go, I suppose I'll let her dole out whatever details she sees fit."

"Not fair," Faith groaned, poking him in the side. "You can't just drop a bomb like this in my lap and then walk away without cleaning up after yourself."

Jed chuckled. "I'll make you a deal. If all goes well, I'll swing by your place this evening for a piece of that blackberry cobbler, okay?"

She gave him another stern look. "And if it doesn't go well? You'll still swing by? You can't leave me hanging like this." When he didn't answer immediately, she added, "I'm a pregnant woman, for Pete's sake, Daddy. This kind of stress could make me go into premature labor, you know. Do you want that on your conscience?"

Jed guffawed and tweaked her nose. She still had the cutest nose; his eldest daughter did.

"What's so funny?" Jasmine and Yvette fluttered into the foyer from outside, arm-in-arm as usual. "And I like your haircut, Gramps," his eldest granddaughter added. "You look like you again."

He hugged both girls and told them how pretty they looked, Jasmine in her fluttery yellow sundress, and Yvette in her tomato-red pearl-snap shirt and black jeans. The best-friend-turned-cousins-by-marriage were practically joined at the hip, but they were as different as day and night in every way. They reminded Jed so much of Courage and Justice at their age. The only time the twins wore matching clothes was during their trick riding performances, and even then, the costumes weren't identical.

"What were you laughing about?" Jasmine asked again, leaning forward to plant a kiss on her mother's stomach. "Hello, baby."

Jed's heart melted a little at the display of affection. "Your mom is threatening to go into early labor, that's all."

"And you think that's funny?" Jasmine asked, her tone sardonic. "What aren't you telling me? Or is this one of those 'we'll tell you when you're older' things? Which is such a dumb strategy, if you ask me. I mean, don't you think that will just drive us curious kids to go look stuff up for ourselves? And do you know how dangerous it is these days for girls our age to go looking stuff up on the Internet? It's a scary world out there, Gramps."

"It really is," Yvette confirmed with an emphatic nod. "Scary and gross."

Faith rolled her eyes. "You girls could talk a nudist out of his skin."

"Mom!" Jasmine practically shrieked. "You can't say nudist in church."

"And talk about gross," Yvette remarked. "A nudist without skin? Can it get any more disgusting than that?"

Faith frowned at Jasmine. "You won't let me say nudist in here, but Yvette can? Did you make these rules up, or did God?"

"Why is everyone saying nudist today?" Jasmine bemoaned, covering her ears and darting toward the doors she'd just come through. "My ears are burning! I can feel the fires of hell licking at my heels from standing so close to all you evil people."

"You can't say hell in church, Jazzy!" Yvette declared, raising her voice to be heard above Jasmine's indignant rant. But the girls were starting to giggle uncontrollably, and Faith held both hands up at her sides in surrender.

"Do you want a couple of teenage girls for the afternoon, Dad?" she asked as she eyed the girls with equal parts adoration and annoyance.

Relieved that his granddaughters had effectively redirected themselves away from the topic of the hour, he took that opportunity to shoo everyone outside where he could put on his hat and make his excuses to leave. He needed to be home long before Charlotte showed up. He'd left his breakfast dishes on the drainer, and he didn't want to be unwrapping takeout food in front of him. If he'd learned anything from helping Charlotte in her catering business over the last few years, it was that presentation was everything.

FORTY-FIVE

Grateful for the chance to sleep in past dawn, Abby lay in bed after her alarm went off, listening to the sounds outside her window. Birds were singing, insects buzzing, and every few minutes a car passed by. It was a whole different song at six AM than it was three hours earlier.

Brrum-brrum.

Twee-twoo-twee-twoo-twee-twoo.

Zzzen. Zzzen. Zzzennnnnn...

The rhythm of life pulsed in her veins, and her fingers tapped out a four-count beat as first one bar, then another came to her.

When I go back
I am reminded of the spirit that I've unearthed.
In the dissonance
Uncovering someone inside me I think I can trust.
When I go back
It feels like nothing's changed and everything makes sense.
And yet, here I am, and there you are
Seven states separating us.

The lyrics of 'Cicada Serenade' drifted lazily through her mind. She'd written the song one lonely night on the road with the Remington Sounder Tour. She'd been desperately homesick and heartbroken over how things had ended with Mike, and her misery had flowed out of her into the nostalgic lyrics about home. It spoke of growing up, of sacrifices made, of longing and remembering and aching for what might never be. It was the same song she'd almost shed tears over the night her Nashville dreams had unraveled before her eyes.

But this morning, now that she and Mike had finally found their way back to each other, the song took on a whole new meaning.

How could I have known that I would travel this far?
The days trailing behind me like ghosts,
The ghost of who I thought I was,
And the ghost of who I thought I'd be.
I'll hold their hands and let them walk beside me...

There's still so many things that we don't know
But now we have the space to grow.
To grow.
To go home....

Abby still had to make peace with her father, she knew, but this morning, she felt better than she had for months. No, years. Her dreams might have crashed and burned, but it no longer seemed like all was lost. Mike still loved her, and he wanted to marry her when she was ready. Sooner than later, if he had any say in the matter. He'd made that abundantly clear. And she was home, in a place where she could find her footing.

Maybe not home at Seven Virtues. Maybe not home in her father's good graces, yet. But home in the hollow, the place her heart longed for.

She'd find the way back into her father's embrace, too. She was confident of that. Despite the hurt and resentment she'd unwittingly harbored all these years, she knew he loved her, and she believed that his was an unbreakable, unconditional love.

Abby thought back on her escape from Nashville, how low she'd fallen into the darkness of despair. That was where she needed to change the most if she was ever going to get her wings working again. Running was not an option. Hadn't her flight out of town proved that to be true? Nothing had been resolved by taking the coward's way out, or by burying her head in the sand—or in Cass's guest room—and hoping all would mend itself while she sequestered herself away.

"I'm not a runner," she murmured into the quiet room. "I'm a warrior."

Abby sat up. "I'm not a runner," she repeated.

She kicked her covers off and stood up, one fist in the air. "I am a warrior." She said each word individually, emphatically.

Cass's groggy morning voice came through the bedroom door. "Then it sounds like it's time to armor up, girlie."

Startled, Abby let out a little squeak of surprise. "Sorry!" she said, pulling the door open. "I didn't mean to wake you."

"You didn't," Cass assured her with a wave and a yawn. "I have to get all gussied up for church. Gotta look good for Jesus, right? Want some coffee?"

Abby grimaced. "You know, I think I'll pass. I'm a little too keyed up already. The caffeine and sugar might do me in."

Cass straightened and cocked her head at Abby. "And just why are you all keyed up at this ungodly hour, might I ask? Good news with your daddy, I presume? I wasn't going to ask until this evening after I got home, but here you are and here I am." She gestured back and forth between them in the narrow hallway.

"Not my dad," Abby said, trying in vain not to smile. She kept her left hand behind her back. "He wasn't home last night. I waited on his front porch for at least an hour. But…" She drew the word out before continuing. "Mike came looking for me last night."

Cass's penciled in eyebrows rose in question. "Should I make my coffee first for this? Should I be sitting down?"

Abby hesitated, then nodded. "Maybe you should sit down. I'll make you coffee while I talk." She had time. She was up a little earlier than she'd planned to be. She could at least give Cass the bullet points.

Careful not to let Cass see her ring, Abby kept her back to her as she scooped grounds into the Mr. Coffee machine Cass insisted she'd never replace. Within moments, the water inside began to boil, and while the coffee brewed, Abby pulled the carton of cream from the fridge and set it next to the sugar bowl already on the table.

She told Cass how Mike had found her sitting on her daddy's porch, then how he'd followed her back here so they could talk.

"You two came back here?" Cass asked, glancing around the space as though they might have left some kind of evidence. Abby had straightened the sofa and all its cushions for that very reason. "To *talk?*"

"Get your mind out of the gutter, Cass. It's the Lord's day and you're getting ready to go to church," Abby chided. But she'd expected a whole lot of teasing from her friend. Cass had made it abundantly clear what she thought of Mike and Abby as a couple.

"Go on," Cass prodded, then reached for the steaming mug Abby handed her.

The mug Abby held with her left hand.

The mug she wouldn't let go of until...

"Oh, my Great Aunt Tiddlywinks!" Cass exclaimed, sloshing the hot coffee all over both their hands.

"Oh Cass! Ouch! Hot-hot. I'm sorry," Abby gushed, setting the mug down and grabbing napkins from the holder in the center of the table. She shoved them at Cass before shaking the quickly cooling liquid off her own. "Are you okay? That was not the smartest move I've ever made."

Cass seemed to have a difficult time finding her voice, but she tossed aside the napkins and grabbed Abby's left hand. Her wide-eyed gaze went from the sparkling ring on her finger to the sparkle in Abby's eyes and back again, before she finally said, "Is this what I think it is?"

Abby grinned and nodded, suddenly choked up herself. "I said yes," she managed to squeak out.

Cass jumped to her feet and enfolded Abby in her voluminous embrace, the fragrance of honeysuckle and vanilla filling Abby's nostrils as she leaned into her friend. Cass was crying, Abby realized, and she pulled back to look at her.

"I'm so happy for you, honey," Cass told her, taking Abby's face in her soft hands. "Love shouldn't stand in the way of your dreams. It should help pave the way for them. And I believe you and Mike can find a way to do that for each other." She pulled her close again and hugged her hard. "Forgive my weeping," she said against Abby's hair. "I feel like a proud mama right now."

Together, they cleaned up the coffee mess while Abby gave her a few more details about the night, then asked Cass how her's had gone.

"Well, I don't have a ring on my finger," Cass said coyly. "But we did get called out for a little PDA last night."

Abby rolled her eyes. "Oh no. What did you do, woman? Is Badger okay?"

Cass laughed, her delight obvious. She pressed her hand to her bosom. "I didn't do anything wrong," she insisted. "I was just standing there next to the bar, and this big, burly man came up behind me, wrapped his arms around me, and kissed my neck." She lifted a finger and pointed at a spot just below her right ear. "I swear I can still feel it."

"Please tell me it was Badger," Abby groaned, although she was having a hard time imagining the guy showing anyone any affection beyond a nod and a handshake.

Cass giggled and patted Abby's cheek. "Of course, it was Badger, girlie. It wasn't much, not for most people, but it was the first time he has ever done anything like that in public." Her cheeks were pink with happiness as she continued. "There was this guy, not someone I'd seen in there before, who pulled up a stool next to mine. I was polite at first, but then I tried to make it clear that I wasn't interested."

"What you call polite can sometimes be misconstrued as, oh, you know, flirting?" Abby said with a gentle smile.

Cass waved her words away. "Oh, please. I'm just friendlier than most. But anyway, my hero caught on to what was happening and rescued me. Staked his claim for all the world to see." She sighed and drank the last of her creamy coffee. "I'm so in love, Abby," she gushed.

"Who called you out on it?" Abby asked, wondering with disgust who the fuddy-duddy was.

"That awful Jenny Stuben. She's between husbands or boyfriends again. I can't keep up with that girl, but she's always had her eye on Badger. Probably because he refuses to reciprocate." Cass rolled her eyes. "Anyway, she actually shouted at us from three tables away. And do you know what Badger did?"

"Oh dear. No. What?" Abby was enjoying this story almost as much as Cass was enjoying telling it.

Cass pressed her palms to her cheeks. "That man of mine turned me in his arms and planted a great big kiss right on my mouth," she all but squealed. Then she clarified, "I mean, we've kissed before, mind you. But never like that in front of everyone at his work. Or in front of anyone, anywhere." She stilled for a brief moment, as if weighing her next words, then said, "I've always worried that he might be embarrassed of me."

Abby's heart swelled at the uncertainty in Cass's words, especially coming on the heels of her effusive gushing. "I can assure, no one who knows you and loves you—and I repeat, no one, Cass—is embarrassed of you, you hear?" She reached over and squeezed Cass's hand.

FORTY-SIX

Charlotte stood on his doorstep at 11:41 AM, two minutes early, but by the time he'd opened his front door and invited her in, the clock on his wall said 11:43 AM. The woman was nothing, if not true to her word.

The table was already set with white plates and blue-tinted glasses, a delft bud vase in the center with a small bouquet of purple coneflowers and small white Shasta daisies he'd grabbed from one of the flowerbeds on either side of his front steps. There still wasn't much in them, but Prudence had been dropping off starters of what she claimed were low-maintenance plants from the big garden at Seven Virtues since late spring, and he'd dutifully found places for each of her offerings.

"What a pretty table," Charlotte declared politely as she crossed the front room to the eat-in kitchen area. His dishes were lightweight and break-resistant, something he'd purchased with the knowledge that he was getting older, and dropping slippery wet dishes was something that happened more often than he'd like to admit. But he didn't say as much to Charlotte. He didn't want to highlight their age difference anymore than was already obvious.

In her early sixties, Justice had said when she'd first told him about Charlotte. Jed would turn seventy-one in September. He'd have to work up the courage to ask the woman her age at some point in their conversation, he supposed.

Charlotte sat while Jed held her chair for her, then laid her napkin in her lap while he got situated across from her. It felt natural, this seating arrangement, he thought. Across the table from each other, face to face.

"Shall we ask the Lord to bless this food?" he asked. When he reached across the table to take her hand, she placed hers in his without even a moment's hesitation. The way she'd been doing all week.

Jed was reluctant to release her hand when the prayer was over. "Thank you for coming," he said, giving her fingers a gentle squeeze before letting go. He explained where the sandwiches were from, then asked how the Lynxwilders' visit with Sarah's family had gone earlier in the week. He'd spoken briefly to Courage in church that morning, but with his attention on Charlotte, he hadn't garnered much information from his daughter.

Charlotte smiled sadly. "Believe it or not, it wasn't great. Her sister is an awful human being, I guess. I met her briefly last Monday, and she wasn't very friendly. I assumed she was just tired from the road, and I was ready to duck out, anyway. But from what I hear, that was a good day for Marla. They were supposed to leave yesterday, right? But Thursday night, over a meal that Sarah and Courage had worked hard all afternoon to prepare, Marla said cruel things about Sarah. Something about her never having been any good in the kitchen, and that she'd done a good job making sure Joe hadn't married someone who could cook any better."

"I beg your pardon?" Jed stiffened in his seat and set his fork down with a scoop of potato salad still on it.

"I know. Vile, right? But don't worry," Charlotte said with a wink. "Your daughter's husband set things straight, once and for all, yes indeed. Farmer Joe smacked the table hard enough to scare the devil out of them all. Even their morose corpse of a daughter—have you met her? She reminds me of that Wednesday Addams child from the movies, but all grown up and well on her way to becoming Cousin It."

Jed was still stuck on the fact that his daughter had been so maligned by someone who was supposed to be family.

"Anyway," Charlotte continued, becoming more animated as she spoke. "Joe stood up at the head of the table, turned to Marla's namby-pamby husband—Troy, I think is his name—and told him that he and his wife and daughter would need to find another place to spend the night, that they were no longer welcome under his roof unless they could learn how to behave like civilized members of the family."

Jed sat back in his chair, thrilled to hear of his son-in-law's response. If Joe wasn't going to put up with it anymore, it had to have been pretty bad. The farmer was what his daughter called "an oak tree of a man." Steady and collected, difficult to rile. Presumably, then, Troy and Marla were so far out of line, Joe had seen fit to send them packing. Literally.

"Oh, it gets better," Charlotte told him when she saw his relief. "I guess Marla scoffed at his demands, and then had the audacity to tell him to sit down and eat his food."

"Who is this woman?" Jed asked, aghast. And kind, gregarious, loving Sarah. Marla was her sister?

"I know," Charlotte repeated, practically giddy with the telling of it. "I guess Marla is the oldest of the three sisters, and when their mother passed away, Marla took over as matriarch, even though Sarah and Lorraine were already in their teens, and she's never let either of the younger two forget how much she sacrificed for them."

"I see," Jed said, nodding slowly. But his thoughts were no longer on Marla, Sarah, and Lorraine. His mind—and heart—went to Faith and the burden of motherhood that had been thrust on her when she was only twelve. Never had he heard her complain about the sacrifices she'd had to make. In fact, the only time he caught a hint of regret when she talked about the years after Caroline's death, was how difficult it had been to be a single parent, and how much she'd taken Jed for granted with having to raise not one, but seven daughters on his own. Faith was nothing like this Marla person, it gratified him to say.

Charlotte must have misunderstood his pensiveness. She sat back in her own chair and covered her cheeks were her hands. "Oh, goodness. Listen to me. I sound like a small-town gossip." She made a face at Jed, and then said, "Forgive me, but I *must* tell you the rest of the story, Jedediah. That son-in-law of yours is something else; I hope you know."

She paused and chewed on her bottom lip, clearly waiting for him to give her permission to carry on. Jed picked up his fork. "Please."

"Oh, thank goodness," she said with a dramatic sigh. "So Joe excuses himself to Sarah and Courage and walks out of the room and down the hall to the guest room where he pulls their empty suitcases from the closet, lays them both open on the bed, and in a raised voice—he wasn't hollering or yelling, Sarah assured me. In a raised voice, he tells them that if they don't get in there and start packing, he'll do it for them."

"Good man," Jed said with a nod, picking up his fork and going back to his meal.

"My sentiments, exactly. But did that make a dent in that woman's thick head?" Charlotte rapped her knuckles on the tabletop. "Marla goes bustling in, dragging Troy along behind her. She's all offended and accusing Joe of destroying her property—I guess he stepped on one of her earrings in the process—but he just proceeded to do what he'd said he would. There was a whole lot of ugly shrieking, Marla calling for Sarah to help—I guess Troy, coward that he is, stayed out in the hallway, presumably shaking in his boots. So Marla is hollering for Sarah to protect her from her out-of-control son—can you imagine Joe Lynxwilder out of control? Ha!"

By this point, Jed was getting quite a kick out of the incredibly awful story. It helped that Charlotte was getting so much satisfaction out of telling it to him; his heart felt lighter watching her warm to his company again. But knowing that his daughter had the protection of a good man in the face of someone like this Marla woman was a boon to his father's soul.

"But guess where Sarah and Courage were while all this was going on?" Charlotte picked up her glass and took a long, slow drink, drawing out the suspense much longer than necessary.

Maybe she actually wanted him to guess? "Where?" he asked.

"They headed out to the front porch swing with a tub of ice cream and two spoons, and enjoyed the sunset while Joe ushered Uncle Troy, Aunt Marla, and Cousin It out to their car, Marla hollering about lawsuits and court cases and bad seeds right up until he closed the car door in her face. Sarah and Courage just waved politely as they drove off."

"I've always thought highly of Joe Lynxwilder," Jed told her. "But he's just shot up a couple of notches in my book."

"Mine, too," Charlotte agreed. "But that's why it worked out for me to stay with them on such short notice this weekend." As soon as she said the words, she seemed to realize that she'd inadvertently kicked the elephant in the room. "Their guest room was open," she added lamely.

Jed picked up the napkin from his lap and placed it on the table beside his plate. "About that."

"About that," Charlotte echoed.

"Forgive this old man, will you, please? The things I said to you were unwarranted and inexcusable."

She, too, carefully folded her napkin and set it on the table, then set her fork face down on her plate and brushed invisible crumbs from her fingertips. "They were," she finally said, her tone gentle, but wary. She fell silent again as she studied him with those silver-gray eyes of hers.

"I am so ashamed," Jed began again when she left the silence hanging in the air between them. "I had just spent the last half an hour expounding on the merits of honesty where my daughters were concerned, only to turn around and condemn you for being true to yourself and honest with me."

"I'm glad you see it that way." Charlotte shifted in her chair, a look of unease settling on her features.

Well? Was she going to forgive him or not? Jed ran his thumb up and down the curve of his fork handle. Tension built between his shoulders as he waited for her to say something. Anything.

"But I have to come clean with you." Charlotte crossed her legs, bumping the underside of the table with her knee, the rattle of the dishes and cutlery only adding to the strain in the room. "I haven't been completely honest with you."

That was not what he wanted to hear. He wanted her to tell him she forgave him, and that she still loved him despite his codgerliness. He did *not* want to hear that she, too, had been withholding the truth from him all this time. Then a voice in his head said, *Try listening to her. Try trusting her.*

"I see," he said, even though he didn't see at all.

"I never intentionally had designs on your place," she began, then sighed exasperatedly. "Oh, who am I kidding?" She straightened in her seat and pushed her dishes to one side so she could rest her elbows on the table in front of her. "Here's the truth, Jedediah Goodacre. The whole truth. I knew even before I met you that I was going to like you. A lot. Don't ask me how I knew; I just did. The first time Justice said your name, I thought to myself, 'Jedediah Goodacre. Now that's a name I could get used to saying out loud every day of my life.'"

Jed's brow furrowed, so many questions racing through his mind. But when he opened his mouth to speak, not one of them pushed to the front, and instead, he said, "You could have gotten a dog."

Charlotte stared at him in confusion for a moment, then she chuckled dryly, realizing he was teasing her. "I know it sounds silly, but the more she and Brandon talked about you, about Seven Virtues Ranch, and about Plumwood Hollow, the more I wanted—no, I *coveted*—what all of you had. It was while they were still at my home that I became determined to come here and see for myself what kind of place this was."

"Is it all it was cracked up to be?" he asked. Jed was certain that there was no place closer to heaven than their little hollow, so he asked in full confidence that she would wholeheartedly agree.

"All, and so much more," she confirmed. "The hollow is more, the people here are more, Seven Virtues Ranch, and all your remarkable daughters are more. And you, sir. You are so much more than what I expected." She laced her fingers together and squeezed, her knuckles between the silver rings on her fingers going pale.

Jed grew still, no longer distracted by his own questions. All of his attention was fixed on her; he didn't want to miss a single word she said. She could hardly look at him as she continued.

"I have been coming here for the last nine months under the pretense of looking for a place I could call home. But the pretense wasn't intentional. It wasn't. I even fooled myself into believing it for the longest time." She picked up her drink and held it between both hands, her rings clinking softly against the sides of the glass. Finally, she met his eyes, and this time, she didn't look away. "But this last week spent here with you shed a new light on things for me. It exposed my motives for what they were."

Jed didn't know what to say. Were these motives good news for him or bad news?

"You want honesty, right?" she asked, peering at him over the top of the glass. She almost looked like she was trying to hide behind it.

"I do. Yes."

"Then here it is." She straightened her shoulders and lifted her chin a little higher. "When I first came to Plumwood Hollow, I thought Seven Virtues Ranch felt like home to me. I heard the music there, too." She glanced down at the contents of her glass and swirled the ice cubes around a few times. "And all this time, I've been looking for a place that felt the same to me. A place I could call home."

Jed nodded encouragingly, but said nothing.

"This last week, staying here with you, I found it again, that sense of being home, that rhythm that settles into your soul and leaves a mark, you see. And it finally occurred to me after I left yesterday..." She paused, swallowed, and nodded solemnly, as if urging herself to go on. "It occurred to me that it's you, Jedediah Goodacre. Home to me is not a place, not a particular property. It's you. You are what makes me feel like I'm home."

"I—I—" His heart was pounding so loudly in his chest that he wasn't sure he heard her right. He wanted her to repeat what she'd just said, just to be sure, but he didn't think it was fair to ask her to do so.

She took a drink and her shoulders relaxed a little, probably relieved that the words were out. When he still didn't speak, she said, "I know you're finally getting to live in your man cave. Of all the men I know, you, above and beyond all others, deserve to spend as many years as you want in peace and quiet." She smiled bittersweetly at the reference to their sparky conversation a few weeks ago. "I know the idea of fitting cantankerous bean pole shepherdess into your world is probably the last thing you could have imagined happening, right?"

"Well, I—I certainly...."

She didn't wait for him to finish his thought. "I get it, Jed. I really do. My proposal wasn't fair to you, to our friendship, or to your plans for the future." She let out a long sigh, and her shoulders drooped even lower. "But I had to ask, you know. I hope you can understand that I had to ask," she said again.

For several moments, Jed was sure his heart had simply stopped beating. His hands tingled, and he wasn't so sure he could feel his legs. Was he having a heart attack? A stroke?

Had he invited Charlotte Ransome to his home so she could watch him keel over?

"No," he said, his voice sounded strangled as he forced it through his tight airway.

"N—no?" Charlotte stammered, clearly taken aback by his response.

Jed shook his head, still working on getting his voice to cooperate. "No," he repeated. Then he pushed to his feet and managed to say, "Excuse me," before he headed from the room and down the hall to his bedroom.

He wanted to kick himself all the way. He should have been more prepared for this moment. He should have had the dang thing with him, on him. And once again, he should have been the one to ask. But apparently, the Almighty was going to give Jed another opportunity to, as Trudy put it, say yes to the dress.

He ducked into the half-bath in his bedroom and glared at his reflection in the mirror over the sink. He looked a little like he'd just eaten something he couldn't stomach, so he took a few deep fortifying breaths, shook out his arms at his sides, then ran cool water in his cupped palms. "Relax, old man," he told himself as he quickly dried his hands. "This is what you want, remember?"

Then he made a beeline for his bedside table, opened the drawer, and withdrew a beautifully handcrafted silver jewelry box. It looked so small in his large, work-roughened hand, and for a long moment, he hesitated. Was he doing the right thing?

The sound of the front door closing softly spurred him to action. "Charlotte?" he called out as he hurried back the way he came, taking care not to give his bum leg any reason to fail him now. A glance at the kitchen proved that it was empty. The dishes had been stacked next to the sink, the chairs scooted in. There was no one in the front room, either. She couldn't have slipped by his room to go to the bathroom; he'd surely have heard her. "Charlotte?"

Starting to panic now, he pulled open his front door so hard that it bounced off the wall and came back at him, almost knocking him in the side of the head. Thrusting an arm up, he took the brunt of the hit in his elbow, sending zinging electrical currents shooting up and down his arm.

With a muttered oath, he shoved open the screen door, his eyes searching for the car she'd come in, but the driveway was empty.

Had she really left so quickly? How long had he been out of the room? And here he'd thought things were going so well.

"Jedediah Goodacre! Did I just hear you correctly? Where is your cuss jar?"

She sat in the rocking chair he now thought of as hers, her tea glass in one hand, her napkin in the other. Her eyes looked a little teary, the tip of her nose a bit pink, but she was smiling up at him... A brave smile, he realized. She was putting on a brave face.

Jed moved to stand in front of her, then he offered her his hand. "Ms. Ransome," he said.

Charlotte frowned up at him, apparently unsure of what he wanted from her.

It didn't matter. *He* was one hundred and ten percent sure of what he wanted from her. "May I help you up?" he asked, his hand still extended.

"Okay," she said hesitatingly, then placed her hand, chilled from the glass she'd just put down, in his and rose.

When he reached for her other hand, she let the napkin drop to the porch unheeded. "I don't trust this leg of mine to go down on one knee, but I thought it might be better if we stood on equal footing for this. Face to face and eye to eye."

"Okay," Charlotte said again, this time a little breathlessly.

"Ms. Charlotte Ransome, I accept your proposal. If you will have me, then yes, I will marry you, and I will share my life and my family, my home and my property with you. Because I love you, and I don't want to spend another day without you in it."

From his breast pocket, he pulled the jewelry box and held it out to her. "It's only a placeholder until we can get you the real deal," he said a little sheepishly. "And we can get this one sized this afternoon if it doesn't fit; the fellow who made it assured me. There just aren't many fine jewelers in this neck of the woods."

Charlotte gasped when she opened the box. "It's beautiful," she whispered, pulling the filigree-style silver ring out and running a fingertip over the hand-hammered setting with its large polished labradorite. "I love this ring," she insisted, clutching it to her chest.

Jed chuckled softly. "Does that mean you'll still have me, then?"

Charlotte handed him the ring, and for a breath of a moment, he thought she was returning it. But then she pried off the ring that was already on her left ring finger and held her hand out to him.

Without a word, he slid the blue labradorite ring on her finger, and to both their delights, it fit like it had been made for her.

"A perfect fit," Charlotte said, holding her hand out in front of her to admire the stunning piece of jewelry. "I think it's a good sign, don't you?" Then she reached up and cupped Jed's face, her palm gentle against his cheek. "I will have you, Jedediah Goodacre. Every day for the rest of our lives."

Jed thought the first time he kissed Charlotte might feel strange, maybe even not quite right....

But he was quite wrong.

They stepped into each other, pulled each other close, and when Jed wrapped his arms around her tall, slender frame, the only thing that struck him as oddly wonderful was that he didn't have to lower his head to press his lips to hers.

A perfect fit, indeed.

FORTY-SEVEN

ABBY SAT ON CASS'S sofa with her guitar, softly singing the chorus of 'Cicada Serenade'. It had become her mantra over the last several weeks, and the song was now as comfortable as her favorite hoodie.

All I can hope is when the wind decides
It's time for me to land
It's in the sweet-smelling shade of the sassafras trees
A cicada serenade in the branches
And home is still out of reach to me,
But if I close my eyes and sing
With the cicada serenade
In the maples on my street...
For a moment, that's home to me.

She kept glancing at the clock, willing the minutes and seconds to speed up. Mike had wanted to take her out on a second first date, but she wasn't ready to be seen in public, at least not until she'd had a chance to talk with her father.

So Mike was joining Abby and Cass for supper, instead, and he'd promised to be there by five.

She still had two more hours to wait.

Mike worked Sunday afternoons and evenings, but because he had to be up early the next morning, they hadn't seen each other at all on Sunday. It felt like a lifetime had passed in the two days.

Her father, too, had remained unavailable, at least by phone, but because Sundays were a big family day for the Goodacres, she'd decided to put off trying to force him to meet with her until Monday. She'd finally gotten through to him that morning, but he'd told her he was out of town. "I'll call you when I get back," he said. "We can arrange something then."

Now here she was, waiting for the men in her life to show up. Not an easy thing to do.

Lying back on the pile of colorful sofa cushions, Abby let her mind wander back to Nashville. How were her bandmates—ex-bandmates now—faring, she wondered. Surely, they'd all found other gigs by now. They'd been together for almost a year, and none of them had even bothered to reach out to her, not even Tad. Abby didn't hold it against any of them, and if she never heard from Bucky again, she'd be okay with that, but it still hurt to be so thoroughly erased from their lives.

She picked up her phone and lazily scrolled through her social media platforms. She really needed to post some updates. Desperate for a reprieve from the constant barrage of questions about her absence on Honky Tonk Row—and not wanting to alert any of her sisters or other Plumwood Hollow folks of trouble in tune town—she'd put up "Going Dark for a Few Days" memes everywhere, along with the explanation that she was working on a new secret project. It had been quite a bit longer than a few days now, and her followers were starting to ask if she was all right. She knew she needed to step in soon, or the rumor mills would start cranking. Abstinence Goodacre was no Taylor Swift, but she had faithful fans and followers who really seemed to care about her and her music.

There was no time like the present, she decided. Abby flipped to her camera and took a few shots of herself lying on the jewel-tone pillows, her long strawberry blonde hair spread out in loose curls under her head. She wasn't wearing much makeup, but the late afternoon light did kind things to her features, downplaying the shadows under her eyes, highlighting her cheekbones and full lips, and turning the pale tips of her eyelashes to gold against her peachy skin. Even her sea-green eyes looked almost iridescent.

Good enough, she thought. She recorded a short snippet of 'Cicada Serenade' with just her guitar and voice, slapped some gentle reverb on it with her new favorite music app, then took her three favorite images and created a short video. She uploaded it across her feeds and stories along with the caption: "Been working on lots of new material. There's magic in these hills and hollers, peeps. Can't wait to share it with you all!" It was true; now she just needed to figure out *how* she was going to share it with her fans.

The responses started rolling in immediately, Abby was relieved to see. She knew how quickly people in the fickle entertainment industry could fall off the radar, so it was encouraging to get so much immediate feedback. She never responded to anything immediately. Rem's publicist had taught her well; set aside an hour a day to respond on social media, and only do one hour's worth. The advice had done her well in keeping her from being glued to her phone twenty-four hours a day.

She was finished by ten minutes to five. Time well-spent, she congratulated herself as she relaxed back into the sofa again. Cass would arrive any minute with ingredients for supper, and Abby could stay busy learning how to make the herb-encrusted chicken from Cass, who had promised to teach her "a few tasty, easy recipes that every adult needed to know."

Her phone rang, making Abby jump in surprise. It fell out of her hand and bounced off her cheekbone, then tumbled to the floor. "Ow!"

She rolled to her side and scrambled to pick up the rascally thing, hoping—and dreading—that it might be her father.

When she saw the name that popped up on her home screen, she sat up slowly, swinging her legs over the side of the couch.

Stena Holder? What on earth?

Should she answer?

The bass player wouldn't be calling her unless it was important, would she?

But did she want to talk to Stena? The girl who had presumably stepped in to fill Abby's suddenly vacant spot on Stan's roster?

She waited too long to make up her mind, and the call disconnected. *Decision made for me*, she thought, and laid the phone face down on the coffee table. An uneasy feeling settled over her, and she slowly sank back into the cushions. "I should have answered that," she muttered, staring down at the device and willing it to ring again.

Of course, she could always call back... but that might make her look desperate.

"Well, I am kinda desperate right now," she admitted, but still didn't move from where she sat on the edge of the sofa.

The phone began ringing again, and this time, Abby snatched it up immediately. With only a glance to make certain it was Stena again, she answered it. "This is Abby." She should have answered her phone using her full name, but unless someone else had Stena's phone, the woman already called her Abby.

"Abby! I'm so glad you answered. I was hoping you would if I called right back." Despite the sultry rasp of Stena's voice, she sounded positively giddy over connecting. "It's Stena. Do you have a minute?"

"I do," she said, biting back the desire to pretend she was too busy to talk. "What's on your mind?"

"Listen, I know things got rocky for you the week we met. I should have reached out to you sooner, but honestly, I didn't know what to say."

"Um, thanks." How else was she supposed to respond to that?

"But now I *do* have something to say, and when your status update popped up in my feed just now, the one about your new material, I had to call you immediately."

"Okay," Abby said warily.

"I need you. I want you to be in my band. Or I want us to be in our band. Can you come back to Nashville? Please?"

Abby pulled the phone from her ear and stared at the screen. What kind of joke was this? Her palms were beginning to sweat. She pushed the speaker button and got to her feet, no longer able to sit still. She headed into the little hallway so she could pace. "I don't understand," she said, slowly, haltingly. She could hear sounds of activity in the background on Stena's end and wondered where she was calling from.

Stena laughed, low and throaty. "Listen to me, Abby. Listen. I'm serious. Okay. Remember how I told you that Stan was going to come see me play that night I was going to gig with you?"

"Yes," Abby responded when it was obvious from the silence that Stena wanted confirmation. She did her best to keep the scowl out of her voice at the thought of Stan.

"Well, he ended up not showing, and the next day, I learned that he'd had a heart attack."

Abby gasped. "Are you serious? Is he—is he okay?"

"Yes," Stena told her. "But he spent several days in the hospital, and has been told by his doctors that his lifestyle has to change. So he's letting go a ton of his clients, and now he's looking to put together just a few super groups, at least that's what he's calling them. A bunch of solo artists who are just starting to make names for themselves who will perform together—and possibly tour—as one group."

Abby was still stuck on the timing of Stan's heart attack. She'd overheard him muttering about her apartment being on the third floor. Had climbing up and down those stairs that Friday triggered his heart to rebel? "A heart attack," she exclaimed softly.

"Yeah. Scary, huh? But he's doing okay, Abby. I promise."

The front door opened, and Abby ducked out of the hall to see Cass come in with a bag of groceries. "I'll be right out," she told her, covering the mouthpiece with her hand. "I'm on the phone."

Cass waved her off. "We got this!" she said.

"I missed that," Stena said. "Can you repeat it?"

"Sorry." Abby removed her hand and began pacing again. "I was talking to my—my roommate." She wasn't sure what else to call Cass in this circumstance. "She's a great cook, and she's going to show me how to make perfect chicken breast when I get off the phone."

"Oh. Sure. It is that time, isn't it? Am I keeping you?"

"No, no," Abby assured her. "It's no big deal. This sounds like it might be a priority. Anyway, you were saying?"

Stena picked the conversation right back up. "Well, when I found out what Stan had up his sleeve, I got to thinking about you and me, girl, and how amazing we sounded together. I have another friend here, Shelby Tremaine, who is a fantastic fiddle player. Have you heard her play? Mind-blowing."

"Shelby Tremaine? You two are friends?" Oh, Abby had heard of Ms. Tremaine. The twenty-two-year-old was taking the Nashville crowd by storm with her crazy fiddle skills. "Yes, I've heard her. How on earth do you know her?"

"We knew each other before either of us came to Nashville," Stena explained offhandedly. "Our dads were in a band together back in the day, so we kinda grew up together." There was a loud banging noise, and Stena waited until it stopped before she continued. "Anyway, I was talking to Shelby, and we were thinking that we—you, Shelby, and me—could be a super group. I mean, we all have our own solo stuff, and we shouldn't mess with that, but a collaboration? Seems like something that could really benefit all of us, big time." Stena paused, then added, "And it might help smooth the way for you to get back in the saddle here in Nashville, Abstinence Goodacre."

Why was Stena worried about Abby's situation? She still couldn't be a hundred percent sure if the girl was friend or foe. "Well, thank you," she said, trying not to sound as suspicious as she felt.

"And I know you're not living in the area right now, at least according to Stan, but if you need a place to stay, I've got extra room at my place."

Okay, this was sounding too good to be true. What was going on? "Stena, I don't mean to look a gift—" Abby broke off, realizing what she'd been about to say.

"A gift horse in the mouth?" Stena finished for her. "I'm not offended. I know I'm coming on strong, but here's the deal. Ever since you and I played together in that awful little apartment of yours—sorry, but it really was a tragic little place," Stena interjected, with an apologetic note in her voice.

Abby chuckled softly. "Tragic. Pitiful. Disgusting. All the above, yes."

"Except none of that mattered. Once I heard us together? Abby, it's all I can think about. I have had few regrets in my admittedly short life, but not getting to perform live with you is right up there at the top of the list."

Abby frowned, still not sure what to make of all of this. "I agree," Abby acknowledged. "I was really looking forward to having you on stage with me, too."

There was a short silence, then Stena jumped in like she'd just made up her mind about something. "Okay. I'm going to come clean, but you can't judge me for not saying anything before. I'm only telling you this because I can tell you're still not sold on the idea."

"Okay." Abby drew the word out. This was getting too weird.

"Lone River Band. Ever heard of them?" She almost sounded like she hoped Abby would say she hadn't.

"I have," she said with a nod, even though Stena couldn't see her. Their music wasn't something she listened to on a regular basis, but The Lone River Band was kind of a classic element in country music. They'd had several solid hits over the years, and although they'd unofficially retired years ago, they still played every once in a while.

"Yeah, well, that's our dads," Stena explained. "Charlie Holder on bass, and Rick—"

"Oh, my gosh," Abby interrupted. "Rick Tremaine. On drums! Your dads are in The Lone River Band? Why on earth are you two out there working the strip so hard?" she asked. "I mean, sorry if that's too personal a question, but I'm a little mind blown over here."

"I know, which is why we don't really tell people. Our dads have told us both that we need to earn our places in the industry, on our own merit, not theirs, so that's what we're doing."

"Oh, you're doing it, that's for sure. You both are amazing," Abby declared. But something was sticking in her craw. "Why Stan?" she blurted out.

Stena chuckled. "He's a rough piece of work, isn't he? But he was just a new kid in the business back then, but he played a big part in putting Lone River on the map. My dad has every faith in him, and he wouldn't let me work with anyone else."

"I see." So that's why no one else had snapped Stena up. The woman had hand-picked Stan. Or her father had, at least. Abby decided to be up front, too. "I can see that. But you know, don't you, that Stan terminated my contract? I am not really on the best terms with him."

"That's not true!" Stena declared, then shouted to be heard above the loud hammering on her end of the line. "He even suggested I reach out to you."

"He did?" That set her back a little. He *had* been kind to her when he'd left her apartment, hadn't he? In fact, he'd even said he was confident she'd be back, that it might just be timing. Apparently, then, he'd meant it.

"He did," Stena confirmed. "He thinks you're super talented."

"I see," she said again, warmed by the praise from such an unlikely source. The hammering started up again, and her curiosity got the better of her. "What's going on there? You sound like you're in a construction zone."

Stena laughed. "Actually, I am. And I really need to go soon—I'm supposed to be giving my feedback to these guys—but I had to call you immediately or I was afraid I'd chicken out of calling you."

Stena Holder, Charlie Holder's daughter, was afraid to call Abby?

"Anyway, I'm at my dad's condo, the one where he and Rick rented when they first got started. He bought it a couple years back when it went on the market and has been renting it out since. But Shelby and I have taken it over, and we did a major remodel to it. It's gorgeous, if I do say so myself. And this weekend, we're turning one of the four bedrooms into a recording studio; how cool is that? We figure it makes Nashville officially home away from home for us."

"Wow." So Stena and Shelby might be learning the ropes on the surface, but their paths were paved with gold, she realized. Their fathers' gold records. No wonder she'd thought so little of Abby's apartment. She took great care not to let any jealousy seep into her voice. "That sounds amazing."

"And like I said," Stena continued, sounding worried that Abby was still going to turn her down. "You can stay with us if you don't mind having roommates. Even with the studio, we still have one extra room that we were probably going to rent out at some point, anyway. It could be yours, either temporarily, until you find something more permanent, or you can move in and rent it."

A super group of brilliant musicians, a remodeled and updated band house with an in-house studio, Stan Wallenberg back on her side, *and* she'd still be able to keep her own name? How much more could she ask for? It was a dream come true.

"Please say yes, Abby," Stena begged. "I have my heart set on this. On you."

Abby could hardly begrudge the girl for having almost everything in life handed to her, not when she seemed to be generous to a fault with it.

Then Stena sealed the deal with one last *Touché*. "There won't be any Bucky in this band, either."

Abby chuckled appreciatively. "You know how to play your cards, Stena."

"Does that mean you'll do it? You're coming back to Nashville?" Her excitement was contagious.

"What's your timeline? And the room would be great, but what's the rent?" Both were issues, she realized, the glint of her new ring catching her eye. But she'd be stupid to say no, no matter what Stena's response was. "When would you want me there?"

"Can you come next weekend? And we'll make the rent work, promise."

After a moment's hesitation, Abby nodded slowly. "Okay. I can be there next weekend."

Stena whooped so loudly the phone speaker crackled. Abby winced at the shriek, but she was feeling rather giddy herself.

The sound of the front door opening and closing caught Abby's attention. Where was Cass going? Had she forgotten something in her truck? "I'd better go, Stena. I promised to help with the cooking."

"Go. I have to check on my—*our*—studio, too. We'll talk soon, okay?"

Abby said her goodbyes, then headed down the hall and out to the living room. She pulled open the front door and looked outside to where Cass had gone. "Cass?" she called when she didn't see her.

"I'm right here, honey," Cass said from where she stood in the kitchen, reading over her mail. "You walked right past me," she said, when Abby spun around in the door.

"But I—" Confused, Abby pointed at the door over her shoulder. "I thought I heard you go out."

"That was Mike," Cass said. Something in the way she spoke sent a frisson of panic shooting up Abby's spine. "He came in with me. Behind me, actually. I guess you missed him. He was carrying some groceries for me."

"Oh." She suddenly realized exactly what that meant. "Then he... you both heard all that."

Cass nodded. "Yeah."

"Where did he go?" Abby was almost afraid to ask. "Is he coming back?"

Cass straightened the small stack of envelopes on the counter in front of her, then set them aside. Her face was marked by concern. "He didn't say. We tried not to listen, but you had things up pretty loud."

"On speaker," Abby moaned.

"On speaker. And the sound channels out of that hallway like a megaphone. It was impossible not to hear," Cass expounded.

"What did he say?"

"Not much." She waved a hand in a circle in front of her face. "He got this look, you know? Like he didn't know quite how to process everything. He just said he had to go."

"And you let him leave?"

"Honey, I wasn't going to force him to stay." Cass circled the counter and crossed the room to pull Abby into a quick hug. "I'm sorry."

Abby shook her head. "Why are you sorry? I'm the one who keeps screwing things up. Mike and I finally seemed to be getting things sorted out, and then I go and dump cold water on everything."

"Give him his space," Cass murmured, pulling back to look at her. "You two need to learn to trust each other," she gently admonished.

Abby scoffed. "Yeah, but I just proved myself not to be worthy of his trust, didn't I? He just overheard me agreeing to move back to Nashville next week, right after telling him we had a couple of months to figure out a plan for our future."

"And I just heard you agree to move back to Nashville next week, right, even though you told me you'd play at The Smokehouse next Friday night," Cass said, patting Abby's cheek. "Yet, here I am, waiting to get the details about this amazing opportunity, because I want the best for you. And I don't love you nearly as much as that handsome young man of yours does," she teased.

Abby covered her face with her hands. "The Smokehouse," she groaned. "I have to call Stena back right now. I need more time. And I have to make peace with Daddy, and now with Mike again."

"Slow down," Cass said as Abby pulled her phone from her back pocket and swiped it on. "Don't do anything impulsive; that's what's got you in this dilemma right now."

"But I am not going to bail on Friday night," Abby declared. "I'm not going to let everyone down again." Because, of course, once Cass had the go-ahead, the news had spread quickly that Abby would be playing live at The Smokehouse for one night only.

A knock at the door startled her and she nearly dropped her phone again. Why was she was so jumpy today?

FORTY-EIGHT

BEFORE CASS COULD GET around Abby, Mike pushed open the front door and stepped into the room. "Hey, ladies," he said, his gaze going from one face to the other. "I'm sorry I left the way I did." He didn't look sheepish, but Abby could tell he was worried about how they'd receive him.

"It's fine," Abby told him, not sure what to do. Should she go to him and hug him? Wait for him to make the first move? "I'm the one who should be apologizing. I should have talked to you before I made any kind of decision. I was just getting ready to call her back now."

"You're going to go, aren't you?" Mike asked, almost cutting her off. But he didn't sound angry or even hurt the way she'd expected. "You *are* going," he reiterated, emphasizing the word 'are'.

"I—I am still trying to work out the details."

Mike glanced at Cass again, like he was trying to figure out how much she'd told Abby. "We heard the details," he said. "Pretty much all of them."

"I know,' Abby murmured, her voice breaking. "I'm sorry. I didn't handle that right." She toyed with her ring, spinning it around and around on her finger in slow turns.

Mike stepped forward and took her hands in his, stilling her nervous movements. "Abs, stop. You're not hearing me. I want you to go."

"But..." She hesitated, not sure she understood. "You left. Without saying anything."

Cass quietly excused herself and went back to the kitchen to check on the chicken in the oven.

Mike tugged Abby a little closer to him and lowered his voice a notch. "I'm sorry. I had to clear my head, that's all. A quick reboot."

"But I told you we had a couple of months."

"I know." He smiled at her, but she wasn't fooled. His eyes gave away his true emotions. "And I told you I would support you in following your dreams. That I wanted to be the one you come home to. So let me do that for you."

"But Mike, this means I'm leaving again."

He nodded. "I know. It's okay. Give me the chance to make up for the last time." he insisted. "I want to do things right by you."

"But—"

"Do I need to kiss you again to get you to stop arguing with me?"

Abby scowled up at him. "Is that how things are going to be with us? Every time you don't like what I'm saying, you're just going to kiss me to silence me?" But she had to look away quickly to hide the happy blush she could feel warming her cheeks. She could think of worse ways to end an argument.

"Only if you promise to never stop arguing with me." He nudged her foot with the tip of his sneaker. "Hey."

Abby lifted her gaze to his again, and this time, his smile *did* reach his eyes. Even his dimples made an appearance. He took a step closer and rested his forehead against hers. "There's always the alternative, you know."

"And what is that?"

"We could just kiss for the fun of it." He was so close she could feel his warm breath against her temple.

"I like that idea." Abby lifted her face, aching for his lips on hers.

"I don't."

"Daddy!" Abby jerked back, startled to see her father's silhouette through Cass's screen door. Mike startled, too, but Cass just waved from where she stood in the kitchen.

"Hello, Mr. Goodacre. Come in," Cass called before turning to Abby with a sheepish expression. She'd been expecting him, it seemed. "You'll be joining us for dinner, then." It wasn't a question.

Jedediah Goodacre was no fool, Abby knew, and only a fool would say no to Cass Whitehouse's cooking. As he pulled open the screen door, he said, "I seem to have come at the opportune time. Again."

"You have indeed," Cass assured him.

"Sir," Mike said with a respectful nod. He kept hold of one of Abby's hands, but moved back to make room for Jed as he stepped inside the suddenly crowded entryway.

"Young buck," Jed said by way of greeting. But his eyes stayed fixed on his daughter. "Abby."

"Oh, Daddy," she wailed, letting go of Mike's hand to fly into her father's arms. "I'm so sorry. I said things—"

"Hush, child," her father crooned, wrapping her in his embrace. "You have nothing to apologize for. Your wounds are my wounds, do you hear?"

She wanted to argue, but being held like this, his daddy smell all around her like a favorite childhood blanket, she could do nothing but nod against his chest.

She kept her arms around him, but pulled back so she could look up at him. "I'm sorry I didn't come straight to you," she told him. "I should have, and I know that."

"The good Lord works all things together, child," he said, giving her one more squeeze. "Because of the way things happened with you, I was given a glimpse of insight into both your life and my life that I might not have gotten otherwise."

From the kitchen, Cass called, "Ms. Goodacre, would you please bring yourself and your menfolk on in? Supper is almost ready, and I could use a hand with things in here. We'll eat first so this deliciousness doesn't get overcooked. Talk after our bellies are full."

"Always a good idea," Jed agreed, his voice making his chest vibrate against Abby's cheek.

Abby linked arms with him and led him to the table. "Are you here for supper, then?" She shot a look over her shoulder at Mike, who had stepped in behind them.

"It's all good," Mike mouthed, giving her two thumbs up.

Cass put everyone to work setting the table, pouring drinks, and tossing a green salad with her homemade dressing. By the time they sat down to eat, Abby found that, for the first time since coming home, she was ravenous. Relief did funny things to a person, that was for certain.

Cass asked Jed to say the blessing, and when he took Abby's hand in his big, gnarled one, she experienced such a sense of nostalgia that she had to hold her breath to keep from choking up.

"Almighty God." It was how he had begun every prayer for as far back as Abby could remember.

FORTY-NINE

THERE WAS HARDLY A crumb left on anyone's plates when the meal was over. Jed sat back in his chair, satiated in both body and spirit. He was looking forward to giving Abby the gift he'd brought with him, but it could wait while the group of them enjoyed their small talk.

Cass Whitehouse, it seemed, had finally found a man who understood the worth of a good woman. William "Badger" Kane, a man who could rival Jed, himself, for being stoic, had, as Cass put it, 'staked his claim' on her by introducing her as his girlfriend to his mother over the phone on a video chat.

"She invited me to come out to their place with Badger the next time he visits," Cass told them, her face lit up with happiness. He liked seeing the woman that way—she'd seen far too much of the ugly side of selfish men in her life, and it was high time that she had a good man who could put that special smile on her face.

Then there was Abby. His precious youngest child. Jed studied her discreetly as she made doe eyes at young Mike. The sight of it made his ribcage tight. It wasn't easy, seeing her truly all grown up, but knowing her heart belonged to someone who clearly belonged in the hollow meant that she'd have good reason to always come home.

He'd noticed the ring on her left hand, and although it didn't look like a traditional engagement ring, it was on the significant finger, and she fidgeted with it throughout the meal, like she wasn't accustomed to it being there. He was dying to know if it had any special significance, but he'd wait a bit longer; see if she—if they—would tell him about it in their own time.

Jed wouldn't mind another wedding in the family. His pockets might be all but empty, but seeing his daughters loving and being loved by good men made every penny spent worth it. Mike Nesbit, Jed knew, came from good stock, and if he offered Abby the same kind of marriage his parents shared, then Jed had no complaints.

"It's a promise ring, sir," Mike said, startling Jed out of his thoughts. He'd been caught eyeing the bobble, apparently.

Jed turned to Mike. "I see." He didn't, not really. Sure, he knew what a promise ring was. He'd essentially given something of the sort to Charlotte yesterday—

Charlotte. Just thinking her name made him lose his train of thought. He suddenly missed her fiercely. He would have loved to have her sitting here with him this evening, holding his hand under the table while he carried out his plan. But she'd flown back to Colorado today.

"Daddy?"

"Hm?" His daughter was looking at him like he had a second head. He cleared his throat. "A promise ring, you say? And just what kind of promises are you making to my daughter, Mr. Nesbit?"

"Daddy." Abby's voice was now more wary than worried. She placed her hand flat on the table, then turned it this way and that. "It's so beautiful, isn't it?"

"It's perfect for you, Abby," Cass declared from his other side, nudging his foot under the table. She gave him a look that probably meant, 'Straighten up, old man. Don't ruin it now.'

Jed nodded. "It is," he agreed. "But my question stands. What are you promising?"

"I'm promising to love her and support her, and to be here for her," Mike said, his gaze never wavering.

"And I'm promising him the same thing," Abby said.

"What about marriage? Is that not on the list?" Jed looked back and forth between them a few times, but his focus went right back to Mike. "Or is that too old-fashioned for you kids these days?"

"Daddy." This time, there was a warning in her tone.

Mike straightened in his seat. His shoulders went back a little, and although his jaw tightened ever so slightly, he remained seemingly unruffled by Jed's challenging responses. "Actually, Mr. Goodacre, I've asked your daughter to marry me, and she said yes. I would have asked you first, but I honestly hadn't intended—I hadn't believed it possible—that Abby would be quite so ready to say yes to me. This promise ring, one I bought back in high school a few years ago, was meant to warm her up to the idea before I popped the question officially."

"I see." And now, he got it. Charlotte had refused to let him replace the handcrafted silver ring he'd picked out for her from a local silversmith, Trace Graham, who sold custom jewelry online. And out of his garage shop, thank goodness. Jed had gone to him hoping to find something pre-made that would be suitable, but when he'd explained the situation to Trace, the man had whipped out a tray of one-of-a-kind pieces, to choose one. He'd had every intention of getting Charlotte the real deal on Monday when he went to the big city, but she'd insisted that the ring she now wore was more real to her than any ordinary old engagement ring would be. He'd seen the futility of arguing with her too many times over the last nine months to think that he'd get a different response the next day, or the next month, or for years to come. The size and shape of the ring didn't change the weight of the promises behind it, and that, he understood full well. "Well, you could ask me now," Jed prompted.

Mike didn't miss a beat. He pushed his chair back from the table, then pulled Abby up to stand beside him. "Sir," he began. "I have already asked your daughter to share my future, to be my wife when she's ready, to have me as her husband. She has yes to all of it—" He broke off and gave Abby a quick, intimate half-smile; a shared joke between them, perhaps? "Would you give me your blessing to marry your daughter? I promise to take care of her. I promise to love her and honor her and support her dreams." Now it was Mike toying with the ring he'd put on Abby's finger.

"Do I get a promise ring, too, then?" Jed asked, playing just a little more hardball with the kid. Could they really be old enough to marry? He'd married Caroline when she'd been even younger than Abby was now.

"Daddy!" Abby was scolding him now.

Beside him, Cass chortled with delight, but she nudged him again under the table. "You're awful, Jed. Give the poor kids a break."

"I'm just giving you a hard time," Jed assured them, trying not to chuckle at their obvious discomfort. "Sit down, both of you."

When they were seated again, their hands clasped tightly, their chairs scooted a little closer together than they'd been only moments before, Jed nodded. "Yes, I give you my blessing."

Abby relaxed visibly, her shoulders dropping as she let out a long breath. Had she been holding it all this time? "Thank you, sir," Mike said with great decorum. "It means the world to us that you approve."

"I do, indeed," Jed assured them. "But I want to give you something else, too." He pulled an envelope from his back pocket and slid it across the table toward Abby. "I suppose if you're going to marry my daughter, Mr. Nesbit, then it's only fitting that you should be here for this," he said, tapping the envelope.

He had driven more than three hours each way to the Jefferson County Clerk's Office in Louisville and had stood in three different lines to make sure he had exactly what he needed to present his daughter with. He knew it had been above and beyond what was necessary—Trudy had insisted he could download and print out the documents he needed right there in the church office—but Jed had wanted to leave nothing to chance with so important a task. When he'd made it home with plenty of daylight to spare, he'd made up his mind to finish the deed without another day lost. He'd hurried through his day-end chores, called Cass to ask if he could come by that evening, and had been ecstatic when she'd invited him to join them for supper.

"Mike will be here, too," she'd said with calculated nonchalance... and what else? Censure? But now he understood. She'd been warning him to be on his best behavior in the company of Abby's man.

Cass started to rise, obviously trying to be sensitive to this monumental moment, but Jed put a hand on her arm to stay her. "Please stay, Ms. Whitehouse." He hoped she could see in his expression how grateful he was for her in their lives.

Abby pulled the envelope closer but didn't open it. "What is it?" she asked, looking up at him with round eyes. "This looks pretty official," she added, rubbing her fingertip over the Commonwealth of Kentucky Court of Justice seal in the upper left-hand corner.

"Open it."

Her hands trembled as she flipped open the unsealed envelope and withdrew the document inside. She unfolded it slowly, her eyes skimming over the filled out form, then she lifted her confused gaze to his. "I—I don't understand," she whispered.

"It's a petition to change your name," Jed began.

"Change my—Why would I—" Abby broke off, shock and confusion darkening her gaze.

"But only if you want to," Jed added. This wasn't going the way he'd planned, but he hadn't figured on it being easy.

"But, Daddy," Abby began, her eyes filling with tears that she kept trying to blink back. She put the form face down on the table and slid it back toward him. "Those things I said. I was just lashing out. I don't mean them. I don't really believe those things I said about you," she insisted, shifting in her seat so she could lean her head on his shoulder.

"Oh, my sweet Abby-girl," Jed said, putting an arm around her and pulling her into an uncomfortable side-hug. Dining table chairs were not built to accommodate hugs. "I have often wondered, especially over the last few years, if Abstinence was a cruel name to foist on you. It was never intended to be, but I was so lost in my grief, I wasn't able to see clearly about a lot of things."

"I know," she said. "And I've never held it against you. I—I don't really know why I said all those things, and I'm so sorry."

"Enough, child. I give you my forgiveness, if that's what you need from me. But I also want to give you my blessing to do this." He tapped the form gently. "To change your name."

"But I don't want to change my name." She straightened in her chair, shrugging his arm from around her shoulders. Her tears were falling freely now. "I don't understand why you're asking me to do this."

"Abs," Mike murmured gently beside her. He leaned close and placed a gentle kiss on her temple. "Hear him out, okay?"

She turned on him, but he didn't pull away. "Did you know about this?" Abby looked over at Cass. "You, too?"

Jed spoke, his voice raised a little to be heard over Abby's tone. "This was my doing, Abby, and mine alone. Nothing has been made official yet, either. This is simply the petition form that must be turned in to get your name changed."

"I don't understand," Abby said again, her voice breaking. "Why would you think I'd want to do something like this?"

Jed took a deep breath. All day, he'd been attempting to come up with the perfect explanation for his actions, but to no avail. He opened his mouth and said what was on his heart, praying his words would be few and sincere, and that his daughter would hear and recognize the depth of his love for her.

"Your name, Abstinence, was given to you because it was the seventh virtue, not because I needed a constant reminder of my failure. Unfortunately, especially in today's culture, the word has been shoved into a box that has squeezed all the power and scope out of it. Abstinence once was synonymous with temperance—and perhaps we should have named you Temperance instead—which alludes to self-control and speaks of practicing moderation when it comes to self-indulgences."

"I know all of this, Dad," Abby said impatiently, swiping at her tears. "You're preaching to the choir."

Jed turned the form on the table right side up and pointed at a line about a third of the way down the paper. "Do you see this name?"

Abby shot a glance at the document and nodded, but she had crossed her arms and was now chewing on her bottom lip. He knew that body language well; she was listening, but she didn't like what she was hearing.

"Abby-girl," he said slowly, letting the syllables roll off his tongue with great tenderness. "I've been calling you that all your life."

"I know. And I still love it when you do," she acknowledged.

Jed reached over and put his large hand on top of his daughter's head, as if in benediction. "You are and always have been a joy and a delight to me, child. Do you know that?"

She nodded. "I do, Daddy."

"You are not and never have been a regret in my life, not for a single moment. I want you to know that, too."

"I know," Abby whispered, still sniffling. But she was listening more attentively now.

"You are no longer a child, and I no longer have sway in your life the way I did when you were. But I can give you my blessing in this marriage you and Mike will one day enter into. And I can give you my blessing in this way." Jed tapped the paper again. "The decision is yours. You can do nothing, and nothing changes. Or you can put this petition in that envelope and drop it in the mail and make it official. There's no hurry, no deadline. You can take as much time as you want to think about it, or you can drop it in the mail right now. It's all up to you."

Abby reached a tentative hand toward the paper and let her eyes glide over it again. The tension in her shoulders seemed to ease.

"Abigail," he said, getting a little choked up at how closely it resembled Abby-girl. He cleared his throat and pressed on. "Abigail means 'A father's joy' child, and that's what you are to me."

Cass sniffled softly beside him, and Jed glanced over at her.

"Don't mind me," she said, waving away his attention. "I'm just over here taking it all in."

Jed turned to Mike. "I expect you to fulfill every one of those promises you made to my daughter, and more."

"Absolutely, Mr. Goodacre." Mike nodded earnestly while Abby refolded the petition and slid it back inside the envelope.

Jed continued. "But I only need one promise from you, Mr. Nesbit."

"Sir?"

"Keep bringing my daughter home to those of us who love her most. And I don't need a promise ring. A handshake will do just fine."

"You have my word, sir." Mike stuck out his hand to seal the deal.

Cass dabbed at her cheeks with her napkin. "Dessert, anyone? I made us a scrumptious raspberry cream torte."

A phone rang, and all four of them paused to listen. "I think that's yours, Dad," Abby said, her voice still a little wobbly.

He reached behind him and pulled the phone from his back pocket. When he saw the name on the screen, he had to bite the inside of his lip to keep from grinning like the lovesick fool that he was. But he certainly wasn't going to answer Charlotte's call right now. He shoved the phone back in place, but forgot to turn the sound off, so it continued ringing in his pocket. Jed pretended not to hear it.

"Who is that?" Abby asked, eyeing him suspiciously.

"Mind your own beeswax, Abby-girl."

"But you are my beeswax, Daddy. Who is it?" she asked again, her eyes lighting up with mischief. "Is it your girlfriend, Ms. Ransome?"

Jed shot her a droll look. "Now, what would make you think that?"

"Oh, please." Abby rolled her eyes. "We live in a small town, remember? You don't think word hasn't trickled down to me about you and a certain shepherdess from out of state?" she teased.

Jed turned to Cass. "I'd love a piece of that torte, Ms. Whitehouse," he said, doing his best to ignore his daughter.

"Coming right up," Cass told him, getting to her feet. "Abby, grab some dishes and help me serve up dessert." When Mike started to rise, she put a hand on his shoulder. "No, no," she said. "We girls have got this."

While Abby ran hot water over the dishes in the sink, Cass pulled from the fridge a pretty layered cake covered with her famous buttercream frosting and fresh raspberries in a pretty design on top. Jed's mouth watered in anticipation.

"This is Badger's all-time favorite," Cass said with a little shimmy of her shoulders. She began slicing the cake and transferring the wedges to dessert plates. "Do you think it would be weird if I made my own wedding cake?" she asked as she handed two of the plates to Abby.

"Woman, you can do whatever you want," Abby said, as the two of them returned to the table. "It'll be your wedding." Wiggling her eyebrows dramatically, she asked, "So, does that mean we'll soon be hearing wedding bells ringing in Plumwood Hollow again?"

Cass set one plate in front of Jed and one in front of Mike before taking hers from Abby. "Yours or mine?" she asked with a sassy wink in Jed's direction. "Or your daddy's?"

Abby snort-laughed, a sound so sweet to Jed's ears. He couldn't wait to get home and call Charlotte. He had so much to tell her.

~ ~ ~

Did you enjoy your visit with the youngest—and oldest—of the Goodacre family? Isn't it such a joy that Jed is getting his own happily ever after, too? **Something About Abby** wraps up this series about the seven Goodacre sisters, but if you still want just a little more...

There's a WEDDING SEQUEL!
Whose wedding is it, you ask?

Pick up **A Wedding at the Ranch** today and find out!

Have you met the Gustafson Girls yet?
Read the whole heartwarming Contemporary Christian Romance series about sisters, second chances, and, of course, happily ever after.

Juliette & the Monday ManDates: The Gustafson Girls Book 1 .

JULIETTE IS PERFECTLY CONTENT with her evenings at home alone, especially when they include Chinese takeout and sappy RomComs.

But her sisters think she's teetering on the brink of spinsterhood. So they've come up with an intervention plan: weekly blind dates until Jules finds her white knight... or until they run out of single guy friends.

They're calling it The Monday ManDates.

Juliette secretly doles out nicknames for each new Monday man. There's TheraPaul, Frisky Frank, and TAZ the Rock Star, for starters.

Then there's Officer Manly Man, the police officer with a penchant for pulling Juliette over when she's at her very worst.

With a lineup like that, positively identifying her happily ever after seems like a long shot.

Then again, maybe she's looking for love in all the wrong places.

~ ~ ~

"Finally, a book with interesting characters... witty, emotional, REAL, sexy, and Christian without being self-righteous! More, please!" **Reader Review**

Pick up **Juliette & the Monday ManDates** today
Or keep reading for an excerpt...

A Note from Becky

Dear Reader,

Have you enjoyed getting to know Jedediah Goodacre and his seven lovely daughters and their families? What about the indomitable Ms. Charlotte Rawlings? Isn't she something else? Well, I sure have fallen in love with this family, this little town, and the folks who call Plumwood Hollow home. And I'm looking forward to the wedding in **A Wedding at the Ranch** now, aren't you?

I like to say that I write characters you'll want to hug, but that's the one problem with books, isn't it? It's hard to hug a fictional character! So instead, I write *books* you'll want to hug... heartfelt and wholesome Contemporary Romance, Women's Fiction, and even some Romantic Suspense.

If you're looking for fiction with relatable characters and redemptive storylines, then I hope you'll check out my other books and series, too. Or come visit me online at **BeckyDoughty.com** and subscribe to my newsletter for the latest book and audiobook news and updates and other subscriber-exclusive stuff.

Where hope lives and love triumphs.
Becky Doughty

An Excerpt...

Juliette & the Monday ManDates

Chapter 1

JULIETTE STARED WIDE-EYED INTO the rear-view mirror at the red and blue lights flashing behind her. Her palms began to sweat as her heart rate sky-rocketed, and it took her several minutes to pull her little PT Cruiser out of the dinner-hour traffic.

She waited, both hands gripping the steering wheel, as the officer approached her window. Finding it still closed, he tapped on it, and she jumped, letting out a tiny squeal. "Sorry!" she called through the glass, turning the car back on so she could operate the power windows. She worked the knobs, sending the backseat window up and down twice before she finally managed to get hers open. "Sorry," she repeated, peering up at the very tall officer whose eyes were hidden behind his sunglasses.

"Please turn off your engine, ma'am." His voice was firm, and Juliette scrambled to comply.

"Sorry," she muttered a third time, afraid now to look up at him. She toyed with the keys in her lap, sensing his eyes boring into the top of her head. She was sure she'd smell burning hair at any moment.

"May I see your license and registration, please?"

After wrestling with the latch on the glove compartment, she withdrew the paperwork for her car, then reached into the back seat to grab her purse from off the floor. Out of the corner of her eye, she saw him take a step back and put a hand on his holster.

The idea that she might be pulling a weapon struck her as funny, and she had to bite her lip to keep from giggling. Her hands trembled, making it difficult to slide her license from its pocket in her wallet.

"Is everything all right, ma'am?"

"Yes, Officer." The late afternoon sun setting in the sky behind him made her squint. She couldn't tell if he was looking at her or not, but she caught a glimpse of her warped reflection in his sunglasses. "I'm just really nervous, I guess."

"Why are you so nervous?"

"I—I don't know," she stammered as she handed over her license. "I've never been pulled over before, and I'm trying not to freak out."

"I'm not going to hurt you."

"Oh. Good. Thanks." She grimaced. It sounded as though she'd been afraid of just that. "I mean, I know you're not going to hurt me. At least I think I do. I meant thanks for trying to reassure me. I can't help it, though; I get nervous easily." She should just close her mouth. She wasn't making things better by talking.

"Do you know how fast you were driving?"

"Um, I think so." She wrapped her damp fingers around the steering wheel again. "Actually, I'm not sure."

"Ten miles over the speed limit." His voice remained calm, patient, rattling her even more. "Do you know what the speed limit is here?"

"Um, I think so," she said again, a hot flush creeping up her chest and neck. "Actually, I—I'm not exactly sure about that either." Her voice cracked into a whisper.

The officer cleared his throat. "Ma'am, I'm a little concerned. You don't seem to know some pretty important pieces of information that someone who gets behind the wheel of a car should know." His patronizing tone irritated her. "The speed limit here is 35 miles per hour. You were driving 45." He paused, just long enough to make her squirm, before continuing. "Were you in a hurry to get somewhere?"

"No, not really." She shook her head and forgot about keeping her mouth shut. "I was just hungry, and I wasn't paying attention to how fast I was driving."

The officer chuckled, a low rumble that made her stomach flip-flop uncomfortably. "You were speeding because you were hungry? That's a first."

Her grip on the steering wheel tightened; he was mocking her. *Jerk*, she thought to herself. "Well, it's the truth." She tried to glare at him, but the sun made it difficult, and she had to turn away again.

He leaned down to look around the inside of her car while she fumed in her seat. As if satisfied there was nothing suspicious about her, he straightened again, tore off a page from his ticket pad, and handed it to her, along with her license.

"Look, Ms. Gustafson. Believe it or not, I appreciate your honesty. But being distracted is a dangerous way to drive, much more so than driving too fast because you choose to ignore the speed limit. Did you know that most accidents happen when a driver is distracted? Let this be a wake-up call for you. It's why we give tickets; not necessarily to punish drivers for bad behavior, but to encourage them to drive better." He pointed at the pink form she held. "Just follow the instructions on the ticket."

She couldn't believe it. He was actually lecturing her! First, he mocked her, then he lectured her. No longer nervous, she was offended. She nodded, her lips clamped shut, afraid of what she might say if she let any words slip out.

He patted the roof of her car. "Drive safely now, Ms. Gustafson."

"Thank you, Officer," she managed to squeeze out, her upbringing forcing her to be polite. "Not for the ticket, of course. Or the lecture." Why, oh why, couldn't she just stop talking? "I mean, thank you for wishing me safe driving. Thank you for saying 'Drive safely now.'" Her voice trailed off. She stuck her keys in the ignition, turned on the car, and rolled up the window without looking at him again.

"Imbecile," she muttered, not sure if she was referring to him or herself.

A ticket. Her first ever. She didn't know whether to cry or celebrate. And today, of all days. Today marked six months of life without Mike.

Juliette tucked her feet up underneath her as she nestled into the corner of her over-stuffed beige couch. This was her spot. It had always been her spot, and at this rate, it probably always would be. She maneuvered the TV tray over her knees until it was positioned just the way she liked it.

"Another wonderful meal with me, myself, and I. I can eat whatever I want, whenever I want, however I want, wherever I want. No one can tell me otherwise, and I like it this way." Juliette raised her plastic fork in a defiant salute, then stabbed it into the middle of The Green Dragon food on her tray. She spun the utensil until it was loaded with noodles and shoved the whole bundle into her mouth. She couldn't close her lips around the bite, but she didn't care; she just chewed with her mouth open.

"Delicious!" she exclaimed when she could speak again. "It's you I love, Mr. Chen Yu. Only you." She pointed the remote at the television and pressed play. A terribly acted romance-novel-come-to-life started up again where she'd left it to go pick up her takeout. The heroine was overly made up and vacuous. The male lead looked like he'd been shellacked from head to toe, not a hair or muscle out of place. Even his jeans were pressed. She actually wanted the woman to leave him. The story line was not making her cry, nor giving her anything else to relate to, and it was sucking all the joy out of her favorite food.

Just as she was debating whether she could stand another second of the sappy dialogue, her phone rang.

At first, she tried to ignore it. Then she thought it might be Mike and contemplated throwing the thing out the window. She let it ring instead, and the call eventually went to voicemail, beeping rudely at her. Sighing dramatically, she turned up the movie, preferring to see it through to the bitter end than to be stuck with her thoughts of Mike.

A few minutes later, the phone rang again. "Are you serious?" She pushed the TV tray away and scrambled for the purse she'd dropped on the floor at the end of the couch. It was Renata. "What do you want?" she muttered under her breath, while she considered whether she could handle talking to her sister right now.

Either she was calling to make sure Juliette wasn't drowning herself in the bathtub, or she was calling to try to coerce her into going on another family outing to Pizza Haven or the local dog park. "I don't even have a dog! Or a family, for that matter. Or a man." She sighed and brought the phone to her ear.

"Hi, Ren." She knew she sounded miserable, but she didn't care. Regardless of how she answered the phone, Renata believed Juliette was seriously depressed, and if she sounded otherwise, her sister reminded her she didn't have to fake it with her.

"How are you, sweetie?"

"Why do you call me sweetie?" Juliette voiced the first question that popped into her head, belligerence tattering the edges of her words. She softened her tone just a little. "In fact, you call all of us that."

"Do I?" Renata asked. "It must be because I think you're all so sweet. And actually, I don't call Phoebe that. She'd rip my head off and drop-kick it into outer space."

"Hm. Did you two have another run-in?" Juliette smirked at her own ridiculous question. Renata and Phoebe never had anything but run-ins.

As though reading her thoughts, Renata declared, "We don't have run-ins. We just think differently. But I didn't call you to talk about Phoebe. I called to find out how you're doing."

"I'm fine." Juliette opted for cryptic. She'd hadn't turned down the movie and was struggling to focus on what Renata was saying.

"You're fine? Really? What is that noise? Do you have company?"

"I'm fine. Really. The noise is a movie. No, I don't have company. Any other questions?" Juliette rolled her eyes as the two main characters on screen started moving toward each other across a parking lot in slow motion.

"You're starting to sound like Phoebe." Juliette could hear the disdain in Renata's voice, and it made her bristle.

"That's not such a bad thing," she said, defending their younger sister.

"Oh relax. I don't mean it's bad. I just mean you don't sound like you, because you're acting like her." Renata sighed. "Again, I didn't call to talk about Phoebe."

"What did you call about, Ren?" Juliette couldn't decide which was worse, this conversation or her movie.

"We had a G-FOURce yesterday."

All ears now, Juliette grabbed the remote and paused the lovers mid-lunge. "What? Why didn't anyone call me? I didn't know." She didn't remember scheduling a meeting with her sisters.

"Wait." A terrible thought occurred to her. "Renata, why didn't I know there was a G-FOURce yesterday?"

"Because we needed to meet without you. We're having a follow-up tomorrow, though, and you need to be there for that one."

"What's going on? I don't like the sound of this. In fact, I'm not sure I really want to be there." Juliette's mind was spinning. They'd met without her. That meant they'd met to talk about her. "This is another one of your interventions, isn't it?"

Renata didn't deny it. "We're worried about you, sweetie."

"Stop calling me that! I'm not your sweetie, Renata. I'm not your child, and I'm not some empty-headed twit who needs to be called placating names." Juliette pressed her forehead into the palm of her free hand and closed her eyes, immediately ashamed of her uncharacteristic outburst. "Look, I don't need an intervention, okay? Yes, I'm sad. Yes, I'm even slightly depressed. When I think about Mike, I get hot and sweaty, but not in a good way. I get sad, and then angry, and then wonder what's so wrong with me that he couldn't love me like I loved him."

"Wouldn't," Renata interjected. "Love is a decision, Juliette. That's why John and I are still married after all these years."

Ah yes. Mr. and Mrs. Perfect. "Regardless, my reactions are normal. I'm not on the verge of suicide, and I'm not going to go be a hermit on some isolated mountaintop. I just need a little time to lick my wounds and heal up a bit."

There was silence on the other end of the phone. "Ren? You still there?"

"Tomorrow. Five o'clock. Your place. That way, you can't ditch us. Come straight home from work, Juliette. Don't dawdle." The phone went dead in her hand.

"Yes, Mother," Juliette muttered. She glared down the sofa to her spot at the other end, where her food waited patiently, trying not to congeal. Her plastic fork had been knocked to the floor in her scramble for the phone and was nowhere to be seen. She didn't really care; she wasn't so hungry anymore.

"I need a dog," she said. "One that will love me unconditionally. And eat my cold leftovers."

***

Keep reading Juliette's happily ever after in...
Juliette & the Monday ManDates: The Gustafson Girls Book 1